# Light Years from Paradise

## Einstein's Double-Take

A novel by Frank Lewandowski

PublishAmerica
Baltimore

ISBN: 1-4241-5403-0
PUBLISHED BY PUBLISHAMERICA, LLLP
www.publishamerica.com
Baltimore

Printed in the United States of America

# A Note of Thanks

Writing is a solitary occupation but it takes the support of many people for a novel to see print. I deeply appreciate my wife, Sandy, for her patience during the hundreds of hours I worked on this story. Thanks to our son, Michael, for working on the initial book cover design.

Many thanks to Mike Read and Carol Orsburn for their invaluable feedback, encouragement and inspiration throughout the creative process. Thanks to Terry Thompkins for his insightful critique and Sarah Crespo for her kind words and suggestions. Thanks also to Larisa Clopton for sharing her enthusiasm for all things sci-fi and fantasy.

# Pronunciation Guide to a Few of the Names and Terms in *Light Years from Paradise*

A'laama (Al omm' ma)
Daj Minj (Dodge Min-j)
Umni Ott (Umm' knee. Ott like in tot.)
Unfoonaba (Oon fan a' ba)
Zama Elle (Zama as in mama and Elle as in the letter L.)

# Prologue

The bartender had never before seen an old man. The stranger who arrived one evening had once been tall but he now had stooped shoulders. He had brown, leathery skin and a thick mane of white hair. His appearance both frightened and fascinated the barkeep, who couldn't take his eyes off the visitor as he shuffled into the pub, leaning heavily on a gnarled walking stick that was black with age. His appearance was unlike anything the bartender had even seen. At first, he assumed the lone figure was an alien. But no, he was too obviously human to be of another species. What had caused him to look that way, to walk that way, some unfortunate mishap? Then it dawned on the server that this was an elderly human. He vaguely remembered a documentary he had seen many years earlier about how centuries ago people had aged like this. Their bodies had slowed down, become worn out and finally died. The bar man shuddered as he recalled the graphic depiction of the aging process and all it had entailed. That was before humans had learned to stay young through tissue regeneration, periodic blood filtering and growing new organs from a few of their owns cells. In modern times, people lived for centuries in youthful bodies. If they eventually got tired of biological replacement parts or if they wanted to enjoy super-human strength, hearing or vision, they would opt to have electronic parts integrated into their bio bodies. The bar guy had seen a number of such cyborgs but never an old human. Had his guest actually allowed himself to get that way?

Once the drink man got past his initial shock, he puzzled over why the man struggled to walk with the help of a wooden stick. Why not just get around in an antigrav chair like many more able-bodied people? The man's clothes were a different style from any he had ever seen. Obviously not from any of the local star systems. The visitor eased into a booth facing one of the ports that looked out into space. The pub occupied a tiny portion of a massive, interstellar space station, one that prided itself on having five different such watering holes. The station, an isolated city-state, floated in the black expanse between star systems. The visitor spent some time just gazing at the activities outside the station. One ship was docking while in the distance another was decoupling from the station and slowly moving away from the enormous metal structure before engaging its powerful engine. The inky darkness of space was alive with countless billions of diamonds and sapphires. The man pulled a pair of macro binocs from his coat pocket and studied the stars for some time. He was so intent the barkeep hated to bother him. Finally, he cautiously approached the booth.

"What'll you have?" he asked in heavily accented Interstellar Standard.

"Double shot of Biimannian resa, straight," the elder replied, turning away from the port.

"Biimannian? It's rare so it'll cost you. We get a shipment about once a decade. We have lots of fine local liqueurs that come in every two or three years."

"No, Biimannian. I'm good for it," said the old man, flashing a cosmic debit chip the size of a small coin.

The bartender brought the drink and the man tossed it down, slamming the glass on the table. He went back to gazing out the port. Sometime later, the patron hobbled over to the bar and sat down on a stool. "I'd like another," he said, again flashing the chip, which the proprietor scanned for payment.

"Don't think I've seen you in here before, Pops," he said. "I take it you don't live here in the condos with the other retired star travelers."

The man shook his head. "No. I'm not from around here. Been traveling the stars almost all my life, and even at my age, I still can't stay in one place too long."

"How do you get around?"

"Have my own ship."

The bartender whistled. "I hear they're expensive."

"They are, to get a good one. I retired…reasonably well."

"I take it you don't fly it on your own?"

"No, no. Have a pilot on retainer."

The bartender left him to tend to his other customers, although the evening's crowd was a fairly light. Once business slowed down, he headed back over. "So…if you don't mind my asking, how long you been traveling the stars?"

The man closed his eyes and thought a moment. "I was born planetside…it must have been twelve, thirteen hundred standard years ago. Planet-bound years that is. Of course, since time slows down when you're aboard a ship traveling at close to light speed, my physical age is just a fraction that amount. But…I honestly can't remember how old I am. Been to dozens, no scores of planets in my time."

"So…tell me something. I hope you don't mind if I get a little personal but I'm curious…with all the anti-aging techniques they have these days…." His voice trailed off while his customer stared at him. The host's face turned red.

The man laughed. "I don't mind growing old. After centuries of traveling the stars I've got time to slow down and reflect, to appreciate all my experiences."

Suddenly, he recognized his guest. "Say, are you the one they call the Story Teller?" he asked, reverently.

The elder smiled again. "I'm the one. Been spending the last few weeks here on your station telling small audiences about a few of my adventures from centuries past. Guess I'm kind of a novelty because I actually speak with live audiences rather than holding holo conferences. I've spent the last few decades going from station to station and planet to planet telling my tales as a way of amusing myself."

"Out of all the planets you've visited, d'you have a favorite one?"

The man closed his eyes again and thought for a moment. A smile crept across his face. "Al'aama," he said. "It would have to be the planet Al'aama. Ever heard of it? About sixty light years from here."

"Is that the same thing as the Al'aaman Republic?"

"Not exactly." The elder waved a gnarled hand and a hologram appeared. It was a flag. A black background with several stars of various degrees of brightness forming some sort of constellation. "The Independent Republic of

9

Al'aama is an interstellar nation consisting of the Al'aaman solar system and several neighboring ones. It's a regional power in that sector. But I'm referring to the capital of the republic, the planet Al'aama." The man waved his hand again and the flag disappeared. In its place, a blue and white planet contrasted with the black void of space. Flanking the orb were two suns, one much smaller and dimmer than the other.

"I've vaguely heard of it. Supposed to be a feisty little place."

"Their leader eons ago was feisty, too."

"How long ago were you there?"

The old man wrinkled his already heavily-lined brow. "Must be… at least eight or nine centuries. At that time, there was no interstellar nation. Just the one planet. And they didn't even have starflight capabilities. It was an enchanting, exotic world. There were lush jungles, tall fern trees…."

The bartender glanced around. Several of his patrons were calling it an early night so he had the time to listen further to the man's stories. "Tell me about your adventures there."

"Be glad to…."

# I: The Eye of the Cyclops

# 1.

Starship Captain Erik Houston hadn't planned to become a hero, especially not a dead one. As his life began to ebb away, his thoughts wandered back to an earlier portion of today's battle:

Arrows whizzed past his ears. Star people fired their stunners. Their allies, the A'laamans, shot ener pistols at hundreds of primitive Batu. Shouted orders and the din of battle filled the air. The captain choked on the thick dust that hung like a cloud. After hours of intense fighting, the high tech side appeared to be winning. Abruptly, he felt pain slicing into his calf. A stray arrow had met its mark. He began to stagger. Two crew members rushed over and supported him under his arms, helping him limp to the safety of the huge metal landing craft that was serving as the allied command center. He took a seat on the floor and joined several other wounded who were awaiting treatment. He craned his neck to glance out the port and watch the the battle. By the time a med tech removed the arrow and treated the wound, the captain was getting edgy. At his soonest possible moment he retrieved a belt buckle-sized force field generator, making sure this one actually worked. He clipped the device onto his belt, grabbed the stunner and headed back outside, despite the loud protests of all medical personnel within earshot.

Knots of tribesmen galloped into the jungle. Erik waved several of his troops to follow him as he scrambled after the Batu, pain shooting through his leg with each step. Two braves shot arrows at him and another launched a spear. All weapons bounced off the iridescent energy field that surrounded him.

He crashed through some brush and into the jungle. The same braves who had shot at him were still ahead. He fired his stunner. Again. A third time. First one tribesman dropped. Then another. There were still dozens of Batu fleeing with at least that many Al'aamans and star people giving chase. He was about to track down more of the enemy when he heard a painful moan. The sound seemed to be coming from about ten yards away. He looked around until he saw a female warrior lying on the ground. A metal animal trap held her ankle like a ferocious set of teeth. He crept closer to the woman.

Ice gripped Erik's stomach. The warrior was Umni Ott, the brave who only a short while earlier had held a knife to the throat of the A'laaman chiefexec's teenage daughter, Omma.

The warrior turned her head and looked at him. "Star man, you have me where you want me!" she wheezed. "Just get it over with and kill me!"

He frowned and looked into her eyes. "I'm not going to kill you."

"Why not? I was trying to kill your people."

He swallowed hard as he thought about Omma. He said nothing but crouched down beside the fighter. Using a large stick for leverage, he was finally able to pry open the jaws of the trap enough for the warrior to remove the remains of her ankle. She groaned with relief. He examined the ankle. The trap had cut through her moccasin and had deeply penetrated her flesh. The shoe was soaked with blood. He pulled some supplies from a small pack he was carrying.

"Why are you doing this?" she demanded. "I'm your enemy!"

"We don't *have* to be enemies."

"You're insane, Star man!"

He used a cleansing cloth to wipe away the blood. She flinched at the fiery burning from the antiseptic. He gently rubbed some salve on the torn ankle. At first she gritted her teeth but her expression quickly eased. "Hey! What kind of medicine is this?"

"It contains tiny organisms that will gradually heal your wound and re-build your flesh. I'll give you something for the pain."

"N-no, I'm fine!"

Ignoring her protests, he gave her a pill and let her take several swigs of water from his canteen. Next, he looked at the woman's left hand. It was swollen, red and badly blistered. By now, the hardened warrior could no longer stand it. She shrieked: "Leave me alone! I don't *deserve* your help! I almost killed that baby-faced girl!" Her right hand picked up dust and stones, which she threw at him. He froze in his tracks and swallowed hard.

"Leave me alone! Go!"

Erik, still thinking of Omma, was inclined to give the Batu her wish. Instead, he said quietly, "I'm not going anywhere."

The tribeswoman tried to start dragging herself away. Realizing that her ankle was now feeling somewhat better, she tried to stand by balancing on her good foot. She tried to hobble then quickly fell. Instead of slamming to the ground, she landed in Erik's arms.

"You're a sly one, Star man. I hate you! I hate you!"

He laid her down on the ground. He got another type of salve from his pack. He gingerly applied some to the woman's injured hand. She looked at her hand in wonder. The pain began to ease and she could almost see her flesh returning to its normal color.

"Why are you doing this? I hate your people."

"We don't hate you. We're just trying to get you to stop attacking us." He marveled at his own words, as if he considered himself an Al'aaman.

She looked puzzled. She finally allowed herself the luxury of a faint smile. Her expression changed as she heard some thrashing around in the brush nearby. She turned her head and saw a couple figures approaching from the distance. Members of her tribe.

"You need to go…. Go!" she whispered. "My tribesmen will kill me if they know you helped me!"

The captain scrambled off into the brush. While the two braves were still off in the distance, the woman scooped up some dirt and rubbed it on the wound. She clenched her teeth in pain at the burning sensation her action caused. The braves hurried over to her.

"Umni! What is this we just saw!" cried one of them, a male.

"That's right!" added the other, a female. "We saw you talking with that star man. And he looked as he was helping you! Have you turned against *your own tribe?*"

"You know what the chief does to traitors," continued the male, raising his arm as he prepared to lance the wounded lady with his spear.

15

"It's not what you think!" Umni replied. "I fought bravely for our tribe today! You know that!"

"No, you've turned your back on your own people and are consorting with the enemy," accused the female. "That's treason!"

The male was about to plunge his spear into her when he stopped in mid-motion and abruptly fell forward, crashing to the ground. Erik stepped out of the brush, stunner in hand. He quickly fired at the female antagonist, who hit the dirt as well.

"Let's get you out of here," he said. He picked up the tall warrior and began carrying her. The woman, who was lean and muscular, still weighed enough that it was quite a struggle. At first the brave squirmed a little and protested vocally. But the medication was already beginning to make her drowsy. Once she began to relax a little, it became easier to carry her. He moved along at a deliberate pace, knowing he could instantly set a force field around them if any other Batu showed up. The edge of the jungle was less than a hundred yards away. He quickly became out of breath and slowed his gait considerably. After several minutes, he became weary and laid her on the ground. He tried hoisting her over one shoulder by her waist. He was soaked with perspiration and soon became out of breath again. His lower back and right shoulder were beginning to ache. His lungs burned. The edge of the jungle seemed miles away.

"How you feeling?" he asked.

"A little better," her speech slurring. The warrior looked at him, studying his face with her heavy eyes as if she were still trying to understand him. She moved her lips and said, in barely a whisper, "Thank you."

He kept listening for sounds of any additional warriors and scanning the foliage for any signs of motion. He used his pocket heat-sensing device to scan a wide area. There was no one else for quite some distance. The pain shot through his wounded calf as it knotted in a cramp.

"D-don't have to carry me. I can walk," said the delirious Umni. She tried standing on her wounded ankle. He caught her before she hit the ground. This time she didn't protest. He tried carrying her again but he had to stop after a short distance. The medicine was further relaxing her, making her feel more and more like dead weight. The jungle perimeter was close but felt distant. He eased back down.

"Why don't you rest?" he said. "You can use my pack for a pillow. I'll stand guard over you."

"Hey…rescuer man. What's…yer name?" asked the woozy Umni.

16

"Erik."

"G'night, Erik." He slid his pack under her head. Her eyes closed within seconds.

He sat on the jungle floor and watched the brown-skinned Umni. She was breathing heavily. She had been a tough opponent, as were her people. He gulped some water from his canteen. He was soaked with perspiration. It had seemed like a long battle, one he hoped was winding down. He planned to call Montoya, his second in command, but wanted to rest first. He leaned his back against a fern tree, unaware of the sets of eyes watching him from above. A small purple creature slid down the tree trunk. It lowered itself, spider-like onto his shoulder. He finally noticed but it was too late. He tried to pull it off but it was already sinking its deadly fangs into his skin. He cried out and rolled from a sitting position to a prone one.

Umni, who was lying nearby, opened one eye then closed it. She opened both eyes. She tried to rise to her feet and found that, due to the magic pills, she could now stand on the ankle with difficulty. Her eyes scoured the ground until she found a large stick. She limped over to him. She tore the creature off his shoulder. The animal hit the ground. She beat the attacker repeatedly with the stick, smashing through its hard shell. Within moments, the flattened creature was lifeless, oozing a clear gel. Retrieving a knife from her leg sheath, she cut open the man's shirt sleeve. His shoulder was already deep red and swollen. It was beginning to turn purple. The warrior made two v-shaped cuts in the shoulder. She began squeezing the shoulder and sucking on the cuts. She hated the bitter taste of the poison. She spat some out and went back to sucking the wounds.

Erik was still partially conscious. His face was twisted in pain. He opened his eyes for a moment but soon fell unconscious. The woman desperately continued her work. After several minutes, he looked a little better. She returned to her task. The jungle was beginning to spin around her. She collapsed to the ground.

Sometime later, the groggy Erik became vaguely aware of a sound. He gradually realized it was breathing. Labored breathing. He opened his eyes a sliver. Umni was lying on the ground. Her chest slowly rose and fell as she struggled for air. Erik was breathing with similar difficulty. The sound of each breath resounded in his ears. He closed his eyes. Summoning all his strength, he wheezed: "Umni." Several seconds passed. He thought he heard her stir. "Umni," he repeated.

"Star man," barely a whisper.

"Y-you didn't have to...."

"It's okay," she wheezed. "You honored me" (Breath) "by sparing my life." (Breath) "I wanted" (Breath) "to save you."

"That venom" (Breath) "...how bad?" he asked, opening his eyes wider than before. She opened her eyes, too. They were only a couple feet apart, staring into one another's orbs.

"Fatal," she said somberly. (Breath) "Almost always" (Breath) "fatal. Sorry if I" (Breath) "if I did too little." (Breath) "I really" (Breath) "tried...." (Breath) "You're a" (Breath) "good man." (Breath) "...Deserve to live...." (Breath)

"Umni!" He reached for her hand and tried to grasp it. It was going limp.

"See you" (Breath) "in the afterlife," (Breath) "Erik...." She closed her eyes and stopped breathing.

The fatigued soldier closed his eyes and felt his life slipping away. A bright light flooded his eyes as his mind replayed the events of the past few months, beginning with the ship's voyage to the planet A'laama....

# 2.

Captain Houston smiled. Entry into the Quartran solar system was progressing well. His ship, the *Initiative*, had passed through the system's outermost edge, the gravitational lens. The captain had dispatched a couple of automated probes to take holos through the lens. He had always been fascinated with the warping of space by gravity. The gravity of each star created a lens that served as a natural magnifying glass, allowing much greater close-ups than a telescope alone could provide. Probes could peer through the lens and examine details of planets in other star systems. Details down to tens of yards across. As the ship had penetrated farther into the system, it had passed through the Oort comet cloud. The *Initiative* pressed on, finally beginning to reach the outermost planets, each of them billions of miles from the two suns. The starship had been gradually decelerating, having scaled back from just below the speed of light.

The captain was a tall, fortyish man with powerful shoulders. He had dark brown hair that sometimes looked black and ended in a few curls that fell across his forehead. By late afternoon, he had a five o'clock shadow that gave his face a grey appearance.

He hurried down one of the ship's hallways and burst into the ship's exercise room. "Planetfall's in about a week!" he announced.

"That's great," said dark-haired Lt. Fred Montoya, looking up from his exercycle.

"Are we back in normal time yet?" asked Communications Specialist Luci Strong between puffs of breath. The petite woman with braided, blond hair was hard at work on a stair-step machine. A thin stream of perspiration darkened the back of her shirt.

The captain nodded. "Our speed has dropped low enough that the difference between shipboard time and planetary time is negligible."

"It will take a while to get my planet legs back," said the slim Montoya, ship's chief science officer and doctor.

"That's why we all need to keep exercising," said that captain. "Although this world will be easier to walk on than some we've visited. Its grav is only 78% of standard, so we'll all have an extra spring in our step."

"Don't know if I'll like seeing natives as tall as pro basketball players," chuckled Daj Minj, who was about to start a workout on an electronic weight machine. His wispy mustache and light brown hair were showing a few flecks of grey.

"As tall as...*what?*" asked the captain, wrinkling his brow.

"Oh, you know Daj. Always throwing in some obscure historic reference," Luci sighed.

"Okay, so what's basketball?" asked the skipper.

"A sport the ancients played," Daj replied. He waved his hand and a few seconds of a fast-moving game appeared. The clip ended and the visual disappeared. He continued: "It's never gone totally extinct. I'm just saying that crew members who are shorter than average like Luci and me may feel lost on a planet of giants."

Luci nodded between puffs.

The captain rolled his eyes before recalling it had been a few missions since they had been on a low grav world."We can expect the natives to be *several inches* taller than most of us. That's about it."

The captain and his crew belonged to a First Contact group, serving as the initial Association contact for a given colony. Several ships each served in a First Contact capacity. Other crews specialized in follow-up contacts, typically decades after the first one.

"Anything else we should know about this planet?" asked Daj.

"Planetside," said the captain, "both suns are usually in the sky at the same time, meaning the sky is extremely bright and there's a greatly increased danger of sunburn. We'll definitely need protection, including sun lenses," he said, referring to heavily tinted contact lenses that would protect their eyes. "At any given time, there's almost always at least one sun in the sky so this planet only experiences night about once every three weeks."

Montoya nodded and stroked his Van Dyke beard.

The captain asked: "Luci, how are we doing analyzing the broadcasts we've monitored?"

"It's been the toughest I've ever encountered. Now that we're entering this sector, there's been a lot of audio interference due to the local clouds of dust and gas. We've been able to pick up a few signals from one small, isolated area on the planet and even those have been extremely weak."

The captain shook his head. It was the same story every time the ship left the more heavily colonized area of space known as the Local Bubble, which was relatively free of massive dust and gas formations. "Have we been able to gather enough samples of their language for our cosmic translators so that we'll be able to talk to these people?"

"I think so. I've learned that they call both their planet and their city 'Al'aama.' It means to be snug and cozy."

He rubbed his chin with his thumb and forefinger. "Odd name for a city or a planet. And they're both called the same thing?"

"That's right. Their word for city and their word for planet are synonymous, too. If the natives mean one, they often mean the other," she said.

The skipper looked even more perplexed.

Luci continued: "And they call their ruler the Chiefexec of the Planet, even though the colony consists entire of just *one city.*"

"*That's it?*"

She nodded. "Most of the audio and video we've monitored have shown that several of their top leaders are women."

His arms at his side, the captain unconsciously clenched his fists. Over the years, he had dealt with a few planets that were patriarchies, many that had a combination of male and female leaders, and a few matriarchies. The matriarchies had by far been the most vexing....

Several days later, Houston was gazing out the port at the primary sun in the distance and the vast sweep of the galaxy in the background. The star's sister, a dwarf, was too dim for the unaided eye to see at this distance. Today, visibility was good with no dust or gas clouds obscuring the view. The captain thought about the vastness of space and how it would take an eternity to explore it all. The more man learned of its enormity, the smaller he looked in trying to explore his small corner.

The captain thought of a familiar verse: *"When I consider the heavens, the works of your hands, the moons and stars that you've made, what is man that you are mindful of him? Or the son of man that you visit him?"* He thought of the Maker of all that is, lifted up his eyes and worshiped.

After a few minutes, his thoughts drifted back to the landing preparations. Luci had completed the broadcast monitoring and there was now enough language in the system. Houston had even listened to some of the raw speech. The overall sound was like the standard language. But every other word seemed like slang or jargon. Or maybe it was just the thick drawl. He increased the playback speed, which made things worse. The captain waved his hand and the sound cut off. Thank God for the cosmic translator!

The captain again thought of his need to send a videocast announcing their imminent arrival. Protocol dictated that a First Contact ship give the natives advance notice so they could prepare—mentally, emotionally and otherwise. But how could an isolated culture get ready on short notice for an event that had never before happened? Regional headquarters was to have sent a message a decade (planetary time) earlier, but who knew if it had been received due to the region's electromagnetic disturbances? He had told HQ repeatedly to always send an unmanned message capsule sufficient years in advance of their ship, but throughout the decades and centuries, the response had always been the same: Budget cutbacks. Since his ship had entered the Quartran system, he had tried several times to contact the planet's leaders but had gotten no response. Had the message still not gotten through? He would keep trying....

Sometime later, he strode over to his over-sized command chair on the ship's bridge. He eased into the soft like-leather. Forward ports and large video screens displayed the view in all directions. He spent several minutes taking in the sights then announced: "This is your captain. As you have opportunity, feel free to go to the nearest starboard port for a view of a gas giant and a couple of its moons. At our closest approach, we'll be within twenty thousand miles. And as a special treat, this one has rings." Erik gazed at a screen that displayed the sight he had just described. Surrounded by the blackness of space was an orange, striped ball and its colorful rings. In plain view against the slightly flattened sphere was a tiny brown marble, one of the moons. Another moon was a small, barely visible dot slightly above the planet.

Erik had previously ordered two automated probes dispatched to study the system's planets and moons. He continued to look at the gas giant while he made a verbal entry into the ship's log.

Next, he reviewed some 3-D still shots one of the probes had taken through the gravitational lens. One planet, orbiting a star three light years away, showed some visual signs of prior colonization, including a handful of cities. The Association had for years monitored audio and video broadcasts from that planet. These new visuals further confirmed its candidacy for a First Contact.

The captain puzzled over the next set of 3-D's. They were taken of a world that was two light years away, one of the most human-habitable planets he had ever seen. The probe had zoomed in on verdant forests, clear blue lakes, snow-capped mountains. But there was no sign, anywhere, of a settlement. He wrinkled his brow. He waved his hand through the air, thus ordering the ship's artificial intelligence to scan through the billions of additional images the probe had taken. He was trying to learn whether there was anything, anything whatsoever, that implied structures of unnatural origin. Within a nanosecond, the search came back negative. No visuals of any buildings. Or highways. Or bridges. No brush fires set for clearing forest land or jungles. The probe had also scanned for night photos as it looked for the twinkle of city lights. But when the planet rotated away from the sun, its surface was as dark as an unlit room past twilight. And no one had ever detected an electronic message coming from the planet. There was no evidence whatsoever of intelligent life. The place appeared pristine and totally vacant. The commander shook his head. All other star systems for light years around appeared to have been settled or at least visited by humans at one time or another. How had such a gem of a world, such a beauty of an orb, ripe for colonizing, been missed? He would make a strong recommendation to put it on the A-list for a Future Colony.

He thought about their present destination, now only days away. There had been no record, anywhere, that a ship had ever been dispatched to colonize the planet. Its lone city had been discovered via a previous First Contact ship's visual reconnaissance through a gravitational lens. The origin of the Quartran IV colony had piqued his curiosity the entire voyage. He hoped to soon have some answers.

# 3.

"No space aliens are landing on my planet!" snapped Zama Elle, Chiefexec of the Planet.

"But we may not have a choice!" shot back Science Director Tanna Bern. "Do you want to anger some interstellar authority? They could also have some powerful weapons."

The chiefexec bit her lip.

Just moments earlier, Tanna had startled her boss, crying: "Madame Exec! An alien space craft has entered our solar system!"

Zama had slammed her hand down on her desk. She had been home for the evening, reading some online reports. Her personal video screen, the size and shape of a small, handheld makeup mirror had startled her by abruptly flashing crimson. Her stomach had tightened and mouth had instantly gone dry. She'd never before had a Red Alert during her administration. She glared back at the 3-D image of her science director. Tanna was thin and had straight, medium brown hair that abruptly ended just past the nape of her neck. "You sure?" the leader replied.

Tanna looked pale. "Yes. The past several days our astrogazers have been tracking a small object. It started out in deep space and is moving toward us at a significant fraction of the speed of light. It is gradually slowing down and should arrive here within two days."

Zama felt the *thump-thump* of her heart. She could feel her blood pressure rising. She took a deep breath, certain that the bio-electronic implant in her arm was already shooting meds into her bloodstream to help her cope with this shock. "And there's...*no possibility* this is some sort of *natural* phenomenon?"

"Not something that *fast*, Ma'am."

The leader sighed. "Looks like we'll be getting some visitors," she finally said, her voice trembling even as she tried to act nonchalant.

"Yes, Ma'am," agreed Tanna, sounding equally uncertain.

The chiefexec again went uncharacteristically silent. Tanna felt a thousand needles in her spine while she awaited a further response. Finally, the science director continued: "Madame Exec...should we try to *contact* them?"

"Yes! Tell them we don't need them here! The sovereign planet of A'laama has stood alone for three centuries. We'll continue along fine without them."

"Ma'am...we...we can't send that message."

"Then say nothing. I'm sure they'll get in touch when they're ready."

"They've already been trying."

"How's that?"

"We've been receiving some short messages but the static is so heavy they keep breaking up."

The exec sat straight up. "What have they been saying?"

"Not sure. We keep losing every third or fourth word and the speaker has a heavy accent."

"Keep me posted."

"Yes, Ma'am."

The chiefexec ended the call. The video screen reverted to looking like a mirror. The screen was a total information and communications device, serving as a combination 3-D picture phone, 3-D television and personal computer. The leader pushed her hand through her thick hair and tried to put the conversation out of her mind. She nervously went back to her online reports. Her fingers toyed with her fine, gold necklace, something she often did when deep in thought.

She was able to block out thoughts about Tanna's call fairly well until the following day when word of the approaching celestial object leaked out. Before long, speculation was all over the media. The following day, the news reported an upsurge in impromptu temple services and included interviews with excited citizens feeling The Prophecy was about to be fulfilled. Zama gritted her teeth and concentrated even harder on her work. Finally, needing a break, she swivelled her chair to face the room's wall-sized video screen. She snapped her fingers and the screen sprang to life, filling with an over-sized 3-D image of a man wearing a suit and a woman in a skirt suit.

The man boomed in a bass voice: "This evening we have with us the Madelin King, author of the best selling online book, *Interstellar Orphans*. Madelin, I've heard that title refers to we A'laamans. Is that correct?"

"That's right, John. We're orphans because when our Founders' ship crashed here centuries ago, many of their scientific, historic and cultural records were destroyed. Much of the information we have of our pre-history comes from traditions the Founders preserved. Oral histories about their various planets of origin. So, what we know about other planets and the human race's past is fragmented. We have few roots. I hope that since a visit from space seems imminent that our guests will help us fill in some of the gaps...."

The exec shook her head. She waved her hand and the video screen switched to another channel. More talk about the space invaders. She tried a different station. Same thing. She snapped her fingers, turning off the video screen. She turned back to her desk and tried to resume her work.

Across town, a tall, bony man with teased hair sat in a plush lounge chair in a penthouse atop the highest skyscraper in A'laama. His hair was longish and stuck out in all directions. Dark with streaks of grey. He had only a few strands in the front of his head but an abundance in back and on the sides. His face was scarred from a battle with acne that had peaked decades earlier. He fidgeted but couldn't get comfortable. He hopped up from his chair and briskly moved his lanky frame across the thick, carpeted floor, his upper body leaning forward at an angle.

He quickly reached the wall-sized picture window. He opened the sliding glass door and stepped out onto the balcony. He gazed at the city below, its skyscrapers seeming to reach up to him. This was his city. He owned this town. He peered disdainfully at the bustling streets hundreds of feet below. Tiny vehicles and smaller dots moved quickly to and fro. He thought about how the cars and the people looked like little insects. He wished he could put two of his fingers together and crush several of them at once. He pictured stomping on them with his feet and laughed in a sinister way. He leaned over the railing and spat, hoping it would hit someone far below.

He went back inside, closed the sliding door and ambled back to his seat. The man waved the glass in his hand. A well-tanned brunette woman in a black evening dress and high heels appeared. She refilled the glass with a mixture of intoxicant and ice. A blonde lady in a red evening gown wiped his brow then stepped away. The man sipped on his drink then made a sour face. "Too much ice!" he snapped.

The brunette hurried back over, bowed and returned moments later with a replacement. The man held the drink up to the light and peered at it. The lady anxiously awaited his verdict. He swirled the glass slightly with his hand, causing the ice cubes to spin in little circles. He held the drink up to his nose and sniffed, inhaling the fragrant aroma. He took a sip. A second. No negative reaction. The brunette stepped away, relief on her face.

"Good drink, Sylvia," he said. "Take the rest of the night off."

She smiled, briskly thanked him, turned on her heel and left.

"The rest of you, too. Get out of here," he said to the other women.

Once the room was clear, the man punched a code into his personal video screen. He was on a private channel that couldn't be traced. "This South Vineyard stock from '92 is the best," he declared to the man who had answered.

"Even better than '91," his counterpart agreed. "More of a fruity flavor. Sweeter. Less woody."

"Indeed," said the man with the wiry hair. "So...the whole world continues to love Zama Elle," he mocked. "She's still up in the polls. Got a standing ovation at her last speech. What is it about this woman everyone likes?"

"She's a good speaker. And she knows how to play the media," opined the man at the other end.

"Naw," the electric-haired man dismissed with the wave of his hand. "Her speeches are mediocre. She says what the masses want to hear. She is somewhat photogenic and she smiles a lot. But it takes more than image to make a chiefexec. Her popularity makes it hard to push our agenda. Since she's been in office, she opposed our every move. But it will be a whole new scenario now that these space aliens are coming. It could be the beginning of the end for her. And it could be our golden opportunity...."

The face at the other end of the line grinned. "This does give us some opportunities to exploit. If she buddies up to these off-worlders, we'll accuse her of being unpatriotic. If she opposes them, we'll say she's anti-progress. Things are finally about to swing our way."

"Yes. Yes, indeed," agreed the wiry-haired man. He placed his drink on a coaster and made a steeple with his hands.

"But what if we're unable to turn the public against her?"

His partner gritted his teeth before replying. "Don't worry. We have other ways to deal with Zama Elle."

# 4.

 

Farmhand Robert Miller had arrived early that morning at his employer's spread. He was ready to begin the numerous chores. It would be a good idea to get as much done as possible before it got hot. Robert knocked on the door to announce his arrival. There was no answer. He waited a minute but no one came to the door. He knocked again and waited. Silence, except for the house pet running around frantically and howling. That crazy mongrel. Robert walked down the porch steps. His eyes swept the yard, but his bosses were nowhere to be found. He strode over to the barn. The lock on the door was broken. The door opened with a creak. He pushed his way inside. He felt his stomach turn to ice. At first he was speechless but finally managed a shout.

The youth pulled his video screen from his pocket and punched in an emergency code. "P-police?" he cried, his trembling voice breaking. "I'm at the Eddlesbeth farm, 3331 Windmere Road. Hurry! Something terrible's happened!" Within minutes, a squad car roared up the long drive and screeched to a halt by the barn.

Sergeant John Saachi exited the car and trotted over to the open barn door. He immediately noted signs of forced entry. "What's the trouble, son?" he asked the white-faced teen who was standing in the doorway. The speechless youth pointed. The officer rushed into the barn. Sprawled on the floor were the lifeless bodies of farmer Joe Eddlesbeth, his wife, Sarah, and their son, Tony. All three had cuts and bruises on their faces, heads and hands. Saachi whistled. He hadn't seen anything like it in a long time. There was little crime in this small, farming section of Al'aama. And violent crime was almost unheard of. Yet, here was evidence of violent murders, within a barn of all places. Even stranger, many of the gannao the farmers raised were missing. The anguished bleating of the remaining animals filled the policeman's ears. It was incredible that someone would kill three people over a few head of livestock, especially a variety so commonly raised as the gannao.

The sergeant audioed in his report. He learned that there had been a few other gannao thefts in the area in recent months. This fact and these killings moved the sergeant's supervisor to consider this no longer a local issue. He alerted the regional police headquarters downtown in the hopes they would send a detective squad as well as some additional officers and squad cars to better patrol this large, rural area. As the sergeant concluded his survey of the crime scene, he noticed in the corner of the barn a couple broken arrows. Strange. What was *archery equipment* doing at the scene of a bludgeoning triple homicide?

# 5.

Captain Houston stood gazing at the planet below. It had five continents. The world's polar ice caps were tiny. The area near the equator was too hot for human life. The only habitable zone was over 2,000 miles north of the equator but still a torrid area. Most of the planet surface within Erik's gaze was dark. But illuminating one small section on the next to the largest continent was a tiny patch of light. Within minutes the ship's orbit would take it past the light and there would be nothing but darkness. At least for several more minutes until one of the two suns lit up the world. Then, eventually darkness again. Then another sunrise, this one caused by the second sun. Then more darkness. Finally, the spot of light would re-appear and the process would repeat. He couldn't get over it. Just one city—one!—on the entire planet. There were no signs of advanced civilization anywhere else. He had never seen the like. The city was the planet's only source of media broadcasts.

The *Initiative's* technicians had used heat sensing, but other than the city, the only town of any size consisted of a few thousand people some thirty miles to the northeast. The heat-seeking device did reveal a few hundred thousand additional life forms spread over an area of tens of thousands of square miles but the captain thought these were mostly herds of animals and perhaps a few small human villages. Other parts of the planet had small groups of living creatures each numbering in the tens or hundreds, but these were also just as likely to be animal groupings. The captain turned his thoughts back to the lighted city below. Its shape reminded Houston of a tiny eye, causing him to think of the planet as a giant Cyclops. The captain was concerned that he had still been unable to set up communications between his ship and the planet. It turned out the larger of the two suns had an unusual amount of sunspot activity, disrupting his attempts. Yet he had really hoped on sending the landing party to the planet tomorrow. He would try one more time tonight....

"Hey, there." The captain recognized the female voice without having to turn around. It was Luci. He turned away from the port to face her. Her blond hair was brushed out to its full shoulder length.

"Hi," he replied. "Have you had a chance to audio the Association?"

"Tried several times but I'm not sure we transmitted successfully. Still dealing with that bad space weather."

He nodded. "The sunspots? All right. But stay on top of it."

That evening, on the planet surface twelve-year-old Grana Maar was sitting at an audio console talking with other amateur operators. It was an interesting way to meet people. Sometimes she heard from operators who lived all the way on the other side of the city! She had tried finding a source of conversation tonight, but so far no one seemed to have their "ears" on. She was about to give up when a loud voice broke in.

"Hello, there!" said a man's voice in a strange accent.

"H-hello," said Grana.

"Greetings on behalf of the United Association of Planets," said the rich, bass voice. Grana blinked her eyes. "My name is Erik Houston, captain of the starship *Initiative*. We come in peace! At this moment, we are orbiting your beautiful planet and would like to land tomorrow and meet with your leaders."

Grana, her microphone button open, let out a piercing scream that hurt Houston's ears. She dropped the mike and ran out the room shouting: "Mama! Mama! Come quick!"

That night and into the next morning, A'laaman video screens all over the city were abuzz.

"The aliens are coming!" Debbie Rann cried into her personal screen.

"Aliens?" repeated Donna Marx.

"You know. The space people."

"Do you think they'll be friendly?"

"Don't know. What if they're hostile?"

Donna called another friend, creating a three-way call. "Gloria, this is Donna. What do you think about these space men?"

"Been expecting them. It's all in the Prophecy."

"What?"

Debbie broke in: "I heard the head space guy called a young girl over in Bataamiville."

"No way!"

"Yes!"

"My husband's working the late shift. I'll have to call him and tell him."

The visitors from space were the talk of the entire city that night and into the next morning.

# 6.

Chiefexec Zama Elle was sitting at a desk in her private study, online as she worked on the last-minute details of tomorrow's State of the Planet speech. She was a polished, effective speaker. And, a rarity among politicians, she insisted on writing her own speeches. Her concentration was so intense that an unexpected musical chime from her video screen startled her. She reminded herself to change the setting back to either color mode or vibrate. The chiefexec touched a corner of the screen. "Yes," she said.

"Madame Exec."

"Yes, Alisa," she said to her chief of staff, whose face appeared on the screen.

"Sorry to call so late in the evening, Ma'am. But I didn't want you to be blindsided right before your speech."

The chiefexec sighed. "Is that clones' rights group agitating again? Let them try one more implosion threat and I'll have the *whole organization* arrested!"

"No, it's *much bigger* than that," she said with the obvious emotion. The chief of staff was normally well composed. "Have you seen tonight's news?"

She shook her head. "Been tied up on this speech."

"A couple of our citizens have been contacted by *people from the stars!* It's been all over the media."

Zama frowned.

"Our scientists have traced the source of the broadcast and it did, in fact, emanate from a source that's orbiting a few hundred miles over our heads."

"And these…*star people* chose to initiate their communications with *private citizens* rather than with me?"

"Apparently so."

"What did they *say?*"

"T-that they come in peace and want permission to land and meet with our leaders."

"It would be nice if they'd ask *me* first! Get Evva Barr on the screen. Tell her to figure out what to say to calm the public. And tell all the major stations we need to get her on the air as soon as possible."

"Ah…Madame Exec, I don't think we can *demand* air time from private media."

"This *is* an emergency. Tell Evva that's how I want it handled. I'll also make sure to discuss the space visitors in my speech."

"Very good, Ma'am. Should we send the space people a message?"

"They've snubbed me. I'll wait for *them* to contact *me.*"

"Thank you, Ma'am."

The exec clicked off the video screen. She ran her hand through her mane.

Her screen alerted her to another call. "Madame Exec," began Science Director Tanna Bern.

After Tanna's call, Zama thought about putting her screen on Do Not Disturb but she felt a need to stay available in case there were any breaking developments. She went back to struggling with her speech. Finally, she gave up and went to bed. It took a long time for her to fall asleep. When she finally did so, she had a nightmare about a fleet of starships invading the planet.

The next morning, the chiefexec was rushing to get ready for her speech, due to start in less than half an hour. She rapidly brushed her light brown hair. The brush gently sprayed conditioner, a must on a low grav planet where hair would otherwise tend to either stick straight up or frizz outward.

The room was teeming with various tiny robots going about their chores. Some of the miniature machines were too small to even be seen. Thousands of organo-bots, which were actually tiny living creatures, were busy eating dust mites and allergens. Numerous non-organic bots were sanitizing the area. Several others, looking like small, metallic insects, were crawling the floor and scaling the walls, seeking micro-sized audio devices and video cameras that could have been planted by media people or political enemies. One of the tiny machines spotted such an intruder and shot out a beam of light, disintegrating it.

All this was unseen by the chiefexec. She looked in the mirror then turned toward a shelf on the wall to the left of her vanity and ordered: "Microbots, quick trim plus Scarlet # 37 on the nails and Bronze Blush # 22 on the face!" Dozens of gold-colored, inch-high robots swung into action. They slid down strings to the vanity. The nail specialists ran toward the chiefexec's hands, which she had placed palm down on the vanity. Some of the robots used the hose and brush attachments at the ends of their arms to apply and spread nail color on each of Zama's fingernails. Another tiny group raced toward her feet and were about to start on her toenails. "No, gang, that won't be necessary," she said. "I'll be wearing closed-toed sandals." The toenail specialists headed back up to the Microbot shelf. Meanwhile, the fingernail-painting robots were followed by others that had tiny blow driers instead of hands. Other specialized machines were scaling Zama's face as if it were a cliff. The little devices had boots that clung to any surface. They gave her the tickling sensation of small insects crawling on her. She had long since gotten used to the feeling. The mini-robots quickly trimmed her eyebrows and eyelashes, vacuuming up the debris and plucking a facial hair or two. Others brushed colored powder onto the chiefexec's face. When the multiple crew members had finished all their tasks in less than a minute, they hurried back to the vanity and stood in line at attention while the exec inspected their work. "Makeup, forget Bronze Blush # 22. Let's go with Sun Blest # 43."

The makeup robots hurried back into motion, squirting tiny streams of quick-drying liquid to wash off their previous work. They then applied the chiefexec's new choice of color. She inspected again. "Looking good, team. Looking good. Oh. Lipstick, to match the nail gloss!" The lip specialists hurried up her arms, climbed up her hair, scurried down her face and quickly began painting on the lipstick using tiny brush attachments. Within thirty seconds, the job was done. Zama smiled a toothy grin. They hadn't gotten lipstick on her teeth this time. "Good job," she said. "Microbots, back to the shelf!" The crew of tiny robots hurried back to their home where they would stand and wait for days, or years if necessary, until she called on them again.

She jumped to her feet, knocking into a standing figurine, a six-inch-high 3-D photoid of herself. The motion-sensitive image came to life and began energetically walking back and forth, stabbing the air with an index finger while repeating a fragment of a speech she had once made on the legislature floor. The present-day Zama's eyes widened as she watched the tiny figure. The photoid had captured a moment in time, showing a Legislae Elle who was slender, had hair several inches above shoulder length and was wearing a crisp pants suit. She had a rosy face and spoke with energy, confidence, authority. Had the image really been taken only five or six years earlier?

Her thoughts flashed back ever further. She had grown up in a suburb. Her late mother had been a business exec but Zama had always interested in the legal field and public policy. She was head of the debate club in high school and studied law in college. She later spent nine years as an attorney, three years as a judge and four years as a legislae before becoming chiefexec three years ago.

Returning to the present, she wondered when she had developed the beginning of a double chin and when her previously thinner face had started looking round. She had always been tall and lean but lately had been developing a stomach. She even looked pale by Al'aaman standards. At least today she looked good in the tailored skirt, jacket and blouse outfit. Most other people would be dressed in their typical light, wrap-around outfits to cope with the intense, two-sun heat. But especially today, she needed to look like a chiefexec.

She stood up and headed toward the door, stopping long enough to listen to a few seconds of an audio broadcast. *More* about the imminent arrival of the visitors from space! She shook her head.

She headed out the door, which locked automatically behind her. She was in a narrow, lighted hallway and stepped into the cube-shaped accelevator that was always there for hurried mornings like this. She took one of the several upholstered seats, buckling in. It was a straight shot from her vanity room door to her office, but they were separated by seventy-five yards of hallway. She leaned back in the seat and pushed a button. The cab jerked into motion with a burst of acceleration, pressing her head and back against the high, cushioned seat. Nausea momentarily gripped her. Within a few seconds, the vehicle began automatically decelerating. When it braked to a stop, Zama was at the other end of the vast executive complex and only a few steps away from her main office. The vehicle was several times quicker than she could get there walking full speed. The tall, athletic Zama could always *run* down the mansion hallways, but that would be too undignified for a lady exec and still not a fraction as fast as the device.

She got out, stood up straight and ran her hands over her outfit, anti-wrinkle wand in hand. The car would wait there in case she needed it for her return trip. She opened a hidden door that led into an obscure hallway. She made a couple quick turns down short corridors and bounded into her spacious office. Video crews and makeup people were bustling around. The boss strode over to her massive desk, made of red-colored ironwood. The native wood shined up to a mirror finish and was one of the hardest natural substances on the planet. Nothing short of laser saws could cut and shape it. She pulled out her plush, high-backed chair and slid into it.

A makeup person frowned. "Madame Exec," she said, "with all due respect, these colors won't look right to the folks at home."

Zama shook her head and sat there helpless while two makeup artists quickly undid the Microbots' work.

"Madame Exec," said Alisa, bustling into the room. She looked as if she had gotten even less sleep than Zama. Shoving a paper-thin, tablet-sized video screen onto the desk, the chief of staff continued: "I've got your morning briefing. More details on the star people."

"At least my staff is keeping in me in the loop," sighed the leader.

Just that moment, she saw her firstadvisor ambling toward. *Here comes trouble,* thought Zama Elle.

"Madame Exec! Madame Exec!"

She looked up to see Adae Betelgeuse hurrying toward her. Zama had long been thinking of replacing the older woman.

"What is it?" snapped the exec.

"Haven't I been telling you all the signs are there? Last week, the moon lined up with both suns...."

"Yes, yes. That's called a triple eclipse, Betel. Happens once every 127 years."

"And haven't I been telling you for months now that the old-time prophecy is about to come true...?"

"Betel...."

"That just as three women, the Founders of our Planet, came from the stars and started our civilization, so three men would come from the stars...."

"Betel, we'll talk later! I'm about to address the planet."

"Ma'am," said Betel, "look at this!" She slapped on the desk a tablet-sized video screen displaying one of the online newzoids: "Star men Talk with

Citizens!" She punched a few tabs and pulled up another, which read: "Invasion from Space Imminent!"

Alisa was again vying for attention: "Madame Exec...."

The chief executive sighed deeply and ran a hand through her hair. "All right. All right," she said quietly. "Everyone needs to stay calm."

"Ready, Madame Exec?" called one of the news directors, looking smart in his tailored suit. "Ready in five, four, three, two one...." He pointed at the leader, who was abruptly aware that all cameras were now live.

She took a deep breath, looked directly into the main camera and said: "Good morning, fellow citizens. I'm here this morning to talk with you about the state of our planet. First of all, I know something important is on the minds of many of you, but I want to ask all of you to remain calm...."

At that moment there was a blinding flash and a 3-D, color image of a man filled the space in front of her. "Greetings, Chiefexec Elle and people of the planet Al'aama. I'm Erik Houston, captain of the starship *Initiative*. We come in peace. With your permission, we'd like to send a landing party to your fair planet...."

The head of state just sat and stared.

# 7.

Captain Houston was pacing the floor. He always felt nervous before landing on a new planet. How would the government and the citizens receive them? You always needed back-up plans and contingency plans and a backup for the backup....

Yet the whole idea was to visit the planet, find out about its civilization, help in anyway possible. Let the inhabitants know there were other populated planets out there, although it took many years, especially planetary years, to communicate from one to another.... And communications! Why had every possible thing gone wrong with paving the way in advance of their landing? He had made several attempts to discretely contact the chiefexec directly but somehow the signal had bounced and he had ended up contacting ordinary citizens. Now the entire populace was alarmed.

As the captain paced, he went over a mental checklist of everything the landing party needed to do before heading planetside. Confident that all items had been handled, his thoughts ran through all numerous protocols involved in a First Contact visit. The captain had run many such visits over the years and was anxious for the current one to go well. On the ship's previous layover at an Association world, the officials had commended him and implied he was in line for a promotion. Erik smiled and had a gleam in his eye as he thought of the possibility. Coming back to reality, he shook his head and realized it was time to get moving. He exited his cabin and strode down the hall to Montoya's room. He knocked tensely on the door. The senior officer popped his head out.

"It's time," the captain said.

"Let's go meet the natives."

The captain and the first officer rounded up the other landing party members. As was his custom before each planetary visit, he had everyone stand in a circle and join hands. He led the group in prayer, asking God to guide the mission, doing His will through the crew. He asked that his crew and he be effective in helping the natives. And he asked for protection for all his people and that they might all successfully complete their visit. After the captain's prayer, a couple other landing party members took their turns.

The three men and three women walked in silence down a long hallway and through an airlock that led to one of the ship's several landing craft. Houston took the pilot's seat. Each crew member took a seat. The gentle force that served as a protective restraint system surrounded them. The captain opened the starship's starboard doors, revealing the pitch blackness of space, a portion of the jeweled Milky Way and the blue and white planet below. He eased the lander through the hatch and closed it. He engaged the craft's engine, slowly accelerating. The starship quickly faded to a tiny toy. Within minutes, the lander was plunging through the planet's atmosphere, the crew members' vision obscured by the clouds. As the ship descended, the captain felt a knot in his stomach the size of one of Minj's basketballs. They broke through the clouds. Below was a building that looked like a large, silver-grey gem stone set on a vast, light blue cloth. Spread out in all directions was a crowd of numerous gnat-sized creatures. The captain made the craft hover in place for a moment as the crew and he took it all in. Then he swallowed hard and slowly continued the descent. The building and the people rapidly grew larger as the ground came up to meet them. Houston eased the little ship down as gently as if an infant were onboard. They stopped smoothly. A flawless landing as usual. As it normally did, the ship would continue to hover a few feet above the ground while a long ramp would allow the landing party to exit.

As everyone arose from their seats, the skipper had some final words:

"Remember, we've left civilization behind. We're in the frontier. Being isolated for hundreds of years can do strange things to a culture. The natives may have developed some unusual customs. Or they may have lost many of the technologies their ancestors took for granted. We've got to be ready for anything."

Minj's face was visibly perspiring. Montoya just stood there and stroked his beard. Luci and the other ladies were poker-faced. They each took turns stepping through a disinfecting chamber that would kill many of the germs they could potentially pass on to the natives."Okay, guys and ladies," Houston said. "Ready?"

No one responded to the contrary.

"Here goes."

He hit a button and a round doorway appeared. Bright light flooded the landing craft. The intensity would have been overwhelming were it not for the crew members' dark sun lenses. Looking through the hatch, the star visitors saw a sky lit by a huge, extremely bright sun and, in another part of the sky a tiny, dim one. In the distance was a large building in some geometric shape, its walls all made of mirror glass. There was a tiny reflection of the landing craft.

They also noted a sprawling crowd and, much closer, an entourage of officials. Erik stepped forward, almost bounding out of the craft. Montoya and Minj followed, with Luci and the other two ladies farther behind.

Captain Houston glanced back and noted that all six members of the landing party were now out. He touched a button on a control pad to activate the vehicle's force field. The air around it began to shimmer, causing many in the crowd to gasp.

The star visitors looked straight ahead as they advanced but their peripheral vision continued to note the crowd. None of the natives were talking as they continued staring at the space people advancing toward their top leaders. He spotted the ruler from a long way off. She was finely dressed and looked dignified. She stood up straight, had a piercing gaze and carried an air of authority. She seemed to radiate power and confidence.

Chiefexec Elle took a few steps forward, trailed cautiously by other members of her group. Armed security agents began to form a semi-circle around the planet's dignitaries while reporters with video equipment pressed as far forward as the guards would allow.

The captain and the others in the landing party looked uneasily at the huge crowd surrounding them. The people were tall. The visitors noted skin of various dark hues: tan, mocha, olive, bronze, cocoa, ebony. The abundance of such shades may have been due to the intensity of the suns' rays when both orbs were in the sky. Yet, Houston didn't spot any sun lenses in the crowd. Apparently everyone was *used* to the extremely bright days and could function normally without assistance. Many of the natives had hairstyles that stuck out oddly or were frizzed per a typical low grav world. Others had straight hair.

The captain's eyes focused on the limo, now being joined by the official vehicles of other of the planet's dignitaries. He strode toward the executive vehicle. The others in the landing party followed closely behind. His eyes shifted from the top leader to the crowd and back again. Virtually all the natives wore light-colored clothing made up of long swatches of cloth that were wrapped around the body and tied. Some people wore their wraps at about knee level, others somewhat above the knee. The natives also wore various types of sandals. No doubt their garb was in response to the intense heat from the double sun. It must be 120 degrees Fahrenheit! Yet none of the locals seemed to be perspiring.

# 8.

An hour earlier, a morning news anchor had been shouting: "The star people are orbiting our planet and are about to land!" Video screens all over the city were tuned in to the show. In Central Media Plaza downtown, hundreds of people were standing near the 100-foot-tall video screen that was tuned into the show. Around the corner an equally large screen tuned into another news show also talked of the imminent arrival of visitors. Around another corner a third screen carried a broadcast from an additional station. Al'aama's citizens, some frantic and some excited, noted that the starship captain who had spoken last night with the young girl had talked about meeting *the chiefexec*. This morning, the captain had addressed her directly. Thousands of curious men and women began flooding the highways and the solar electric trains as they headed toward the leader's mansion in an effort to witness this historic event. Others had begun camping outside the grounds since the previous night.

Crowds began to pour onto the grounds, with more people constantly arriving. Chiefexec Elle stood at the edge of the vast lawn and surveyed the crowd. No doubt every media outlet on the planet was here as well, down to the smallest audio station and the tiniest online newzoid. The exec's staff had been reporting that all work on the planet had come to standstill. Everyone was either on their way to the grounds or glued to their video screens.

She wasn't sure what upset her more, having her speech put on hold by the abrupt burst of communication from the space ship or these star men having the audacity to visit her planet. A couple hours had passed since the star captain's transmission. The chiefexec had given her permission for a landing party to arrive. What more could she have said, "No, you do not have permission to land. Keep on orbiting our planet indefinitely"? But what if their intentions weren't peaceful, despite what the captain had claimed?

The chiefexec went back to scanning the sky, watching for the arrival of the landing craft. She kept straining her eyes but didn't see a thing. Finally, members of the crowd gasped loudly and pointed overhead. Zama shaded her eyes against the double-sunned sky. She could see it, too—a tiny dot in the distance that was rapidly growing larger. When the craft had enlarged to a fairly good size, it had seemed to hover overhead then slowly descended, softly coming to a stop near the edge of the mansion's sprawling lawn. Moments after the ship stopped moving and the crowd surged toward it.

The leader's personal security chief immediately audioed his group leaders: "Keep them back! Keep them back!" Armed guards ordered the onlookers and media people away from the landing craft. Burly robots also ordered the crowd back. The mechanical agents had foam arms and looked ready to push people away if there appeared the need. Long moments passed while there was no visible sign of the star men disembarking.

The planetary leader continued to stare at the craft, which looked like a toy in the distance.

"That little thing's a starship?" scoffed one official.

"Naw. I've heard the big ship's orbiting in space. This is their lander," said another.

Zama frowned and set her jaw.

Another dignitary stage-whispered: "Maybe if Chiefexec Elle looks mad enough, they'll turn around and go back home."

She ignored the comment. She waited a moment longer, fidgeting with her jewelry and shifting from one foot to another. Abruptly she launched off, double-time toward the alien vehicle, her long legs rapidly closing the gap. The crowd stood in awe-struck silence as they watched their leader boldly close in on the landing craft.

"Where's she going?" cried Alisa, her jaw dropping.

"M-madame Exec!" shouted Security Chief Thal into her earpiece. "It may not be safe!"

"I'm not afraid of these space people," she replied. "If they planned to attack us, I'm sure they would have done so by now."

"I don't like this," Thal snapped at two of his deputies."Get me three dozen officers, fully armed and get them caught up with the chiefexec. Now!"

As her superior closed in on the lander, Alisa barked out orders for a driver to steer a limo across the vast lawn to pick up the chief executive. Within moments, a long, white vehicle appeared. Several of the bolder administration members piled into it. The car began edging its way through the crowd. It was a deluxe, elongated version of the local solar electric cars. Several carloads of security agents also started out toward the big boss lady. Meanwhile, she had gotten within thirty yards of the lander. She stopped walking as suddenly as she had started. She was the ruler of this planet. Let the intruders come to her. Her belated entourage began to draw closer.

She stood and waited, massaging her hands as if she were washing them. The little ship appeared solid. There was no obvious port and seemed no way in or out. The ship sat there with no signs of life. All of A'laama stared. Finally, a large, round section of wall dissolved and a steep ramp emerged.

The first space man bounded out of the craft. Two more rapidly followed. They were sporting backpacks. As they moved toward the chiefexec's vehicle, the officials were puzzled by the bounce in the space people's steps. Zama squinted at the visitors through air that shimmered from the heat. The part of their eyes that should be pigmented were—black! Three other people, all women, left the ship. The large, round exit vanished and the ship's skin was again solid.

Zama, who was wearing the same skirt suit from her failed broadcast attempt, had advanced no farther. Finally, the men and the chiefexec were only a few feet apart. She looked at the head of the delegation. He was a few inches shorter than she. He was rather muscular, fortyish and had dark hair. Her eyes probed his mysterious, sun lens-darkened orbs. He had an earnest appearance she found disarming despite her suspicions.

The captain looked more closely at the exec lady. She was a few inches taller than he but not quite as tall as some of the bystanders. She had light brown hair past her shoulders. She came across as a no-nonsense person and seemed somewhat perturbed. Almost as if the visitors were invading her turf. His eyes focused on some tiny blue lights that were flashing below the skin of her left forearm, some kind of electronic implant. He glanced at the distant crowd and thought he could detect similar implants on many of the people. Some on the left arm. Some on the right. Some on an ear or a temple. Some people were looking at their arms and were seeming to speak to them. Were some of the implants built-in comm devices? Some flashed red lights, some other colors. In the dead silence, he thought the planetary leader's arm was quietly humming.

The lead spaceman swallowed hard and, in what he hoped was a universal gesture of friendship, extended his right hand to the chiefexec. The boss lady, fully aware of all the media equipment trained on her, firmly grasped the spaceman's hand. The crowd let out a collective sigh then began to cheer.

All six space people waved to the crowd, which cheered even louder. After several minutes, the response died down. The space captain, switching on the cosmic translator, took a deep breath. He paused a moment before speaking. It always took a while for space travelers' lungs to adjust to breathing planetary atmosphere after spending months at a time taking in the filtered, re-circulated, purified air aboard a starship. The more Erik breathed, the more his lungs burned. He swallowed again, took another breath and in a somewhat raspy voice said into his mike: "Greetings, Chiefexec Elle and people of the planet Al'aama!"

A long silence ensued. The head of A'laama shut off her mike and boldly said to Houston: "Captain, I was insulted that you chose to initiate contact with our planet through private citizens rather than through me. I'm the ruler of this sovereign planet!"

The captain looked at the ground. He raised his eyes back to the level of hers. "Madame Exec, you have my deepest apologies. We actually did try, *several times*, to contact your office directly but we ran into severe sunspot trouble that caused our signal to bounce. We did not in any sense mean to slight you or your office."

There was a pause while the cosmic translator rendered the captain's words into the native language. She heard the translated words but remained poker-faced. She looked at the captain and opened her mouth to respond.

The mood was abruptly interrupted by chief advisor Betelguese, who had elbowed her way through the crowd and had somehow eluded even the security personnel. "It's true, it's true!" she bellowed. "The Prophecy has come true, Madame Exec! Three men from the stars!"

The chiefexec, already embarrassed by the strangeness of these star people, turned away from Betel. But several audio and video reporters were already beckoning to her for further comments. Meanwhile, the chiefexec noted that the three landing party members following behind the first were women. They had the same unnaturally dark eyes as the others.

After Betel's outburst, the long silence resumed. The leader did not make any effort to speak "mike on" with Captain Houston. Instead, she glared at these short, pale men with their bouncy manner of walking, dark eyes and strangely raspy voices. Houston and the others had become uncomfortably aware of the large number of uniformed men and women with handheld, metallic weapons surrounding the landing party.

A long, silent moment passed during which Houston glanced out of the corner of his eye at Montoya and Minj, who were right behind him. The other two men slowly followed his lead in sliding their hands to a pocket from which they withdrew a hand stunner, just in case. Each man's other hand was on a button that could activate a personal force field if needed for protection.

Within that same split second, the security guards surrounding the group raised their metallic hand weapons. Just as quickly, the three spacemen raised theirs. The two groups looked eye to eye. No one flinched; no one blinked. The captain felt ice in his stomach. He wasn't seeking a confrontation but was only being cautious. He had lost crew members on two previous missions due to incidents caused by suspicions of those planets' natives. As tension continued to mount, he wished the chiefexec would call off her troops. But she did not do so. In fact, the natives seemed quite determined to stand their ground.

"You all right, captain?" asked a gravelly voice in his ear. It was Irv Malvo, his security chief who was monitoring the situation from the ship as it orbited high above the planet.

"Affirmative," the captain replied through clenched teeth.

He was about to casually drop his weapon as a gesture of good faith. Just then, the hoarse voice of Betel punctured the silence. "You...spacemen!" she bellowed.

The chiefexec groaned and shook her head.

"You spacemen," the older woman repeated, "resolve this standoff. Fulfill the Prophecy by calling fire down from heaven! Call fire down from heaven!"

The chiefexec's jaw dropped. A few members of the crowd, perhaps intending to mock the spacemen, perhaps because they had no idea what *to* say, began to chant: "Call fire down from heaven! Call fire down from heaven!" Betel gestured to the crowd and continued leading them in their chant.

"Captain!" cried the voice in his ear. "Should I *do* anything?"

Houston thought a moment. He spied a large, decorative boulder that sat far away from any people. "See that big rock in the distance?" he asked quietly.

"Yes, sir."

"Give the lady what she wants."

"Aye, sir."

Malvo fired a powerful energy burst that shot like lightning through the planet's atmosphere and hit the boulder dead on. The huge rock seemed to explode but was instantly vaporized. When the smoke dissipated, a deep crater appeared. The crowd gasped and the people closest to the scene scrambled away helter skelter.

"Erik...no! I saw that thing *move!*" cried Minj.

"You mean we've just disintegrated a *local life form?*"

Chiefexec Elle swallowed hard and began to tremble. She raised a quivering arm, pointed a finger at the landing party and said to her guards: "Arrest these people!"

The captain glared at her. He switched off his microphone and said in a low voice, "All right. We'll go along with this, Madame Exec, just to show you we mean no harm. But this detention better be short lived. And I won't tolerate your hurting my people."

Zama looked him in the eye but said nothing further as the guards pointed their weapons and gestured to the landing party to start walking. The fickle crowd began to boo and jeer at the prisoners.

"A lot of good that prayer did," the first officer muttered as they were led away.

"God doesn't always answer immediately," the captain said quietly.

# 9.

"Captain, I want the truth!"

A short-haired, burly male interrogator was glaring into Houston's eyes, his face just inches away. "Why are you here?"

"I *told* you the truth," he said, staring right back at his antagonist. "We're here on a peaceful mission. We want to learn more about your planet. And we want to help you." It was difficult saying these words so emphatically without detracting from their meaning. Houston was growing weary. They had been over these same questions for what seemed like hours but the interrogator wouldn't let up. He only hoped his crew members, especially the ladies, weren't undergoing similar experiences.

"If you mean us no harm, then what is *this?*" asked the man, resting the stunner in the palm of his hand.

"It's for defensive purposes. We thought you were going to shoot us. And we weren't going to kill any of your people. It's set to stun."

"But it is *capable* of killing people," the man insisted for at least the third time.

"Yes. But it's not set for lethal power."

"*You* need to demonstrate how these devices work."

"I don't *have to* do anything!"

"So, you refuse my orders, Captain? We can make life unpleasant for you and your people."

The captain pushed the chair out and stood up. "My security people are continually watching us from space and they won't allow you to harm us."

"Sit down!" the interrogator bellowed, pushing him back down into the chair. He returned to examining the other objects in the box. "And what is *this?*" he asked, holding a small object the size of a key chain.

"Look, I don't have to tell you anything further. I've already told you enough! We come here in peace, wanting to share some of our tech with your people but if you try to *force* it from us, I have the authority to cut short our mission and the help we give you will be minimal."

"Captain, you try my patience!" growled the man, slamming his fist into his hand."Let's try this again, Captain. What does this do?"

"It's defensive also, and it's not even a weapon. When activated, it surrounds me with a protective energy field that weapons cannot penetrate."

"Then why didn't you activate it instead of reaching for your weapon?"

Erik hesitated, knowing the man had a good point.... "We thought you were going to shoot us," he repeated.

"And what is this?" He held up an object the size of an ancient hearing aid.

"That's my comm link. I use it to communicate with my crew on the ship and here on the planet. And as I told your chiefexec, if you try to hold us indefinitely, our crew will begin to worry about us and will find a way to rescue us!"

The man's eyes flashed. "What will you do, disintegrate us like you did that rock? That sounds like a threat to me, Captain. We're not afraid of your threats!" He arose from his seat, turned and walked out of the room, taking with him the box that held Houston's possessions.

The captain sat in the uncomfortable chair for what felt like additional hours. He was then marched to another room and given a physical. The doctor said he was worried about the inhabitants of the planet being contaminated by "space germs" and jammed a series of hypodermics into the captain's arm. After some more waiting, the interrogator returned and without speaking handed him the comm link, the cosmic translator and a couple other items. The captain asked for the remaining equipment. "No, we're keeping it so we can study it," the man replied.

The captor strode out the door, carrying the box.

Sometime later, three female armed guards marched into the room. The lead guard motioned for Houston to exit the room and walk into a hallway. One guard walked in front of him while the others followed behind him, the closer one poking his ribs with her handheld weapon. Erik noted that all three women were tall and had deep tans. Each guard had blond hair halfway down her back and worn in a pigtail. The group reached a cell. The lead guard pulled a tiny electronic device from her pocket and punched a button. She motioned for the captain to walk forward into the cell. He did so and she punched another button. The guard motioned for him to watch her. She retrieved a coin from her pocket and threw it toward the cell. A blue bolt of electricity noisily zapped the coin, which now sat melting on the floor. The leader looked at Erik to make sure he got the picture. He now got a better look at the guards, including the ones who had been behind him. The women were triplets! He was so startled it took him a moment to realize the two other male landing party members, Minj and Montoya, were also in the cell.

"Captain!" said Minj with relief.

"Are we glad to see you!" said Montoya. "You all right?"

Houston nodded. As the three men commiserated, he found out their experiences had been similar to his. "How about those three guards?"

Said Minj: "They're like holos of one another."

"Clones?" asked the captain.

Montoya, the medical officer, nodded.

Now that the guards were gone, Houston switched off the cosmic translator, another device the natives had thankfully not confiscated. He punched in a code on the comm link. He set up a visual and sound block in case the guards came by.

"Luci?"

"Erik! I'm glad to hear you! How are you guys?"

"We're fine," he said. "Tired, but fine. Are you and the other ladies okay?"

"Surviving. We were each interrogated and that was kinda scary, but they didn't hurt us. Hopefully, they'll leave us alone now."

"I hope so, too. And don't worry. I won't let this drag on indefinitely. If I have to, I'll get us out of here."

"I know."

The men continued to sit in the cell for hours.

"Wonder how long the Ice Queen will leave us in here," Minj wondered.

Erik set his comm link to re-dial the chiefexec's frequency. The woman at the other end yelped in surprise when a 3-D of the star man abruptly appeared in front of her. "Captain! I-I'm in a meeting. C-can you wait until I get my earpiece?"

He complied, then said: "Madame Exec, you've disrespected my crew and I, treated us roughly and now you're keeping us locked up. This violates interstellar law. If we're not out of here within twenty-four hours, we'll break out on her own and leave your planet. We'll report that you're an uncooperative world that's not interested in becoming part of the interstellar community."

Her face reddened and she bit her lip. She sighed. "Be patient with us. Your arrival has been a shock to all of us. We're still sorting this out."

"I suggest you not take too long. Twenty-four hours maximum." He terminated the call, frustrated for the thousandth time at how each planet he visited was its own independent fiefdom. He began to pace the floor.

Montoya heard one of the guards walking further down the long hall. Turning on his translator, he called: "Hey, when do we eat?"

One of the identical guards walked toward the cell, offered to check on that then returned sometime later with trays of food. Houston retrieved another pocket-sized device, a food analyzer, and pronounced that the items were all okay to ingest. The glasses contained a clear liquid that the men took to be water but it turned out to be much thicker and had a sweet, fruity flavor. Minj drained his right down. The plates of food each contained a flat, chewy substance that was warm to the touch and something that was light blue colored and leafy. Montoya took a bite of the leafy item and spat it out.

"This stuff is bitter," he said, taking a swig of the fruity liquid.

"At least the analyzer shows they're not trying to poison us," said Minj.

"Well, maybe not on purpose," Montoya replied, taking another gulp of the clear juice as he still tried to wash the bitter taste from his mouth.

The captain quickly ate his meal then settled onto a bunk to sleep. It had already been too long of a day....

# 10.

Thousands of people continued to camp on the mansion lawn. Some were actively protesting the star people's arrival. Others voiced concern over their treatment. Still others remained from a sense of history being made or from simple curiosity. The mansion continued to experience a record-breaking volume of video screen inquiries. The situation threatened to cause the business of the executive branch to grind to a halt.

Deep within the structure, Communications Director Barr looked out over a hostile sea of reporters. She was short by A'laaman standards, stockily built and had curly, dark brown hair that was shading toward grey. She was wearing a light grey skirt suit and dark-colored top. Her left hand was twitching nervously as she prepared to start the press conference, her second so far that day.

"I'd like to begin…" she said.

"Madame secretary!" called a female reporter who stood up in back of the room. "Where are our visitors from the stars? Are they still being unlawfully detained?"

The communications director bristled. "It's not unlawful!" she insisted. "Our constitution clearly gives the chiefexec emergency powers...."

"What's the emergency?" countered a male correspondent. "Our visitors said they came here with no hostile intentions. The administration bullied them into making a stand to make them look bad." Several members of the press murmured in agreement.

Evva replied: "Our sole intention has been to protect our citizens...."

"Madame secretary," cried another female, "when will we be given access to the star people? When will they get to make a statement?"

"In due time you'll have an opportunity...."

"Madame secretary!" interrupted a fourth reporter.

Evva's head felt like it was splitting by the time she called an end of the proceedings some forty-five minutes later. She trotted down the hall to meet with the rest of the cabinet. She sheepishly opened the door to the long, high-ceilinged room. She was five minutes late; the others were all seated and the meeting had begun. The chiefexec nodded somberly at Evva as she rushed to her seat.

The leader pushed back her hair with one hand while the other rested on the long meeting table made of red ironwood that had been polished to a mirror finish. Her cabinet members sat in high-backed chairs. "We need to figure out what to do with the star people," she said. "What do you think they really want from us?" She looked tensely around the room.

"Madame Exec," said portly, white-haired Education Minister Harald Filb, "there may be a lot we can *learn* from our visitors."

"Yes," said Science Minister Bern, a gleam in her eye, "think what technological secrets they could reveal." Tanna's ears were poking through her baby-fine hair, drawing attention away from her rather prominent nose.

"But," said Social Analyst Lil Nemms, "their culture seems radically different than ours, even based on what little we know of them. They seem...strange."

"You're absolutely right," said the chiefexec. "I don't trust these invaders. We know nothing about them or the societies on other planets...."

"And it's our own fault!" cried Tanna. Several mouths hung open and Madame Exec's face was hardening. "That's right. We've always known that there are many other inhabited star systems yet we *choose* to remain ignorant about them. I've been fighting for years for funding to set up a couple electronic eyes and ears to monitor other planets' broadcasts."

"We've been over this before," said the boss lady.

"Ma'am, I've asked every chiefexec over the last ten years…."

Zama Elle dismissed Tanna's comments with a wave of the hand, causing the science director to look like she'd just eaten a lemon. The chiefexec lowered her head and let out a deep sigh. "All right," she said reluctantly, "I know we can't postpone this matter any longer. We need a vote of the council." The cabinet members abruptly straightened up in their chairs. "I propose the following resolution to be voted on by the council: We will release our visitors under the cabinet's supervision and question them on the nature of their mission."

Parliamentarian James Oppel said loudly and in a serious tone of voice: "A vote is about to be cast by the leaders of the Three Great Tribes. Leader of the Caab tribe, what say you?"

"Aye," said the tribal leader.

"Leader of the tribe of Batami, what say you?"

"No. I agree with the chiefexec. I'm leery of these people."

All eyes in the room now rested on Chiefexec Elle. For several moments she said nothing, finally raising her head. "And as leader of the tribe of Paol, my vote is a reluctant aye," she said. The leader of the Batami tribe stared daggers at her leader. The room erupted into animated conversation.

The chiefexec took advantage of the lull in the proceedings to summon Chief of Staff Conway to her side. "Alisa," she said quietly, "my firstadvisor, Betel, is well past retirement age." Zama had inherited her from the two previous administrations.

Alisa smiled her usual tense smile. "Consider it done."

"Now, for her successor. I have in mind a lady who has been one of my counselors over the past several years. Kelly Farji."

Alisa thought a moment. "Yes, Dr. Farji. Former legislae. Advanced degrees in stellar theology and bio-ethics. Known for her wisdom. I take it that I should give her a substantial raise?"

"Make her an offer at your soonest convenience."

"Yes, Ma'am."

# 11.

The three guards approached the cell where the men from the stars were being held. The prisoners had learned that the guards' names were Lila, Lola and Leela. The head guard, Lila, turned off the electronic gate, motioning for the three men to don their backpacks and exit. Captain Houston quickly switched on the translator. "Where are we going?" he asked.

"Not allowed to say, sir," she replied. The men had learned she was the most outgoing of the three women.

The guards blindfolded the men. They led the prisoners rather briskly down the hall, then turned into another hall, then another. There were a few steps; the women were careful with their charges there. Abruptly the group seemed to be outdoors. The men felt a warm wind on their faces. Erik smiled, grateful for the fresh air after days of confinement.

"Duck down," Lila's voice said as all three guards used their hands to protect the blindfolded men's heads as they entered the car. Houston noticed "his" guard has rather large hands, but not unusually large for someone of her height. The car's electric motor began whirring and the car lumbered off.

After about a five-minute ride, the car came to a halt. The guards helped the men out. This time, the star men did not have the sense of being outdoors. In the distance, an air conditioning unit was humming. They were inside now, perhaps in some underground parking facility. The guards walked the men down a short series of hallways and helped them step over the threshold of a door. The door closed and there was the slightly stomach-jarring sensation of moving upward, as in a vertilift. The lift stopped moving and the guards walked the men out the door and down a series of hallways. Finally, after what seemed like several minutes of walking, the group entered a room and the guards removed the blindfolds. They were in a plush suite with a few comfortable-looking chairs and couches. A long table covered with a fine table cloth was laden with plates of several varieties of food and large containers of chilled beverages.

"Relax, gentlemen," said Lila, smiling. All three men noticed for the first time that she had a beautiful smile. "Feel free to eat, drink, rest."

"What happens now?" asked the captain.

"You'll be meeting with our leaders," she replied. The guards exited, closing the door behind them, although the men had no doubt they would be waiting right outside the door, weapons at the ready.

"This is a little better," Montoya said uneasily.

Minj nodded.

The captain began to pace the room while the other two men ate ravenously and downed some beverages. His equipment showed that the room was bugged. He laughed. The natives could listen in all they wanted. What good would it do them if they couldn't understand the language?

The men took turns showering, laser shaving and changing clothes. The suite contained three bedrooms. Each was sparsely furnished, with a wall-sized video screen as the main embellishment. None of the screens worked. The captain chuckled again. Did these people really think they could keep info from their visitors so easily? He used his comm equipment to monitor local 3-D videocasts. The space people's arrival, of course, dominated the news sites. The captain switched to a few minutes of a pro-sports match but he had trouble following the rules. Another source was broadcasting a drama about some love triangle. He even looked up some online want ads. Job openings included longevity specialist, gene splicer and clone psychologist.

He had learned that if he began to ease toward a sitting position, a comfortable chair would slide out from the wall. If he moved toward a reclining position, a bed would appear. The suite appeared climate controlled but was set to an infernally hot temperature with no obvious way to change it. There was some electronic equipment behind the walls. From time to time it buzzed, hummed or beeped for a moment. The captain would later observe that the windowless suite had artificial lighting that simulated a standard day. The rooms would gradually get dark at night, except for intentionally turning on a lamp, and get light in the morning.

What seemed like a couple hours later, the guards returned. This time, they didn't blindfold the men. The guards led them down another unending series of hallways. Finally, the group stopped walking.

Standing before them was a woman wearing a cream-colored, sleeveless wrap outfit that was adorned with some gold insignias. She was the tallest lady the men had seen on the planet, towering over Minj, who looked up at her. She had auburn hair barely long enough to cover her ears and neck. The official had the same deep tan as most of the natives. Covering her face and arms were an explosion of even darker spots. Freckles. An area near her left ear flashed with some red lights that seemed to come from within the ear canal, freakishly lighting the canal for a moment. This was likely a communications implant, appropriate for someone who could never afford to be out of touch with either her staff or her superiors.

The officials' eyes narrowed as she looked at the visitors: "The chiefexec and her cabinet will see you now," she said through a tense smile.

Two halves of a section of wall parted. The official walked through the opening. The guards beckoned for the men to follow but did not themselves enter. The men stepped in and the wall sections came seamlessly back together without making a sound. The men stood before a long, shiny red table surrounded by about a dozen seated men and women ranging from early middle age to elderly.

The dignitaries stared at the visitors but did not address them. Erik moved his gaze from one leader to another. One was a brown-skinned woman with long, straight hair that was chestnut in color. She looked serene and had large, brown eyes. Another was a balding, tan-skinned man with white hair and a goatee. Another was a lady with almond-shaped eyes and high cheekbones. An implant outlined the left cheekbone and flashed with red lights.

The woman in the cream-colored tunic, Chief of Staff Alisa Conway, was the first to rise to her feet as the chiefexec strode into the room. The planetary leader wore a knee-length white wrap of high-quality cloth, a burgundy sash, and sandals that laced halfway up her calves. Burgundy polish adorned her fingernails and toenails. She took her seat, followed by the cabinet members. The spacemen were still standing and the room had no unoccupied chairs. No one said a word for a long moment as the chiefexec visually examined the spacemen like a scientist would a lab specimen. Finally, she said: "Greetings, gentlemen. I trust you've enjoyed your stay."

The captain, arms at his sides, unconsciously clenched his fists. "Madame Exec," he began, a little louder than he intended, "we've spent the day and a half in confinement. To be blunt, our spirits have been a little dampened. And we've been particularly concerned about how this confinement has hurt the morale of our women." Chiefexec Elle bristled at the last remark. The captain continued: "We mean you no harm, yet your treatment of us so far hasn't been very hospitable. We have highly developed technology. We had intended to share some of it with you but instead you've tried to force info from us. You have the potential to gain great benefits from our visit. But if you continue to treat us badly, what we'll be willing to do for you will be limited."

The chiefexec shook her head. "It was you who invaded our sovereign planet," she said quietly. Several cabinet members looked agape at their chiefexec. She looked at Houston a moment then sighed. "Captain," she said, "surely you can understand our concern. We've built a civilization here over centuries. We've always stood alone, without any outside support or…interference. Then, unexpectedly, you show up. How do we know you're truly peaceful?"

"So far, there's been cause for distrust on both sides. I'd like to tell you why we're here." He waved his hand and a 3-D image of an ultramodern city appeared. The leaders gasped. "Madame Exec and distinguished leaders of the planet Al'aama, we represent the United Association of Planets, a confederation of worlds that communicate and cooperate with one another on cultural and scientific matters." The captain waved his hand again and the first image was replaced by one of an evening setting depicting a lush garden area interspersed with various buildings. Three silvery moons of various sizes hung in the twilight sky. "As I said, we come in peace, and that is the truth," he said, boldly looking the chiefexec directly in the eye. She held her gaze for a moment before they both looked away. "The Association includes several dozen planets," the captain continued. He waved his hand again and the image changed again to show a red planet with a dual sun in the background. Additional hand waves over the next several minutes revealed shots of various other worlds. "Each planet has its own unique culture and each planet sends it greetings," Houston continued. The next image depicted a small group of dark-haired, dark-eyed children waving. Most of the cabinet members smiled.

"Skip the PR," said Zama "What do you want from us?"

The captain held his composure."We want to learn about your culture, invite you to join our association. To exchange knowledge and ideas. And we want to help your planet develop."

The chiefexec whispered to Chief of Staff Conway: "I knew it! A larger invasion is just around the corner."

The captain smiled. He waved his hand. The officials gasped as all lights went out. Suddenly, they were someplace very different. Crowds of people in exotic-looking outfits were walking around at ground level. Some individuals were darting through the air like insects but without any visible means of propulsion. One launched into the sky directly in front of them. Ground level showed what looked like machines, each several acres across, that projected into the sky what appeared to be translucent buildings made of light. Each structure was a different pastel color: blue, green, pink. Many of the towers pierced a bank of clouds that resembled a ceiling high overhead. The virtual tour swept the audience upward through the clouds, which then became a floor as many of the towers continued hundreds or thousands of feet higher. This blended into scenes showing various people strolling ankle deep through clouds as if they actually were a floor. Toward the tops of the various monuments, large clusters of tiny dots hovered as if they were swarms of insects.

Abruptly, the officials felt like they were rising. Rising upward inside a tube of light that looked dozens of yards wide and hundreds high. As they flashed upward, the audience could see tiny people on various floors milling about. The visitors shot past multi-dimensional sculptures that were each several stories high. Indoor rivers spilled thousands of feet to form waterfalls that created their own clouds of mist. There was even an indoor rainbow. Near the waterfalls, some of them tiered, scattered individual humans and small groups of them, looking like mites due to the sheer scale of their surroundings, flew to and fro. Some had wings strapped to their backs and were gliding through the indoor sky.

The A'laamans caught fleeting glimpses of vast, multi-level indoor parks. Atriums the size of A'laama's entire downtown. Multi-storied, floating transports the size of city blocks moved here and there within the atrium. The

A'laamans' ride upward continued as the pastel-colored buildings shrunk down to miniatures then disappeared. The sky outside the building rapidly grew medium blue. Indigo. Black. The spectators ooh and ahhed as the horizon dropped away and a curved surface appeared. Below was a shining dark blue and green semi-sphere surrounded by a thin, light blue envelope. Tiny lights winked on and the sky soon looked like black velvet encrusted with a billion diamonds and sapphires. Space. They continued to rise as if riding a beam of light that acted like an enormous vertilift going...where? Various cabinet members stared up and pointed. Approaching was some sort of jewel in space. No. A building. An enormous one.

Now they were inside. Their feet sunk into plush carpet. The ornate furnishings looked like some sort of lobby. Everything was now back to human scale. Even the people looked normal except for their odd clothing. And their tremendous diversity. Some were extremely tall, thin and had elongated limbs, resembling praying mantises. Other people were short and squat. There was every skin color from ghostly pale to coal black, a far wider palette than even on A'laama. Yet everyone was obviously human. Had these different types of people somehow naturally adapted to millennia on various high grav and low grav planets, as well as a number of different solar and temperature conditions? The A'laamans were vaguely aware of some audio that had been droning on to accompany the video, but they were too swept up in the experience to focus on it.

The lights flashed back on, snapping the dignitaries back to reality. Every A'laaman mouth was hanging open. Every set of eyes was maxxed wide. The chiefexec appeared to have stopped breathing.

After a moment, she mumbled: "T-hat's nice, Captain, but how do we know this isn't system generated...." No one appeared to have heard her.

Minj, the ship historian, broke in: "There's a wide range of maturities among the cultures within our Association. A relative handful of planets have settlements dating back fifteen hundred years or more. But our sociologists say it takes multiple thousands of years for a given planet to develop a truly global civilization with populous nation-states on all major land masses and numerous large cities. The only planet that *truly* fits that description would be the mother planet from which *all* of our ancestors originated...."

Nemms stuttered for a long moment before she could speak. "Getting back to your...interstellar association, doesn't the relative slowness of your ships and communications make it unwieldy to operate?"

"Valid point," said Minj. "Visual and audio communications between and among member star systems can travel no faster than light. Communications are constantly sent between star systems and among all Association member planets. Each planet has large organizations that do nothing but send and receive communications to and from other star systems. But because the distance between stars is so vast, any type of two-way or multi-way dialog takes many years. Matters of policy that must be considered, revised, voted upon by members can literally take centuries. The Association members share scientific data and knowledge of one another's cultures. There are a limited number of ships traveling between star systems bearing cargo, ambassadors, scientists, exchange students, adventurers and travelers. And there are some ships like ours, visiting inhabited systems, trying to find what's become of colonies planted long ago. A stage play or video that's a hit in one star system may be beamed into space then years or decades later become a hit in other star systems. Over many centuries, we've developed what we call a *virtual civilization*. We share in one another's cultures, but on time delay. Physically, each inhabited world is still relatively isolated. They're like *islands among the stars*."

Chiefexec Elle nodded. "No wonder it's taken you so long to catch up with us."

The captain added: "The majority of human civilization is thinly spread across an area reaching about fifty light years in all directions. After more than two millennia of starflight, we still haven't scratched the surface in that area, which is just a tiny dot in the cosmos. Ancient writers at the dawn of spaceflight would craft fictional tales about empires ruling entire galaxies, which consist of *hundreds of billions* of star systems. The systems humans and automated probes have actually visited so far numbers less than a thousand."

Science Director Bern's fingers had been flying across her video screen as she entered various numbers. She looked up and said: "There's debate over the exact size of our galaxy, but if you use commonly accepted figures for its length, the width of the disk and its thickness and account for the spiral arms…I come up with some 5.6 trillion cubic light years as the volume of the entire Milky Way. You say that humans have done a partial exploration of an area with a radius of 50 light years, or about 523,000 cubic light years. So, after two thousand years in space, we're beginning to make our mark on less than one ten-millionth of the galaxy."

The captain nodded. "Many of the stars are expected to burn for billions more years but they would have died of old age before we've even explored a significant fraction of the Milky Way."

Montoya added: "And our galaxy is just one out of *hundreds of billions.*"

The room fell silent for a long moment. Contemplating things on so vast a scale made one feel very small. The captain thought of quoting a scripture or two but held back. After all, he knew nothing yet about this world's belief system and the leaders seemed like they were just beginning to trust their visitors. Besides, the *Initiative* wasn't a mission ship....

The chiefexec broke the spell by asking the star men some other questions. Sometime later, when Houston and his senior officers had fielded all of the officials' questions, he decided he would try to switch gears with the discussion.

"Madame Exec," he said, "so far we've told you a lot of things about ourselves. Now, if we may, we'd like to ask you a few things about your culture."

"In due time, Captain," she said. "For now, this interview is over." She arose from her chair and turned to leave.

The moment she saw the backs of the three men heading out via the re-separated wall segments, the chiefexec sprang to her feet and exited the plush chamber from another direction. Her legs propelling her down a hallway, she thought: *Didn't need the history lesson. But I want their tech.*

The next day, on the far outskirts of A'laama, teen Jaylene Farber rose early as she did every morning. As she shuffled to the kitchen, no one else in the family seemed to be around. She tended to sleep a little later than the rest of the family. Everyone else had undoubtedly gone outside to start their morning chores. She quickly grabbed a breakfast bar and headed toward the barn to feed the family's herd of gannao. This was the first of several such tasks she would need to accomplish before leaving for school in a couple hours.

As she neared the barn, Jae heard a noise, including frantic bleating by the gannao. This puzzled her because they were normally such docile creatures. Had some small animal found its way into the barn and frightened them? Perhaps it was even her pet, Mauser, who had a habit of howling at the gannao. As Jae strode closer to the barn, the commotion grew louder. She was convinced she heard hushed voices in an unknown dialect. Instinctively grabbing a long-handled farm implement that was lying nearby on the ground, she crept up to the barn and cautiously opened the door a foot or so.

Caught by surprise were two muscular, roughly-dressed men and a woman. Each man was carrying a gannao, animals the size of a large dog. The female companion was about to pick one up. The bleating of the animals was deafening. Instantly, Jay pushed an emergency button on the video screen in her pocket then boldly tried to lance the nearest man with the sharp farm implement. The woman put down the gannao and picked up an archer's bow lying on the ground. Jae launched her weapon at the man. He deftly sidestepped it. The female archer let an arrow fly. At such close range, it hit the girl with tremendous force as it penetrated her chest just below the breastbone. A look of horror frozen to her face, Jae fell forward onto the ground, further driving the arrow into her body. The three invaders each grabbed a gannao and fled.

Jae's parents, responding to her emergency alarm, hurried to the barn. Her father, laser pistol in hand, shot at the fleeing rustlers. They hurried away before he was able to score a hit. Jae's mother screamed as she saw her girl lying face first on the ground. She gently rolled her over and saw the growing dark patch on her shirt and the arrow deeply embedded in her chest.

# 12.

Tanna ran out of the meeting, her flat, serious shoes making the process easier. She pulled her round video screen from the deep, wide pants pocket that served as a purse for many A'laaman women. Still moving full speed while holding the screen in one hand and pulling her hair into a ponytail with the other, she said: "Hey, it's me. Yeah, these space jocks are amazing. Yeah. They've got to be centuries ahead of us. I don't care what we have to do. I want that tech."

An hour or so later, Security Chief William Thal looked down the hall in both directions before striding over to Science Director Tanna Bern's office. William was tall, lean and muscular. He had blond hair and a meticulously trimmed brown goatee. He stopped a moment to pick a piece of lint off his suit coat then knocked on Tanna's door. He waited a long moment for a response then cautiously opened the door. Bern was talking on her video screen but motioned for him to come in. He stepped inside but did not advance any farther so that he would not appear on the other person's screen. Bern was wearing an earpiece.

"Yes, Ma'am. Yes. Yes, I'll keep you posted, Ma'am. Thank you." The call concluded.

"Old Iron Pants?" William smirked.

Tanna nodded. "I used to think we were friends but she always shoots down my ideas."

"There *are* no friends in this business," he spat. "Only allies and enemies. And the two can change from day to day."

The science director nodded. "She humiliated me at our cabinet meeting. Brushed aside one of my pet projects in front of all my peers. Yet I'm the only one who appreciates what we can gain from these star people. I'm the only one who's asked them any intelligent questions. Zama Elle and the others just sat there clueless."

"At least nightfall will soon be here," William said.

"That's right," said Tanna with a mischievous grin.

"Any luck with the space people's equipment?"

The science officer shook her head. "Can't get any of it to work. I asked our technicians to take the items apart so we could examine them. But they're all held together using some sort of molecular bonding. Even lasers can't penetrate them."

The security chief shook his head. "So we're at a dead end."

The science director nodded. "Do you have enough officers for tonight?"

"Yes," replied the security chief.

"Good. I'm looking forward to it."

"Until then," said William, rising from his chair and bowing, tongue in cheek to his counterpart.

# 13.

After meeting with the cabinet, the men from the landing party had gone back to their quarters. Less than an hour later, Chief of Staff Conway returned and commandeered them for a conference with the native media. All six star visitors were there, allowing the men and women a chance to visit one another and compare notes for a few minutes before the meeting began.

Once the men returned to their suite, the captain stayed busy having long comm link conversations with the ship's crew. He also periodically contacted the ladies of the landing party. Montoya used his comm link to tap into A'laama's communications media to catch up on local news. The arrival of the landing team and today's press conference dominated the broadcasts and online chatter. The veteran star traveler was always amused at the differences in how his cohorts and he were portrayed from one world to another. Minj worked on learning the Al'aamans' language using his cosmic translator.

Later, the three men got together and started playing a video card game. Star travelers, who spent months and sometimes years in space, frequently played video cards and other games to help pass the time. The men began to wager, using rolls, pieces of native fruit and juice glasses as chips. Well into the second card game, the table was filled with stacks of glasses and piles of rolls and fruit.

"So, how's it going to manifest itself this time?" Montoya asked.

"What?" asked Minj.

"Why Einstein's Law, of course," Montoya replied. The captain rolled his eyes.

"I'm not superstitious," Minj replied.

"Come on, you *know* it works," said Montoya.

Minj shook his head. "We're dozens of trillions of miles from the next inhabited planet yet somehow you believe in these cosmic coincidences that have a near zero chance of happening."

The captain smiled.

Montoya continued: "That's just it—they're not coincidences. These things are *meant* to happen."

"What *things*?" asked Minj. "I'm not experiencing some weird déjà vu being on this planet. It's just as unusual as any of the others we've visited. But we've never been here before. We've never been within several light years of here. There's no great big cosmic surprise waiting to sneak up on us."

"You're wrong," Montoya insisted. "It's happened before...on some of our previous voyages."

"All right, when? Where? Give me time and place."

Montoya hesitated. "I-I'll have to go check my datamaster, but I know it's happened. And it's happened to other crews down through the centuries. What about...?"

Minj interjected: "No...don't tell about some stellar legend. I don't want to hear any more of these fairytales." Raising his voice, he said: "There *is* no Einstein's law!"

A knock sounded at the door. Startled, the three men jumped. The captain ambled over to the door and opened it.

In stepped a woman with shoulder-length, dark hair and the same deep tan as most of the natives. She was wearing a dress, one of the few variations the men had seen from the light wraps many of the A'laamans wore in response to the double-sun heat. The lady was a little shorter than most on the planet. Erik noticed his eye level was about the same as hers.

"Good afternoon, gentlemen," she said enthusiastically. Her face was beaming, reducing her eyes to mere slits. As her smile faded a little, he was able to note the fullness of her eyes, which were large and expressive. Her eyes were green, but the left one was brown around the rim. Some blue lights flashing near her left temple indicated an implant. One in that location might indicate she was a scholar, with the implant making available vast libraries of knowledge the lady could access at will.

"My name is Kelly Farji," she said. "I'm Chiefexec Elle's new firstadvisor. She has asked me to personally be in charge of your stay here."

"Captain Erik Houston. Nice to meet you, Ma'am," he said, sticking out his hand. She clasped it warmly.

"Dr. Fred Montoya."

"Hi. I'm Daj Minj. Ms. Farji, based on your name and appearance, I'd guess you to be part Irish and part Italian. Although…I think I detect a hint of Brazilian in your facial features. I'm mostly of Ukrainian descent."

She stared at him wide-eyed. "I-I don't know what any of that means. I'm 100 percent A'laaman going back twelve generations. Prior to that, I don't know."

The captain shook his head and grinned. "Daj is our expert on ancient, as well as modern civilizations," he chuckled.

"I see," Kelly said, still looking puzzled. "First, you'll be pleased to know that you will no longer be under armed guard." The three men looked out through the open door and Minj even walked through the doorway and looked down the hall, which was empty in both directions.

"So, we're no longer considered a security threat," Montoya said dryly.

"Well no, uh…not that you ever were," she said diplomatically. "But from now on, you'll have reasonable freedom to move about the exec mansion, except for the areas that are restricted to everyone but government employees. Is there anything more we can do for you?"

"Yes," said the captain. "We can't seem to get the temperature much below ninety degrees Fahrenheit."

Kelly's brow knit. "But…that's what we consider to be cool, sir."

"If you can at least get it under eighty, that would be great."

"Okay. So refrigerate your suite…and the ladies'."

"And," the captain continued, "the rest of my crew, those who were not in the landing party, have been aboard ship for three months. I'm requesting that they be brought to your planet in shifts and stay a couple weeks or so at a time. They need to breathe *fresh air* again, see *real sunlight*, wander in some *open spaces*."

The official paused, making a mental list. After a moment, she continued: "Your objective is to learn as much as you can about our planet, is that correct?"

"That's why we've crossed several light years," said Houston, still smiling.

"Very well, then. My boss has recommended that we take you to a ceremony this evening that will help you understand more about our culture. It starts shortly. I apologize for the short notice."

"Lead the way." They followed her through the door way and down a hall. She turned crisply and led them down another hall, then another.

"This is a lot easier when you're not blindfolded," said the captain. The other two men laughed.

A high-pitched beeping sounded from behind them, prompting Daj to jump out of the way. A short, squat robot on wheels zipped by, followed by three smaller ones. As the machines continued down the carpeted hallway, Kelly's eyes narrowed in disgust. "What's wrong with them? They have their own lane!" she cried. Another robot, rolling across a wall as if it were a floor, had its eye-pod on a metal goose neck and was rapidly moving it around. It saw the high official glaring at it then withdrew the eye pod back into its body.

Kelly led the group a little farther down the hall then stopped, looking to make certain no other human or machine was nearby. She then pressed on a portion of the wall. A hidden doorway opened to reveal a lighted passageway. She stepped quickly through the door and beckoned for the men to follow. The doorway closed behind them, blending back into the wall.

"I apologize for the secrecy but we're going to leave the mansion grounds through a back exit because of the media and the public. They're still camped out on the grounds."

The hallway continued for some time. It seemed familiar. They reached some stairs that led to a vertilift. After descending for a moment, they exited the vertilift and walked into a small underground parking garage.

The advisor led them to a vehicle. It was much smaller than one of the limos and had no official marking to indicate government service. The lady gestured for them to get in. The electric motor started and the car purred to life. She drove up a long, winding ramp. When they finally emerged above ground, the men could see the back of the mansion beginning to recede in the distance. The men immediately noted that the sky, which they had not seen in two days, looked much dimmer than what they remembered it. They realized that one of the suns was not in the sky and the other was close to dipping below the horizon.

"So, Al'aama is about to see its first nightfall in three weeks," Montoya noted.

"That's right," said Kelly. The men also noticed that the sweltering heat they had previously experienced outdoors was gone. The advisor turned on the car's heater. Warmer air began to flow through the vehicle. The car entered a city street and blended into traffic. The vehicle passed several blocks of distinguished stone and brick buildings that looked as if they had stood for generations. "Government buildings," Kelly explained. Those structures eventually gave way to newer-looking ones that had a business-like appearance. Some were skyscrapers. Other buildings had no doors but had fairly open fronts with broad archways as entrances. The star men assumed this architectural feature was in response to a climate that was hot at least *most* of the time. Many of the buildings had vertilifts on the *outside*. The roofs of virtually all buildings, both government and business, had built-in solar energy collectors. She had told them that fusion was another power source.

Back at ground level, Kelly's vehicle passed a road crew wearing work pants and shirts. Their host turned her car down a road that led to a wooded area. The remaining sun was beginning to set and the sky gradually turned various shades of yellow, orange and crimson.

She parked the car and everyone exited. She led the way to the building then stepped inside. The structure had no roof. As the four people entered, it became apparent that the structure was some sort of stone amphitheater. The entrance was near the top of the seating and the building had been built into the ground. Houston estimated that it could seat several hundred. The men noticed some sort of somber yet inspiring a capella music wafting through the air.

"This reminds me of the ancient Gregorian chants," said Montoya, "except that they're being sung by a choir of men and women. I must say, the women's voices add dimension."

Kelly smiled.

"Gregorian chants on *this* far-flung world. Einstein's Law at work again," said Minj.

The captain frowned at Minj. Kelly's eyes widened at the sound of the strange-sounding phrase, "Einstein's Law."

She led the group to a row of seats and took one. The captain saw Luci and the other female landing party members were across the way with another female Al'aaman official. The two groups of star people waved to one another. Across the way, in a prominent seat near the front sat the chiefexec, clad in a long, formal-looking robe tied with a waist sash.

Following Kelly's example, the men sat down. The seats were all tilted upward at an angle that caused one to look up toward the sky, which was turning deeper shades of purple as the sun faded over the horizon. As the last rays of the sun disappeared, hundreds of well-dressed men, women and children began to stream into the amphitheater and took seats. A narrow shaft of sunlight poured through an ornate opening in the wall, creating a shadow on the floor. The shadow intrigued Erik. It looked like...his eyes snapped away as a sharp cough from a couple rows over distracted him.

As the unseen choir continued their musical chants, stars began to dot the sky. The visitors noticed that there was a wide aisle between each row of seats. Kelly got out of her seat and knelt on the carpeted floor, facing the ground. The captain motioned for his crew members to do likewise. After a couple minutes, he opened one eye then the other and cautiously glanced around. Everyone was on their knees. Even the chiefexec humbled herself. He closed his eyes and tried to imitate the piety surrounding him.

After several minutes, Kelly returned to her seat, followed by the star men taking theirs. The musical chants increased in volume. Everyone looked into the nighttime sky, which was aglow with the hundreds of stars. The stars seemed so close Erik thought he could reach out and touch them. For long moments, he said nothing.

Finally, in a hushed, reverent tone, he whispered to Kelly: "So what more do we need to do?"

"Nothing," she whispered back.

The inspiring singing continued while everyone kept gazing at the stars. Finally, a close-up of the star field was projected onto a screen as the intensity of the singing increased. This went on for perhaps fifteen or twenty minutes until finally, people began to leave.

"That's it?" asked Erik.

"That's it," she echoed.

"It was beautiful. But why?"

She increased the volume of her voice to allow the other two men to hear. "Once every three weeks, at the beginning of the night, we gather to remember where our ancestors came from. And to observe the beauty of the stars themselves. The stars and their glory remind us that this universe didn't happen on its own. It was designed and made."

Erik nodded.

"Our chiefexec was moved by the talk you gave our cabinet about the vastness of the galaxy and interstellar space," she continued. "I understand it made quite a hit with the entire cabinet. Since you're in awe of the cosmos like she is, she thought you would especially appreciate our service tonight."

The captain smiled, surprised the chiefexec had found the discussion inspirational; she had been the first to return to hammering the spacemen with questions right after those remarks.

As Erik pondered Kelly's words, she gestured toward a doorway and the group exited. Once outside, Minj and Montoya went back to gazing at the stars, pointing out to one another ones they had visited. Kelly and Erik walked a short distance away.

"So tell me, Captain," she asked, "what is this Einstein's Law you and your crew keep talking about?"

He was startled. He thought: *Keep talking about?* Regaining his composure, he replied: "Einstein's Law is an ancient superstition. It's a subject of tall tales spacemen tell one another on trips between the stars. Except that in Montoya's case, he actually *believes* the stories."

She persisted, "What does Einstein's Law actually claim?"

"Are you familiar with Einstein's Theory of Relativity?"

"The layman's version."

"Einstein's Law is a distortion of the theory. The 'law' claims that the warping of time by traveling at close to the speed of light will, at some point, come back to haunt the star traveler. The idea is derived from the even more ancient Murphy's Law, a bit of folklore that stated that everything that could possibly go wrong would, at some point, do so.

"What an odd belief."

"I agree. I've been traveling the stars almost half my life and have never once run into an example of the Einstein's Law."

"Now, Captain, is that because you're a non-believer?" she laughed.

"No, it's because I'm too practical."

"But I take it you do believe in order in the universe."

"Yes, but *intelligent* order. Not based on some fairytale."

"And that's the whole idea behind our worship, the intelligent order of the universe," said Kelly. The stars provided enough light that Houston could see the ear-to-ear smile that turned her eyes into mere slits.

The captain continued: "There's actually a whole spectrum of belief. For some people, it's almost a religion. But for others, Einstein's Law doesn't necessarily have a *negative* connotation. It's just an observation that the warping of space and time can produce some ironic effects, some paradoxes we limited human beings have difficulty grasping."

They stopped talking a moment as they tried to ponder something so great and complex.

"Tell about your concept of G—" Erik began.

But she seemed to not hear him. "It's getting cold," she said, turning away.

The captain noted that temperature had, indeed, plummeted following sunset. Kelly pulled a colored handkerchief from her pocket and shook it a few times. It unfurled into a large, thin cloak. "Here, wrap this around you," she said. "This cloth is made from a plant that produces a chemical that creates heat." Erik took the cloak and followed his hostess' suggestion. She then produced another cloak for herself. Minj and Montoya were still involved in their discussion, so they ignored her offer of cloaks. Everyone got into the car. Kelly put on the heater and drove back to the executive compound. On the way, Erik noted some white flakes floating through the air that he was convinced were snow. He marveled at the remarkable changes that took place on this world once both suns were down.

# 14.

"Stargazer. That you?" came a masculine whisper from the shadows.

"Over here, Big Protector," another shadow responded quietly. William and Tanna stepped out into a slightly better lighting. They were both dressed head to toe in black, including black stocking caps. Three security officers all dressed in a similar fashion also emerged from the deep shadows.

The group stood about twenty yards away from the starship landing craft that had arrived days earlier. An iridescent energy field still surrounded the vehicle. At a signal from Security Chief Bern, one of the guards raised his handheld weapon and fired at the ship. A beam of light shot toward the ship but was deflected and went off in another direction. A second guard threw a rock full force. It hit the protective wall and glanced off. The group walked closer to the craft. The third guard aimed another ener pistol. Nothing. The shield appeared impenetrable. The guard threw his gun. It hit the iridescence with a thud and dropped to the ground.

"The things we could do if we had access to this baby," Tanna sighed.

"Have you made any progress in dissecting the aliens' equipment?" William asked.

"Still working on it," she whispered back. "My people have used our most powerful lasers but so far, nothing. I can't even tell what those things are made of. Not metal. No known atomic elements. Are these people able to create new ones?"

"Just get it done. We'll soon be under some major pressure to turn these things over."

"My people won't let us down," she said.

The security chief dismissed the guards, who each walked off in a different direction.

The curious science director walked back toward the landing craft, amazed at how it hovered a few feet above the ground. She walked over the vehicle and passed her hand through the open air under it. She pulled a tiny flashlight from her pocket and looked underneath the lander. She even crawled under the ship, which remained suspended a few feet over her. She crawled back out and got back to her feet, rejoining the head of security.

"Have you noticed how it seems to be floating a little lower than it was the first day?" she asked. "And how the air around it doesn't shimmer quite as much as it used to? I think if we wait a couple days and come back, we'll have our shot."

William smirked with glee.

# 15.

Kelly was back the next day. As she entered the suite, Houston was reading a native, online book using the cosmic translator. The device stored the information for future use, as well as displaying summaries on a palm-sized screen for Houston to read. She spent some time fascinated at watching the captain and Minj "read" using the palm-sized gadgets.

She greeted Montoya as he strolled into the room sipping on a dark-colored glass of a nutritional supplement. The doctor, who had been steadily losing weight the past several days, didn't have the heart to tell her that the local food didn't agree with him.

Finally, she asked: "Is there anything else you need, Captain?"

"Yes," he said, his arm muscles knotting. "My crew and I had some of our belongings confiscated when we arrived here, and we've never gotten them back."

"I'll look into this for you," she offered. "Anything else?"

"Last night was the first time we've actually been out to see any of the city," said the captain. "Other than that, virtually all we've seen are this suite and, of course, the jail cell where we spent our first three days. I'm beginning to think you don't appreciate having us here."

Montoya switched off his cosmic translator and said to the captain: "Or they're still figuring out what to do with us."

Kelly looked at Montoya, puzzled by his strange-sounding, untranslated speech. She then looked back at Houston, appearing concerned that her guests weren't enjoying their visit.

Erik continued: "I know we're free to move about the mansion, but we need to get to know your city and its people."

"Captain, I apologize. Be patient with us. It takes time to get used to something as monumental as unexpected visitors from the stars. I'll remind our chiefexec of your requests." She then left the room. She returned sometime later, still without the equipment. She stayed briefly then left again.

"Let me get this straight," the captain said to the two other men. "Kelly comes in and tells us that as many crew members as we'd like are invited to a banquet and dance in our honor tonight. How do these people feel we can trust them with bringing most of the crew planetside when they can't even return our personal items?"

Montoya responded, "We have no way to fall back on our personal force fields or our stunners if we need them. What if they turn on us again like they did the first day?"

"That's right," said Minj.

The captain nodded. "I hate those items in the hands of strangers. If we don't soon get our equipment back, we may need to find a way to get it."

There was a knock at the door. It was Kelly. She bounded through the door with her usual energy. "So, Captain, how do you gentlemen feel about attending our banquet and dance tonight?"

"We'd be honored," said Captain Houston.

"Looking forward to it," said Montoya.

"I really don't dance," said Minj.

"Well, you don't have to," said Kelly with a smile. "There will plenty of good food, a number of our leaders to talk with…."

He looked more at ease. "I'd be delighted," he said.

"And what about the rest of your crew, Captain?"

Houston crossed his arms. "I'd be willing to bring half my crew to the planet for the evening," he said. "The rest would need to stay aboard the ship. After a couple weeks, the two halves of the crew could switch and the first set would go back to the ship."

"Sounds reasonable," said Kelly.

"But I'll only allow half the crew to come tonight if you agree to some conditions," said Houston. "There will be absolutely no interrogating. No frisking. No taking of personal items. What our crew arrives with...*stays* with them."

"Sir, I'll have to check...."

He looked directly into her eyes. "Tell the chiefexec those are my conditions."

"Yes, sir."

"And what about our missing equipment?"

She hesitated. "Still looking into it."

Houston frowned.

Changing the subject, Minj told Kelly how hard he had been studying the Al'aaman language.

"He has a gift for languages," Montoya offered.

Minj nodded. Kelly and he each took seats at the table and he began to practice the language. She encouraged his efforts. At one point he was attempting to pay her a compliment but instead her face turned red. After that, everything went well for a while until he said something with a sincere face but she began to laugh hysterically.

"What did he say?" Montoya deadpanned, distracted by the commotion.

"You don't want to know," Kelly replied, still laughing.

"Minj, go back to using the translator for this party," the captain said with a smile.

"But I'm starting to get good," said Minj. Kelly shook her head. He continued with his language lessons for a while and avoided making any more major faux pax. Then it was time for her to leave to allow the men time to get ready for the banquet. She hurried down the hall, still chuckling over what Minj had inadvertently said to her.

After she left, Montoya said: "Okay, Daj. You've impressed Kelly with what a whiz kid you are but soon it will all be in vain. I'd say we've almost have enough of the natives' language in the translator. Soon I'll be able to clone some brain cells from each crew member, record the entire Al'aaman language into the cells, then integrate them in each of our brains. The Al'aamans will marvel at how we've all suddenly become fluent in their language."

"It's a good thing we've got more than one doctor so you don't have to operate on yourself, Fred," Erik quipped.

# 16.

Chiefexec Elle was staring her security chief in the eye. "William, I'm tired of this insubordination."

He pulled back. "Madame Exec. What do you mean?"

"First I find out that you authorized interrogations of the star people that were a lot tougher than I had intended. And now you claim you no longer have the spacemen's articles in your possession."

He paused before answering. "On the handling of the…aliens, I'm sorry if I…overstepped my bounds."

"Well you did. Now where's their equipment?"

"As you correctly stated, Ma'am, I don't have the items."

"Find them!"

"Director Bern has been conducting experiments, trying to see how they work. Their tech could be a tremendous benefit."

"She told me even our top scientists can't find a way to make the devices work. You're wasting your time and antagonizing our visitors. I want these items retrieved and brought to me…now!"

"But we were only trying to protect you...."

"Save it, William. I'm convinced these space people have no intention to harm us, and I've been one of their biggest skeptics. Do you have some hidden agenda?"

"Ma'am, I've served you well. How can you say such things?"

"Skip the act. I want you to personally hand me these items within the hour!"

"Yes, Ma'am."

Sometime later William, his head down, knocked on Elle's door. "Madame Exec," he said in a deep voice.

She looked up from the online report she was reading. "Come in."

The security chief placed a cloth bag on her desk. "I've got them. The items you asked for."

She looked up at him. "And...they're *all there?*"

"Yes, Ma'am."

She didn't bother to open the bag and went back to her reading. He stood for a long, awkward moment in front of the big boss' desk, shifting his weight from one foot to another. Finally, the she looked up again.

"Don't ever pull a stunt like this again."

"No, Ma'am."

"That will be all." He turned and shuffled out the door. Zama unlocked a metal cabinet, placed the bag in a drawer and locked the cabinet. She would return the objects to the captain as soon as she could, but she wouldn't really have an opportunity at the banquet that was starting in a couple hours.

The security chief stomped back to his office. He took a seat at his desk and remained there for some time. Eventually, he was drawn to the window. He stared out, watching the last of three additional alien landing craft touch down on the expansive mansion lawn. Now even more of those offworlders were arriving, he thought. He watched a small knot of people disembark from the landing craft, joining others who had arrived a few minutes earlier. *They're taking over!* thought William. And there was the chiefexec and her entourage greeting the arrivals as if they were celebrities! He noted the leader was surrounded by a number of his guards, though probably not enough for her to be truly safe from these heathen and their strange ways. The security chief planned on having plenty of agents at this evening's banquet and if any of these space people made a false move....

Hundreds of men and women in formal attire filled the ornate banquet hall. Captain Houston wore his dress white uniform. The ship's other officers wore similar attire. Surrounding the visitor was a large circle of natives. Although the administration had strictly limited the number of media people attending the banquet, several reporters, electron notepads in hand, were scribbling away and a few videographers were filming the space group. Chief of Staff Alisa Conway observed the scene and frowned.

Security Chief William Thal stood near a far corner of the room, speaking into his video screen in departmental jargon to his top deputies, most of whom were plain clothes. He instructed them to keep the aliens in view at all times and report anything suspicious.

After instructing his crew, William's sharp eyes roved the room until he spotted her. There, in the distance, was Tanna, mingling with several other cabinet members. She was in mid-sentence when she caught William's long-distance gaze. She returned his look, non-verbal signals passing between them unnoticed by anyone else, Tanna all the while not missing one nuance of her conversation.

In another part of the room, Minj and Montoya had been able to avoid many of the curious A'laamans. They were off in a corner. Montoya had used a small device to short out any electronic bugs. The two crew members were speaking quietly, translators off.

"Sometimes the captain's too soft," said Montoya.

Minj looked cautiously around, making certain no crew members were within earshot. "What do you mean?"

"You know Erik. He's an Association man, a diplomat. He's more worried about not offending the natives than he is about our own safety."

"C'mon, Fred...."

"I'm worried that the A'laamans are still hanging on to our weapons, our force field generators. Nothing good can come of that."

"The captain's trying to get our stuff back."

"It's taking too long," said Montoya. "I think we may need to take matters into our own hands."

Minj's voice dropped to almost a whisper. "Meaning...?"

Montoya glanced out of the corners of his eyes and lowered his voice. "Tonight, once everyone's having a good time, we'll sneak out, find the equipment and get it back."

"I don't know...."

"We can't let these people keep it any longer. We've got to do something!"

Minj was about to respond when he noticed Erik walking toward them. "There you go again with that Einstein's Law!" Minj cried.

Montoya rolled his eyes.

The captain heard the remark and laughed. Almost immediately, another sight distracted him. The chiefexec was walking toward him. But when she got within a few feet he realized it was someone else…but someone who could have passed for a twin, or at least a sister. Erik shook his head.

The captain saw Luci from the corner of his eye. He turned around and looked straight at her. She was wearing a long, light blue gown, the first one the captain had seen her wear since their last planetary visit. He walked over to her, first switching off the translator.

Balding, grey-haired Irv Malvo, security chief for the *Intitiative*, hurried over to the duo. "Captain Houston, you old salt!" he growled, smiling as he clapped Erik on the shoulder and shook his hand. The captain noticed Irv was passing something to him. It was a palm-sized kit containing a force field generator, a stunner and some other key items that were counterparts to the ones the A'laamans had taken from the landing party. The captain nodded and smiled, sliding the packet into his suit coat pocket. Irv slipped Luci a packet that she dropped into her purse, all the while continuing to talk with Erik. The security boss was already making the rounds to the other landing party members.

Montoya, after receiving his packet, quickly pulled Minj aside and said: "Our plan is still a go. It's dangerous for them to keep our equipment."

Minj nodded.

He spotted Alisa Conway on the other side of the vast room. "The Great Stone Face is here," he said, nodding her direction.

"Why do you call her that?"

"She never smiles."

"She does too."

"It's a fake smile. Bet I can get her to smile for real."

"You're on."

Minj crossed the large room then casually strolled up to the official while Montoya kept watching from a distance. He observed her politely acknowledge Daj, who tried several times to engage her in conversation. She maintained the usual bare-toothed facade, nothing more. After a few minutes, Minj gave up and walked away. It was Montoya's smile that was genuine when Daj got back over to him.

Alisa came up to Erik and Luci, saying: "We need to take our seats. The chiefexec is about to arrive." Luci and the other landing party members followed the captain to their assigned table. The highest dignitaries of Al'aama were all seated at the table, awaiting her arrival. The landing party's table was in a place of honor, closest to the leader's. Everyone sat waiting in anticipation of her arrival. Conway snapped her fingers to create a sound amplification and announced: "Ladies and gentlemen, the Chiefexec of the Planet Al'aama!"

Everyone rose and stood at attention as Zama entered the room. Wearing an ivory-colored formal evening dress, the confident Zama strode into the room.

Following behind her was a young lady a few inches shorter. She had a small build and almost looked petite by A'laaman standards. She had thick, medium-brown hair with auburn highlights. Her hair flowed halfway down her back and ended in some bouncy curls. Her round face was beaming. She seemed proud of her formal gown and jewelry, having the bearing of a princess. She moved quickly, radiating life and energy. She waved to everyone as if she were greeting her loyal subjects. Several of the dignitaries waved back.

Trailing behind was a great brown bear of a man in a tuxedo. He had dark brown hair past his collar and halfway covering his ears. The mass of hair was extremely curly, forming numerous ringlets. The hair was almost falling into his eyes, which were slits and seemed almost too small for his face. Those eyes were alert and constantly moved around the room. He had a serious, no-nonsense demeanor like the chiefexec. He gave the impression of protecting the two women and could have easily been mistaken for a bouncer.

Zama strode with dignity to the head table and remained standing. Creating her own sound amp, she said: "Ladies and gentlemen, this evening we are here to honor the arrival of our visitors from the stars!" She said this with a smile. "Tonight, Captain Erik Houston and twenty-four of his crew members are here. They will be spending some time on our planet. Let's welcome them!" She applauded, prompting everyone else in the room to do so.

Watching from a table of other leaders, Kelly was beaming.

The applause continued until the chiefexec waved for everyone to stop. She continued: "Tonight we have prepared a special feast for all of you. The meal will be followed by music and dancing. Have a wonderful evening, everyone!"

Within a few minutes, the head of state and those at her table were being served some steaming food from silver trays. The original landing party's table was the next one to be served. A waiter placed a large silver tray in front of Erik and removed the lid. A foot-long creature with the appearance of an elongated grasshopper lay in a pool of brown liquid. He glanced at the other tables and noticed everyone there was being served the same thing.

Luci wrinkled her nose. "Erik…" she said.

"These people constantly come up with new ways to torment my insides," said Montoya.

The captain discreetly waved his palm device over the creature. The food analyzer pronounced it as good to eat and actually nutritious. "Listen, everyone," Houston whispered to his table mates, "I know this isn't the most appetizing food, but it's probably some sort of delicacy here. We need to each eat at least some of it." Houston sent a text message to that effect to the handhelds at the other crew members' tables. He looked around the room and saw several slow, reluctant nods.

"Where do I start?" whispered Minj. "This…thing's eyes are staring up at me!"

Erik and the other crew members watched people at adjacent tables. The natives grabbed the over-sized insect by the neck, twisted to the right and pulled the guts out, putting them on the plate. Then they would each pick up the creature with two hands and bite off pieces and chew them. Houston imitated those from the other tables. The crew members followed Erik's lead.

Luci twisted the head off her insect, pulled out the guts and almost gagged at the pungent odor that was exuded. "The things I do to make the Association happy," she muttered under her breath.

The captain took a bite of his insect. It had a crunchy texture and a surprisingly sweet taste. "Hey, this is good!" he said with surprise. He took another bite and the others followed suit. When most of the people at his table were about halfway through eating the giant insects, waiters arrived with another course consisting of an object that looked like a blue, feathery sphere and a blob of clear jelly-like substance.

Luci broke off a piece of the feathery substance with her fork. She moved the fork to her mouth. Once inside her mouth, the substance seemed to turn into fine powder. Luci's mouth became very dry and she was unable to swallow. She struggled with the mouthful of food for several moments then began to turn red and choke. She grabbed a tall glass of the clear liquid that was the main beverage on the planet. She drained the glass within seconds. Once she had taken a drink, her color returned to normal.

"I'm not that hungry," Montoya said.

Minj was tapping the jelly-like substance with a spoon and watching it jiggle.

"Daj, quit playing with your food," Luci teased. Minj smiled.

Erik said: "I've passed the analyzer over all these other items and they all check out okay, except for that," he was pointing to a garnish that looked like small red leaves. Minj had already picked up a forkful but discretely put it down . "That's a good idea," the captain said. "That stuff would have given you a lot of problems if you had eaten it." Minj and Montoya looked at one another.

The table of star travelers survived the rest of the meal without incident. The waiters then cleared away the dishes and gave each person a plate with a long, curling tube or stem that appeared to have liquid inside. The natives each bit off one end of the tube, spat it out then sucked on the tube as if it were a straw, draining the liquid inside. Luci thought the biting and spitting was rather disgusting. Erik's table followed suit, each person biting the tip off his or her tube then spitting. The other tables of star people followed the lead of Erik's table. The star travelers' actions were somewhat more pronounced than those of the natives, who glared at them as if they were heathen. Minj, the last to try the item, cut off the tip with a knife and began imbibing. The captain and the others were pleased to note that the liquid they were imbibing was cool and refreshing. It had a pleasant, unique taste.

At the end of the meal, the chief exec and her two younger companions approached the captain's table. "Good evening, Captain Houston and crew members," the chiefexec said, filled with pride. "I'd like to introduce my son, Andy, and my daughter, Omma."

The young man nodded to the group but remained poker faced. His sister, still smiling, bowed slightly. "Andy is a junior at A'laama University, and Omma is a freshman." The captain's jaw dropped. He thought the ruler looked too young to have children these ages. The two youths exchanged a few pleasantries with the captain and crew members before moving on to another table.

During the meal, William had spotted Tanna, who was seated several tables away. He discretely looked toward her from the corner of his eye. She noticed his attention, flashed a half-smile in his direction then spooned some food into her mouth. She dabbed her lips with a napkin then looked down at the table.

William shifted his gaze. He glanced from one table of space people to another, his eyes narrowing as he watched each table for several moments. He lifted a bit of food with a utensil and chomped down hard.

After the dessert, the waiters cleared the remaining dishes. Meanwhile, a band had been setting up. Alisa invited the star visitors and anyone else who felt the need to walk through some brief dance lessons taught by an instructor. The basic types of dance weren't much different from those with which the space travelers were familiar—some slow dances, some waltzes, some free-form fast dances—not much different from the types of dances that had been done on many other planets over thousands of years. Then the band began to play. Several people coupled up and headed for the floor.

The captain was speaking with two A'laaman officials when he noticed the chiefexec step onto the dance floor. She looked elegant in her cream-colored gown, gold necklace and matching tiara. He looked closely and was convinced this was actually her. Not some relative or a clone. Her dance partner was about as tall as she and handsomely dressed. They began waltzing. The couple swept across the floor. Erik was spell-bound. He tried to continue his conversation but was obviously not concentrating, the cosmic translator making it that much more awkward. The two dignitaries finally excused themselves and walked away.

Erik kept watching the top leader. Her refined-looking partner had a full head of white hair. They danced a second dance, a slow number. He was saying something and she was laughing. The next dance was another slow one. After that song, they walked off the floor and continued to talk. Another official came up to the skipper and started a discussion.

William was scrutinizing that offworlder captain when he glanced at his ring chronometer. It was time. He reached into his pocket and casually pushed a tab on his video screen.

In another part of the hall, Tanna felt a warm flash on her wrist. She glanced at the mini screen that was built into her bracelet. It displayed a red dot. She pushed a tab to return the message. She excused herself from her discussion and strode toward an exit.

At that moment, a flash of warmth emanated from William's wrist screen. He spotted a blue dot. He punched in the code for his chief lieutenant.

"Jim. I've got some official business. You're in charge now."

"Affirmative, sir."

William headed off in a different direction than Tanna.

A hundred feet away, Montoya glanced cautiously around the room. Everyone seemed preoccupied. Even Alisa was on the dance floor, gyrating to a fast song with an even taller man. The chief of staff was smiling widely.

"At least someone knows how to make her smile," Montoya said, digging Minj in the ribs with his elbow.

Minj frowned.

"Let's get outta here," said Montoya. He led the way and Daj fell in behind him, shaking his head.

Taking a roundabout route, the two made their way toward one of the expansive exits from the grand ballroom. So far, so good. No one seemed to be watching. They strode down a long hallway, down another, then another as if they were heading back toward their suite. Down one hallway, they passed the director of science and the chiefexec's *security chief*. Montoya's spine felt like ice. But the two officials seemed preoccupied. The star men waited a couple minutes then began to retrace their steps. They branched off down another hallway.

"I've located our equipment," said Montoya, glancing at a handheld screen.

"Where?"

"The Dragon Lady's office."

"Alisa?"

"Bigger."

"The chiefexec?" Minj squeaked.

Montoya nodded.

"No!" cried Minj, freezing in place. "The captain will have our heads!"

His buddy roughly grabbed his shoulder and pulled him along. "C'mon! We've got to do this!"

The two men were approaching the door to the chiefexec's over-sized suite. They looked up and down the hall. Montoya reached into his pocket and pulled out an electronic device the size of a pen. He twisted it slightly. "There," he whispered. "That will knock out their surveillance."

He pushed a tiny button on the device. The locked door to the power suite swung open. The two hurried through Alisa's office, closing the door. They continued on into the top exec's office. Montoya checked the device, which picked up the electronic signatures of the star men's equipment in a nearby locked filing cabinet. He put on a pair of gloves that allowed his hands to reach right through the cabinet, grab the bag and pull it out without disturbing the drawer or the lock. He reached into the bag. The missing equipment at last! Minj and he quietly closed the door to the suite and locked it. They tip-toed back through Alisa's office, closing and locking that door.

They would actually have gotten away with their heist were it not for two security officers who happened to be coming around the corner and saw them leave the chief of staff's area.

"Halt!" one of the men yelled. The guards drew their handheld weapons. Minj just as quickly reached his pocket and grabbed his personal force field generator. Montoya did the same. They activated their fields, rushed past the guards then fled down the hall.

Minj and Montoya ran off full-speed, the two security officers in rapid pursuit. "Don't fire!" said one guard to the other. "What if someone else comes down this hall!"

"We'll just have to take that chance," the other officer replied. "The chiefexec's security is at stake. Hurry! They're getting away!"

Both officers fired. Beams of light shot out at the intruders. The first shot missed the fleeing star men, hitting a wall and burning a small hole into it. The second shot hit Montoya's force field and angled off it, hitting another wall. The officers fired again but the shots were equally ineffective. The two spacemen turned at an intersection and fled down another hall. "Where are you taking us?" Minj asked as they continued to run.

"To that secret passage Kelly showed us," Montoya replied.

"These are security people. You really think they don't know about it?"

"You have any better ideas?"

The two star men turned at another intersection and finally lost their pursuers, but they were hearing shouting farther down the hall. No doubt there were now many officers searching for them. Minj started stopping every fifty feet or so and tapping on the wall. "What are you doing?" Montoya demanded.

"Maybe there's more than one hidden passage."

Upon his third try, Minj's experiment worked. A door opened in the wall. Minj and Montoya ran into it. The door closed behind them.

A half dozen security guards rounded the corner and ran down the hall, arriving at the point where the culprits had vanished. Several of the agents looked around, puzzled. Two of them had hearing enhancement implants that allowed them to hear the invaders behind the walls. The same officers also had occular implants that allowed them to locate the offenders, at first via heat sensing then in full color, 3-D.

Meanwhile, the two star men scrambled through the hidden corridor. They used their pocket devices to link to their orbiting ship's AI brain, which transmitted a detailed map showing them the closest way out of the mansion.

They followed one hallway, then another. They went down a few steps then found a narrow vertilift. They took the lift down three floors and hurried down a hallway that was to be their passage to freedom. They burst through a door and out into the nighttime air. A small army of uniformed figures, weapons drawn, stepped out of the shadows.

"Check mate!" said the chief officer grimly.

# 17.

Science Minister Bern and Security Chief Thal were surveying the four alien landing craft. All were protected by energy fields. Bern was clearly frustrated. "We still haven't figured out what makes *this thing* work," she whispered to Thal. "We've tried everything we know and we're at a loss."

William Thal shook his head. "I wish we could get inside one of these ships just to see what it's like."

Tanna silently pointed toward the one craft they had eyeballed a couple days earlier. It was now hovering only about six inches above the ground. And the energy field surrounding it was faint. "I think this is our lucky day," she whispered. She began rapidly hitting buttons at random on the keypad to the force field, the one piece of equipment William and she had held back from giving the chiefexec. Abruptly, she noticed that the closest ship no longer had an iridescent glow surrounding it. Could it be?

The two officials crept closer, wearing night vision goggles and shining their hand lights. There was no obvious way to enter the vehicle. It looked like one continuous sheet of metal without so much as a seam or an outline to indicate a door. Tanna walked around the lander and began banging on it at random. Easily at first then with increasing energy. William joined her. Nothing happened. Tanna attacked the metal skin with a pen-sized plasma torch. The intense heat did not even discolor the surface. Finally the duo skulked away. A low, whooshing sound came from behind them. They turned in disbelief. A round doorway had appeared, looking in the dark like a small cave entrance. The duo crept up the ramp, entering the vessel. There were half a dozen seats arranged in a semi-circle. In front of the foremost seat was a control panel.

"Should we...?" Tanna whispered.

"Don't know," said William, suddenly feeling much more cautious. "Let's not touch anything. Let's just get out of here."

"Wait a minute. I'm not in a hurry." She walked over and visually examined the controls. "None of these craft have any exterior solar panels. Do you think they use nuclear power?"

A few hundred miles in space, the *Initiative's* assistant security chief responded to an alarm that was sounding aboard the starship. He hurried to a monitor. Two people were aboard one of the landing craft and the system did not recognize the retinal scans of either. Tanna, meanwhile, had settled into one of the high-back chairs and continued to eye the control panel.

"Attention, invaders!" boomed a thunder-like voice. "You are not authorized! You must leave immediately!" The voice seemed to come from everywhere.

William, who had become increasingly anxious, was only too happy to oblige. He turned to leave.

"C'mon," said Tanna. "This is fascinating."

"Let's go. They're on to us."

"Some brave security guy!"

"I can't leave without you."

"Attention! Natives of the planet Al'aama! You are not authorized. You must leave immediately! This is your last warning!"

"I'm with you," said the science director. "Let's get out of here before they fry us like they did that rock last week!" She quickly stood up and turned to walk toward the exit. She tripped and fell into the control panel. There was a loud hum and the engine of the landing craft sprang to life.

William and Tanna stared apprehensively at the landing craft's console as it began to glow. Lights were flashing rapidly as the two intruders tried to hurry toward the exit. The hatch was closing. They lunged for the door but it was too late. The craft began to angle skyward, throwing them off their feet.

"Do something! "shouted William. They each scrambled to get into a seat. Where was the safety harness? Once they sat down, they felt held in place by an invisible force.

The science director's arms reached in vain for the control panel.

The security boss glanced out a window and saw the city retreating below them. Even the skyscrapers looked like toys. Yet somehow there was no sense of motion.

Tanna wrenched free of the invisible force, grabbed what looked like a control throttle and pulled it back. The craft began to plunge downward! She kept working the throttle with one hand hitting buttons with the other but was unable to gain control. The ship was weaving erratically over the city. Finally, it plunged downward at a steep angle. William felt his stomach dropping as he saw the buildings of the city rapidly rush toward him. Tanna was still frantically trying anything that looked like it would help. Suddenly, the craft began to slow abruptly as if an unseen hand were controlling it. But the braking action was too late and vehicle slammed into a city street, having narrowly missed a commuter train that was going by on a nearby track.

# 18.

Captain Houston had spent much of the evening talking with various members of the administration. The politeness of several had barely masked their skepticism. Others seemed genuinely curious. Kelly had appeared and talked with him for a while, supportive as always. A few other officials had also seemed genuinely positive.

For the first time that evening, the captain stood alone. He was sipping a glass of punch when he spotted the chiefexec again. Her formal dress and statuesque appearance gave her a regal air. Their eyes met. She headed directly toward him.

"Good evening, Captain," she said. She offered her hand and he gently held it. She smiled, her face hinting at a blush. Her skin was soft and scented.

"Good evening, Madame Exec," he said.

"I've been enjoying the band this evening. May I have this dance?'

"Certainly, Ma'am."

They walked onto the dance floor. He was about to place his hand around her waist then noticed it was the same height as the middle of his stomach.

She looked at him sweetly.

He engaged. The chiefexec began leading, taking big steps with those long legs. He felt as if he were being pulled around the floor. He broke contact and stepped away.

He saw empathy in her eyes. She slipped off her flat-heeled shoes and pushed them off the dance floor with her foot, reducing the small height difference. "Relax," she said soothingly.

He took a couple deep breaths while she patiently waited. He tried again. She was letting him lead. And the steps were smaller. He tried not to hold her too close, attempting to show respect for her and her office. She seemed to know what he was thinking and smiled. It didn't fit the tempo of the music, but he reached his right arm high and playfully twirled her. She skillfully ducked under his upheld arm. They continued to glide across the floor. He dipped her, hoping he could hold on to the tall lady without dropping her. He brought her back up. She was now smiling, showing a perfect set of white teeth. For the first time, he was enjoying being around her. The song ended too soon.

Just as another was beginning, she stiffened. She pulled away and her face hardened. The shocked captain removed his arms from around her. One of her earrings was an audio receiver and a mike was built into her necklace. She had just received two sobering messages.

Meanwhile, the captain's face twisted as he heard a couple urgent messages in his comm link earpiece. The chiefexec and the captain glared at one another.

Taking a step away from her, he turned off his translator. "Montoya! Where are you?" he shouted into his comm link.

"Behind some walls, sir...."

"What??"

"Inside a secret passage."

"Listen, keep your situation as low key as you can...under the circumstances.... I'll call you later! Houston out!"

The leader's eyes cut him like daggers.

"Madame Exec, I realize two of your people's lives are in danger. I'd like to help...."

"I'll handle this myself!"

"I can get you to the crash site quicker...."

"Very well, Captain," she said coldly. "We'll take a back way out of here so my guards won't follow us. That is, if they're not all trying to find your people!"

They hurried to a little-used side exit from the ballroom and began winding through some corridors. Then it was down a vertilift, through another hallway and out an exit leading to the mansion lawn. Zama, who had retrieved her shoes, slipped them off again and carried them in one hand, hiking up her long gown with the other. She was practically running with Erik to the nearest of his landing craft. The captain pushed the button to open the hatch. He offered the chiefexec a hand to help her walk up the steep ramp but she insisted on walking on her own. He gestured toward a seat. He took the pilot's seat and started the craft. He would be running on instruments rather than using lights in order to make the flight as unobtrusive as possible in the dark night sky. He had learned that Al'aama did not have any air traffic so the lights were not a necessity. The ship rose. Zama was so upset she was trembling. Within seconds, the craft was lowering back to the ground. There had been no sensation of motion.

Erik lowered the ship onto a nearly deserted parking lot across the street from the accident. A small crowd had gathered and was caught up in the watching the emergency personnel. The passersby didn't even notice the arrival of the landing vehicle, which the nighttime darkness partially camouflaged. Houston and Zama jogged over to the site, blending in anonymously with the other onlookers. It was the wee hours of the morning. Emergency medical workers were already pulling the bloodied Tanna and William from the wreckage. The battered duo barely looked human. The chiefexec swallowed hard. The captain felt her grip his arm, her nails almost penetrating his suit coat. He heard the clatter of teeth and turned to see that she was shivering. He pulled off the coat and helped her put it on. She looked at him, a touch of gratitude softening her anger. They pushed their way through the crowd. Several med techs were working on the two limp bodies. The chiefexec grabbed the arm of one of them.

"How are they?" she asked.

The tech looked the woman in the eye. "I don't think they're going to make it, lady."

Her countenance dropped.

"I need to get in touch with Montoya," said the captain.

"You mean that…that man of yours who broke into my office?" the chiefexec growled.

"We need Montoya because he's our medical officer. He may be able to save these people."

"How do I know he won't make them worse?"

"Look at them! How could they possibly be any worse?"

She bit her lip. "Very well. Call your medicine man. But no more tricks!"

Houston strode away, kicking a stone. It bounced for some distance. He reached for his comm link and punched in a code.

"Fred! Where are you? Is Minj still with you?" snapped Houston.

"Yes. We're just outside the mansion. We've been captured but we're okay. We're both wearing our force fields."

"So…you got our equipment back?"

"Yes."

"I'm glad you're both okay. Well, you two follow my homing signal and get down here right away. Bring your medical bag."

"W-where are you, Captain?"

"On the other side of town at an accident scene."

"What happened, sir?"

"Just get over here! Two people's lives are in danger!"

"First I've got to get back to our suite to get my medical bag. Then how do I get to you?"

"Fly one of the landing craft. We're right across from a big parking lot that's mostly empty at this hour. You could set down there."

"But, Captain, it would be difficult to break away from here without hurting some of the chiefexec's guards."

"Don't worry. She's going to order a truce."

"She's agreed to that?"

"She will. Otherwise, those two officials won't last the night."

# 19.

It was a standoff. The guards had quickly learned that their weapons couldn't penetrate the star men's force fields. And now that Minj and Montoya knew they were waiting on a call, they refused to move when the guards ordered them to march off. Eventually the guards quit barking orders and just stood there helpless while the star men waited. About five minutes later, the head security officer answered his field audio. "You the officer on duty?" a female voice shouted.

"Yes...."

"This is Chiefexec Elle. Are the two star men with you?"

"Affirmative, Ma'am."

"I need you to accompany them back to their suite then let them go!"

"What! Ma'am, are you aware...?"

"I'm aware of everything. Just do it! Now! Two VIP's lives depend upon it!"

"Yes, Ma'am."

The guards quickly escorted Minj and Montoya back to their suite.

Montoya retrieved his medical bag. The security people showed them the quickest way from there to the area of the mansion lawn where the landing craft were located. Minj flew the craft to the coordinates Erik had given them. From the air, the two star men were able to see the crater the other craft had created by its high-speed impact. Minj touched down in the parking lot the captain had suggested. They exited the ship, Minj set the force field and they hurried to the emergency personnel who were still on the scene. The skipper and the chiefexec were nowhere to be found. Montoya switched on his translator. "Where's the two officials who were injured in the crash?" he demanded of one of the officers.

"They were taken to the hospital, two blocks that way," the officer said, pointing. "Not that there's much of them left to save!"

Minj and Montoya ran the two city blocks. The men saw a large building ahead topped with a blue 3-D sign in Al'aaman script. Montoya pointed his translator at the sign. It was, indeed, a hospital. He pointed the device at a sign on the ground level and learned that it said: Emergency Room Entrance. The men flew through the door. Breathless, Montoya identified himself to the desk clerk. The hospital was expecting him. He was told to take the vertilift to the third floor and take the corridor to the left until he passed the nurses' station, then he was to turn right. A male doctor in blood-stained scrubs met him. "Dr. Montoya! I'm told you're somewhat of a miracle man! These two people need a miracle tonight! Come with me!"

Minj left his friend to his medical work and started looking around for the nearest waiting room. Meanwhile, the captain and the chiefexec were in a different lounge. They stood on opposite ends of the otherwise-deserted room, occasionally staring one another down. Over time, the captain noticed she seemed to have been inching closer. And was her expression actually starting to soften? Finally, they were only a few feet apart. He looked into her eyes and they were wet. She caught him glancing at her. Humiliated by her display of emotion, she turned and stormed away.

"You all right?" he called.

"Tanna is my friend," she whispered, not caring whether he heard her. She trotted down the hall to the ladies' room, her heels rapidly clicking on the floor. She returned sometime later, composed and poker-faced. She tried to ignore him and took a seat at the far end of the room. He moved to within two chairs of her. She moved farther away. He shook his head and left her to her thoughts.

An hour or so later, Montoya found them and gave them the news. The two officials had stabilized and were going to live. The chiefexec hugged and kissed Montoya. The captain slapped him on the shoulder. A short time later, an exhausted chiefexec sat down in a chair and closed her eyes. Erik got a warm cloak from the nurses' desk and laid it over the high official. He then carried a chair over to her, lifted up her feet and rested them on the chair..

"My, aren't we being familiar?" she moaned sleepily.

"I'm trying to make you comfortable."

"Go away."

He took a chair at the opposite end of the room.

The next thing Zama knew she was inhaling the scent of her favorite hot morning beverage. There were some savory food smells as well. She opened her eyes. The captain was holding a tray of her favorite breakfast items. He placed them on a nearby coffee table. She smiled. "H-how did you know what I like?"

"I videoed Kelly," he replied.

"Thank you." She looked at him. He was still in his dress uniform from the previous night but he now had a morning beard stubble. "Anything new on Tanna and William?"

"Montoya says they're progressing well," Erik replied. "They may be able to go home in a few days."

Her eyes opened even wider. The two officials had been considered *dead* just hours earlier. She pushed the second chair away with her feet and pulled the blanket off. She still wore her formal gown from the previous night but it was now full of wrinkles. Her formerly well-coiffed hair was in disarray. Zama lifted the tray to her lap and began to eat. "How did you pay for all this?" she asked between bites.

He laughed. "I didn't think about that until I got to the checkout. Fortunately the lady recognized me from your news coverage and said it was on the house."

"You didn't say who it was for...."

"Of course not. I kept your secret."

"Good man." After she had cleaned her plate and drained her cup, she asked: "What time is it?"

"A little after ten in the morning."

She looked panicked. "I've got to go brush out my hair and then I need to leave...."

"May I take you back to your mansion?"

"No. I'll have my people send a limo." She grabbed his arm. "Thank you for staying here with me. And thanks for breakfast. That was very kind...."

Before he had a chance to respond, three men and two women in dark, formal-looking outfits strode over to the couple. "Madame Exec! I'm glad we found you," said a burly male officer. "We've been worried about you." The group stepped between their leader and the captain, muscling Erik out of the way. He ignored the indignity and stepped back.

"Is everything okay?" asked a blonde female officer, her green, penetrating eyes drilling holes in the spaceman.

"Yes, everything is fine," Zama replied. "Thank you once again, Captain Houston. I've got to get going now." She hurried down the hall with her entourage.

A few days later, the two government officials were deemed well enough to leave the hospital. Large crowds were on hand, as well as many members of the media. The crowds cheered as the duo emerged from the exit, riding in automated wheelchairs. The chiefexec was also on hand, as were the captain, Minj and Montoya.

"Look, there's Chiefexec Elle!" said one reporter. They all rushed over to her.

"Madame Exec," yelled one reporter, "do you have any comment about Directors Thal and Bern being released from the hospital?"

"I'm glad to see they've recovered so well," she said tensely. "Other than that, I have no comment."

Erik spotted Zama and walked over to greet with her. She looked him in the eye, turned and walked away. His stomach dropped as if on a fast vertilift. Moments later he was burning with anger.

The reporters now spied him and rushed to his side. "And here's Erik Houston, captain of the starship that brought the visitors to our planet. What are your comments, Captain Houston?" called one newsman while several others mobbed him.

He tried to rapidly shift gears and not let his anger and bitterness show. He deadpanned: "This accident was a tragedy. I'm glad to see the two officials have recovered so well. My technical crew will continue to investigate the cause of the accident."

Then the media people spotted Montoya. They hurried over to him. "Dr. Montoya!" called one. "These officials were considered dead yet somehow you brought them back to life. Can you tell us how you did this, sir?"

He spent some time fielding questions. The photogenic Montoya, with his dark hair and Van Dyke beard was a major feature on the news that day. Many

Al'aamans came to regard him as a hero. Yet some video news shows and online newzines continued to blame the star visitors for the accident. Any of the favorable buzz around the doctor and other space people irritated the chiefexec. She wasn't through dealing with them yet.

The next day, Captain Houston learned that it was, indeed, a systems failure that had caused the landing craft to launch into the sky when the two government officials obviously did not have clearance. The craft had also been initially unresponsive to long-distance remote control when Irv's second in command had tried to land it safely. Houston appeared on the news to explain the equipment failure and apologize for the disaster, something the captain hated to do given William and Tanna's unlawful entry. Some Al'aamans appreciated the captain's honesty. Others expressed distrust for the star people. The topic kept blogs and editorial offices busy for the next several days.

The captain's stomach had tightened into a ball over being summoned to an audience with Queen Zama. He had received a call from a harsh-sounding Alisa Conway demanding he show up at a certain day and time. He arrived fifteen minutes early dressed in a semi-formal uniform. The chief of staff pointed to a seat then promptly went back to her work. She made several calls using her ear implant, her ear canal again developing that freakish red glow. She then worked with some online files. She stopped and pulled out a tube of lipstick. She freshened her lips, using a small video screen as a makeup mirror. She pursed her lips and looked at her teeth. Then she closed the lipstick case with a loud click. She shot Houston a look with eyes that could be registered as lethal weapons. After several grueling seconds, she turned her attention elsewhere.

The captain glanced at his wrist chronometer. The chiefexec was already twenty minutes late. Alisa made another video screen call. The captain and she periodically exchanged looks. The big boss was now twenty-five minutes late. Thirty minutes. Forty. Houston stood up.

Before he could say a word, the gatekeeper snapped: "The chiefexec wants to see you!"

"When?" he demanded.

"When she's ready!"

Deflated, he sat back down. Ten more minutes passed. An intercom buzzed. "Yes," said Alisa. "Yes, Ma'am." Her eyes moved back to the captain. "Go in," she said.

The captain opened the door and stepped into the vast office. Without a word, the chief of staff closed the door behind him. The captain marched toward the over-sized desk. The chiefexec was standing with her back to him and her arms folded. She stayed riveted some distance away and was staring out the window toward the mansion lawn.

"Good day, Captain," she began icily, her back still toward him. "Sit down."

"Been sitting long enough," he said through gritted teeth.

"As you wish." She said nothing further for an eternally long two or three minutes. The captain shifted his weight from one foot to the other. Finally: "I...appreciate your apology to our people."

"Thank you."

"And...you treated me kindly at the hospital." More silence. She turned his direction but looked at the floor. "Nevertheless," she said in a voice almost too deep for a woman, "I'm thinking of asking you to you leave our planet."

He saw his chance for a promotion evaporate, which upset him even more than her demeanor. But he said, calmly: "That's your prerogative."

"Yes, it is." She strode over to her desk then took a seat. He finally sat as well. "Our people and the media are sharply divided on whether your visit here has been a blessing or a curse. Some view you as friends. Some even see you as heroes. But others point out that there's been nothing but trouble since you came."

"Two of your senior officials would not even be alive right now if not for us. How do you feel about us?"

"I, too, am conflicted. You've caused us trouble but you also have some knowledge that we would find useful. But...we haven't yet learned to trust you."

"You...haven't yet learned to trust *us*! You confiscated some key pieces of our equipment and wouldn't give them back!"

"I had gotten it back and was going to give it to you the day after the banquet! You had two of your people break into my office!"

"I knew nothing about it! But two of your people broke into one of my landing craft and flew off with it!"

"It was an accident! And I knew nothing about what they were doing."

"You knew nothing about it!"

"Don't raise your voice to me! I'm the chiefexec of this planet!"

"You're the ruler of a city state. You don't know what goes on five miles past your border."

"So why don't you leave?"

"There must be a thousand other planets that would be more hospitable!"

"How dare you!"

As the volume of the argument rapidly escalated, Alisa began to hear the shouts through the door. The chief of staff heard further loud, high-pitched squeals and grunts and was afraid the two were physically hurting one another. She pushed a button to call Exec Security, grabbed a heavy desk ornament and flung open the door. Within seconds, five dark-suited guards, weapons drawn, appeared behind her. They all stood there, mouths agape. Their chiefexec and that space alien were both sitting in their chairs, red-faced, laughing hysterically as tears rolled down their faces. Alisa shook her head. The absurdity continued for a moment before the duo realized they had an audience. They looked at the cluster of stone-faced people standing in the doorway then burst into more laughter.

The normally refined Zama wiped her tears on her sleeve, brushing away the captain's offer of a handkerchief. Once the chief executive's laughter subsided, she looked at the star man again and smiled. It was the nicest smile he had even seen on her. Even better than the night of the dance. She looked him in the eye again and held out her hand in the sight of all the witnesses.

"Friends?" she asked.

"Friends!" he affirmed. She grasped his hand and shook it firmly.

# 20.

"You wished to see me, Madame Exec?" Tanna asked.

"Yes. Come in."

She limped into the chiefexec's office, leaning heavily on a walker cane. The big boss pushed a button to close the door. "Sit down."

"Yes, Ma'am." She eased into a seat.

"I'm glad you've recovered so well. How are you feeling?"

She put her hand to here forehead and grimaced. "Getting better. I've got a couple weeks of therapy left."

"I'm sincerely glad to hear that. But you know why you're here, don't you?"

"Yes, Ma'am."

"You and I have been friends a long time. We worked well together in the past. But friendship is based on trust. Working relationships are based on trust. And I've learned that I can't trust you. You withheld the star people's possessions in defiance of my orders. You were involved in secret experiments using their equipment and you broke and into one of their private landing craft. Without these actions, there would have been no accident! And one other thing," she said, jabbing a finger at the official, "the star people claim they broke into my office only because they thought we *weren't going* to return their possessions. If you had even turned them in sooner, prior to my insisting on it, *none* of these things would have happened. I have no choice but to let you go. I know you have a family so you will receive a severance package. But as of today, you are no longer a part of my administration. I'll be having this same type of conversation with William Thal. And I'm making sure he fires all the security officers who were your accomplices. You may pick up your belongings at your office. Good day, Tanna."

The ex-cabinet member slowly rose to her feet, silently opened the door and limped out. Once she was out of sight of her former boss and Alisa Conway, she squared her shoulders and straightened up to her full height. She folded up the walker cane and placed it in her purse. Striding boldly down the hall, her eyes ablaze, she hissed: "You'll live to regret this, Zama Elle!"

On the other side of the mansion, Captain Houston was holding a similar meeting with two of *his* officers. "Fred, I realize you were able to save those two government officials' lives. But I should have you two court martialed for breaking into the chiefexec's office!" a red-hot captain Houston snapped. "You did this in defiance of my orders! You two turned yourselves into fugitives! We lost her trust and you sabotaged our entire mission. She was furious when I last spoke with her. We almost had to scrub this mission. I've never once had that happen on my watch!"

Minj didn't say a thing and hung his head.

"But, Captain," said Montoya.

The skipper looked at him, eyes ablaze.

"I felt it vital to our security to get our equipment back. Look what happened when that was delayed."

"Point well taken, Fred. But don't forget I'm the captain here! I'm responsible for everything that takes place on this mission. You should have discussed your concerns with me in greater detail. I wasn't going to let this drag on much longer. Guys, I appreciate your concern for our safety but you needed to go about this another way. Don't ever let this happen again!"

"Yes, sir," said Minj.

"Aye," said Montoya.

"Now, as punishment for your insubordination, I'm busting each of you down one full rank! Plus, you will each be confined to your quarters aboard ship for the the next three weeks. Irv has already sent officers to escort you back to the *Initiative*. And you two can be glad your punishment isn't a lot worse. That is all, gentlemen!" The two stood up to leave. The captain opened the door to reveal two of his security officers. The chastened men shuffled out the door and the officers escorted them down the hall.

Later, the captain was having a comm link conversation with his security chief, who was also the ship's chaplain. "Irv, there are two philosophies star captains go by when it comes to dealing with natives of these planets we visit," he said. "One school of thought is to just arrive on the planet, gain all the knowledge about the place that you can, then leave. Sure, that makes for quicker trips, and the Association likes that because more planets can be visited. But I don't go with that theory. I feel we were sent here to *help* the natives. They may have missed out on a lot of technological development and there may be other ways we can assist them."

The older man thought a moment. "Captain, don't forget these are fairly short trips. You're here a few months then gone again. Off to some other planet in another star system. It would be easy for you to care too much. Become too attached to this planet and its people."

"You've traveled the stars a lot longer than I have. What do you think?" asked the captain.

"You're going about it the right way. Yes, you open yourself up to being hurt when it comes time to leave people you've grown attached to, but I think we have an *obligation* to help. I've heard the locals haven't been too cooperative."

"Their ruler is hardheaded, but I think she does care about her people. We've reached a truce."

# 21.

A couple days later, Kelly showed up to invite the visitors to a parade in their honor. A number of the little solar electric vehicles filled with waving dignitaries drove by the grandstand where Chiefexec Elle and several of her top officials sat with Erik and all crew members currently on the planet. Following the vehicles were school marching bands and cheerleaders, then clowns and acrobats. Several people passed by riding what looked like a giant caterpillar that meandered from one side of the street to another.

"Is that an actual life form?" asked the captain. "It's huge!"

"They're rare," said the leader. "Occasionally one will wander from the wilderness to the outskirts of the city. Our people will capture it and put it in the zoo. A few of them have been trained for parades like this. Those creatures are actually quite docile."

After the parade, a group of young school children performed some simple songs for the visitors. Erik smiled and waved at the kids. Several of them shyly looked at the floor. One smiled at the captain. A little girl waved back at him. Kelly, who was sitting two seats away, had noticed how much he was enjoying the kids. She looked at him and smiled. He caught her glance and returned the smile. The chiefexec, who was sitting between them, caught her firstadvisor's glance. Kelly looked away.

The big boss thought about the differences between her counselor and her. The chiefexec was in her mid-forties and had worked hard for years to build her career. Although a skilled politician, Zama was somewhat reserved and definitely had a private side. At a younger age, she'd had a slender build that had gradually been eroded by middle age and too many hours at the office. Although many people thought of their chiefexec as good looking, she was also not considered a great beauty.

Kelly was bright and had been a prodigy. She was in her late thirties, had gotten into public service early and had risen through the ranks quickly. She was outgoing, somewhat full-figured and many considered her attractive. The chiefexec shook her head when she realized she was mentally comparing the two of them in this context. After all, the star people, even at their best were just business partners. She'd gain what she could from them then they'd be free to leave. She returned her attention to the festivities.

Realizing her boss was no longer watching her, Kelly glanced at Erik from the corner of her eye and smiled once again.

Meanwhile, an animal expert had arrived to show off some examples of native wildlife. One creature's body looked like a pink, fluffy ball with a smaller ball for a head and another for a tail. The creature appeared to be sneezing over and over again. "That's how they bark," the expert explained. Luci tried to pet the creature but it lunged at her, almost biting her finger.

"You have to watch them. They can get vicious if they don't know you, the trainer explained.

The next animal was an elliptical-shaped creature made of what looked like semi-transparent jelly. The trainer stood the creature on one end and let it go; the animal flopped end over end several times, negotiating some distance in the process. "Kids love these," the trainer laughed.

"This next animal is called a dropper," said the trainer. The dropper was a dark-colored creature that had two legs, two arms, a squat body and a head. The trainer released the dropper, which quickly climbed up on the canopy of the grandstand then jumped off, landing on its feet on the grandstand floor. The dropper climbed a second time and jumped again. It then repeated the act.

"What an odd creature," Luci said.

"Many people own droppers." The trainer smiled. "They help rid your home of quantacida and ypitammin."

After the animal exhibition, Kelly took Erik and his crew on an official tour of the city. First, they surveyed the stately government district then the business area, which boasted a number of skyscrapers. Some towering buildings stood with little visible means of support. Architects were able to take a little more artistic license on a lower grav planet such as Al'aama. Some of the buildings the star people visited had interior courtyards and lush gardens. A few skyscrapers each had an entire wall consisting of an enormous video screen. One wall was covered with a gigantic picture of a woman's face and was apparently advertising some brand of cosmetics. After about half a minute, the image dissolved and another took its place.

The business district contained several broad avenues lined on either side with tall, arching vegetation known as fern trees. The trees were branchless for over half their length then opened up into many feathery branches making the overall tree resemble a fern. The fern trees provided some degree of shade for pedestrians walking along the sidewalks. Erik and his crew saw some major highways that crossed the city and were crowded with thousands of the small, solar electric cars. Kelly also had them ride on a maglev train system that crossed the entire city. Beyond the business district was an industrial area with various automated factories. There was also an area devoted to nothing but massive solar energy collectors, helping supply the main power source for the city. Beyond the solar equipment was a wide green space followed by one suburb after another featuring houses with large, immaculately landscaped lawns.

Erik remembered looking at the lights of Al'aama from space and his thought at the time that the city was shaped somewhat like a giant eye. He now learned it was shaped more like a spider. Well beyond the metro area proper were several deep mines and strip mines, as well as a few residential communities, all connected to the metro area by trains and highways. In between each set of "spider legs" was an extensive area of undeveloped jungle. Some Al'aamans enjoyed hunting and camping in many of these areas. Located even farther out from the center city was a farm district, which surrounded the area like a cocoon. Beyond the farms, civilization abruptly ended and the wilderness began. However, in some areas the tourists saw workers driving landozers and rock pulverizers to clear land for additional farms. Metro Al'aama seemed large and efficient yet comfortable and livable.

The next day, the tour went into greater detail. Kelly accompanied them to an automated factory, then a scientific research facility. They visited a two-hundred-eighty-year-old institution, Al'aama University, one of several in the city. It was a virtual university, with all classes broadcast remotely to students' video screens. Many recorded the lectures and viewed them at their leisure. Class projects were handled via live video conference. Students primarily only met physically to participate in sports teams and for social events. This meant few students lived or ate on campus. Most either lived at home or rented junior apartments, often subsidized by their parents. Some young people skipped college altogether by getting knowledge implants then going directly into the workforce at age eighteen or so.

The visitors discussed in detail with their hosts specifics of what was accomplished at each of these institutions. Whenever appropriate, the visitors politely let their hosts know that they had some insight into their field, if the hosts were interested. On the first few such visits, the leaders running the institutions were somewhat taken aback by the offers, as if the star people were assuming they didn't know their respective fields. But gradually, word seemed to get around that the visitors were knowledgeable and genuinely trying to help, so eventually some of the officials began to take them up on the offer. Then the star people began to start receiving requests for them to visit and counsel with various leaders. By this time, Montoya and Minj's time of punishment was over, so they returned planetside.

Kelly gave the visitors permission to roam A'laama at will. Erik led the landing party on various self-directed tours. Numerous downtown buildings were interconnected by webs of overhead walkways and underground corridors. The group began to encounter a group of A'laamans known as paele, or "pale ones." They tended to stay indoors in the climate-controlled environment, away from the blazing Ava sun. Erik and his crew were shocked to see so many pasty-skinned people, having rarely come across them on A'laama. He recalled seeing few light skin tones in the crowd the day his people had landed on the planet. Apparently not even such an historic event could draw many paele out of their man-made caves.

The peale kept tabs on the rest of the world via the ever-present video screens. Because they were able to work, sleep, exercise, buy groceries and seek entertainment all without ever leaving the comfort of a building, many of them did not go outdoors for weeks at a time. Erik considered them the ultimate example of the cocoon that was A'laama. The group made up a full eight percent of the population.

As the star people continued to explore the world of the paele, they descended deeper into the bellies of buildings. Many stories below ground lived a sub-group of paele. The ones the crew had encountered so far had been prosperous professionals. But deep underground, the environment changed. Corridor walls were now made of concrete block that had once been painted white but were now discolored. The lighting was dimmer and the paele began to take on a scruffy appearance. The star people retraced their steps and ascended back to ground level. They were actually grateful to get outdoors into the intense heat and blinding sunlight.

After several weeks of the star people's touring, some of them even began to give guest lectures at the university and other colleges. Montoya would give a lecture on a scientific topic, Minj would give an overview of interstellar history or Luci would talk about the latest applications for electronic communications. Chiefexec Elle kept hearing such positive reports on the star visitors that she was glad she had decided to let them stay.

"We're going to visit the place where our history all started," Kelly said. Historian Minj especially perked up. They got into her vehicle and crossed much of the city. Finally, they reached a massive building near an old stone tower. "This is it," she said. "The Founders' Museum."

The structure contained much open space and had a high ceiling. Their guide led them to the main exhibit. The museum had been built around an enormous crater. Considerable metal and other debris was strewn about the perimeter. Apparently the site had been kept in its original state. The crater was at least a couple hundred yards across and more than fifty feet deep. The group had to walk up one flight of stairs to traverse the mounds of dirt the impact had created. It took a few more sets of steps to reach the bottom. The visitors gasped as they looked into the enormous pit. Near its center were the remnants of a huge space vessel. The ship was broken into three major pieces and a number of smaller ones. The communications antennae were broken off. The ship's mid-section was blackened with fire. The visitors felt they could still smell the acrid smoke.

"Starship Class VE-2. Definitely a type used during that era," Minj confirmed.

"The survivors had no way to send a message about the crash," Luci observed.

Kelly explained that this ship was the *Endurance*. It had started out on the longest manned interstellar voyage that had ever been attempted, a thirty-light-year journey beyond the frontier of civilization. The prize was one of the most earth-like planets that had ever been discovered. But severe drive system trouble had forced it to divert to another star system two light years short of its goal. A binary system whose fourth planet was a relatively earth-like, low grav world. She showed them a lighted map depicting the two systems.

Erik felt like someone had knocked the breath out of him. Now it was clear why the Association had no prior record of the A'laaman colony. And why the beautiful world he had observed through the gravitational lens had never been settled.

Most of *Endurance's* crew had been in Cold Sleep during the voyage. As many as possible were awakened prior to the emergency landing. The vessel has been designed to orbit a planet, not land on the surface. The ship had been able to dispatch two lifeboats toward the planet before being forced to crash-land on the surface. The life boats and their passengers had never been found. The survival rate of the crew still onboard at the time of the crash was an estimated eighteen percent. Over sixty percent of the survivors were women, primarily due to the location of the women's compared with the men's Cold Sleep tanks. After spending some time examining the wreckage and even going inside it, the group climbed back up out of the crater.

The next exhibit consisted of video survivors had taken after the crash. The smoking crater was in the background. In the foreground was more debris. Here was part of bench-type seat. There some broken glass. Elsewhere some twisted shards of metal. Dazed, wounded people wandered by. Others were heard moaning off-screen. A few medical personnel were treating some of the worst victims. The video panned to reveal more debris. Battered parts of various robots. Damaged control consoles and electronic equipment. A detached, human arm. The footage became more graphic. The star women moaned for their host to turn off.

"I can't stand to look at it, either," Kelly said, shuddering.

She walked rapidly to another part of the hall, explaining how once children began to be born on the planet, the first few babies were girls. It was several years after the founding of the new colony that the first boy baby was born. By then, the pattern was already being established in which many of the leaders were women. This tradition had continued throughout A'laaman history."

They then moved on to the next exhibit, a bronze statue of three women. "These ladies were the main leaders who emerged from among the survivors. They weren't prominent in the immediate aftermath of the crash but over the years came to be considered the greatest leaders of that founding generation.

Their names were Nanci Batami, Dyana Paol and Viola Caab. Each of the women started a family that grew into one of the three leading tribes of our society. Any woman who is descended from one of these Three Founders is given a place of great honor."

The captain asked: "Isn't your chiefexec a descendant of one of the three women?"

Kelly smiled. "She is. She's a descended from Dyana Paol." The men looked at a lone statue of Dyana, who was depicted as a tall, lean woman with long hair. "Dyana was known for her fiery temperament."

Erik smiled. Their hostess led the star men to various other exhibits that showed how the early settlers had lived and how the city had developed.

Finally, she led them outside to a long sidewalk that led to an old stone tower about half a mile distant. She hurried off at a rapid pace while the others struggled to catch up."We'll be soaked by the time we get there," said Erik, whose shirt was already growing damp as he glanced up at the two-sun sky. Once Kelly arrived at the landmark, she waited for her guests.

"And this," she said, "marks the very spot where an important event took place. Four years after the colony was founded, a severe drought had wilted all the crops. The settlers were running out of food and some of them felt they were only weeks away from perishing. One day, an angel appeared to some of our ancestors and told them everything would be all right. That soon some cool rains would come. The crops would miraculously spring back to life and the colony would survive and begin to thrive. A few days later, the angel appeared to others and gave the same message. And before long what the angel had predicted came true. The colonists were saved. And since then we've grown into this great city."

Montoya looked skeptical but the others were fascinated.

"I've studied the histories of dozens of planets and your story is not all that unusual," Minj said. "Very few colonies have died out over the centuries. A variety of planets have histories describing similar stories to A'laama's. And when you consider that in each case the colony was a self-contained unit and that any potential help was years or decades away by the fastest ship, it makes these stories all the more remarkable."

The captain nodded. "I've heard many such tales over the years and most of the ones I've heard have a ring of authenticity." Minj and the star women nodded while Montoya looked away.

"So, now you know a little more about us," said Kelly. "Given our ancestors' traumatic arrival on this planet and their initial difficulty in sustaining the new colony, succeeding generations desired for our society to be secure. So we grew into Al'aama, the self-sufficient, comfortable city where everyone is able to feel safe."

The captain said: "Our ship's sensors have done an analysis. You built your city on one of the greatest single concentrations of resources this world has. You have a lake, minerals, excellent agricultural land...."

"Yes. It's amazing when you consider the colonists overshot their intended landing area by over two hundred miles," Kelly added.

"Tell us exactly what the angel said," Minj requested, still recording everything.

"Okay, here's the exact wording of the Prophecy," Kelly replied. "*You had planned to go to a world fresh and green and have instead come to this torrid place. You have traveled from afar to come to this world and at times your efforts have seemed for nought. Fear not, for you shall not perish. Rejoice, for you and your seed shall live. Within ten days the rains shall come and the drought shall end. Your land shall be green again. Your little group shall not perish but will take root and grow and bear fruit in abundance. You who started so small and weak shall become a great and mighty people.*"

"Did the angel tell the colonists anything else?" asked Luci.

Kelly got a mischievous look in her eye. She smiled broadly and quoted: "*And this is the sign that these things shall all come to pass: three women shall arise from your midst to become great leaders. And just as three women came from the stars, before three hundred years pass three men shall come from the stars and call fire down from heaven.*"

All six star visitors looked at one another. Kelly turned toward the men and continued: "And it just so happens, gentlemen, that your arrival on this planet took place two hundred ninety-nine years, five months after our ancestors first set foot on Al'aama."

# 22.

Fin Wasiling and Tab Moulton had parked their vehicles at the end of a remote road that came to dead end, the abrupt termination of the civilized world. Beyond the road lay a stretch of cultivated fields and, beyond that, the beginning of the wilderness. Waisling had bought a new ener rifle and was anxious to try it out on some large game. The animals in the Inner Jungle were too small and too used to humans. The men crept along the edge of some farmer's field until the crops abruptly ended. Their boots began to tramp through the tall grass and brush of a field grown wild. There, a couple hundred yards ahead, they spotted their destination: the Outer Jungle, rarely visited by A'laamans.

As the two hunters crossed an invisible barrier, a signal from each man's bio-electronic implant tripped an alarm that sounded at the nearest police station a few miles away. One wall of the station was filled with a grid displaying the entire sub-precinct. Yellow dots represented each of the sub's tens of thousands of citizens, all tracked by their implants. As long as the individuals stayed within the outer boundaries of greater A'laama, the dots remained yellow. When anyone strayed outside that area, his or her dot flashed red.

Two dots turned red and began pulsating. "Look at that!" cried one of the dispatchers. A telescopic camera picked up a visual."Two of 'em. Just as bold as can be."

"Let's wait to see what they do," said his coworker.

The violators continued advancing toward the jungle. After a few moments, they crossed The One Hundred Yard Barrier, the A'laaman margin of safety that marked the official difference between innocently wandering away and breaking the law. Enforcing the Forbidden Zone was the hidden reason behind A'laaman society virtually mandating electronic implants of some sort for everyone: adults, youths, even children. Someone having no implant at all was considered immoral. Police were able to track anyone who violated the out of bounds rule. At least most of the time, this was the only reason Law Enforcement tracked average members of society. But occasional periods of governmental abuse had flared up over the years. Many A'laamans were vaguely aware of the tracking but considered it a normal part of life. And the large majority had such a comfortable lifestyle they had no desire to go near the forbidden area.

"They're officially in the Zone," the first dispatcher sighed. "Who's available to send after them?"

"Cars One-Nineteen and Two-Thirty One."

"Send them both," said the first man. "We need to make an example of these guys."

The two Al'aaman hunters were now on the edge of the jungle. They stepped between two fern trees and entered a different world. They knew many Al'aamans considered this a dangerous area but they were tired of tracking prey in the tamer jungle within the Al'aaman perimeter. They had hiked several hundred yards into the jungle for this hunt, something they had always been warned not to do as children because of the violent Non-techs. Such tales had been so firmly planted in the minds of Al'aamans that many refused to hunt or camp even as adults.

But Wasiling and Moulton didn't believe those old tales. The two men were carrying some lumber and tools, which they would use to a build a tree stand, like they had often done in the Inner Jungle. The men planned to set up the stand on a major branch of a bakonga tree. The two hunters were wearing camouflage and a scent that would neutralize their own. After they had begun working on the stand, they thought they heard a sound in the distance but finally concluded it was nothing, only a single animal too small to be worth the bother.

Abruptly, a half dozen officers, guns drawn, stepped out of the brush, startling the hunters. Two of the cops trained their guns on the lawbreakers. The others, weapons drawn, looked in all directions, almost as if they were expecting visitors.

"Waisling, F. and Moulton, T.!" the sergeant cried. "You two are guilty of flagrantly violating the law by entering the Forbidden Zone."

"But, officers, we're just here to do a little hunting," Moulton protested. He cursed to himself, noting that his jamming device had failed to throw the cops off their trail.

"Hunt in the Free Zone," snapped the sergeant. "Now give me your licenses."

"What?" cried Waisling.

"Do as he says!" barked another officer, one of two who were pointing weapons directly at the men's chests. The men retrieved their hunting licenses and handed them over.

"The fine is five hundred units each," the sarge continued. "And if this happens again, you boys will be doing some jail time."

Moulton whistled at the severity of the penalty.

"This isn't fair!" cried Wasiling.

"We're trying to keep you safe," snapped a female officer. "There are Non-techs around."

Wasiling rolled in his head in disbelief. "Bunk! Those are kids' stories."

"No, they're real," said the lady cop."Haven't you heard about all the murders out this way?"

The sarge glared at her. "Enough talking, you two! You're under arrest." Two officers snapped ener cuffs on the prisoners while another confiscated their weapons. The police led their captives out of the jungle at gun point, marching them to the waiting squad car hundreds of yards away on the deserted road . "And pass the word along to all your hunting buddies," he cried.

That night, 3-D's of forlorn-looking Moulton and Wasiling appeared all over the video and online news, much to their chagrin and that of their families. Some of their neighbors and coworkers avoided speaking to them for the next several days.

# 23.

The chiefexec and the star man strolled toward a stand of giant fern trees on the back lawn of the mansion. The captain stopped, leaned his head back and stared at the tops of the trees. Some of them must have been eighty or ninety feet tall.

Chuckling to herself, she gently nudged him forward. The captain took a few steps and the temperature fell at least thirty degrees, making it comparatively chilly for a two-sun Al'aaman day. Shivering, Erik marveled at this zone of coolness. Zama was wearing a knee-length sun dress and a floppy-brimmed hat to help keep the remaining sun out of her eyes.

She spread a large table cloth on the ground and motioned for him to sit. He did so then continued contemplating the fern trees. From a distance, they appeared sky blue but close-up, they were almost transparent. He kept looking at one of the trees, certain he was seeing water move through the trunk. He was convinced of it when he saw what looked like a bubble as wide as his hand following the same path as the water.

A metallic robot, balanced on one wheel, rolled over to the duo. Erik was watching his companion, who was gazing at the electronic servant. She seemed to be directing it by her thoughts. A door opened in the robot's mid-section and a tray slid forward. "Luncheon is served," it said, almost sounding human. Erik smiled.

The lady took the covered dishes and set them down on the tablecloth. The tray retreated back into the robot. Erik noted another non-verbal exchange between woman and machine. The robot bowed then rolled away in reverse. It stopped about twenty feet from the two diners but was still facing them. Erik could even see a tiny reflection of the chiefexec and him in that large, red eye. Her eyes flashed and she frowned at the butler.

"Cedric. Some privacy, please," she said aloud.

"Yes, Ma'am." The robot swiveled exactly 180 degrees. A panel in the its back opened up, revealing a smaller red eye.

"Cedric," she snapped. The panel slammed shut.

She shook her head."Security. They're obsessive. Captain, as a way of showing my appreciation for all you've done for our people, I've had my chefs prepare this special meal."

His stomach tightened. The chiefexec pulled back the cloth covering a bowl, revealing some clear, golf ball-sized spheres that looked like jelly. "Try one of these."

He discretely waved his handheld food analyzer over the bowl. The device pronounced the items safe. He watched her pick up one of the spheres and pop it into her mouth whole. She did not chew. Apparently the item melted in the mouth. He followed her example. The ball of jelly did, indeed, melt on the tongue. The explosion of flavors delighted him. It reminded him of a mixture of fruits, but unlike any he had had previously experienced. Next, she lifted the cover on a dish that looked like thin strands of spaghetti the color and apparent texture of grass. The analyzer pronounced this item edible, too. The chiefexec scooped some of the food into her hand and popped it into her mouth. This time she chewed, seeming to really enjoy the flavor. He followed suit. The item *tasted* somewhat like the *scent* of a rose. He smiled.

"That's a tasty dish, isn't it?" she said. "I love yammick brains, too."

She uncovered a dish filled with dried leaves. The analyzer went off the charts. "Madame Exec, with all due respect, I'm afraid this next item would prove too spicy for me."

"It's really very good."

"I hope you won't be offended...."

She shook her head and smiled. "No, no. That's fine," she said with a wave of her hand. She grabbed a large handful of the leaves, chewed them thoroughly then grabbed a second handful. She then took a couple swigs from her beverage glass. "Ah, delicious!" she pronounced. He thought he saw burn marks develop at either side of her lips, yet she kept eating the spicy dish.

She caught him staring at her nose. It had a fairly obvious bump or knot. He had noticed it on several other occasions but today couldn't seem to take his eyes off it.

"I'm sorry," the captain said, realizing his faux pax.

"Got it in a street fight," she said, looking down.

His shook his head. "When were you ever in a street fight?"

"In my teens." She was staring at the ground. Silence descended on the couple.

Finally, she said: "There's something I've been curious about, Captain. How old are you, really?"

He looked off into the distance. "Around four hundred standard years," he said.

Her eyebrows shot up and her jaw dropped. Recovering, she quipped: "You don't look a day over three-fifty."

He laughed.

She shook her head and smiled. "I realize your starship travels at close to light speed so you travel in slowtime. I don't mean how many calendar years have you been alive but how many...what do you call them, shipboard years? How many years of life have you actually *experienced?*"

He took a deep breath before speaking. "My life's been fragmented. I've spent so many short pieces of it in so many different places. I graduated from the Space Academy twenty of my years ago so in terms of years I've actually lived. I'm...forty-two. Forty-three? No, forty-two."

She laughed. "You and I are in the same demographic."

He noticed she had gradually moved closer. They had started out facing one another but now she was almost sitting beside him. "You've shared much of your tech and I'm grateful. Our scientists have been fascinated by what they've learned. But anytime you learn one new fact, it begets ten more questions. There's one thing that concerns me."

"What's that?"

"Your people seem less anxious to share information lately."

Erik looked down at the tablecloth then cleared his throat. "Madame Exec, whenever a starship visits a planet for the first time, there are...certain *protocols* on how much information we can share with the inhabitants."

"I see. You whet our appetites then leave us wanting more so we'll join that, that...*Association* of yours..."

"We want to help. But we're approaching the limits of what we're able to reveal. And, as much as I hate to say this, our mission to this planet will probably soon be over...."

She slid a couple feet away. She stared straight ahead for a moment. Finally, she said in a low voice: "I know you're following orders. But I do hate the thought of you leaving soon."

He swallowed. "Sometimes our departures come a little soon for me, too."

He had earlier noticed a smooth, rounded decorative boulder that must have been at least eight feet across. Suddenly, it moved! He dropped his beverage glass. "Did you see that rock!" he exclaimed.

"That's not a rock. That's my pet, Illimi," she said. "Come here, Illimi. Here, boy!"

Erik swallowed hard as he recalled the incident on the day the crew had first arrived. He'd asked Irv to disintegrate a large "rock" on the mansion grounds. Had it actually been one of the ruler's *pets*? Yet if his hostess were reminded now of that incident, she didn't show it. The "boulder" slid close to the chief executive, who stroked its crest. Near the crest appeared two deep, dark blue liquid pools, apparently the creature's eyes.

"Here, pet him," she said.

Erik rubbed his hand across the top of the creature. It actually felt wet and slippery to the touch.

"Now, sit on top of him."

"What?"

"He likes you to sit on him. Watch." The lady gracefully slid onto the creature, taking a seat near the crest but behind the eyes. She held out her hand to help Erik onto Illimi's back. A long, bass-like sound emanated from deep inside the creature. "That means he's happy. C'mon, boy. Take us for a ride." The creature began to slowly glide across the lawn.

Erik smiled. The lady started to slip off to the side of the animal. The captain held on to her waist a moment to steady her. She looked back at him and smiled.

He still hated the idea of leaving soon. He foresaw wrapping up the visit in the next couple weeks. Then it would be back to the stars. A couple months of shore leave on the nearest Association planet would be followed by a new First Contact assignment, taking the crew and him who knows where. Despite the difficult beginnings, the A'laama mission had turned out well. The delegation from space had gained the trust of many of the leaders, shared some helpful knowledge and planted a seed for a future relationship with the Association. The star people had learned a fair amount about the planet and its culture and had even solved the mystery of why that earth-like orb two light years distant had never been settled.

The captain prayed silently. *Lord, is our mission here complete?* he asked. *Have we done everything you want us to?*

A thought had been nagging at the captain throughout the mission. And it was growing stronger while he was praying. It concerned him to see the Al'aamans always staying within their gradually expanding city as if it were a cocoon. Despite his employers' protocols against becoming too involved in a host world's internal affairs, despite some warnings in the back of his own mind, he felt the need to challenge the provincial mindset. He swallowed hard.

"Madame Exec…" he began, "in ancient times, a top executive was often called a president. A president was not merely the ruler of a city. She…or he…was the head of a nation comprised of hundreds of millions or even billions of people. A mayor is the traditional term for someone who is the leader of a city. Do you feel that term would better suit your job?"

"I disagree," she said. "Al'aama is divided into 37 different municipalities, each with its own mayor. And there's our capital district, Batamiville, with its own mayor. And we not only have all these cities and towns but over 200 distinct neighborhoods, many with their own political leaders. Miles beyond our metro area are several small, semi-autonomous mining communities and a handful of relatively isolated suburbs, each with their local leaders. But I'm the head of all of that. I'm the chiefexec."

Erik swallowed. "Okay. Maybe Al'aama is more like an ancient county or maybe you're like a small nation."

"An ancient…what or a small what?"

"You rule over one large, metro area. You don't also rule over other metros tens or hundreds of miles away, right?"

"That's correct. But there are no others. This is it."

"Everything I've learned about your early colonists leads me to believe they thought big! They had vision. They gave your office the title of Chiefexec of the Planet because they believed that some day a leader like you would literally be ruling the whole world. I admire the technological society you've developed from humble beginnings. But in some ways, your people no longer seem to think big…."

She sat there glaring at him. "Captain Houston, I am the ruler of this planet!" she exploded.

"You are not the ruler of this planet!"

"The people elected me and made me chiefexec."

"But you don't rule the entire planet. Have you ever been outside the city?"

"Yes. When I was growing up, sometimes we'd play in the woods on the edge of town."

"And where are those woods today?"

"They're an industrial park."

Houston shook his head. "Were you ever further outside the city than those woods?"

"No," she admitted, pouting a little.

"Then how do you *know* what's there?"

"Empty wasteland. *Everyone* knows that! Eventually, as the city continues to expand, we'll tear out some of the wasteland and build farms and roads and houses."

"But what about the *rest* of the planet?"

"I told you. It's wilderness."

Houston shook his head. He waved his hand and a three-dimensional sphere appeared. It slowly rotated. "This, Madame Exec, is your planet as it appears from space. On this video, I've sped up the rotation considerably for effect."

She gasped.

"This is a nighttime view. Now if you'll wait a few moments.... Ah, there."

"What's that little lighted area? "

"Your city as seen from space."

The patch of light was so tiny it would be easy to miss if not for its sharp contrast with the darkness of the planet's surface. After a few moments, the light disappeared, giving way to a planetary surface that was utterly dark. For long moments, there was nothing but darkness. Then one of the two suns arose, gradually lighting a portion of the planet.

He waved his hand again and zoomed in on some details. A range of jagged mountains stood before them, exceptionally tall mountains on this low-grav planet. Towering, snow-capped masses of rock thrusting against the sky. The captain waved his hand again. Before them was a beach. A sea bird cried overhead. Large waves crashed into the shore. Water in various shades of blue stretched as far as the eye could see. It seemed to even go beyond the horizon. Another scene change. Now nothing but sand in all directions. Sand and no signs of life. Dunes the height of small skyscapers. The captain waved his hand again. The great desert disappeared. Now the landscape was a plain of ice, white and barren. The sky looked like it was on fire. But the flames were every color of the rainbow. It was a rare visual phenomenon that could be formed by ice crystals in the air when all conditions were just right.

They were abruptly back at the picnic.

He looked over at her. Her mouth was hanging open. Her eyes were wide. She didn't appear to be breathing.

"You okay?" he asked.

"Yeah...yeah." She shook her head in disbelief.

"And that, Madame Exec, gives you a small taste of the rest of your planet. Would you like to see a little of what lies beyond your city?"

"Yes...Yes, I would." Her eyes were still wide with wonder.

"Tomorrow morning we'll fly one of my landing craft and visit one of those distant sites."

The color drained from her face. "I-I don't know...."

"Okay, we'll explore closer to home. We'll use two of my anti-grav belts and fly to...."

"Captain," she interrupted, grabbing his arm. "Let's...take this slow. Can we...see what's just beyond us?"

He looked at her. "Okay. I have a ground vehicle...."

She looked relieved. "That's better."

"What time shall we leave tomorrow?"

"Not tomorrow! So many meetings...."

"Just tell me when."

She retrieved her electronic calendar from her pocket. "I'm going to busy...."

"What about the weekend?"

"Not this weekend. I'm throwing a surprise 90th anniversary party for my great-grandparents. They look so young for their mid-one tens. After that, another busy week...."

He grunted in disgust. "Too busy to even see some of the planet you supposedly rule...."

"You impudent space alien!"

"What's the matter? Afraid to take such a big step?"

"I'm not afraid of anything! We'll go the second day of next week. I'll give you one day to prove whatever point you're trying to make. One day, no more!"

"You're on," he said, firmly shaking hands with her. She gripped his hand with all her strength, her eyes piercing his.

Later that day, both the metro police chief and the new security chief were in the chiefexec's office, passionately trying to convince her not to go on that foolhardy trip with the space captain. Police Chief Bil Franklin was a large man even by A'laaman standards. He wore an immaculate burgundy uniform with much gold braid and a wrinkle-proof white shirt. He was pacing around the office suite and raised up to his full height before addressing the leader, who was also standing.

"Madame Exec," he began, "you put me in an awkward position. My department is in charge of enforcing the Forbidden Zone yet you'll be breaking the law by crossing into the Zone."

"And that's a problem because…" Zama countered.

"Because of the example it will set. Many people may think that if it's okay for you to cross into the Zone, it's all right for them to do so."

The boss lady bit her lip. She thought about the research she had done immediately prior to this meeting. She had learned that three or four generations earlier, so many small groups had been moving into the deep wilderness that A'laama had created the Forbidden Zone to stop the population trickle from becoming a flood. Eventually, censors were installed to alert the police when citizens tried to cross into the Zone. At first, the law had been laxly enforced but punishment had later become more swift and sure.

In the early years, those who left the area were assumed to be harmless, but over time, they developed a reputation for violence. A'laama then installed censors that would alert the police to anyone crossing into the the perimeter from the wilderness. But the Non-techs were rumored to be at least two or three days' journey away by foot. Attacks by the group became so rare that the censors for incoming people fell into disrepair and eventually were turned off. Over time, the Non-techs became the subject of children's stories and fairytales. The chiefexec had read the police department's online reports that for many years there were at most, one or two suspicious attacks per year that could be attributed to the outdoors people. None in some years. Yet in the last six months there had been fifteen (Fifteen!) such incidents, several resulting in deaths.

She decided this was not the time to give the two officials a history lesson. Arms folded, she stood her ground.

"Times are changing," she said. "Maybe we've looked at this the wrong way. Maybe there shouldn't be a Forbidden Zone."

"But it's for our safety," the chief of police insisted. "You're aware of all the assaults, livestock thefts and killings that have been taking place along our northern perimeter."

The head of state nodded.

"At first, we attributed it to gang activity, but now we're convinced it's Them. The Others."

The new head of exec security jumped into the discussion. "And now, you want to take a vehicle into the north…."

"Northeast."

"Same general area. And the day you want to go! It's the worst possible day! Haven't you seen the forecast?"

"Of course I have. Are you questioning my decision?" she snapped.

The security man shook his head. "It's my job to protect you. My crew and I can't do that if you go to some distant place and we have no way to go there with you. You'll be taking a huge risk."

The chiefexec steeled her shoulders. "I'm sticking to my decision and that's final. Good day, gentlemen."

"But…but…" Police Head Franklin sputtered.

The security man threw his hands into the air. They both shuffled out the door.

Once they had gone, the boss woman pulled out her desk chair and plopped down into it. She couldn't admit to either of them that her stomach was in knots as she anticipated tomorrow's activity. She closed her eyes as a moment of panic gripped her. She shook her head, hoping it would also shake her fear. A moment later, she began to feel better. Her implant had sent just enough soothing med streaming into her bloodstream. She released the electron lock on her desk and pulled open a deep drawer. Her nostrils drank in the aroma of the ironwood that composed the desk. She reached to the bottom of the drawer and retrieved a hand-sized bundle wrapped in a velvety cloth. She folded back the cloth to reveal a sleek, silvery item. She balanced the warm metal in her hand as if to weigh it. It was lighter than she had recalled. The safety lock was still in place. She gripped the device and pointed it at a distant wall and imagined pulling the trigger. The ener pistol had belonged to her late husband, who had been somewhat of a sportsman, as had her own father. She had never fired a weapon in her life.

The chiefexec's limo transported the captain and she across the city, past the farming district to the far edge of Al'aaman civilization. Her security detail had expressed great concern over the trip and insisted on going along. She refused. Captain Houston said the vehicle wasn't large enough to accommodate several people and the trip would only last the day. As she prepared to exit the limo, the head of state noted that some media vehicles had followed them. She wasn't concerned about them going any farther because there were no more roads. Some of the G-men made another attempt to talk her out of going, but she assured them there was nothing to fear. Just as the driver was bringing the limo to a stop, Erik heard a female voice in his comm link ear piece.

"Luci. What's wrong?" he asked quietly, cupping his hand to his mouth to help muffle his voice. He glanced warily through the glass that separated him from the boss lady. The chiefexec kept looking straight ahead.

"Erik, I-I don't think you should head into the wilderness. Not today."

"Their leader's got a tight schedule. We almost didn't get to do this."

"But...the sunspot activity's off the chart. We could lose communications...."

"It'll just be a short trip."

"But what about the chiefex—"

"We've stopped. They're about to open my door. Houston, out."

A security officer opened the chiefexec's door and helped her out. Zama graciously accepted the proffered hand and stepped out of the car. Next, a guard opened the captain's door. The chiefexec glanced at him then stuck her nose in the air.

The captain tried hard not to clench his fists. He trudged off through some low brush, leaving the fuming leader behind. He quickly reached his craft, which sat in a nearby overgrown field. He punched a button on his control pad, causing the door to swing open. Inside sat a vehicle with huge tires. Within moments, the long-legged chiefexec had caught up with him. "It's designed for different types of terrain on a variety of planets," he said in a monotone, not bothering to look at his guest. Minj had had it right, after all. Ice Queen. He got into the vehicle and drove it down the hatch, which doubled as a ramp. He then used his remote control to re-close the hatch and reset the vehicle's force field.

He pressed a button to open the passenger side door, which raised up like that of an ancient Delorean. "Get in," he ordered.

"I'm the chiefexec," she said.

"All right, *please* get in, your majesty."

"Yessir, m'lord," an edge in her voice.

He shook his head and pushed a button to close the hatch. "What's that?"

he asked disdainfully, pointing at the voluminous, black animal skin bag she had laid at her feet. "We'll only be gone a few hours!"

"Change of clothes, a few disinfectants…"

"Disinfectants!" he scoffed.

"I don't like germs."

He buried his hand in his thick hair and was about to rip out a handful. "I'm sure you didn't take disinfectants on your camping trips as a girl."

"Did, too!"

He thought about going a couple miles, pushing her out the door then driving away. He started the ATV and it lumbered off. At the end of the clearing was a thicket of wild prairie grass at least nine feet tall. Its color was goldenrod rather than the light blue of A'laaman lawns. He steered directly into the grass. It brushed against the vehicle with a loud swishing sound as he plowed ahead. As the vehicle bounced and jarred her, Zama held on to the side of her seat.

The grass eventually gave way to patches of fern trees. They looked somewhat like the ones Houston and Elle had sat under during their picnic, a mostly pleasant memory that seemed a lifetime ago. He wheeled the vehicle between trees. The ground was fairly rugged and the truck was bouncing along. Occasionally the woman would let out a surprised and not particularly pleasant yelp. Served her right, he thought.

After a few minutes, she yelled: "Captain! I'm not sure this was such a good idea."

He wondered whether, if he drove recklessly enough, she'd get car sick. "Aw, we should be on a first name basis by now, your highness. Call me Erik." She ignored him. He blushed in shame at his own attitude. Why did he have to think that way?

The vehicle continued to roll through the greenery. After about fifteen minutes, she wasn't crying out as much. They came upon a creek bed. He sent the ATV charging down the bank and splashed into the water, which gushed in all directions. Some splashed through under the door, wetting their shoes. The passenger shouted louder than she had in a while. He looked over. She was laughing hysterically and clapping her hands.

Dumbfounded, he brought the vehicle to a halt. He turned and looked at her. Her eyes were smiling. His anger melted away. "You've got a crazy side after all, Zama. If I can call you that."

"You may, Erik." She laughed again.

He kept grinning, heading deeper into the jungle. The fern trees were now so thick they were blocking out the light from both suns and it was actually dark. The vehicle's automatic lights came on. A fairly large six-legged creature was staring at the vehicle. It charged. Zama gasped. Erik, undaunted, sped away.

After traveling for about another half-hour, they arrived at a hill. "Okay, we're going to take that hill," he said.

"What? No, I don't think…" she cried. But he was already gunning the engine. He built up some speed then began charging up the hill. The angle of ascent grew steeper.

"What are you doing? No! No!" she screamed. The vehicle kept grinding its way up the hill, finally starting to slide a little. When it was less than ten yards from the top, the back wheels began to spin. Then the wheels started sliding backwards. "We're going to die!"

"Don't worry. I'll get us out of this." He kept working the vehicle and began to make up the ground he had lost. Finally, the front wheels cleared the top of the ridge. Moments later, the back wheels hit level ground.

"We made it!"

"Told you."

They continued onward, eventually coming to a clearing. He parked the vehicle. He got out and helped her out. The bumpy trip had caused her hair to fall into bangs that were almost touching her eyes. Her shirt was coming out of her pants. She smelled a little like perspiration, despite Erik having run the climate system. She almost seemed like a regular person, not some stiff aristocrat.

They were now at a high enough elevation that they were able to look back some distance. Zama had half-expected to see a distant silhouette of the towers of A'laama. Instead, the duo saw only jungle behind them. They got back into the ATV and continued through the clearing. The jungle soon picked up again. About half an hour later she startled him by yelling and pointing. He stopped the vehicle. About fifty yards away was a small stone house. They drove closer and noted that the house's door was gone and the roof had caved in.

"Well," said Erik, "it looks like you city dwellers aren't the ones who have explored the farthest on this planet."

She grabbed his arm. "Let's get out of here."

He looked at her.

"We need to leave *now*."

# 24.

Daj Minj had been intrigued with the crash site ever since the group had visited it with Kelly several days earlier. He had told the captain and her that he wanted to learn more about the crash and its survivors, the Founders of Al'aama. He had gone back to the museum and looked in detail at some of the exhibits. He had talked with the museum's curator and had done some searches on the database. He was gaining much background information.

Something about *this* world's past especially intrigued him. Daj glanced at his wrist timepiece, which not only displayed the hours of the day but also kept record of the planetside year. The device worked effectively even when the star man was aboard ship traveling at close to the speed of light. A touch of a button allowed him to jump back and forth between shipboard and planetside calendars. It was currently 4156 A.D. in the Interstellar Standard calendar. The year was 299 in the Al'aaman calendar. The natives used the standard year length that had been used on virtually all civilized planets for millennia. This allowed for a common way of measuring time from one planet to another. Each planet had its own natural year, the length of time it took that planet to revolve around its sun. Al'aama revolved around its two suns about once every two and a half standard years. But, like most planets, Al'aama still measured time using the standard year rather than the local, planetary year. In the same way, the planet's inhabitants used many other ancient standard measurements such as for distance, speed, etc. All of this was additional proof that the Al'aamans had a common heritage with the rest of interstellar civilization.

As Daj continued his research, he especially wanted to find out about the original settlers. Who were they? Where had they come from? And who were these mysterious three females who had had such a strong influence on the early colony? He began to put some of the pieces together. He learned that not only were the Three Founders revered for their leadership but also because they had each produced a large family, contributing to the colony's survival. In the A'laama's early days polygamy had been encouraged due to the limited gene pool. Each of these Founders had had two or three husbands at a time and each of the three women had produced eight to eleven children. In fact, statues of each of the Founders made during the early generations of the colony invariably depicted them either holding several children or surrounded by a large group of children. But in modern Al'aama, it was no longer politically correct to depict the Founders as having had many offspring. The old-time statues were housed in the museum's basement and were unseen by the public. The Founders' descendants had grown into great families that became the three leading tribes of Al'aama. After a couple generations, the colony had progressed back to having nuclear families each with one husband and one wife.

One day, after Daj had spent several hours of reading various facts on the database, his eyes were growing weary and he was almost numb from information overload. Suddenly, he read something that made him sit upright in his seat. Then he went back and read the information again. He crosschecked the information on the screen against another source. He stared back at the screen. He split the screen and checked a third file, then a fourth. He compared the written information with various 3-D stills and videos. He jumped out of his chair and ran out of the room, shouting something incomprehensible to the curator, who stared at him in shock as he headed for the exit.

He ran the several blocks back to the exec mansion, hurried through the corridors and burst through the door of the star man's suite. Montoya was sitting in a chair, reading one of the natives' online books.

"Where's the captain?" Daj sputtered, out of breath.

"Took the chiefexec for a drive into the wilderness," said Montoya nonchalantly.

"Ms. High Maintenance? Why would he do that?"

"Beats me."

"Where's Kelly?"

"Haven't seen her," said Montoya, becoming annoyed.

Minj looked at his longtime friend. "I need to go back to the ship on leave."

"But our rotation isn't up for another week."

"I need to go now."

"I've tried contacting the captain a couple times today and haven't been able to reach him. As the next ranking officer I can grant your request. But would you mind telling me what this all about, Daj?"

"Personal matters."

Montoya was curious but decided not to press the issue. "All right. I'll arrange to have a shuttle pilot take you to the ship."

Minj was shaking as he headed to him room to pack a few items. Einstein's Law had bitten him after all.

# II: The Wilderness

# 25.

"I'm not leaving. Not until I look through this house." Erik hopped out of the vehicle and jogged through the overgrown grass.

She reluctantly slid out of the truck and raced after him. "We need to leave," she called, her long legs beginning to close the gap.

"Gimme a minute." As he reached the house, she caught up with him. She still looked alarmed.

"Don't worry," he said. "I've got a weapon in case some stray animal has wandered inside." They reached the dilapidated building. He stepped through the doorway. She stayed outside. He walked a few steps into the structure. He turned around to see her standing in the doorway, backlit by the two suns. He walked back toward her and held out his hand. She took it and followed him into the building. The house was small, consisting of a couple rooms, one with a stone fireplace. There was no furniture.

After few minutes, they left the ruined house and walked back toward the vehicle. "Look at this," he said. The dirt was marked with a few different sets of footprints, ones that looked fairly recent. They heard some rustling in the brush behind them. Erik drew his stunner and looked cautiously in the direction of the noise. No one was there.

A giant insect with a three-foot wingspan flew out of the nearby jungle and headed toward her. Erik grabbed a stunner and fired at the creature. It instantly dropped to the ground and began thrashing about. He quickly changed a setting and pulled the trigger. The creature burst into flame.

She turned away. "Take me back," she demanded again.

He sighed. They had only been a gone a couple hours. But he realized they must be getting close to that human settlement of several thousand strong he had detected from space. Humans the chiefexec thought were hostile. "Okay," he said.

They headed back to the vehicle. He started it and immediately noticed a dark screen that should have been lit. It was the global positioning system that had been bouncing signals off the orbiting starship. He pulled his comm link from his pocket and tried calling the ship. He heard only static. He tried calling Montoya. Same result. Minj. Nothing. Luci. The same.

Erik grimaced.

"What's wrong?" she asked.

"Communication's out."

Her eyes grew wide.

"Don't worry," he said. "We'll just go back the way we came."

She looked at him. "*The way we came?* There are no roads to follow. We made our own road!"

"I have a compass. Travelers have used them for thousands of years. Besides, I have a good sense of direction."

"I guess so. You found us out here in the middle of space," she said, smiling weakly.

He swung the vehicle in a wide arc and got it heading the opposite direction. Gradually, he realized the scenery wasn't looking familiar. Finally, he stopped the ATV. There was a lake ahead. They hadn't passed one before! He hoped it was a mirage.

"We're going the wrong way," she declared.

"I know."

"Go that way," she said, pointing in a diagonal away from their current location.

"Over there? That's ridiculous."

"Are you saying I'm wrong?"

"Yes. You sure you're not trying to throw me off?"

"No. I really want to get out of here."

Several additional miles of unfamiliar scenery rolled by. "I'm hungry," she said.

He reached into his pack, tossing her a food bar and a foil beverage pack. She nodded her thanks.

He pulled out his comm link and again tried calling several people. Nothing. He took some readings on his compass, pausing a moment to think about whether he wanted to drive farther and take the chance of moving even farther from the city. He looked at his wrist chronometer. They had been gone five hours! He set an emergency code on the tracking device so that as soon as communications were functioning again, they would be found.

He resumed driving, skirting the edge of the lake. About every half-hour, he stopped to take a compass reading. He finally determined he needed to change course. He did so and they proceeded for some time. Finally, he checked the time again. Eight hours since they had left the city, yet a round trip should have only taken half that time! He stopped driving then turned and looked at his passenger. "I don't know how to tell you this but...it looks like we're going to have to spend the night in this wilderness."

She shook her head. "The whole day's shot and we're lost in the middle of nowhere!" They turned away from one another, each folding their arms. Long minutes passed.

"It won't be as bad as it sounds," he said. "I can sleep here in the vehicle and there's a tent that you can sleep in...."

She rolled her eyes.

"It'll be all right," he insisted. "I've stayed out in the wild before...."

"Have you ever been lost like this?"

"No."

She pulled her personal video screen from her purse. Instead of looking mirror-like, it was totally black. She threw it to the floor.

"So, what happens when there's an occasional bad sun storm?" he asked. "Doesn't that ever knock out communications in your city, too?"

She sighed. "Yes...once in a while it does, at least partially. I'm sorry." She retrieved her screen and slipped it into her pants pocket.

He parked the ATV in a clearing. They got out and sat on the ground. They said nothing more for a long time. Finally, she leaned her back against the vehicle and stared into the jungle. He did the same. The jungle contained many of the tall, arching fern trees interspersed with the somewhat shorter, grey-barked ironwoods. The ironwoods were branchless and looked like elongated cylinders. A breeze was blowing, ruffling their hair. After the wind died down, they heard odd sounds and cries from the various forms of life. He gasped and pointed. Then it happened again. They both watched as a tree raised a few feet higher and slid several feet to the left.

She shrugged. "Ironwoods do that once in a while. The jungle I played in as a girl had some that would move on occasion."

"But...it is a form of vegetation, right? It's a plant, not an animal?"

"Of course it's a plant. It doesn't act like an animal, does it?"

Erik shook his head. "What about its roots?"

"They don't have roots."

"Then...how do they feed themselves?"

"They use a vacuum mechanism."

He looked at her, wrinkling his brow. Then he saw a giant insect like the one that had flown toward her, fly near another ironwood. A hole opened up in the side of the tree. The tree sucked in the insect and the hole closed again.

She laughed. "I love to watch them eat."

They continued to gaze at the jungle. Eventually, he noticed a high-pitched humming that grew louder and louder. Finally, he had to cover his ears.

"What *is* that?" he shouted over the noise.

"It's the fern trees. They sing to one another," she shouted back.

He looked at her. "They *sing?*"

"Yes. That's what it's called. They rub their leaves together quickly to make a kind of humming noise."

"And they're considered plants?"

"Yes, they're plants. Don't they have plants on other worlds?"

He entered the vehicle and got some earplugs. He offered a pair to her. She shook her head and smiled. He also retrieved some packaged meals and beverages, which he shared with her.

"I wonder if that stone house was built by Non-techs," she mused.

"By who?" Erik replied.

"Non-techs. There are stories that, generations ago, various people left Al'aama and headed into the wilderness. When I was a kid we would sometimes camp in the jungle near our house and tell one another scary stories about the Non-techs. They were supposed to be fierce people and all of us kids feared them even though none of us had ever seen one."

Their conversation faded away. He looked over at her and pictured her as a little girl in a sun dress. Carefree, picking flowers in a field. She placed one

140

in her hair. She looked right at him and smiled. She stuck her arms straight out to the sides and began to twirl around faster and faster until she fell over, dizzy. Abruptly, the young girl was gone and Zama was an elderly woman. Her long hair was a ghostly white, her skin brown and creased with wrinkles. He shivered at the abrupt transformation.

"What's wrong!" cried a female voice. He jerked back to reality. Staring into his eyes was the present-day Zama. He was breathing heavily and perspiring. He turned away. Already he was having those same feelings he always had before departing a planet. Realizing he'd be going back to shipboard time where he'd age ever so slowly. Planetbound people like Zama would remain in planetary time and race through their lives. Yet, time would feel "normal" to both. Some star travelers, when they left a planet, would crassly refer to the natives as "the dead." Others would call them "temps," knowing they'd never see them again.

He turned back toward her. "Our lives pass so quickly," he said. "It's like telling a story." A breeze ruffled their hair again and caused some dust to kick up into a little whirlwind.

She cocked her head, causing her hair to fall to one side. She pursed her lips and continued to eye him for a moment then turned away and stared off toward the horizon. After a while, they resumed conversing off and on. Mostly small talk. But he seemed distant.

"I'm going to sleep," she announced.

He walked a few steps away from the vehicle and threw a cloth square on the ground. It inflated into a tent, complete with a built-in sleeping bag and pillow. She said goodnight and walked over to her tiny quarters. He went into the vehicle, set a force field around it and the tent. He leaned back in his seat and closed his eyes, the singing from the fern trees still humming in his brain and the light from the two suns glaring in his face.

The next morning, he awoke a little sore from having slept for several hours on one of the vehicle's reclining seats. Immediately, he noted the intense light from the two suns. The days during these double-sun periods seemed to last forever. He had a headache behind his right eye. He stretched his arms then groggily stepped out of the ATV. He walked the few paces over to the domed tent. He heard her stirring. She poked her head out of the tent. Her hair was in disarray and she had dark circles under her eyes.

"G'morning. You all right?"

She nodded but didn't look very convincing. She dragged out of the tent, still wearing yesterday's clothing, which had as many wrinkles and creases as a y'uoonga fruit. Her makeup had worn off. He went into the vehicle, got a cold juice pouch, came out and handed it to her. She took it and nodded. He sat on the ground beside the tent, enjoying the stillness of the morning. She sat down beside him. Her shirt had shifted, revealing a prominent marking that looked like a pink star burst on her left shoulder.

"Birthmark," she said defensively.

He looked away, embarrassed. Minutes passed. He was unable to read her mood. "Just out of curiosity, was there ever a Mr. Elle?" he blurted out, hoping he hadn't offended her. Twice.

She didn't seem to mind. "Yes, I did have a husband," she said. "We were married a long time. He had skin cancer and died not long after I became chiefexec."

He nodded sympathetically. He had learned many of the natives succumbed to skin cancer, given the overpowering strength of the Ava sun.

"It was really hard for the kids at first," she continued. "They missed their dad. I missed him, too. Still do. What about you, Captain. Have you ever been married?"

He dropped his juice pack, sending a red liquid gurgling out through the straw and making a tiny stream in the dirt. He paused a moment before answering in a deep, quiet voice: "Me? Naw. I've come close a couple times but I've never married. It's hard for us to develop permanent relationships. We move around so much. A few months on one planet, then several months aboard ship getting to the next one...."

"I see," said the chiefexec, her eyes shifting away. "W-what about your crew?"

"Sometimes crew members fall in love. Some marry, have families...meaning they'd have to leave the First Contact group. But since I'm the ranking officer, it really wouldn't be ethical for me to have a relationship with one of our ladies...."

"Your personal rule or your Association's?"

"Both. Sometimes an officer may meet a woman on shore leave, fall in love, get married. Many of us just remain single."

"Doesn't leave you many options, Captain."

"No, ma'am."

Silence reigned for a time. Then, without warning, he asked: "That dignified-looking man you were dancing with the night of the banquet. Are you...?"

She laughed and shook her head, sending her hair flying to and fro.

"Legislae Clayton? No. We've been friends and political allies for years. But that's all. He's married and his wife is okay with him dancing occasionally at an official function. She doesn't dance."

Erik turned his head, his face reddening.

"I actually haven't gone out since my husband passed away," she volunteered. "A few men have expressed interest but they seemed more focused on my money and power. Not on me as a person."

He turned back toward her. "That's too bad. I... I think you have a lot to offer."

"Thank you." She smiled widely then shyly looked away.

"What was he like?"

Her eyes dropped to the ground. Her fingers began fiddling with the fine gold chain that adorned her neck. "He was a quiet man. A good man. And very kind. Sometimes I didn't appreciate him...." She began to twist the necklace and looked off toward the jungle, avoiding his eyes.

Silence hung like a cloud. He reached over and picked a few small rocks off the ground. He began to whip them at the overgrown grass in the distance. She continued looking toward the jungle. "Did you love him?" he asked.

She turned her head to face him. Her eyes earnestly looked into his. "Yes. Yes, I did love him. Still do." He picked a foot-long strand of grass from the ground and stuck it in his mouth. His eyes scoured the ground for additional stones to toss.

After a while, she looked at him and asked: "Why did you become a spaceman?"

He dropped a pebble and smiled wistfully. "I had an uncle," he began. "Actually, he was a great-great-great uncle. I don't know, maybe more greats. It went back several generations. When I was growing up, the family would talk about him from time to time. Everybody had stories about him. But I had never met him. Not until I was sixteen. Because he worked on an interstellar merchant ship. It would follow a certain route and he could only get back to see his family for several months once every twenty years or so. Of course, he barely aged. So, when I finally met him, here was this relatively young guy, he was probably younger than I am now, and he had seen many generations of his own family. Like being a time traveler. And he had visited dozens of star systems and seen so many things...."

"So, I decided that I was going to attend the Space Academy and have a career traveling the stars. But what I didn't realize was that on a First Contact ship, you get much less chance to get back to your native planet. It's more like once every fifty or sixty years. So...I lost track of my extended family. They all moved to other star systems or they died.... I haven't seen any of them in at least a century...so now, my shipmates are my family...." He choked up.

She slipped her hand into his and gave it a squeeze. They said nothing for several minutes as they continued holding hands. "Interstellar orphans," she murmured, recalling the title of that best-selling online book from months ago.

He had never read it but nodded just the same.

They remained silent for a while. Finally, he got up and pushed a tab on the tent, causing it to fold back into a small square of cloth. He then shut off the force field surrounding their immediate area. He helped her into the vehicle and was about to get in himself.

They heard some rustling in the nearby jungle. His left shoulder burned with pain.

She was aghast. "What's that?" she cried, pointing at an arrow sticking out of his shoulder and the wet, dark patch that was growing on his shirt.

"Warning shot," he grunted.

"A *warning?*"

"I think so. They probably could have killed me."

"W-why would someone *do* this?"

"We may have invaded their territory. Looks like we've found your Non-techs."

"Oo-hhh. You look badly hurt," she said.

"I'll need to take care of this wound," he acknowledged. "Go into the vehicle and pull out a small white case that's hanging on the wall beside the driver's seat."

She did so. He opened the kit and took out a pair of pliers. He clamped on the arrow with the pliers and shouted as he pulled the arrow out of his shoulder. She cringed. He opened a bottle of pills, took two out and washed them down with a drink from one of the foil packs. He rolled up his shirt sleeve, opened a packet of ointment and rubbed it over the wound. She noticed that almost miraculously, the color started returning to his face.

"Why don't you rest?" she said.

He nodded."I'm setting a force field around the entire area, so if they do come back, they won't be able to hurt us."

He retrieved a pillow from the vehicle, lay on the ground and soon fell asleep. She sat down beside him, leaning against the truck. After he had been sleeping for some time, she heard another rustling in the brush. Out rushed a bronze-skinned woman with hair halfway down her back. She wore an animal skin outfit and had different colored stripes on her face. Zama screamed. Erik snapped awake. The woman placed an arrow in a bow, aimed, pulled back and let it fly. The arrow hit the force field and bounced off. She quickly pulled another arrow from a quiver strapped to her shoulder and fired. Nothing. She tried a third. Same result.

The woman shouted something guttural, turned on her heel and bounded away. Erik leapt to his feet. He hit a button to suspend the protective shield and tore after the woman. He chased her the short distance into the jungle and onto a path between fern trees. As he ran, he reached out for her. His hand was inches away from her. Abruptly she turned, grabbing his extended arm. She flipped him over her shoulder. He grunted as his back slammed the ground. She pounced like an animal. He tried some wrestling moves. Her fingernails dug into his flesh like little daggers. He hung on to her with difficulty. She sunk her teeth into his arm. He cried out and let go of her. She flipped him over. Pinned him to the ground. Pulled a knife from a leg holster. Raised the blade into the air.

Zama, with surprising boldness, had run behind Erik . Wielding a branch she had from the jungle floor, she smacked the woman on the head. The warrior's body went limp. Erik looked up in gratitude.

"You all right?" she asked.

"Yeah," he replied between gasps for breath.

She paused and looked at the branch in her hand and at the woman lying still on the ground. "What have I done? I've really hurt her."

"I think she'll be all right. She's still breathing. She'll have quite a headache, though. Let's go back to the car so I can get her some medication."

The foliage rustled in several locations at once. Three male warriors and two females tore out of the brush. They brandished weapons. Zama froze. He pulled her away from the brave she had wounded with one arm while reaching for the stunner with the other. A moment later, Zama produced an A'laaman ener pistol.

The warriors stepped closer. Zama waved it at the armed braves, who looked at it quizzically. Her hand trembling, she squeezed the trigger. She shot wild, firing into the air. It hit a leafy branch that crashed to the ground, knocking over the would-be attackers.

Erik and Zama's legs burst into motion. Other warriors appeared from between trees. They tore after the couple. The pursuers launched arrows and spears. The star man stopped a moment and turned, the versatile stunner shooting a stream of fire at the pursuers. The fighters shrunk back. Erik hustled to catch up with Zama. They were almost out of the jungle. In the distance was the vehicle. Just as they burst into a clearing, braves appeared from the opposite direction. The fleeing couple abruptly halted. The chasing warriors from behind caught up. They were surrounded.

A man clubbed Erik on the head with the butt of his spear. Two others hit him with their own weapons. Zama screamed. A female warrior clamped a powerful hand over her mouth. The braves raised their spears into the air and were poised to use them on Zama when a loud shout pierced the air.

The warriors halted in mid-motion as a tall, striding figure emerged from the brush. She had shoulder-length blonde hair streaked with gray. She wore a finely detailed cloth outfit, an animal-skin belt and ankle-high, animal-skin boots. She stood tall and carried an air of authority. The warrior queen began shouting orders at her braves who scrambled off, two of them carrying away Erik's limp body. Zama screamed again as they took him away. Another tended to their fallen sister.

The tribal chief strode up to Zama and wrenched the ener gun from her hand. She held the prize in her own hand, stroked the shiny metal then slipped it through her belt. The chief gestured and shouted orders. The two remaining tribes people, one male and one female, grabbed their captive by the shoulders and marched her some distance into the jungle. She was panting and her heart was pounding like rapid hammer blows. After she had been walked a couple hundred yards, she stood at the base of a small hill that had been hollowed out into a cave whose front consisted of metal bars. The braves opened the gate and flung her inside. She hit the dirt floor with a thud and moaned in pain. The braves slammed the door and locked it. They then hurried away to continue the bidding of their leader.

Zama was alone. She grabbed the metal bars and shook them. They were quite secure. She was worried for Erik, hoping they wouldn't kill him. Part of the time she observed what she could see of the jungle and took in its unusual sights and sounds. For some time, there was no sign of the wilderness people. Finally, she heard what sounded like a trumpet in the distance, followed by the loud shouts of what must have been hundreds of people. She also heard some high-pitched squeals that sounded like animal noises and running. Then more animal squeals and shouts by the humans. Sometime later, dozens of warriors approached the cave. Some of the brawnier ones were carrying animal carcasses while others were dragging them. She was nervous that so many of these wild people were approaching, although they seemed in a jubilant mood.

A male warrior opened the lock and heaved in a couple dead animals. They were bleeding and Zama thought they smelled disgusting. Many other braves also threw carcasses. Now she understood. The cave wasn't a jail, it was a temporary storage place for fresh meat! After the tribes people were done throwing in their kill, they locked the door and left her alone again. The sounds of the hunt repeated and later the warriors showed up with even more meat. This time they began to remove the other carcasses and went to an area nearby to drain the blood, butcher the animals and dig several large pits. They started fires in the pits and used long spits to skewer and roast the animals.

Sometime later, a female warrior came up to the cave. The bars were wide enough that the brave was able to slip Zama a slab of cooked meat. The food was still hot and she almost dropped it. She nodded her thanks. Her benefactor also handed her a narrow, ceramic water jar, which Zama gratefully accepted. The lady started walking away when she abruptly turned around, grabbed an arrow from her quiver and shot toward Zama, who ducked instinctively. The arrow hit dead on, piercing through a small, oval-shaped creature, which was now pinned to the outside wall of the cave, a couple feet from where Zama had been standing. The woman walked back toward the cave, pointed at the hapless creature and said: "Unoofanaba. Don't touch it. It's poisonous." Zama barely understood the words due the woman's heavy dialect. The woman made an ugly face at her kill, shook her head and walked away.

Famished, Zama sat down and devoured the meat, burning her mouth. She gulped down most of the water but spared a little for later.

After the city woman experienced some additional solitude, the chief arrived with a contingent of four warriors, two males and two females. Two members of the group were armed with spears, the other two with bows and arrows. This group looked stern. One of the braves unlocked the door and yanked her out of the cave by the arm. After pulling Zama some distance by the shoulders, one of the braves pushed her down into a sitting position on a wide tree stump. She hit her tailbone on the stump. One of the female warriors began saying something to her while the chief stood in front of her, her arms folded and face grimacing. The dialect was still hard to understand but the anger and gestures made translation unnecessary.

The chief stepped in front of the inquisitor. She pulled the captured ener gun from her belt, aimed at a high tree limb and fired. The branch came crashing down.

"Five of my people are injured because of this thing," she cried, waving it in Zama's face. "Plus you knocked out one of my best braves with your club. I ought to just kill you." She swung her free hand, lashing Zama's face with such strength that it almost knocked the captive out of her seat.

Zama's face wrinkled with pain. Her heart was racing. The chief and she glared at one another. The tribal queen stuck the gun back in her belt.

Finally, the prisoner asked: "H-how is the man I was with? What have you done with him?"

"Silence! I'll ask the questions! What do you mean by invading Batu territory in the middle of our sacred hunt?"

"W-we knew nothing of your hunt. We were exploring new territory and got lost."

"Where are you from?"

"From some large tribes to the south."

"Say goodbye to your tribes from the south. You'll never see them again." Zama swallowed hard.

"Why did your man chase down my brave and fight with her? And why did you hit her with a club?"

She abruptly realized she had *no idea* why had he run into the jungle after the woman! She was suddenly angry with him, even though she had no idea whether he were even still alive.

She swallowed hard and explained that they had hit the woman in self-defense, because she had attacked them and had wounded Erik with an arrow. She explained that they intended to carry the woman away to administer medical assistance after their attack on her. There were many more questions and some of the old ones were repeated.

Finally, Zama exploded: "You've asked me enough," she insisted. "The man I'm traveling with and I are *very important* people. If we don't get back home then *our* people, who are much larger and more powerful than your tribe, will come looking for us. They'll deal with you for the way you've treated us!"

The leader's nostrils flared. She raised her hand, ready to strike the prisoner again.

"Wait, Chief!" cried the male brave. "What if she's telling the truth?"

The chief's arm froze in mid-motion. "If you're so big and strong then where is your tribe?" she asked.

148

"I told you, far away. What happened to the man I am traveling with? Is he all right?"

The Batu ignored her question then escorted her back to her quarters. One warrior unlocked the door and opened it while another pushed Zama inside. The door slammed shut and the lock clicked. The warriors turned and left. The right side of her face burned and felt swollen from the powerful slap. One of her teeth felt loose. She was too exhausted to stay awake, too pumped with adrenaline to sleep.

# 26.

Erik felt like his head was splitting open. He cracked open one eye and could tell he was in a tent. He was lying on some kind of pallet and his head was elevated. There was a cold compress on his head. He arms and back ached. He closed his eyes again. He heard voices around him but was too fatigued to care what they were saying.

Suddenly, he had one thought: Zama! He abruptly sat upright. Pain exploded throughout his head and he fell back down again, groaning. A female brave walked over to him and said something. She stroked his hair and got him another cold compress. He opened his eyes farther. A male was grinding something with a porcelain mortar and pestle. He mixed the powder with water, poured it into a mug and handed it to the woman who had put the compress on Erik. She walked over to him and held the cup with one hand and the back of his head with the other. He resisted.

"It's for the pain," the woman said.

The newly implanted language cells in Erik's brain weren't perfect in dealing with the tribe's dialect, but at least this was close enough to the A'laaman language for him to understand. He nodded, but even that much head motion caused pain to shoot through his head. He quit resisting and took a few sips of the remedy. It tasted bitter. He looked to his side and saw two braves standing over him, one male and one female, each holding a spear.

"That woman I was with…where is she? Is she all right?" he asked.

At that moment, the chief strode into the tent. She looked down at him. "If you're well enough to ask questions, you're well enough to answer questions," she said.

She badgered him with the same inquiries she had thrown at Zama. Finally satisfied that the two prisoners' stories matched, she turned on her heel and left. The exhausted Erik went back to sleep.

When he awoke, his head hurt somewhat less but his arms and back were still sore. He opened his eyes and saw the guards were still in the tent. The other two people were gone. He reached into his pocket. Everything he needed for an escape was gone! He looked and saw some of his equipment on a low table at the far end of the tent. His pallet lay on the ground and he spotted a small rock on the dirt tent floor. When the guards weren't looking he slowly picked up the rock then whipped at the end of the tent opposite to where his equipment lay. The guards heard the noise of the rock hitting the side of the tent and hurried over to investigate. Erik did a quick roll off the pallet and went into a crouching position, grabbed his stunner off the table and fired at each of the guards, who crumpled to the ground. Erik grabbed his force field generator, set a field around himself, stuck his equipment in his pocket and hurried through the tent flap. His head was screaming with pain but at least he was out of the tent and protected by the invisible shield.

Braves who were outdoors saw him jogging away and began to chase him, yelling for him to stop. Some threw spears or shot arrows after him to no avail. He found a hiding place under a large rock outcropping and hid there while the warriors rushed past him. He waited there for some time, resting and waiting for the chaos to die down. He crept farther. Finally, he spotted her from about a hundred yards away. He advanced a little at a time, ducking behind trees, rocks, or foliage as needed to avoid detection. When he was within ten yards of her, he ran out into the open.

Standing in front of her was a brave with a spear, the same woman who had wounded Erik with the arrow and later fought with him. He was surprised to see her fully recovered while he still needed to nurse his sore body. She was yelling something at the captive and kept jamming a spear through the bars and jabbing at her. Zama had to keep jumping out of the way to avoid the weapon piercing her.

The outdoors woman heard Erik's foot snap a twig. She turned away from tormenting the woman in the cave and faced the source of the noise. The escapee's face was red with outrage at the brave's cruel treatment of Zama. He shot the warrior with his stunner, having set it on an intermediate setting that would knock her out. He took from his pocket a tiny object the size of a grain of dust and placed it in the woman's hair.

Zama cried: "I was afraid they'd killed you!"

He switched the setting on the versatile stunner and shot out a heat beam that melted the metal lock on the door. He swung open the gate. She hugged him so hard he thought she would break his ribs. He paused a moment and looked at the fallen warrior, then at Zama then back again. He wet his fingers with the remaining water in her flask then went over and wiped some of the war paint off the female brave's face. He then looked at the two of them again, rubbing his chin.

"What are you *doing?* Let's get outta here!"

Before she could say anything further, one male brave had come up from behind her and grabbed her wrists and while another grabbed her ankles. She screamed and struggled as they carried her off. Erik started after Zama's captors but became overwhelmed by the throbbing in his head. He collapsed to the ground.

# 27.

Zama was sitting on a wooden cart, her hands and feet bound with rope. The trip bounced her and pushed her this way and that without her being able to steady herself. At one point the cart hit a rut, banging her tailbone and knocking her on her side. Several six-legged creatures were pulling the cart, part of a caravan that was winding its way though the jungle. After what seemed like hours, the jungle abruptly ended and the path continued into a clearing. The trip continued through a field, then over a wooden bridge that spanned a rapidly flowing river. About a mile past the river, Zama noticed a settlement on the horizon. As the cart drew closer, she was able to make out a tall, wooden stockade. Eventually she realized it covered a large area, perhaps a number of acres. As the caravan approached the fence, two massive gates swung open to accommodate the returning tribes people. The cart passed rows of small, family-sized tents, then much larger tents that must belong to tribal elders. In the center of the village was a massive tent, probably the chief's. As the cart moved farther into the settlement, the tents began to get smaller again. Finally, the cart came to a cultivated field and stopped.

A stern-looking man walked around to the back of the cart. He produced a knife and slit the rope that bound her hands and feet. He pushed her off the cart. She landed hard on her feet. He threw some sort of native outfit at her. She reluctantly put it on over her own clothes. She saw a number of people laboring, apparently doing some kind of manual harvesting of grain. The man began speaking to her in the tribal dialect. The more she heard the language, the easier it was becoming for her to understand. He was ordering her to watch what the laborers were doing and start doing the same thing. She complied. Over time, she became soaked with perspiration and her back was aching. What seemed like every couple hours, she was given a cup of water. There was no food. One time, she tried to eat some of the harvested grain and man slapped her face. She recovered and returned to her task. In the distance, she saw fires blazing in another part of the camp and many braves gathered around the fires. The hunters seemed to be feasting, rejoicing in the spoils of the hunt. As hours passed, the laborers, with no overseer any longer in sight, lay down to sleep. Zama lay down and closed her eyes. She ached all over and was ravenous but was too excited to rest. Gradually, the fires died down and the talking grew less and less animated. Finally, the fires were out altogether and she had the impression the camp was at rest. Perhaps the warriors would be too exhausted from their hunt and too bloated from gorging to notice if she carefully slipped away.

She retraced the way the cart had brought her. Finally, she reached the wooden stockade. She found a thick section post and struggled to climb it. At first she kept slipping, but with some effort, she was finally able to progress. She reached the top of the wall and pulled herself over. She dropped to the ground in the slightly slow motion way that marked such as low grav planet. The impact of her feet caused a small cloud of dust to puff out of the ground. She had twisted her ankle. She began to hobble away, feeling pain with each step. She eventually made it to the wooden bridge that spanned the roaring river. She thought she heard a howling sound in the distance. Looking back, she realized several braves and some baying, furry creatures were in pursuit. Someone must have seen her prior to her clearing the fence. She moved as fast as her ankle pain would allow. She looked back at her pursuers. They were still in the distance but now seemed a little closer. She was hoping they were so far behind her that they wouldn't notice what she was about to do.

Having come to the end of the bridge, she began hurrying down the slope beneath the span. The river was flowing rapidly below her. The water churned and swirled. As she continued down the slope, she realized the land was dropping off abruptly and for safety's sake she dare not go much farther. The roaring river was now kicking up a spray that was beginning to get her wet. She again hoped her pursuers hadn't seen her. She noticed that the slope ahead was a vertical drop and the river was hurtling over the cliff with a mighty roar as the water plunged hundreds of feet to a pool below. She gasped at the sight. The city girl had never seen anything like it. She froze with fear as she continued to watch the mighty waterfall. She pulled the native tunic over her head, revealing her own clothing. She tossed the tunic into the nearby river and watched it rapidly move downstream then abruptly disappear over the falls. Her hair, skin and clothing were becoming soaked by the spray. Fearing the falls more than her pursuers, she slowly began to make her way back up the slope, warily looking for the braves and their animals. By the time she had almost reached the bridge, she thought she heard the warriors and their beasts close by. She climbed up under the bridge and hung on to one of the piers while struggling to keep her feet in place on the muddy slope that led to the churning water below. She heard the posse overhead, human feet and animal paws pounding on the wooden bridge. Continuing to struggle to keep her footing, she waited a long time to see if the group would come back.

Finally, she eased up the slope enough to stick her head up to bridge level. She scanned the horizon in all directions for several long moments before hurrying onto the path that led away from the village. Her clothing and hair were soaked and her ankle was more sore than ever. She struggled to walk as rapidly as she could. When she couldn't take the pain anymore, she sat down beside the path and took a quick break.

Upon struggling back to her feet, she looked behind her while starting to walk forward. She walked right into...*someone*, apparently a muscular man. Zama screamed. The man clamped a powerful hand over her mouth. She turned her head and met a piercing set of eyes. Eyes belonging to a fierce-looking man with a shaved head and a bare chest. McTeague.

The warrior boss stood within inches of Zama. She looked away from his heartless stare. She swallowed as she eyed the posse accompanying him.

"So, woman, you're not so tough without your weapons," he said, yanking on her hair. She yelped in pain as her head and neck jerked back. At the warrior's signal, one of the male braves pinned their captive's arms behind her while another wrapped a rope around her wrists and waist. The brave handed his boss one end of the rope. "You're not getting away this time," the leader sneered through badly discolored teeth. "If I have to lead you like an animal, so be it." He pushed the woman forward. As she began to walk, he got ahead of her then began to pull on the rope. It chafed and burned her waist and wrists. Her sore ankle was now quite huge. She stumbled forward, painfully trying to keep pace. She fell. He yanked hard on the rope, which cut into her as he pulled her back to her feet. The suns were beating down on her and she was soon pouring sweat. Rivulets ran down her face, her back.

An eternity later, that the stockade doors swung open to admit the group. Zama's clothing was soaked and she was panting. She was beyond limping and now dragged her sore leg behind her. "Tell Chief Laura I've returned with the runaway," McTeague barked at the guard who stood, spear in hand at the entrance. The brave ducked into the tent, returning moments later.

"The chief says you may enter," the guard said in a deep, serious voice.

The official brushed past the man, practically dragging his captive. He turned around and held up a restraining hand to the posse that was following them. "The chief and I will handle this alone," he said. He pulled the woman through a series of rooms, stopping in a spacious area with a high ceiling. On a large, high-backed chair sat the chief. Several braves, some males and some females, fanned her. Zama's captor released his grip on the rope and pushed her to the ground before the chief's throne.

Chief Laura's face hardened and eyes narrowed as she viewed the panting woman. "If it isn't the chief without a tribe. You thought you could escape from us so easily," she gloated. "You claimed to be so big and mighty. Where are your loyal subjects?"

Zama raised her head and glared at the chief.

"Bow your head!" ordered her tormentor, slapping her on the back. The blow jarred the woman, knocking her video screen out of her pocket and onto the floor. The bad sun storm having ended, the screen sprang to life. "Madame Exec! Are you all right?" cried a tiny, 3-D image of Kelly, startling the chief and her attendants.

"Madame Exec? Madame Exec! Come in!" shouted a miniature Alisa.

"Silence!" the chief yelled at the screen.

"Maybe her people *do* have a way to rescue her," mused the bald McTeague.

Chief Laura seemed unnerved. "Throw her into the cell for now. If she's that important, perhaps we can charge a ransom. No matter what happens, we won't give her up without a fight. And throw that talking mirror in with her!"

A muscular guard pulled Zama to her feet, and walked her out of the chief's tent to a concrete block structure about fifty yards away. He kicked open the door. A wave of torrid air hit them. He pitched Zama into the building. She hit the dirt floor with a thud. He whipped her video screen in after her. It smacked her in the back of the head. She moaned in pain. The guard closed the door, sending the windowless room into pitch darkness. The only sounds were her labored breathing and the rapid pounding of her heart. Her ankle hurt intensely and her arms, shoulders and mid-section had a number of deep cuts and severe brush burns from the rope. Still bound, she was unable to get comfortable. Her dry tongue clove to the roof her mouth. The room seemed like a furnace.

Suddenly, she was on her hands and knees, crawling up a mountain of sand. It was the desert the captain had shown her. One on another part of the planet. Had he sent her there? She faded back to ugly reality. She felt on fire from head to foot. Her throat felt as dry as a clay pot in the sun. Water. She craved water. Life-saving water.

Perspiration trickled down her face. She stuck out her parched tongue and twisted her face like a contortionist. Finally one drop then another of the salty fluid reached her tongue. She was desperate for more. As the minutes passed, sweat began to stream down her face. She kept trying to direct the precious liquid to her mouth. One drop burned against her cracked lips. Frustrated, she allowed herself to cry. As she sobbed, several precious tears ran and made it to her mouth. The air seemed to grow heavier and her breathing became difficult.

Summoning all her strength, she whispered: "Great Maker…don't let me die." She passed out.

# 28.

Meanwhile, in Al'aama, Kelly and Alisa were speaking with one another via video. "Dr. Farji! Did you hear what I just did? The chiefexec's life is in danger!"

Kelly nodded solemnly. "We've got to rescue her!"

"Where *is* she?"

"Our people have traced the signal. She's in the outback, dozens of miles beyond the farm district."

"We have no way to get there!"

"I know," Kelly sighed. "But don't worry, Alisa. Captain Houston will save her.

"Your blind loyalty may cost her life, Dr. Farji."

Kelly ended the call in a huff. She contacted the nextexec, second-in-command of A'laama.

The chief of staff made Red Alert calls to the new head of exec security and the metro chief of police. The security official cursed in Alisa's ear but abruptly apologized. The security man promised two dozen mounted officers ready to leave from the farm district within the hour. The police chief agreed to round up a similar number of the toughest officers, those from the gang unit and crowd control. In a little over an hour, an armed militia was riding six-legged beasts into the wilderness, fixed on the signal from the chiefexec's arm implant.

Back in the jungle, Erik was lying face down. He moved a little and moaned as a voice cried out from his comm link. "Captain! Captain Houston! Come in! It's Irv." The security chief had paged his skipper several times since communications had been restored. Houston still did not respond. The security chief got a visual fix on the captain. The injured man began to stretch his limbs. He rubbed the back of his head and groaned.

"Sir...you all right?"

Erik hit a button on the comm link. "Yeah. A little rough."

"What happened?"

"Some men clubbed me. That was yesterday but it was a severe beating.... Still haven't fully recovered."

The security officer shook his head. "I'll send Montoya. And what about the chiefexec?"

Erik suddenly sat upright. "The chiefexec?"

"Yes."

Houston lowered his head. "I-I tried to save her. She was carried off by some of those tribes people. I-I've got to find her!"

"I'll send Montoya and Minj."

"Tell them hurry!" ordered the captain.

When the two crew members found Erik, he was sitting against a tree and rubbing the back of his head. Montoya treated him and gave him some pain medication. The famished patient devoured a nutrition bar and a couple juice packs. After the captain rested a while, the doctor offered to take him to the landing craft where he could lie down.

"She's my responsibility," he insisted. "I got her into this."

Montoya laid a hand on his shoulder. "You really should stay behind," he said firmly.

"I'm going. That's an order," he snapped. The doctor reluctantly helped him stand up. He closed his eyes and the world seemed to go in circles for a moment. He put his hand on the rough tree trunk then opened his eyes. He took a couple steps forward on his own, then took a few more."Get me an anti-grav belt," he commanded.

Within moments, the three were rising into the air, levitating through a hole in the jungle canopy. Within minutes, they were over the sprawling tent village. The rescuers followed the signal from Zama's video screen. Montoya pointed to a small concrete block structure. They began their descent. Several warriors saw the star men begin to lower from the sky. Some pointed and shouted. Others grabbed spears and bows. The scene below looked like an ant hill that had been stirred up with a stick.

"Force fields, boys!" yelled Erik. They each set their personal fields while they continued to hover well above the concrete building. A hail of spears and arrows arched up at them. None of them quite hit their marks. The invaders patiently waited as the defenders began to exhaust both their immediate weapons and their energy. After a couple minutes, the stream of arrows and spears dropped to a trickle then ceased entirely. The star men waited a moment longer then suspended their force fields and resumed lowering to the ground, rapid repeat firing their stunners. The braves started dropping until the smarter ones fled.

Inside the concrete bunker, some distant noises startled Zama awake. She tried to ignore them and fell back to sleep. A short while later, she heard the noises again. There seemed to be shouting that was getting closer. The door burst open, flooding the area with light. She tried to cover her eyes with her arm. She realized someone was hoisting her into the air, someone who felt strong yet gentle. She looked up to see the face of Captain Erik Houston. He carried her outdoors, where Minj and Montoya were firing their stunners at a number of defending tribes people. Several braves hit the ground.

Her stomach felt like it were falling. Erik and she had become airborne, as had his two crew members. Was she hallucinating?

As the four people rose higher, Minj and Montoya continued firing at the braves below. Some of the warriors launched spears and arrows, all of which stopped in mid-flight instead of hitting their quarry. She leaned her head against the captain's shoulder and closed her eyes.

Moments later, the group lighted down at the landing craft. Montoya hoisted Zama onto his arms, giving the exhausted captain a break. After they entered the craft, the doctor attended to the chief exec. Erik collapsed onto a cot.

The chiefexec took a mental survey. Her entire waist and rib area felt lacerated. The left side of her head was throbbing. She had soreness and intense burning in dozens of places. But she was alive. Thankfully alive.

Meanwhile, the A'laaman posse was advancing through the tall brush on their six-legged beasts, having gone a few miles into the wilderness. The group leader's video screen rang loudly. He retrieved the device. "The chiefexec's been rescued," he yelled loudly. "The chiefexec is safe!" The patriots cried out and shouted with all their might. Some fired their ener rifles into the air.

Back at the landing craft, the chiefexec opened her eyes. She was lying on a surprisingly comfortable hospital bed. Montoya was looking down at her. "I'm glad we got you out of there, Madame Exec. I've given you something for the pain and some other meds to help you heal more quickly. I'm sorry you've gone through so much."

She felt too weak to respond. Finally, she opened her eyes and gestured toward a pitcher of water. Montoya poured some of the valuable liquid into a large cup. She quickly drained it. She put the cup down and he refilled it. After drinking the second time, she closed her eyes.

Next thing she knew, she was sitting in a seat of the landing craft, which was airborne on its way back to Al'aama. The star men had even recovered her gun, which she had placed back in her pants pocket holster. As Minj piloted the craft, the captain sat there in silence, both fists balled. His crew and he had picked up the ATV and were carrying it aboard the flying craft.

The air ship hovered then eased down on the lawn of the exec mansion. A large crowd had gathered, reminding him of the day his crew and he had arrived on the planet. The vehicle eased gently to the ground. The ramp from the landing craft lowered.

Zama arose from her seat, marveling at how much better she already felt. As she put pressure on her sprained ankle, she noted the swelling had gone considerably and the pain had greatly decreased. But the ankle was still tender. She held onto Erik's arm as she walked down the ramp but let go of him as soon as they were outside the craft.

She waved with as much energy as she could muster. Many people had holographic signs over their heads saying such things as: "Welcome Home, Chiefexec Elle!" and "At Last You're Safe, Madame Exec!" But the crowd began to boo and jeer as soon as they saw the star men. Some had holographic slogans such as: "Star men, Go Home!" and "Leave Al'aama— Troublemakers!" One of the protesters hit Montoya in the head with an over-sized egg, its lilac yoke running down his face as a foul stench filled the air. Members of the crowd threw several other missiles at the star people but missed.

A phalanx of the chiefexec's guards stepped between her and the star men. Zama reached between two guards and pulled Erik to her side. Walking as fast as she could with a limp, she hung on to his arm for support and hurried toward the nearest mansion entrance.

"Where we going?" he asked.

"My office."

His face was hot. He felt like a young school boy being hauled off to the face the principal.

Despite their chiefexec's limp, the guards could barely keep up with her. The captain and she arrived at her office suite. The couple, grimy and disheveled, hurried past the speechless Alisa Conway and slammed the door. The chief of staff wrinkled her nose, as much from the rank stench of sweat and dirt as from their totally undignified appearance. The muscle-weary chiefexec eased into the seat behind her massive desk. He took a chair in front of her.

They said nothing for a long moment. The captain stared at the floor. "Our mission has been doomed from the start," he sighed. "First, that crash of the landing craft a couple months ago. Now, this...this *debacle* of a field trip I took you on...I-I'm ashamed of what you must think of us. And our Association. The vast majority of our trips have actually been *beneficial* to the planets we've visited. Otherwise, I wouldn't have been allowed to spend the last twelve years as a starship captain. And a *decorated* one at that...." His weary voice trailed off as he continued to speak to the floor.

The chiefexec looked at him, her matted hair falling into her eyes. Her face was streaked with dirt, perspiration and the trails of her tears.

He continued: "I compromised your safety and almost got you killed. Now your people *hate* us. I'll spare you any further difficulty and we'll just go...."

She looked at him incredulously.

"We'll ship out tomorrow...."

She shook her head. "No," she said in a low voice. "You saved my life. And you're not going anywhere."

"Beg your pardon?"

"I don't want you to go. Not until you're truly ready."

"A-are you sure?"

"Sometimes a leader has to do the right thing. Even if it's unpopular. Sticking up for you is the right thing."

He smiled weakly, glad for another reprieve from scuttling the trip before it was quite complete.

"But," she continued, "there's one thing that's been bothering me. After that woman shot you with an arrow she came back a second time and shot at you again. But that time, you and I were protected by the force field. So, why in the *cosmos* did you shut it off and run after her? None of the bad things would have happened if you hadn't chased after that crazy woman. Why did you do that, Erik?"

"Why did you have me drive into that part of the wilderness when you knew of the dangers?" he countered.

Her jaw dropped. "I-I..." she stuttered.

"You brought that gun along because you apparently had some idea those primitives were around. Yet you sent us right into their path. I'll bet that if we had gone south of A'laama instead of north, we wouldn't have run into trouble. Am I right?"

She looked at the floor.

"Yet at the first sign of other people, you kept urging me to take you back home."

"I-I lost my nerve, okay?"

"Why did you have us head that way in the first place?'

She raised her eyes and looked at him, her bangs falling into her eyes. "Because I...wanted to see firsthand what my people are up against," she said in a low voice.

"What do you mean?" he asked, calming a little.

"Those heathen have been stealing our crops and livestock. They've killed several of our people."

"I had no idea."

"We've tried to keep these things quiet. But who *are* these people? Can they really be the Non-techs? They can't be descended from the Founders like we A'laamans. They must be native to this planet."

"Are you kidding? That woman who was trying to lance you at the cave looks like you. Sure, she's much darker than you from being outdoors so much. Otherwise, you two could pass for sisters!"

"I do *not* look like that wild woman!"

"She's a twenty-five-year-old version of you."

The chiefexec vigorously shook her head.

"And the reason I ran after her is this." He reached into his pocket and pulled out a tiny dot the size of a grain of dust. "This is a tracking dot. My intention was to stick it on her. When I broke you out of that cave I was able attach one of these tracking dots to the woman's hair. This bug will always remain in place. It will transmit audio and video to us. That way, we can keep up with her and at least some of her people. And their plans for any future raids."

"I see," she said.

163

"We can help you develop a plan for dealing with them."

She drew back in her chair. "*What qualifies you* to do that? Isn't your job mainly PR for that Association?"

"In theory. But some of the societies we've visited have been much less hospitable than yours. At times we've had to fight our way out of some tough predicaments."

Zama frowned. Embarrassed, she recalled that *her* administration had not been very hospitable to the star people at first. "I-I'll think about it," she said. "But you told me last week that your duties here would soon be over."

"I want us to stay here for now and help you."

"I'm an adult. I can handle this."

"My crew and I have all received full *military* training."

The chiefexec wasn't sure what the term *military* meant, but it sounded important. She nodded, realizing the captain and his people could be a valuable resource. "We have a lot to do...."

He eased to his feet. "First eat something and get some rest."

"I will. But since you and I will be working closely on this defense project, we should be able to speak with one another at all times. I want to give you this." She opened a desk drawer, pulled out a pocket-sized video screen and handed it to him. It looked like a thin, rectangular mirror but was somehow soft and warm. She showed him several faint, criss-crossing lines that divided the screen into dozens of fingertip-sized squares, making the entirety of the device its own keypad. She explained that the lines disappeared when the screen was in use. She had a fourteen digit personal code that would allow him to contact her directly, bypassing any staffers or security people. The squares weren't marked by A'laaman letters or numbers, yet they had to be punched in the exact sequence. She demonstrated her code, her long fingers dancing over the tabs. Erik's screen had caused hers to flash purple. She invited him to copy her, but he couldn't duplicate the sequence. She showed him the code again, much more slowly. The captain thought he got it but still couldn't follow his mentor. She grabbed his hand rather tightly and guided his fingers to the appointed spots. He tried to repeat her motions but he still missed one or two digits. Too fatigued to be patient any longer, she fought the temptation to yell at him. She suggested Kelly as a more effective teacher.

He slipped the screen into his pocket. "*We'll find a way* to keep your people safe," he said, turning to leave.

"Hey. We need to meet again soon," she called after him. "I'll video you."

After he closed the office door she stood up, walked over to a wall and touched a hidden panel. A section of wall slid up, opening the way into an adjoining suite, her private sanctuary. As was her habit, she checked the suite's scanner for electronic bugs, audio and *especially* video. The suite was a secret hideaway known only to her security people. But one still couldn't be too careful of media intruders. She walked over to a cabinet and retrieved a glass. She opened the small nuclear fridge, pulled out a cold, glass jug, poured a glass of water and quickly drained it. She poured another and gulped down half. She sat down on a chair beside a pedestal table and punched her choice of meal into a built-in keypad. Within moments, the hot meal ascended inside the pedestal and appeared atop the table. Zama wolfed down the food. After finishing, she punched a button and the dirty dishes disappeared into the table's innards. Her thoughts returned to her trials in the wilderness. Abruptly, she shivered from the stark realization that she *could have died* there.

She thought of the last time she had felt in such danger. At age 16....

She stormed out of the house after an argument with her parents. She spent a couple hours walking, walking until her feet ached and burned. Finally, she stopped staring at the pavement and looked up. None of the streets were familiar. The buildings looked like they had been neglected for decades. One of them had a broken window. Litter and broken glass were scattered on the ground. Vehicles lined both sides of the street. One car had been totally blackened by fire. Another sat on blocks, its wheels having been stripped. She swallowed hard. Abruptly, four scruffy teen guys stepped out of the shadows. Their leader, who had severe acne, wild hair and was wearing shorts and a T-shirt boldly strutted up to her.

"Hey, rich girl. You lost?" he asked, stabbing a finger toward her.

She felt her stomach turn to water.

"Yeah. Looks like you're a long way from home." said a second youth, stepping toward her.

"Please. L-let me go. I'll give you my jewelry," she offered, her voice breaking. She opened the clasp on her gem stone necklace.

"That's not all we want," insisted the leader, stepping uncomfortably close

The teen girl swallowed hard. The four youths drew closer and surrounded her. She eyed the leader, whose eyes were hard as ironwood. A trained athlete, she broke through their ranks and sprinted, her long legs pounding rapidly. Her heart beat even faster. The youths raced after her. The tall leader soon closed the gap, tackling her. She put out her arms to break her fall. She hit the pavement with a thud, badly scraping her arms and face.

The gang boss pulled a laser knife from his pocket. His buddies caught up with him and pulled weapons of their own. She lay on the ground, covering her aching face with her hands. The leader activated his laser knife and moved the blade menacingly toward her. She screamed. Her mouth became desert dry as three other laser knives began to move toward her. The youths were about to do their worst when a loud squeal of tires sent them running....

The modern-day Zama shook her head as if to clear it. She was breathing heavily and perspiring. After taking a moment to come back to reality, she set her personal video screen on Audio Only and punched in a code. "Evva? This is the chiefexec. Get me some air time on tonight's news. I want to address the public. Yes, a couple hours from now would be fine. I want to make the broadcast from my office desk. No, *no* press conference. A statement only."

The exec clicked off the screen. She got up from the table and began to shed items of her filthy clothes, casually dropping them on the floor as she made her way to the shower. A small, flat robot on tractor treads emerged from behind a wall panel and followed her. The mechanical servant extended a metal arm, picked up the discarded clothing and deposited it into a sonic cleaner. Zama touched her neck and was relieved her fine gold necklace had somehow survived the wilderness.

She limped gingerly to the shower on her sore legs and ankle. The water burned like fire as it hit her dozens of deep cuts and abrasions. She tightly clenched her teeth. But her expression softened as the hot water began to ease her sore muscles' grip. As she began to apply some liquid soap, she was amazed at how much dirt she was washing off. She cut off the water and hit a button that turned on an air drying and heat lamp system. She used control knobs to direct jets that squirted some scented, medicated lotion to various sections of her skin. She vigorously rubbed in the lotion, scrunching her face as the medication initially intensified the burning and stinging. As she stepped out of the shower, she held her arms in the air and two metal arms emerged from the wall, wrapping a silky robe around her. She tied the robe's waist sash, sat down at a vanity and ordered this suite's set of Microbots to apply some makeup to help hide her wounds and fatigue. Other tiny bots brushed her long mane to a silky texture.

Still wearing her robe, she padded over to the sanctum's small chapel. It had a cathedral ceiling and a skylight made of sections of glass in various colors. The stained glass composed a picture—one of the prophetic angel appearing to two of the Founders. The simple room contained a padded kneeler and a raised, padded shelf for leaning one's arms and head. The

Chiefexec of the Planet knelt down and sobbed, expressing her relief and thanks for being back home alive and safe. She asked for strength.

She wiped her eyes, got up, and strode over to a drawer that was built into the wall. She chose plain white underwear rather than one of the prettier sets. The panties had a navy blue patch on the left hip, one of several pairs she'd had made that included the official seal of the chiefexec. She chuckled as she always did when selecting one of those. She headed to a walk-in closet and dressed in one of her more slimming skirt suits.

Sometime later, she was sitting at the massive desk in her main office, several 3-D news cameras trained on her. One of the technicians counted down the seconds until air time and pointed at her.

The chiefexec, looking and sounding well-composed, began to speak, as excerpted below:

"Good evening, citizens of Al'aama. Thank all of you for your concern for me over the past couple days while I was in the wilderness. I learned that Nontechs we feared as children are real and they are a threat.

"Although the trip had its negative aspects, going on it definitely broadened my knowledge and I'm now able to approach my responsibilities to you from a fresh perspective.

"One thing I *don't* want you to do is blame Captain Erik Houston or any of his people for the problems we encountered. Yes, we were stranded in the wilderness but it was due to a communication system failure caused by severe sunspot activity. During our two days in the wilderness, the captain was a gentleman and treated me with respect. His crew and he rescued me from danger, gave me some medical care and returned me safely home. Some of you have been protesting against the star people. I appreciate your concern for me and your loyalty. But I ask you to please stop these protests immediately. Remember that the star people have shared a wealth of knowledge with us. *They are our friends.* And I've asked them to remain with us as long as they'd like.

"The wilderness people we encountered are hostile and aggressive, but I assure you we will immediately begin to make the utmost effort to protect you, our citizens.

"Thank you and good night."

The news directors motioned it was fini. She sighed then stumbled off to check the feeds on her screen. InstaNews 5 showed just a few seconds of her speech then spent several minutes discussing her having been alone in the wilderness with the captain. The coverage on HyperNow 3 was about the same and YouKnowFirst was even more sensational. She lowered her head and shook it. She'd just told everyone in the speech that nothing had happened with him. Didn't the media know by now that she tried to live her values? She hoped that at least the general public believed her but she hesitated to check the ImmediatePoll stats.

Her adrenaline wearing off, she shuffled out of her office, leaving her aides behind. She didn't feel she had the stamina at the moment for the accelevator so she took the express moving walkways back to her official quarters. That night, she sat on a plush chair in the privacy of her suite, her feet up on a hassock. She was wearing a bathrobe. It felt good to at last do nothing.

Then she began to notice a severe itching on her arms, face and stomach. The next day, Chiefexec Elle had wanted to hold an emergency cabinet meeting but was too miserable to do so. Overnight, she had developed a widespread rash. Her face was red and puffy and one eye was almost swollen shut. Weed poisoning, her official physician had said. She had been too embarrassed to talk with Erik on the video screen that morning, so she had kept her video screen on Audio Only.

Somehow *he* had not come down with weed poisoning. He said he was fine and sounded well. Later that morning, he brought her some salve that Montoya had made. She was too self-conscious to greet the captain in person and had a staffer take the delivery. She applied the salve to the rash. Almost instantly it cooled the burning, relieved the itch. The rash began to fade within minutes. But she was physically and mentally drained. The safety of her people was important, but the game plan would have to wait a few hours.

# 29.

The tribe's cooking fire had died down. The Circle of Honor sat around the fire. Perspiration ran down their faces and arms. It was said this was a way the body purged itself of toxins. Each brave had a large water skin and occasionally took swigs from it. The group sat quietly, letting the evening meal settle as they stared into the fire. Normally, the mood of these evening gatherings was relaxed, but tonight, the silence lasted longer than normal. There was tension in the air. As was customary, the chief was the first to speak.

"We must not be afraid. We must be brave," said Chief Laura Svensen.

"But, Chief, three gods flew into our camp and attacked us. All because we wouldn't give up some outside woman," said Jonah Bleu, a male warrior.

"Those flying ones weren't gods. They were men." Every face turned and looked at the speaker. It was Umni Ott, the female warrior who looked like Zama.

"How do you know?" asked the chief.

"Because I attacked one of them the other day. I shot him with an arrow and later I pulled my knife on him."

"Then, why isn't he dead? " said Allie Smythe, another female.

"His squaw came up behind me and hit me with a club," Umni admitted, her face reddening.

"That's not it. You had passed out from drinking too much happy juice," said Allie, Umni's chief rival. Several braves laughed.

"You know I don't touch the juice!" Umni replied.

"It sounds like this man uses powerful magic. I believe he really is a god!" exclaimed Bill Gatti.

The tribal leaders began to talk animatedly with one another while the chief tried to speak. She raised her voice in attempt to be heard above the din.

"Silence!" shouted McTeague, jamming his spear into the ground.

"You know nothing at all, any of you!" spat the chief. "One of these so-called 'gods' was a stranger we captured in last week's hunt. There was a man and a woman. The man seemed to have some mysterious powers. But I agree with Umni. He is a man, not a god. Do you remember that bright new star that first appeared in the sky a few nightfalls ago? And how I told you we've been visited from the stars?"

The braves nodded their heads.

She continued, "This 'god' you fear is merely a man! He may know how to do some things we can't do, but *he is a man!* So are his companions who attacked us!"

The tribes people again murmured in assent.

"Now he's trying to scare us away from the land of plenty many miles south of the Great Waterfall. Yet that is where we've found some of the most succulent gannao. I'm not willing to give up such a treat, are you?" The braves all shook their heads and murmured.

McTeague, his eyes turning an eerie shade of red, said: "And don't forget how these men attacked and humiliated us when they stole that squaw away from us. We need to show them that the Batu are strong! We need revenge!"

The group of ten cheered loudly, shouted and whistled.

McTeague continued: "We need to take their gannao, burn their farms and spill their blood! The star men, too!"

Cheers and shouts erupted again, this time more pronounced.

"All right, we agree!" cried the chief. "You will each make a pact with me and swear you will do everything you can to continue to provide this meat for the tribe. And that we will take our revenge for our recent humiliation. This is how we will seal the pledge!" The chief took her wooden walking stick and stuck the end of it into the fire. After few minutes, she pulled it out. The end of the stick was glowing red. She jammed the hot end of the stick onto her muscular left arm and held it there for several moments, gritting her teeth. She passed the stick to the brave to her left, who reheated the stick then repeated the gesture on her own arm. This continued until all ten warriors in the circle had thus branded themselves.

Said the chief, "Whenever you see the scar from this burn, you will remember your promise to the tribe. We will go on the attack! We will have our revenge! That is all, my warriors. Good hunting!"

# 30.

Captain Houston rushed through the door of the Founders Museum to find Minj, Montoya, Luci and Kelly waiting for him. The curator and even the security guards were *outside* the building.

"Daj! Your message sounded urgent," said the captain.

Minj looked somber. He waved his hand and a 3-D image of a short, dark-haired woman appeared. She had dark skin, like that of most Al'aamans and short hair.

"That's Nanci Batami," said Kelly. "Not only was she one of our Founders. She started one of our three great tribes."

"Exactly," said Minj, solemnly. "Now look at this." He pulled a flat piece of plastic from his wallet, pressed on it and a 3-D image appeared, that of a short woman with dark, shoulder-length hair. Her skin was much lighter and her hair was somewhat darker than the first lady's. The two women were also dressed differently. But their facial features bore a striking resemblance.

"That second image is the same 3-D you've been carrying around as long as I've known you," said Montoya.

Luci nodded.

"It gets even better," said Minj, "Look at this." He pressed on the tab again and another image appeared. This one showed Minj and the lighter-skinned woman with their arms around one another. Some members of the group gasped audibly. "So you see, Image # 1, Nanci Batami, after she had arrived on this planet and had baked in the harsh UV rays of your two suns for several years. She was sometimes known as Nanci Botany because she had developed a hardy, miracle grain that helped ensure that there was never again a famine after the one that took place in Year 4 of the colony. Nanci sometimes wrote her online signature as Nanci M. Batami. The "M" wasn't her middle initial because her middle name was Elaine. Image numbers 2 and 3, a botanist named Natalie Elaine *Minj*, as she was previously known *before* crash landing here."

"How is this possible?" cried Kelly.

Daj, explained, his voice cracking: "Natalie, or Nanci didn't obtain the last name of Batami until she married a Ron Batami five years after arriving here. It was her second marriage. Prior to that she was Nanci Minj, a fact that somehow is missing from your records. Her maiden name was Schultz, another missing fact. That's the reason it took me so long to realize the identity of this Founding Mom of yours. She and I were married young, but after a few years, she divorced me. Once we both graduated from the Space Academy, we each wanted different career paths. She wanted to help found a colony on some far-off world. I wanted to work for the Association and visit planets that had already been colonized. We went our separate ways...." Minj lowered his head before continuing: "Our final breakup was really painful. It took me a couple years to get over her. But...with all my travel to different star systems I stayed busy enough that, eventually, I almost stopped thinking about her. Until now...."

Luci walked over to Daj and put her arm around him. Kelly's eyes were wet. Montoya and the captain stood there looking at the floor.

"But...that was *three hundred years ago!*" Kelly sniffed between the tears. "What? How?"

"Daj is *well over* three hundred years old," Erik said. "Planetside years. After Daj and Nanci broke up, she apparently went into space aboard the starship carrying the people who colonized your planet. The ship crashed but Nanci survived and became a leader. Meanwhile, Daj started working for the Association and began to travel to the stars, visiting different planets. Aging very slowly...."

"So…you actually *knew* Nancy Batami?" Kelly said, reverently.

"Intimately," he said, his face reddening.

"W-what was she like?"

"She was a strong woman. Very independent. The personality you depict in your histories is fairly accurate."

"Daj has told us many times about Nat…uh, Nanci on our long voyages," said Montoya. "He's always spoken of her with the highest regard."

"Say, Daj," said Luci, "I think we need to enlarge some details of this Founding Mom image of Nanci. Zoom in on this area."

He did so.

"She's wearing a ring," said Luci.

He zoomed in further, noting the fine details. "Our wedding ring!" he exclaimed. He held up a long chain he was wearing around his neck. At the end of the chain was a ring that matched Nanci's.

"Our records show Nanci as being single when she arrived on this planet," said Kelly. "Now, wait. I think I saw another detail. Let's enlarge this section."

Minj did so, revealing that Nanci was wearing a necklace in the photo. Minj zoomed in even closer. The necklace contained a brooch holding a picture of…Daj's face!

Everyone gasped.

"I'll be right back," called Kelly, rushing away. She returned a few minutes later, carrying an aged, wooden jewelry box. She opened the box and pulled out a metal necklace, black with age. The necklace included a brooch holding the faded photo of Daj! He took the necklace from Kelly, holding it and staring at it in wonder.

"Y-your visit is more historic than we ever imagined!" she said.

"There's even more," said Daj. "The first child born on this planet was a girl born to Nanci."

"That's right," Kelly agreed.

"The baby was born just seven months after the colonist's arrival. Your historic records show the baby was full term, which means Nanci must have already been pregnant at the time the starship crashed here. Not only is it a wonder Nanci and the others survived. It's amazing the baby was unharmed."

Kelly was becoming flushed, realizing the implications.

Daj continued: "The colonists had been in Cold Sleep during the trip and were revived shortly before crashing here. That means Nanci must have become pregnant *before* she went into space. She and I had been trying to patch things up. We didn't break up for good until just one week before her ship left. Right after Nanci left, I found a pregnancy test that showed positive…. She told me there'd been no one else and I believed her. I still do."

Kelly's eyes narrowed. "Daj, I know you're sincere in your belief. And…I hate to put you through this. But for something this significant, we really need *proof*…."

The doc declared: "We need a gen test."

"A gen test on a woman who's been dead for centuries?" asked Erik.

"I know of a way," said Kelly, stabbing the air with her index finger.

The Founders Cemetery contained the remains of the three Founders and most of the other colonists as well the next several generations of their descendants. It was normal to have at least a few visitors wandering through to look at the historic graves. But mid-way through the day, those who attempted to enter the cemetery found guards posted at the entrance explaining that it was temporarily closed. Within the grounds, the captain, Minj, Montoya, Luci and Kelly were standing in front of the mausoleum holding Nanci Batami's remains. Minj religiously read the inscription at the entrance. He then walked up the steps and inside the mausoleum, which was large enough that it doubled as a small museum.

While he was preoccupied, Kelly led the group to the adjacent, smaller mausoleum that honored Nanci's second husband, Ron Batami, and Nanci's children. They stopped in front of a sealed casket that contained the remains of Ami Batami, Nanci's first child. Other members of the group stood off at a distance while Montoya used a laser tool to cut through the casket seal. Erik helped him pull off the lid. They looked down at the skeleton of a woman who had died centuries earlier. Montoya took a long cotton swab from his medical bag, rubbed the swab across one of the skull's teeth and placed the swab in a sealed, sterile plastic bag. The two men replaced the coffin lid and used a molecular bonding tool to reseal the coffin. Montoya surveyed their work. The coffin looked just as it had previously. The group left the mausoleum and caught up with Minj. They gave him some additional time to look at the various tributes to Nanci and read the inscriptions. Finally, he was content and he agreed to leave. The group left the cemetery via a back exit. Moments later, the guards at the entrance were told they could again open the facility to visitors.

Kelly sped back to the chiefexec's mansion with the captain and crew. Once the group was inside the star men's suite, Montoya pulled a testing kit from his medical bag and retrieved the tiny scrapings from the skeleton. He strode off to another room. A short while later, he returned and told the anxiously awaiting crew:

"I conducted the test three different times. Each time, the test showed a positive match between Daj and the skel…uh…Amy Batami. The first child born on this planet was the child not only of Nanci Batami but of Daj Minj as well."

"What's your margin of error?" Kelly shot back.

The doc held her steely gaze. "Virtually zero."

Her eyes dropped to the floor. Her face scrunched in deep thought.

Daj suddenly swayed and grabbed a counter top. Erik guided him to a chair and eased him into it. The others were speechless.

After a long moment of standing there in silence, Kelly asked to be excused and wandered into another room. She sat on a bed for several minutes gazing at the ceiling. Then, despite a large knot in her stomach, she was on her video screen. Upon reaching Zama, she poured out the news about Daj and his tie-in with the founding of the A'aalaman colony. The leader demanded Kelly have administration scientists independently confirm the test results. She also ordered her advisor to prepare a confidential online packet that would come directly to her, bypassing all intermediaries.

"You and I need to verify the truth," the chiefexec said, "but it must not, must not come out."

"We'll bury it in our most heavily encrypted archive," Kelly said. "The star men will eventually be gone and their secret will leave with them."

"That's my girl," the leader hissed through clenched teeth.

Kelly hurried from the room with a new sense of mission. As she passed through the main area of the suite, Erik and his crew were by now in the midst of drinking some liquid intoxicants, not so much as a toast to Daj but as a way of helping them cope with the news.

Minj looked a little tipsy. It was quite a shock to find out about fatherhood three hundred years after the fact.

# 31.

The primitives were poised to attack. Communications monitoring had revealed that they planned to conduct raids at several locations at nightfall. Earlier in the day, hundreds of warriors had left their compound and hiked through dozens of miles of jungle. They had set up camp just a few miles from the farm district. They planned to split up into smaller groups and, once it was dark, hit gannao ranches all along the perimeter, stealing the livestock. Terrorizing. Killing.

Erik stood in a field, watching the Ava sun as it was about to sink below the horizon, heralding twilight then the once-in-three-weeks' night. He checked his heat sensing scanner. The Batu were breaking into groups of twelve to fifteen, heading off in separate directions. He alerted his crew members and the Al'aaman police officers. Each group was staked out at a major gannao ranch along the rim. The defenders were armed and equipped with force fields, night-vision goggles and heat-sensing devices. Erik had chosen a farm that raised a particularly large number of prize-winning gannao. A police captain and he were hiding behind some shrubbery twenty yards from a barn filled with the creatures.

Erik watched the sun dip below the horizon. Soon it grew dark. The temperature started to drop rapidly and the stars began to appear. Before long, the entire sky was alive with huge clusters of bright, blue-white diamonds and sapphires. There were so many stars the sky looked grainy. The stars were even more prominent tonight than they had been the night of the temple service because this time Erik was much farther from the lights of the city. As he continued to look up, he spied a small but especially bright star slowly moving across the sky. It was their starship *Initiative*, passing a few hundred miles overhead. He waved playfully.

"I see you down there, Captain, you rascal!"

Erik jumped. It was Irv, calling to him from space via the comm link. "You old goat!" the captain stage-whispered into the comm link.

The security boss' loud laughter rang in his ear.

"Keep it down," came a whisper. It was the police captain with whom Erik was partnered. He was crouched down a few yards away.

Each of Erik's section chiefs quietly reported in to him, as he had requested they do exactly every half hour. Minj's sector was quiet. So was Montoya's. And Luci's. And the others'. A silvery full moon arose over the horizon. The temperature continued dropping. The police officer retrieved a warm cloak from his pack and pulled it around his shoulders, placing the hood over his head. He held out one of the rectangles of folded cloth, offering it to Erik. The star man shook his head. He could see his breath but his adrenaline had him too wired to worry about the cold. The moon rose higher in the sky. The *Initiative* passed overhead again.

He checked his equipment. The Batu groups were making progress, creeping stealthily toward their targets.

Clouds started to obscure the stars and even the moon. It began to grow darker and colder. Erik checked on the warriors. One group seemed to be on a path that would take them directly to this farm! A few minutes passed. He checked again. "They're heading this way and closing in fast!" he whispered to the lead policeman. "Get ready! They should be here in the next few minutes!" The star captain alerted each of his crew chiefs at other sites to get ready for action soon, too.

As Erik and the policeman kept watch, a cluster of figures appeared a hundred yards from the barn. Within seconds they swooped in on the structure. They broke the lock on the barn door and poured inside. Just inside was a police megawagon, its doors wide open. Officers, weapons drawn, began herding the tribes people into the vehicle. The first braves were caught by the ruse, but subsequent ones broke and ran. Erik and a dozen or so A'laaman police swarmed out of the brush and shot, dropping several of the surprised warriors. Erik spotted McTeague and fired. He missed. The tribal boss circled back and began launching arrows at the defenders. Other Batu followed suit. Two of them lit torches and tossed them to the ground, where they rapidly caught sections of brush on fire.

Umni Ott threw an axe at Erik. His force field kicked on and the weapon bounced off. She spat an epithet and bounded away. The remaining tribesmen quickly realized they were outmatched. They fled helter skelter, leaving without their precious gannao.

Two officers appeared with firefighting equipment and fought to extinguish the rapidly spreading blazes. Others carried each of the stunned Batu into the police wagon. Erik and several policemen remained on alert, weapons drawn, in case the intruders re-grouped and counter-attacked. A few others, using their night-vision goggles, took off after the Batu. They downed several more and painstakingly carried them to the police vehicle. After some time, the stillness of the night returned.

The police had captured nine of the invaders. Two policemen had suffered minor arrow wounds. Property damage had been minimal. Erik checked in with the other groups. Similar battles had taken place at a dozen other locations. Two skirmishes were still in progress.

"We've got to stop playing defense," Erik said to the police captain.

# 32.

Minj was walking down a hallway in the exec mansion when he noticed a lady approaching from the opposite direction. He glanced at her then looked more closely. He did a double take, his jaw dropping. The lady smiled shyly then walked past him. He was so stunned he almost walked past the door to the star men's suite. He got out his electronic key, turned the door then stumbled into the suite. When Captain Houston found him a half hour later, he was sitting on a couch, staring.

Erik shook his head. He walked over to Daj and sympathetically put a hand on his shoulder. "How are you, buddy?"

"Captain, I saw her."

"Who?"

"Nanci"

"*Your* Nanci? She's been dead for well over two hundred years. We've seen her grave. We've seen her children's graves. Daj, look at me. I know Nanci means a lot to you, but you've got to face it. Nanci's not alive."

"But I saw her."

"Let me talk with him, Erik. I may be able to help." Kelly was standing in the doorway.

He smiled. "Sure. Be my guest."

She entered the room and sat down by Daj. Soon they were talking animatedly. A few minutes later they were laughing. Erik excused himself and looked up Montoya to go over some battle plans.

Late that night, it felt good to Daj to lie down in his bed and go to sleep. He was glad for the talk with Kelly that evening. She was always good company. He drifted off to sleep, a smile on his face.

Suddenly, he saw Nanci. Her hair was pulled back in a ponytail the way she used to wear it. She was wearing the necklace bearing his picture. She turned to the side and he could tell she was pregnant. Pregnant with little Ami. The daughter born almost three hundred years ago. The daughter he had never known. Then Daj felt he was looking up. Suddenly, Nanci's face filled the sky. He could see every detail of her face. He looked deeply into her eyes. "I'll never forget you, Daj!" she called. Then she faded away.

He saw a little girl playing. The girl looked up. She had dark hair, dark eyes. Her hair was in a ponytail. She was like a miniature version of Nanci. The girl began to run. "Daddy! Daddy!" she cried. "Daddy, where are you?" Daj realized she was calling...him!

He awoke with a start and sat straight up in bed. He got out of bed, walked into the suite's kitchen and pulled a cold bottle from the refrigerator. It was a bottle of a native intoxicant. He got out a glass and poured a tall drink.

A few days later, he was walking down the hall and saw her again. He felt a murmur in his chest. As she drew closer, he called to her. "Nanci. Nanci!"

The woman slowed her pace and looked puzzled. He practically ran to her. "Nanci, it's me, Daj," he said.

The woman stared at him. "My name's Lisa."

"No. You're Nanci Batami."

She laughed. "I do come from the Batami tribe. Say, aren't you one of those spacemen?"

"Yes," he said. "I'm Daj Minj." He held out his hand and she shook it.

"Nice meeting you, Dodge."

"I-I'm sorry for staring, but the resemblance is...incredible."

The woman smiled.

"So...what type of work do you do?"

"I'm the undersecretary of agriculture. I'm over here a lot for meetings."

Interesting, he thought. A Nanci look-alike who was not a hard-charging, fiery leader like the original Nanci but a government administrator.

"I'm going to be late for my meeting, and the cabinet members don't like to be kept waiting. I've got to go."

He was still staring at her.

"You seem like a nice man but I've got to run."

"Bye…Nanci, uh…."

She began to turn red. She clasped his hand again. "It's Lisa. Goodbye, Daj."

Minj let go of her hand. "Will you…give me your video code?"

She smiled. "Yes, of course." She produced a stylus and quickly scribbled the code on an electronic notepad. She punched a button and the pad printed out a plastic card that she handed to Daj. "This is a message card," she explained. "You push this corner of the card to read the message. See how the card lights up? Well, I've got to go. Video me, okay?" She hurried down the hall. Minj stared at the card. Even his cosmic translator couldn't make sense of the code. It wasn't composed of Al'aaman letters or numbers but of several unfamiliar symbols. He shrugged, realizing Kelly could help him figure it out. He was beaming.

The next afternoon, he was leaving the Founders Museum. He knew it would do him good to stay away because he realized he had developed an unhealthy obsession. But he just couldn't help himself. He walked down the sidewalk and was startled to see about twenty women walking together in a group. Something looked familiar about them. All the women were dressed differently but as the group got closer he realized most of the women were short, they all had dark hair and they all had the same face…Nanci's face! A few of them were speaking and they even sounded like her. He was convinced he was imagining this and thought he was losing his mind. He hurried the several blocks to the exec mansion, virtually ran down the hallways to the star man's suite, rushed inside and closed the door. His heart was pounding rapidly and he was out of breath. What was *wrong* with him, he wondered.

# 33.

Eighteen-year-old Omma Elle, dressed in a leotard top and a skirt, was jumping up and down to the music at the club. Jump dancing was popular among young people. The floor was divided into different-colored squares. Each person jumped in time to the music and tried to stay within his or her square. Some dancers would also throw their arms into the air or wave them. Most participants would stay in their respective areas. Occasionally, someone would lose their balance and fall down, knocking over some of the others. Omma thought this was great fun. The floor was made of a soft material that minimized the chance of injury plus added some extra "spring" to each jump. The regulars all wore knee and elbow pads to help prevent injury. The chiefexec's daughter was one of dozens of people on the crowded floor jumping to the music. As the sounds pulsated and lights flashed, her hair flew up and down.

As the song finished, she left the floor and bounced over to her best friend, Paula, a thin, blonde girl. They each raised their hands into the air and lightly touched palms, the current greeting among young people. Standing next to Paula was her boyfriend, Georj. He had a small waist, broad shoulders and red, curly hair. He nodded his greeting.

Omma, having warmed up on the dance floor, was ready for some high action on the tramps. She peeled apart the adhesive fastener for her wrap-around skirt, revealing a pair of shorts. Without a word, she handed the skirt to Paula and bounded over to the tramps. Dozens of people were jumping around on the large, group one. Omma thought the massive tramping was too rowdy and preferred one of the many individual units. Overseeing the individs were guards with air whistles who enforced the one person at a time rule. Each unit was surrounded by nets strung from the high ceiling. Nets to catch anyone who flew off in an unintended direction. She climbed a ladder to the jumping board. A small crowd had gathered below. She sprung into the air, landing on the board and bouncing higher. Once. Twice. Three times. She launched into the air, flying several feet above the board. She was sailing, falling slightly slo-mo, feet first toward the large tramp below. Her feet hit, sinking down a foot or so before the tension shot her high into the air. She curled into a ball and did a triple somersault, landing on her feet before launching skyward again. She went a little less high this time. She used her muscles to her slow her momentum. She bounced one more time. Two. Three, a little lower each time. At the end of the fourth bounce, she did a mid-air flip off the tramp and landed lightly on the padded floor about ten feet from Paula and Georj. The small crowd applauded. Omma's face and limbs were flushed pink. Breathing a little heavily, she held out her hand. Paula returned the skirt and Omma re-fastened it.

"You were flyin'!" cried Paula.

Omma smiled.

The three of them headed to the dance tramp. Paula and Georj got onto the tramp, and began lightly bouncing to the music. Through several songs, they alternately slow danced and free form fast danced, displaying considerable style and grace. They finally exited the tramp to the applause of the audience. Omma grabbed her tiny purse from a nearby table and the trio hurried over to the bar, joining a group of other friends. Everyone touched palms. The guys and ladies each ordered slam, a frothy, chilled beverage that was served in tall, narrow glasses. It was made from a local herb, had a creamy color and somewhat of a mint chocolate flavor. It was a mild stimulant. As Omma waited for her drink, she realized she had walked into the middle of an animated conversation.

"So, if you believed in something strongly enough, would you be willing to *die* for it?" Omma and the other members of the group stared at Tad, the thin blond guy who had posed the question.

Without hesitation, Omma replied: "If I believed in something strongly enough, I'd risk death for it."

The group members all turned and stared at her. "So...*what* do you believe in enough that you'd die for it?" asked Beta, a thin woman who was one of her sorority sisters. She pushed her long, dark hair out of her face as she awaited an answer.

Omma hesitated a moment. "I-if anything threatened our society...our way of life here in Al'aama, I'd risk death to defend it."

Georj laughed aloud. "What could possibly threaten us?"

"What about all those mysterious killings and thefts taking place in the inner jungle and the farm district?" Beta challenged.

"That's all on the outskirts," scoffed Georj.

"I think it's a threat," Omma countered.

The group quickly downed their slams and ordered another round. As Omma conversed and sipped her drink, she looked up and frowned. There they were again, the security people in their funeral suits, still hovering close to the bar. She hated their presence. They didn't even try to blend in, didn't even try to have any fun. Omma told her friends she was leaving then went to the ladies' room. She had to hurry before a couple of female agents followed her. She spied a high window and wondered if she could fit through it. She carried a metal trash disintegrator over to the wall and stood up on it. Omma boosted herself onto the window ledge. She sized up the window, realizing she appeared just thin enough to fit. She was glad she had gone on a diet. How humiliating it would have been if she got stuck in the window and had to be rescued! She pulled in her stomach, held her breath and slipped through the window, pulling her purse through with her. She dropped slo-mo a few feet to an alley below, landing with surprising grace. So far so good. All she had to do was get to the parking lot....

She glanced around the corner and spied two agents at the front of the club. She trotted down the alley and entered the parking lot from the back. She hurried to her tiny, red sports car. It was low-slung and sleek, the effect broken by the crumpled left fender. She brushed her palm through the air, causing the car to recognize her print. The door slid open and Omma slipped into the seat. It adjusted to custom-fit her body down to microscopic levels. She was thankful her vehicle that had a driver-control option. She hated just punching in a destination and having a car automatically take you there in as safe and boring a manner as possible. Not Omma. This girl was meant to fly.

She engaged the engine and placed her fingertips on the sensitive, U-shaped steering mechanism. A button on the right controlled acceleration. The left was the brake. The car was so responsive the coed almost felt it could read her thoughts. Woman and machine became one.

She tore out of the lot. She rounded the corner onto the street. Two agents pointed her direction. Another shouted into his screen: "Red Brat in motion. Red Brat in motion. Headed down Ava Street toward Number 6 Highway."

Tires squealed as Omma turned again. The sportster zipped down the next road. She whipped onto a freeway ramp. She lightly touched the accelerator button. A burst of speed jerked her back against the high seat. Omma smiled. The steering continued responding instantly to tiny changes in her fingertip positions.

It was fairly dark that night with only the faint Zoe sun in the sky. She looked in her rearview mirror, noting that several black vehicles were already in pursuit. The Red Streak hummed loudly as it flashed along the highway. Omma's stomach tightened as she felt the adrenaline rush. She weaved in and out of lanes, passing larger, slower vehicles. Several black cars were not so discretely following the red one and also weaved in and out. Omma glanced into her rearview mirror. She shifted gears. They were still in sight! Wouldn't they ever leave her alone? She quickly exited the highway, zipping into a well-hidden, private tunnel that led into the sub-sub basement of the exec mansion. She quickly parked, looking in the mirror again as she first brushed her hair then freshened her lipstick. The fusion-powered car had cost her mother a fortune, but man, could it move!

She strode over to a private lift, entered it and punched a button. Within moments, the vertilift deposited her just outside her personal workout room. She changed into some shorts and a tank top she had previously laid out. She pulled out her personal video screen, an elliptical one that had her name etched into it and a flowered border. She pushed a tab to set the screen to project holos of the latest fashion commercials. Omma began free form dancing to the music accompanying the ads while she eyed the constantly changing screen.

After a few minutes, a weary-looking Zama Elle, clad in a fuzzy bathrobe and slippers, appeared in the doorway.

"Mother! What are you doing here?" she called, not missing a beat of the music.

Mom groaned: "I told you to always set up a sound block. I'm only two rooms away!"

The young woman ignored her mother. She hopped onto a treadmill, set it for max speed and grade and began pounding away. Some digital readouts from her arm implant flashed through her mind, telling her how many energy units she would eventually burn at her present speed and what eating and exercise goals she had to hit in order to keep losing weight.

Zama again demanded her daughter's attention. "Did you just get in? What have you been doing?"

"Jump dancing."

"Again? And how many slam drinks did you have?"

"Five."

"No wonder you can't unwind."

"Mother, they're small."

"That stuff's supposed to be addictive…"

"Why aren't you asleep?"

"I can't sleep," said Zama.

"You're concerned about this security thing, aren't you?"

"How did you know?"

"I've been using my sound amplifier when you've been talking on the screen with Chief Franklin and Captain Houston," Omma admitted. She was just beginning to breathe a little harder as she got further into her workout.

Zama glared at her. "You've been spying on me?"

"I'm worried about you. You're under a lot of stress. And I want to be in on this security detail."

"You can't. You're still a child."

"Mother," said Omma, disdainfully, "I'm a college woman. I'm an accomplished athlete. And I want to help defend our city."

Zama sighed. "First your brother tries to argue me into signing up…."

"He just wants to be brave like Captain Houston. I don't think the captain's afraid of anything!" By now, she was beginning to puff harder. Perspiration began to trickle down her face.

"I am chiefexec of this plan…uh, city and I say you're not going into battle, young lady!"

"I just want to help. Who's going to defend us if we don't defend ourselves? Someday the star people will be gone and then what will we do?"

"You're not going to risk your life! I forbid it!" The chiefexec stomped off to her private quarters and poured a drink. Omma pounded the treadmill even harder, a flow of tears beginning to mingle with her sweat.

Hours later Chiefexec Elle, still awake and clad in her robe, wandered through the outdoor garden that took up most of an extensive balcony. She normally loved the sights and scents of the various plants and flowers. But tonight more serious thoughts haunted her. She thought of Jaylene Farber. The farm girl had been two days short of her seventeenth birthday when an arrow had pierced her chest during one of the gannao raids. She recalled Joe, Sarah and Tony Eddlesbeth, an entire family that had perished in another raid. She thought about other families who were now missing members. She thought of the fear and frustration the killings were creating among her people.

She thought about the self-defense force that her police and security departments had assembled. Erik and his staff had been training them for battle. She recalled watching him demonstrate a type of force field. It had proven quite effective against a star man stunner and an A'laaman ener weapon but had still allowed the crew member to shoot at and hit a target.

Her thoughts returned to the present. Andy and Omma also weighed heavily on her mind. Still two children, really. But they were willing to sacrifice so that her people could again feel safe.

She shuffled over to the balcony railing and gazed at the city. Nearby were the stately government buildings. In the distance stood the skyscrapers. She looked into the sky and thought about what her late mother had told her when she had first run for public office—always put the needs of the people first. Even when you had to make some hard decisions. Even when the choices are personal. She stood there for several minutes, looking first at the faint Zoe sun. Then she stared for a time at the crescent moon. Finally, she slipped the omnipresent video screen out of her robe pocket, set it on Audio Only and called the head of police.

"Chief Franklin?" she said softly. "Yes, it's the chiefexec. Sorry to awaken you. Oh…you've had trouble sleeping, too. Thank you for turning down my son when he volunteered for the self-defense force. Now my daughter's interested, too. But I-I've…changed my mind," she said, her voice breaking. "I want you to allow them to join…if they so desire. Yes, yes. I know there's not much training time left. But train them as thoroughly as possible. In fact, I'm sure they wouldn't mind staying late to make up for some lost time. Thanks again." She ended the call.

She placed both hands on the balcony railing, lowered her head and wept. "Help me," she sobbed. "Help us…."

# 34.

The Wilderness Modification crews worked at the frontier of civilization. They had a highly important and respected task, that of clearing out the empty wasteland, preparing for the future growth of A'laama. They tore out trees, drove out animals and otherwise prepared the land to become tomorrow's farms. And the next decade's suburbs. And, over generations, part of the city proper. Only the modification crews were authorized to work inside, although barely inside, the Forbidden Zone.

That morning, Pete Sanchez and his crew were operating giant tree harvesters and rock pulverizers. The harvesters, each the size of a small factory, had several mechanical arms that picked up trees whole and fed them into an enormous maw. An automated sawmill within the monster truck began separating the types of trees, debarking the logs and processing them into various types of lumber that would be used to make homes, barns and furniture. The machinery even had laser saws to cut up the harder-than-stone ironwood. The crews would not completely deforest a given area but would leave various small stands of trees and rows of shrubs for shade, firebreaks and aesthetics. The crews had strict rules and their goal was to thin, not eradicate.

Pete glanced at the wrist implant that served as his built-in timepiece. The crew had been working hard this morning and it was time for a break. He punched a button to signal their video screens. The deafening roaring, buzzing and high-pitched humming of the great machines ceased. His crew members, one by one, took the vertilift from his or her elevated cab to the ground. They followed Pete to the shade of a remaining tree and sat down, each one holding a cold drink. Some pulled snacks from their self-refrigerating lunch pails. The sweet scent of sawdust filled the air.

Just as the crew was starting to relax, Pete fell over, face forward.

"Non-techs!" cried one of the men, noting the arrow protruding from the boss's back.

One of the workers started to administer first aid while two others grabbed ener rifles normally used for warding off stray animals. A half-dozen screaming warriors burst out of the brush, sending a hail of arrows at the group. Within moments it was all over, with several dead workers on the ground and only minor injuries to the fleeing Batu.

Once word spread to modification crews along other parts of the frontier, they began posting armed sentries at all times. Some crews even refused to work, citing a lack of safety. The next day, police sharpshooters at some sites to protect crew members. Meanwhile, the leaders of the modification department talked of a strike. Within two days, the expansion of metro A'laama had come to a stop.

A livid Chiefexec Elle was on the screen to Police Chief Franklin, Captain Houston and all the other leaders of the small resistance army. She had set up an emergency conference call and was looking up at several disembodied, 3-D faces that hovered at eye level. The officials all were seeing a wall-sized face of Zama Elle. Her eyes and voice were grave. "The time has come," she said.

# 35.

Omma, clad in khaki running shorts, a maroon top and athletic shoes, ran along the path leading to the Batu settlement. She carried a pouch with a message to the warrior chief. Omma's legs continued to pump as she felt her pulse pounding and she gasped for air, a headband keeping the perspiration from her eyes. Finally, she could see the wooden stockade in the distance. When she was about ten yards away, a tall male warrior rushed out the gate to confront her, spear in hand. He yelled something at her in an unfamiliar dialect. Omma, being coached by comm link, knew how to word her response.

"I represent the combined tribes of Al'aama," the athlete panted, with all the boldness she could muster. "I'm carrying a message from our chief to your chief."

The robust warrior laughed at her. "You just go back home with your message," he said with a sneer. The gate was still open and other warriors began to notice her. Several male braves stopped what they were doing and eyed the attractive woman, walking through the gate toward her. A crowd began to gather.

"Antoine! Don't stand there like a stump! What does this girl want?"

called a bass voice. It was McTeague. He eyed the stranger suspiciously.

"She says she has a message for the chief," Antoine replied.

"Well, let's take her to the chief!" McTeague continued to stare at the female but beckoned her through the gate. She walked boldly into the tent village, followed by her growing male entourage. The stockade gate slammed shut behind her.

"You young bucks act like you've never seen a woman before!" spat McTeague. "Don't most of you have your own wives? Calm yourselves!" Belying what he just told the warriors, he also eyed up the young woman. He turned around and looked at the crowd. "What did I just tell you men? I'll handle this. Go to your tents, all of you!" They reluctantly began to disperse. He continued to lead the woman toward the chief's tent then at the last minute pointed her to his nearby tent. He was about to push her inside when the chief appeared, having heard the previous commotion. Some of the other men were still nearby.

"Who dares disturb the chief?" she cried indignantly. Several of the remaining braves started talking at once.

"Silence!" shouted McTeague, jamming the butt of his spear into the ground.

"Who *is* this invader?" the chief barked.

"I'm a messenger of the tribes of Al'aama, the land beyond the jungle. Great and mighty Chief, our chief has a message for you."

"I have nothing to say to your chief! Over the past few days, a number of our people have disappeared. Do you know anything about this?" The chief was holding a carved spear and pointed it toward the Omma's neck.

She swallowed. "Your braves are safely in our custody. They have not been harmed."

"We demand you return them to us!" the chief said, spitting on the ground. McTeague and several of the warriors murmured their approval.

"You are not in a position to make demands! Your tribe has repeatedly wronged our tribes by trespassing on our land, stealing our livestock, destroying our property and killing our people! We will no longer tolerate this!" The athlete mentally cringed as veins began to stand out on the chief's neck. "We are several peoples and are much more numerous and powerful than you can imagine! You have stirred our wrath and we are about to avenge all that has been done to us. But even now, you can spare your people much grief by agreeing to never again invade our land!" Now even the braves were reaching for their weapons.

192

The chief raised up to her full height, stepped forward and leaned her face to within inches of the athlete's. "We're not afraid of you! If you're so big and strong, then why have you been unable to stop most of our raids? Not even your star men with all their power have been able to help you. We do not fear you at all!"

The chief spat on the ground again. Several of the warriors spat, too. McTeague raised his spear and pointed it at the young woman..

She swallowed hard, took a couple steps back then proclaimed with a loud voice: "Very well, Laura Svensen, chief of the tribe of Batu. Let all your warriors witness that you have rejected our offer of peace! Our warriors will invade your territory! Out of concern for your children, we will not invade this village but will engage you in battle at eight tomorrow morning in the field two miles south of here. If you do not show, then we will march on your camp!"

"You cannot get into our camp unless we let you through the gate! Our walls are strong and can stop both man and beast," the chief cried.

"Oh, but we have machines that can fly *over* your walls and drop our strongest warriors into your midst! One way or the other, we will fight you tomorrow at eight. And we will win!"

The chief and the warriors were enraged and rushed the woman. The charging warriors somehow ran right through her and collided with one another, several of them falling to the ground. The young lady laughed.

"Chief! S-she's not really there!" cried McTeague.

"I can see that!" shouted Chief Laura, staring at the 3-D image. The real Omma was safe many miles away.

"She—she seems to be made of light. What kind of evil magic is this?" cried McTeague.

Recovering her composure, the chief continued: "No one makes a fool of Chief Laura! Messenger lady, you either show up in person to challenge me or else we won't even go to your battle!"

"I told you before, you have no choice. Eight o'clock tomorrow morning. Be there!" The woman of light faded from view.

Energy beams shot from the sky to the ground, causing explosions of dust and dirt. One beam hit McTeague in the arm, causing him to cry out and drop his spear. "You just wait until I see you in person, little woman. You'll pay for shaming us like this!" he cried.

Chief Laura shook her fist into the air and spat out an epithet followed by the term "star man."

# 36.

Grey clouds hung like a low ceiling. A misty rain was falling. In the field stood several hundred A'laamans. The makeshift army was composed of policemen, exec security agents, volunteers. Sprinkled among the crowd were some of Erik's crew. The chiefexec briefly addressed her small defense force. Nearby, Kelly sipped on a steaming beverage. After their leader finished, the crowd began to disperse.

Erik looked Zama in the eye and reiterated his promise to keep her apprised of all major battlefield developments. She somberly nodded.

As he walked by, Kelly grabbed his arm. He looked into her eyes. They were wet, bloodshot and underscored by dark circles. "I have a bad feeling," she choked. "We need an invocation."

Zama, who had heard from nearby, loudly called the group back to attention. Once the crowd settled down, the boss lady nodded to her advisor. Erik, with his military experience, would be leading the troops. He bowed his head. Kelly laid her hands on it, closed her eyes and began to speak. Once she finished, he looked into her eyes. He looked somber. But she was now smiling.

He smiled back. Zama watched the non-verbal exchange and bit her lip. Kelly gave Erik a hug. The chiefexec held out her arms for a hug, too, but he had already turned away.

She found Andy and Omma trotting over to them. She hugged each of them tightly.

"Don't worry, Mom. We won't let you down," Andy promised.

Omma, silent for once, nodded. Zama hugged her again.

Spotting Erik a dozen yards away, the chiefexec called, her voice breaking: "Take care of my kids." An audible moan passed through the crowd. The exec stuck her hands in her pockets, lowered her head, turned and walked away. It began to rain harder, pounding like dozens of hammers on the landing craft. Zama was quickly getting soaked, her tears dropping along with the rain.

The fighting force split into three groups, each one entering an over-sized star man landing craft normally used for carrying heavy equipment or freight. Troops filed into each transport's cargo hold then took seats on the floor. Everyone was silent as the craft lifted off from the field. They flew over the farm district then over the jungle. The passengers oohed and aahed as the river below them poured over a cliff, becoming the Great Waterfall. Then the ships began to touch down. It wasn't raining here and the ground looked dry. The allies all wore self-drying clothes that now felt fresh and warm.

"This is Captain Erik Houston," he said over a comm link so that people in the other ships could hear him, too. "Let's stay in the ships until I give the signal. The warriors have a surprise for us. You would expect them to arrive from the far end of the field because that's closer to their settlement. But they are hiding in the jungle opposite *this* end of the field, lying in wait for us. We'll have to come out fighting. Stay calm and remember your training. Each of you has been equipped with a shield generator that will automatically turn on if someone tries to harm you. You should all be wearing your body armor. Anyone who does not have it on needs to put it on *now*. You Al'aamans should all set your weapons on *stun* and members of my crew should do the same. Your chiefexec has ordered us to try not to kill anyone if we can avoid it.. We are trying to defeat and demoralize the enemy. Any questions?"

The silence was palpable. "Let's go. Our ship will lead the way and the rest of you will follow."

He donned the telepatch. Each of his crew members would also wear one, enabling them to read one another's thoughts and thus be much more effective in coordinating the battle. He asked each crew member to check in telepathically. All twenty units, counting his, were operational. He hit a button to open the automatic hatch. His group poured out of the vehicle and into the field. As soon as the last person was out of the ship, he set the force field. Minj and Montoya were quickly emptying out their transports.

Hundreds of warriors in battle regalia poured out of the jungle, yelling and brandishing their weapons. A number of the Al'aamans fired pistols called blinders, low-powered lasers used to temporarily blind an opponent. The first ranks of the Batu were thus incapacitated. The A'laamans and star people were about to take aim when they, too, were blinded by flashes of light. The warriors were using polished metal shields to flash the rays from the two suns. The warriors opened fire with their spears and bows. A number of the force fields kicked on.

The warriors' metal sheets were abruptly yanked from their hands and thrown to the ground. Erik heard familiar laughter in his ear piece. Irv must have created some sort of magnetic field. But that could also compromise the shields. He noticed some of their shimmer wavering but after a moment they looked normal again.

He was keeping his eye out for the chief, thinking that if he wounded or captured her, that could bring a quick end to the battle. A number of the warriors rushed him. His shield engaged and the fighters bounced off it.

Many of the Al'aamans and star people had gotten off shots, downing a number of the warriors. The ground exploded near some of the larger groups of Batu. Erik spotted the chief, surrounded by a circle of braves. He charged toward the circle and began firing his stunner. Two warriors dropped. Turning off his shield to allow him greater freedom of movement, he tackled the chief full force but quickly regretted his decision. She proved to be an even tougher fighter than the Umni Ott. The chief pinned Erik to the ground and was about to skewer him with her spear. Someone shot the chief with a stunner. She dropped to the ground and groaned. Erik looked up to see Luci's face.

He struggled back to his feet and surveyed the battlefield. Dozens of warriors were down, none of the Al'aamans or crew members. He set his comm link on broadcast mode and, using the cosmic translator, said in the warriors' language: "People of the Batu tribe! Your chief has been injured! Give up your fight and admit defeat!"

A number of the warriors stopped fighting and looked at where the star man was pointing. The chief was, indeed, on the ground. How could this be? Many of the braves were also unnerved their enemies' attacks being so well-coordinated, almost as if their leaders were of one mind. What kind of evil magic was this?

"You braves! Listen to me!" bellowed McTeague. "This is one of the Star man's tricks! You warriors, keep fighting. All of you!" The group turned back to the fight with renewed vigor. Then Erik led about a dozen crew members wearing anti-grav belts. They took to the air and began firing energy bursts into groups of fighting braves. A number of the tribes people fell and their groups began to scatter.

Upon Erik's tele-command, his crew members changed the settings on their weapons. They aimed at various places on the ground, creating instant, four foot deep sink holes that snared many of the Batu, cries of shock and moans of pain filling the air as the braves tumbled into the craters. Many of the remaining warriors fled.

"Quick, efficient but non-deadly, just like the chiefexec wanted," Erik telepathed to his people. "A little mop-up work and we're done."

Omma felt the allies had already won. She sighed and turned off her shield. A rock-solid arm grabbed her around the waist. She felt the bite of warm, sharp metal against her throat. She gasped a high-pitched whimper.

"So. The lady who was made of light!" a harsh female voice breathed into her ear. "You were bold when you challenged us yesterday. But you're weak as a baby in person!"

The warrior began to yell loudly in an attempt to be heard above the fray. "Star men, listen to me! Listen!" A nearby comrade began blowing a piercing battle horn.

Erik and a number of other fighters stopped to look for the source of the clamor. The bellowing woman was Umni Ott. She held onto a young lady with one arm and held an over-sized bush knife against her throat with another. A thick circle of warriors surrounded them. Erik stopped breathing when he saw the captive's identity.

"Star men, listen!" Umni shouted again. The battle was dying down over a larger area. "You Star men, you other tribes! Do you see *who I have here?* Your pathetic little messenger! She looks a lot like your chief. Could they possibly be *related?* I see your chief is too much of a weakling to even lead her troops into battle! All of you invaders must stop fighting and go back home *or this little girl dies!*"

Erik telepathed commands to his crew and shouted order to the Al'aamans over his comm link. "They've captured the chiefexec's daughter! Stop fighting! I repeat, halt your fighting!" He heard several group leaders echo those same orders to make certain their troops understood.

By the time Umni finished shouting, only the farther reaches of the field had any activity. Everywhere else, the Al'aamans and the star people stood helplessly by. Umni and her cohorts slowly led Omma away while Umni continued to hold a knife to her throat.

"Umni Ott!" shouted Erik from above her. The seasoned warrior ignored him. Erik's anti-grav patrol trailed the knife-wielding brave from the air and began to shout her name as well. This went on for a several minutes and she found it difficult to ignore them. Finally, she shouted: "Stop it! Stop it, all of you, or I'll slit her throat right now!"

McTeague strode cockily over to Omma. "Well, my young beauty, you're not so brave now, are you?" he sneered. "You'll pay dearly for shaming our tribe!"

She looked into his eyes and swallowed hard. There was something horribly wrong about those eyes. She suddenly felt icy cold from head to foot.

About fifty feet away, Andy's face reddened. His muscles knotted. Unseen by Omma's attackers, he picked up a stone and whipped it at McTeague. Andy was throwing uphill, so the rock stung the tribal leader in the back of his thigh. He cried out, falling to his knees.

Montoya raised his stunner and zapped the distracted Umni in her knife hand. She dropped the weapon. Omma stomped hard on her captor's foot. The warrior shouted. Omma broke free. She fired her ener pistol at Umni at close range. The beam hit the same hand Monoyta had. Several tribesmen rushed Omma. She quickly reset her shield. Umni gritted her teeth, rubbing her injured left hand. Omma touched the front of her neck, shuddering as she saw a little blood smeared across her fingers.

Andy sprinted over to her. "Sis! You all right?"

Her eyes flashed with the same intensity as her mother's. "Don't worry about me! Let's tear up these warriors!" The Elle siblings began rapid repeat firing at the nearest Batu. Several hit the ground. The star people and the Al'aamans went back to fighting with renewed zeal.

Erik and his airborne troops continued firing on the braves. He noticed one of the shields die out. It was Andy's! Erik aimed and fired his stunner at the nearby warriors. He shot twice. Three times. Three braves dropped. Others fled. Erik didn't understand how one of the force fields could quit. His crew and he had tested every last one of them the previous night. He landed on the ground near the young man, removed his own shield device and clipped it onto the wounded man's belt. Andy was bleeding, an arm wound.

A surprisingly bad shot. Emboldened by their wounding of one of their enemy, the warriors fought harder.

Meanwhile, their chief was beginning to recover and struggled back to her feet. Luci again shot her. The woman collapsed back to the ground.

A sharp pain felt like it split Erik's calf in two. An arrow had found its mark.

"Get the captain and Andy back to the ship. Now!" Minj telepathed to a couple nearby crewmen. They hurriedly complied, their force fields holding off a hail of arrows from the warriors.

Minj thought of the ancient sport of football. He stuck his weapon in his holster and rushed toward the nearest warrior, who fired at him. The strength of the force field hit the warrior like a brick wall, knocking him to the ground. The brave did not get back up. Minj repeated the technique on another tribesman. Others picked up on his telepathed thoughts and began to use their force fields as offensive weapons as well.

A second wave of several hundred fresh braves poured out of the nearby jungle. Encouraged by the reinforcements, the outdoors people began fighting harder.

Some additional explosions took place near several knots of warriors, causing them to flee. Luci quickly surveyed the battlefield. Despite the warriors' reinforcements, the fighting was starting to become scattered. Yet many of the enemy were continuing to hold their own. She switched on her comm link and translator. First she telepathed to the crew, then shouted to the Al'aamans: "We need to fall back and regroup. Everyone, *right now*, run as quickly as you can behind the landing craft. Then we're going to circle around the vehicles and come back out, charging and firing our weapons, On my signal. One, two, three…go!"

She led the group back toward the vehicle. Her longer-legged colleagues quickly outran her. The group massed behind the vehicles and rushed back onto the field. The warriors, in the meantime, had given chase, thinking their enemy was in retreat. They ran headlong into the now-advancing troops, who were firing at them. A number of braves dropped to the ground. Most of the others turned and fled. Emboldened, the Al'aamans and star crew chased the group, continuing to fire. Many warriors fled into the jungle. Luci felt uncertain about this, realizing the warriors would have an advantage on that terrain and could easily disappear into the foliage, re-group and begin a counter-attack. She couldn't believe it when she saw one of the fighters going after the warriors was…Erik! He was running as fast as he could despite a pronounced limp caused by his recent arrow wound. She repeatedly called him telepathically. He ignored her, focusing on his prey. A couple braves turned around and fired arrows at him. The arrows dropped harmlessly to the ground.

He crashed through some brush and into the jungle. The same braves who had shot at him were still ahead. He fired his stunner. Again. One brave dropped. Another. There were now dozens of Batu fleeing into the jungle with at least that many Al'aamans and star people giving chase.

He was about to track down some additional braves when he heard a woman moan in pain. The sound seemed to be coming from about ten yards away. He looked around until he saw a female warrior lying on the ground. A metal animal trap held her ankle like a ferocious set of teeth. The brave was virtually unconscious from shock and pain. It was Umni Ott! No one else was nearby because the jungle portion of the battle had already advanced beyond them.

He found a large stick and used it to pry open the jaws of the trap. The metal teeth had penetrated her flesh. Her moccasin was soaked with blood. He pulled some medication from his pack and began to treat her wound. After a few minutes, she began to stir. She groaned then opened her eyes. Suddenly, they got very large.

"Star man, you have me where you want me!" she wheezed. "Just get it over with and kill me!"

He frowned and looked into her eyes. "I'm not going to kill you."

"Why not? I was trying to kill your people."

He swallowed hard as he thought of the incident with Omma a little while earlier. He said nothing further but crouched down beside the fighter.

"Why are you doing this?" she demanded. "I'm your enemy!"

"We don't *have* to be enemies."

"You're insane!"

"I just hate to see people suffer."

"You're weak, Star man," she spat.

He ignored her comments and used a cleansing cloth to wipe away the dried blood. She flinched at the fiery burning from the antiseptic. He gently rubbed some salve on the torn ankle. At first she gritted her teeth in pain but her expression quickly eased. "Hey! What kind of medicine is this?"

"Its tiny organisms that will gradually heal your wound and re-build your flesh. You shouldn't even have a scar. Let me give you something for the pain."

"No!"

He put a pill up to her lips. She bit his hand. He dropped the pill, got

200

another. She closed her mouth and gritted her teeth. He forced it into her mouth. She spat it out. He got another. She didn't open her mouth but this time she didn't fight him. He got the pill inside her lips. He saw her swallow. He let her take several swigs of water from his canteen. He looked at her left hand, the same one Montoya and Omma had shot a little earlier. It was swollen, red and badly blistered.

The hardened warrior could no longer stand it. She shouted shrilly: "Leave me alone, Star man! Leave me alone! I don't *deserve* your help! I almost killed that baby-faced girl!"

He froze in his tracks and swallowed hard.

She grew more vociferous. "Just leave me alone! Go! I don't deserve this!"

Erik, still thinking of Omma, was almost inclined to give the Batu lady her wish. Instead, he said quietly, "I'm not going anywhere."

The tribeswoman tried to start dragging herself away. Remembering that her ankle was now feeling somewhat better, she tried to stand. Balancing on her good foot, she took a few steps then quickly fell. Rather than slamming to the ground, she landed in Erik's arms.

"You're a sly one, Star man. I hate you! I hate you!"

He ignored her and set her on the ground. He got another type of salve from his pack. He gingerly applied some to the woman's injured hand. She looked at her hand in wonder. The pain began to ease and she could almost see her flesh returning to its normal color.

"Why are you doing this? I hate your people."

"We don't hate you. We're just trying to get you to stop attacking us." Erik marveled at his own words, as if he considered himself an Al'aaman.

Umni looked puzzled at his response. She finally allowed herself the luxury of a faint smile. Her expression changed as she heard some thrashing around in the brush nearby. She turned and saw that a couple figures approaching from the distance were members of her tribe.

"You need to go…. Go!" she whispered. "My tribesmen will kill me if they know you helped me!"

The captain scrambled off into the brush. While the two braves were still off in the distance, the woman scooped up some dirt and rubbed it on the wound to hide any signs that it had been cleansed. The braves hurried over to her.

"Umni Ott! What is this we just saw!" cried one of them, a male.

"That's right!" added the other, a female. "We saw you talking with that star man. And he looked as he was helping you!"

"You know what the chief does to traitors," continued the male, raising his arm as he prepared to lance the wounded lady with his spear.

"I fought bravely for our tribe today! You know that!"

"No, Umni! You've turned your back on your own people and are consorting with the enemy." accused the female. "You're guilty of treason!"

The male was about to plunge his spear into her when he stopped in mid-motion and abruptly fell forward, crashing to the ground. Erik stepped out of the brush, stunner in hand. He quickly fired at the female antagonist, who hit the dirt as well.

"Let's get you out of here," he said. He picked up the tall warrior and began carrying her in his arms. After a few steps, his muscles ached in protest. He gently eased her to the ground. He was still wearing his anti-grav belt. The jungle canopy was too thick for flying. He pulled off the belt and strapped it around Umni's waist.

"You crazy man! What are you doing?"

"Quiet. This will help me carry you."

He changed some settings on the belt and picked her back up. Because it was now doing most of the work, it was much easier to balance her weight and carry her. At first she squirmed and protested a little but the medication was beginning to make her drowsy. He moved along as rapidly as he could, still limping on his injured leg as he headed toward the edge of the jungle a few hundred yards away. He gradually became out of breath and slowed his gait somewhat. After several minutes of carrying the woman, he became weary and set her on the ground.

"How you feeling?" he asked her.

"A little better." The steely fighter looked at Erik, studying his face and eyes as if she were still trying to understand him. She moved her lips and said, in barely a whisper: "Thank you."

Erik smiled. While he caught his breath, he kept listening for sounds of any additional warriors and scanning the foliage for any signs of motion. He used his pocket heat sensing device to scan a wide area. There was no one else for quite some distance.

"Star man, you don't have to carry me. I can walk on my own." She tried standing on her wounded ankle but was still a little wobbly. He tried carrying her again but he had to stop after a short distance. The medicine was beginning to make her groggy, making her feel more and more like dead weight. He didn't feel he could make it out of the jungle, at least not now. He laid her back down on the ground.

"Why don't you rest?" he said. "You can use my pack for a pillow. I'll stand guard over you."

As the medication continued working, she no longer felt up to fighting it. "What's your name, Star man?"

"Erik."

"Good night, Erik."

He slid his pack under her head and watched the brown-skinned woman drift off to sleep. She was breathing heavily but he knew she would be feeling much better upon awakening. He looked around, observing the sights and sounds of the jungle. He remembered his last trip into the wilderness, the previous time he had tangled with Umni and her tribe. He took a needed rest and gulped some water from his canteen. He was soaked with perspiration. He planned to call Montoya again but wanted to rest first. He leaned his back against a fern tree, unaware of the sets of eyes watching him from above. A sky blue creature slid down the tree trunk. It was shaped like half an oval. Dozens of stubby, black legs protruded from beneath its hard shell. It secreted a strand that allowed it to lower itself, spider-like, onto the captain's shoulder. He finally noticed his stalker but it was too late. He tried to pull it off his shoulder but hundreds of tiny, sticky hairs on each leg held the nemesis in place. It was already sinking its deadly fangs into his skin. He cried out and slumped over.

Umni, who was lying nearby, opened one eye then closed it. Abruptly, she opened both eyes and was suddenly awake. She tried to rise to her feet and found she could now stand on the ankle with difficulty. Her eyes scoured the ground until she found a large stick. She limped over to Erik. She tore the creature off his shoulder. The animal hit the ground. She beat the attacker repeatedly with the stick, smashing through its hard shell. Within moments, the flattened creature was lifeless. A clear gel oozed from its body. She then turned her attention to Erik, who was lying on the ground. Retrieving a knife from her leg sheath, she cut open his shirt sleeve. His shoulder was already deep red and swollen. It was beginning to turn purple. The warrior made two v-shaped cuts in his shoulder. She began squeezing his shoulder and sucking on the cuts. She hated the bitter taste of the poison. She spat some out and went back to sucking the wounds. Erik was still partially conscious. His face was twisted in pain. Umni desperately continued her work. After several minutes, she noticed the star man's shoulder looked a little better. She went back to her task with determination. A few minutes later, she began to feel the jungle spinning around her. She collapsed to the ground.

Sometime later, the groggy Erik became vaguely aware of a sound. He gradually realized it was breathing. Labored breathing. Someone else's breathing. He opened his eyes a sliver. Umni was lying on the ground. Her chest slowly rose and fell as she struggled for air. Erik was breathing with similar difficulty. The sound of each breath resounded in his ears. He closed his eyes. Summoning all his strength, he said weakly: "Umni." Several seconds passed. He thought he heard her stir. "Umni," he repeated.

"Star man," barely a whisper.

"Y-you didn't have to…."

"It's okay," she wheezed. "You honored me" (Breath) "by sparing my life." (Breath) "I wanted" (Breath) "to save you."

"That venom" (Breath) "…how bad?" he asked, opening his eyes wider than before. She opened her eyes, too. They were only a couple feet apart, staring into one another's orbs.

"Fatal," she said somberly. (Breath) "Almost always" (Breath) "fatal. Sorry if I" (Breath) "if I did too little." (Breath) "I really" (Breath) "tried…." (Breath) "You're a" (Breath) "good man." (Breath) "…Deserve to live…" (Breath)

"Umni!" He reached for her hand and tried to grasp it. It was going limp.

"See you" (Breath) "in the afterlife," (Breath) "star man…." She closed her eyes and stopped breathing. The fatigued Erik closed his eyes and felt his life slipping away.

# 37.

A short while earlier, in another part of the jungle, several dozen warriors had charged forward, about to re-join the battle by waging a small counter attack. One fired an arrow toward Montoya. The arrow bounced off the force field. He was close enough to the edge of the battlefield that he was able to survey the progress. The warriors who had come out of the jungle continued advancing, firing but to no avail.

Montoya telepathed: "Erik! Where *are* you?"

"In the jungle."

"Can you get back to the battlefield?"

"Can't. I'm tending to…one of the wounded. I need *you* to take over the battle."

"Aye, sir."

Montoya telepathed to his crew and spoke on his comm link to the Al'aamans the following message: "This is Fred Montoya, second in command! Captain Houston is all right but is indisposed at the moment." He ordered some new battlefield tactics. He was becoming concerned that the small proportion of allied wounded was slowly mounting. Only a few of the wounds had been due to failure of the force field generators. The majority had resulted from people turning off their fields to make themselves more maneuverable in battle.

"Montoya again," he announced. "Do not, I repeat, do not under any circumstances turn off your force fields. We're going to win this battle but we want to make sure you get home safely."

Minj chimed in on the comm link. "This is Daj Minj to all personnel. You can actually use your force field as an offensive weapon. Just start running full force into the enemy. It's quite effective!"

Montoya watched as a number of people began to do what Daj had suggested. Many warriors succumbed to the attack. Some began to flee. Montoya retrieved his medical bag from the landing craft. Several of his counterparts, including a couple A'aalman doctors, were doing likewise. The Association doctor found a couple critically wounded people who appeared to have been poisoned. He determined there must have been something toxic on those arrowheads.

Gradually, the action began to dissipate as more of the braves fled before their enemies. Several small fires caused by the braves' flaming arrows were beginning to engulf parts of the field. A few pockets of braves remained and were still fighting. The rest had either been left behind as wounded or had fled. Montoya directed his troops via the comm link and they quickly put an end to the remaining resistance. Once the enemy troops were gone, Fred's crew used some fire fighting equipment to extinguish the blazes. Only a few Al'aamans and star people were still lying on the ground. But it appeared that, overall, the battle had been successful.

Montoya began working from one of the landing craft, which was serving as a makeshift hospital. Several attendants and he continued treating the allied wounded. Given the ferocity of the battle, the number of injured was still low. But some of the wounds were severe and a few were potentially fatal. After several hours, the doctor took a badly needed break.

Minj, who was still wearing his telepatch, thought: "It's been some time since we've picked up on any of Erik's thoughts."

Luci was still wearing her patch as well. Her eyes got big. "He's never come back! And I sense he's in some kind of trouble."

"We need to find him!" cried Minj. The two crew members were still wearing their anti-grav belts. They took off into the sky, following the homing signal from Erik's comm link.

A few minutes later, wearing anti-grav belts, they eased lower, and through a clearing in the jungle canopy, they were aghast at the sight that was moving up to meet them. Captain Houston was lying on the ground, not moving, as was a female warrior. Between them was some small light blue creature that was all smashed at one end and had a clear gel oozing from it. The captain's left arm and shoulder were purple and swollen, as was Umni's mouth and face.

Luci shrieked. "Is he...?"

"Hope not!" Minj cried. "Neither one appears to be breathing." They touched ground. Luci rapidly pulled two respirators from a first aid kit. Minj clamped an oxygen mask over the captain's face while Luci took care of the warrior. Within moments, each of the poison victims began to take shallow breaths. Their two rescuers sighed with relief.

"Montoya! We've found the captain and one of the female braves," Luci called over the comm link. "They're in bad shape."

They heard Montoya curse in their earpieces. "What's wrong with them?" the doctor asked.

"They appear to have fought off some venomous creature that got to one or both of them first," Daj said. "How soon can you get here to take a look at them?"

"Still looking after several of the worst injuries," the doctor replied. "I'll get to you as soon as I have everyone stabilized. Montoya out."

Luci looked at Daj. "It may be up to us to get them to Fred," she said.

Minj went back to the first aid kit. He produced two compresses and laid one on the captain's forehead and the other on the brave's. The swelling did not get any worse from that point.

"How do we move them?" Luci wondered aloud. The warrior woman was almost a foot taller than she and Daj was a slight man, nowhere near as brawny as the captain.

"We have to lay them on something," Daj said. "Let's look around here. And make sure your shield's on. We don't need to be attacked by some jungle creature, too."

Luci shook her head, wondering what had distracted Erik into turning off his shield. The duo quickly walked around, eyeing the jungle floor for anything that could help them build a stretcher. Then Minj came across one of the fern tree leaves. It was about five feet long by three feet wide. He picked up the giant leaf, bending it back and forth at the stem. It was strong, yet supple.

"Hey, look at this," Minj called. Luci looked over at him. "Let's gather as many of these as we can," he added. The two of them collected several of the giant leaves, carried them over to a nearby flat rock and laid the leaves cross ways atop one another, eventually forming a nest. They then picked up the captain, Minj at one end and Luci at the other, laboriously carrying him over to the nest and laying him in it. They then did the same thing with Umni. They set their anti-grav belts to automatically take them back to the former battlefield. Daj placed his arms under one end of the nests, Luci placed hers under the other and the two rescuers slowly rose into the air with their cargo.

When they eased to the ground a few minutes later, they spotted Montoya, who was now working outdoors treating one of the overflow wounded. The doctor rushed over to the crew members. He looked at the captain then at the warrior. He shook his head. "Wish we could have gotten to them sooner," he said quietly.

Meanwhile, a few miles away Chief Laura and a smaller than normal Circle of Honor sat around the fire. The chief remained silent as her eyes passed from brave to brave, surveying the damage. One of her top warriors had a broken arm. Another had a severely bruised face. A third had bandaged ribs. Even McTeague, her toughest warrior, had taken his lumps.

The chief's eyes stopped roving as she came upon an empty space. The one normally occupied by Umni Ott. She had almost single-handedly brought the battle to a halt through her bravery. Yet was she rumored to have gone over to the enemy? Others claim to have seen her die.

The chief thought of the battle that had ended just hours ago. Her people had fought bravely but had suffered miserably. The chief's stomach gnawed at her insides as she thought of the humiliation. The enemy had severely insulted the proud Batu. Instead of killing them outright they had merely wounded them, almost as if they had been toying with them. That's what bothered Chief Laura the most. If you're going to fight me, fight me to the death but don't make me a laughingstock.

The chief had already spoken with McTeague about plans to regroup. There would be another attack. Soon. Before the enemy had time to expect it. The Batu would hit hard. And fast. And totally surprise them with overwhelming numbers. They would show no mercy. Every tribe member beyond childhood would fight for the glory of the tribe.

The chief knew the enemy had advantages. They had their evil tech ways. They had the star men and their magic. But the chief was no longer intimidated. She held up her necklace, revealing the item at the end. The braves looked at the chief, spotted the item, smiled and nodded.

McTeague, overpowering intensity in his eyes, stood up and jammed his spear into the ground.

Chief Laura stood as well, followed by the circle of braves. "Long live the Batu!" she cried, jamming the butt of her spear into the dirt.

"Long live the Batu!" the warriors shouted at the top of their lungs.

"Long live the Batu!" the chief shouted even louder.

"Long live the Batu!" they cried with even more fervor.

"Down with the tech men!"

"Down with the tech men!"

"Down with the star men!"

"Down with the star men!"

Large groups of braves began to approach the sacred circle, joining in on the commotion. The chief soon had half the camp in an uproar. The rally continued until everyone was hoarse. The chief dismissed everyone to their tents.

McTeague stayed behind, helping the chief map out plans that would right the wrongs of the last battle.

The chief smiled as she looked down again at her necklace, which sported a shiny, coin-sized item that had been found after the battle. One of the star men's invisible shields. One of several such prizes.

# 38.

The chiefexec wore black. She was barely able to remain composed as she gave a eulogy at the state funeral to a live audience of thousands. A'laama had come to a standstill and all media were covering the event. Three allies had died in battle. One from severe burning. Two others from poisoning. The leader had wanted to avoid any deaths but knew it couldn't be helped. From the dais, she was pleased to spot Captain Houston in the crowd. She had been sobered to learn of his own brush with death. But that miracle worker, Montoya, had done it again. Over the past couple days, the captain had recovered. He looked thinner and his face was a little drawn. But at least he was alive.

Later that day, still clad in black, she sat at her massive desk. Her face was buried in her hands as she wept over the deceased. Heroes who had fought to protect A'laama.

"Captain Houston to see you," came Alisa's monotone voice.

"Send him in," sniffed the boss, dabbing her eyes with a couple antiseptic tissues. She had purposely not worn any makeup. Her eyes were red and swollen.

She arose from her desk as the captain, wearing a black dress uniform, walked over to her. She stood up and they hugged for a long moment. "So glad to see you," she whispered in his ear. "I was afraid we'd lost you."

"You almost did," he mumbled.

"Not to mention my babies."

He nodded.

She walked to a nearby overstuffed chair and took a seat. He eased into another chair beside her. Silence reigned for a few moments.

"So...the battle," she began. "Overall, a success?"

"Yes," he said quietly. "That tribe should leave you alone for a while."

"Good. Now who are those two people camping out on the back lawn?"

"One of them saved my life."

Zama frowned. "The same woman who tried to kill my baby girl?" she cried indignantly.

"Yes. But I believe she's had a change of heart."

She gripped the wooden chair arms hard with both hands until her knuckles looked ready to pop. "I don't buy it. And Omma keeps having nightmares about that woman and her knife. She'd be furious to know she's staying here."

"I've set a force field around those people. They can't hurt anyone. And that warrior did save my life. I saved her first. Long story. But she can't go back to her people. They'll kill her."

"What a bloodthirsty lot, " she spat. "And who's here with her?"

"Boyfriend. He'd heard we were trying to save his beau so he came to our camp and asked to stay with us while she recovered."

The chiefexec sighed and pushed her hair out of her eyes. "They can't stay here forever."

He lowered his gaze.

"But...I guess anyone who saved your life deserves a favor...."

He stayed with her a while longer then headed back to his suite. Once there, he entered his room, closed the door and made a remote, verbal entry into the ship's log. He recorded the need to again remind Regional HQ to increase the maintenance budget for older equipment like landing craft and force field generators. And some new hardware once in a while would be nice. They couldn't keep running these missions on a shoestring. People's live were at stake.

# 39.

The yacht was close to the middle of the vast, blue lake. The water was calm and reflected the overhead clouds like a mirror. Two leggy models wearing swimsuits were sitting on deck chairs, spraying handheld jets of cool water on their glistening skin. Two other ladies stood nearby, ready to serve more drinks and snacks to the master and his guests. The wiry-haired man gestured to Sylvia, who jogged over to his side. The brunette looked stunning in her white swimsuit. He noted how brown she was getting from the suns. Several shades darker just in the last couple weeks. She smiled at him, which highlighted the mole on the right side of her face.

He led her by the arm to a four-person, 3-D electronic game board where they faced off against another couple. They played for some time. The master and Sylvia racked up several consecutive wins.

"So, legislae, have you given any more thought to joining our coalition?" the kinky-haired host asked the opponent he had just defeated.

"I…believe I'm beginning to understand your position," the lawmaker replied.

"Excellent," the other man said, flashing a smile. "Let's go have a drink."

He led Sylvia to the shipboard bar, followed by the legislae and his date. They each ordered a glass of the finest vintage onboard and carried it back to their lounge chairs, where the two power brokers talked for some time.

Later, the yacht owner retrieved his over-sized video screen from the deck. He frowned as he read several of the latest online news reports. Noting his frustration, Sylvia offered to make him a drink. He shook his head.

He popped out of his chair, strolled over to the rail and gazed out onto the lake. It was a nice day to be on the water. Not as blistering hot as some days. The lake was dotted with several sail boats and, farther away, a couple fishing vessels. A seabird cried overhead. But, as always, the man was unable to relax. He paced around the perimeter of the boat, finally arriving back at his chair. He plopped down into it. His insides were still tearing at him.

He snapped his fingers and Sylvia brought him a drink. He eyeballed it then sniffed the bouquet. One of the blues from '88. An excellent year. Some of his best stock. He sipped on the drink then set it down on a small, round table. He motioned that he needed shade. One of the women set a zone of coolness.

He glanced at his arm implant, its red and blue lights dancing in their pre-set sequence that repeated approximately every 51 days. The device was a fake. He was the only man in A'laama that had a non-working implant so he did not appear on police tracking. People who owed him favors plus a few occasional monetary payments kept the law off his back.

He marveled that for generations the cops had been able to track every last citizen's whereabouts, yet the information had never been used for anything except monitoring incursions into that ridiculous Forbidden Zone. What wasted potential! Some leaders had been advocating terminating the Zone. But he had been its most vociferous proponent. His had been a losing battle…until those mysterious raids on the farm district had begun several months ago. Now people were no longer complacent; they were fearful. His organization had even hired some hunters to stage copycat raids to further alarm the public. He pressured the media to whip up hysteria in an effort to keep the Zone intact. Soon, when the time was right, he would pounce. Overnight, the government would not only track everyone's whereabouts but begin regulating their activities. The power would finally be put to good use. No one would so much as spit without him telling them to do so.

But one force stood in his way—that damnable Zama Elle. Not only had she flaunted the Zone by her overnight trip with that space invader (The wiry-haired man had incited the media to smear her character over that excursion. "Nothing happened," indeed!), but she had gone on the offense against the raiders. Now some A'laamans felt safer. More confident. Less open to the emergency measures he'd planned to propose....

He motioned for all the ladies to back away. He set up a sound block then placed a video screen call.

"Zama Elle has gone too far," he growled into the screen. "She wasn't elected to cater to space aliens. Or to lose A'laaman lives battling some primitive tribe."

The voice at other end agreed. "She's the wrong leader for our time."

The man on the yacht continued. "Society's changing. But it's a bad kind of change. This can't go on. We may soon need to teach Madame Exec a lesson."

"We'll keep it hot for her politically. What else do you have in mind?"

The wiry-haired man was silent for a moment. He gritted his teeth and was hyperventilating. He pulled a zen pill from his pocket and bit it. A bitter taste flooded his mouth. Within moments, waves of calm swept over him. Finally he growled in a low, deep voice: "It may be time to put an end to the Elle administration."

# 40.

Erik stood on the balcony of his suite as a yellowish orb with greyish markings hung in the sky.

"It's a lovely evening," said a melodic voice from behind him.

"It is," he agreed, turning to see Kelly. "Didn't hear you come in. What have you been doing?"

"Talking with Minj and Montoya. Glad to see you're all back. And that you've recovered so quickly."

He smiled. As always, he felt at ease around her.

She strolled onto the balcony and hugged him. The scent of her perfume filled his nostrils. They parted and she stood beside him. She joined him in gazing into the sky. "There's the moon," she said, pointing.

He nodded.

She continued: "The Woman in the Moon. Whoever would have thought that some mountains and craters would look like a human face from hundreds of thousands of miles away?"

He laughed.

She wrinkled her nose. "You can't see a woman's face? Look at the big, expressive eyes, the eyebrows...."

He chuckled. "On most planets, they call it the Man in the Moon."

"Well this is A'laama and we do things differently."

"Does the moon have a name like your suns do?"

She shook her head. "Maybe if we had more than one of them we'd name it but it's just 'the moon.'"

He smiled.

"Do you know why the moon has a face?" she asked.

He shook his head.

"God's looking down at...."

"Your God is female?"

"I didn't say that." She turned away from him and folded her arms. Several moments passed.

She still wasn't looking at him. "We worship the Creator who made everything you see," she said, sweeping her arms toward the skyful of stars, "and his Son, Jesus, our Everliving Savior. I take it you've heard of them?"

"I had that coming," he said quietly in his bass voice. "Of course I've heard of them. Our ship is over 60 percent Christian."

"As are we."

He thought a moment, recalling that the shadow at the temple when he'd first met her had been the image of a cross. He now recalled seeing crosses on other A'laaman buildings, including the hospital where the two officials had been taken the night the lander had crashed. He hadn't paid attention to the religious icons at the time but he now recalled them vividly. He sighed with relief, realizing the main reason he was beginning to feel so at home here. Some isolated space colonies had forgotten God.

She said: "By the way, our folklore says the face in the moon shows God smiling down on his people."

Erik was now the one smiling. "I'm sorry," he said. "I didn't mean to offend you."

She turned back toward him. "I missed you," she said, drawing closer until they were almost touching. A warmth crept over him, contrasting with the coolness of the night.

He swallowed. "Kelly, I...I'm glad to see you," he said, but his voice sounded tenuous.

They paused. Her eyes looked into his. He couldn't meet her gaze. "What's wrong?" she whispered.

"I'm glad you came. But I shouldn't…I really need to turn in. Feel free to stay as long as you'd like."

"Yes. Yes, of course. I know it's late," she said, stepping away. "I-I'll show myself out."

"Goodnight."

"'Night." He turned and walked back into the suite, heading to his room. She spent a long moment continuing to gaze at the moon, a tear forming in one eye. She sighed, walked back inside and left.

Erik, who was lying on his bunk, heard her walk out the door. He gritted his teeth. His fists clenched and unclenched. He knew he had hurt her and felt like a jourke. "Can't get involved," he told himself. "Got to focus on the mission. On helping these people. God, give me strength."

He waved his hand to turn on the wall video screen. He spent several minutes flipping stations then finally gave up, turned out the light and tried to sleep. But he kept thinking how good it had been to see Kelly again.

# 41.

"Lisa, thanks for agreeing to meet me here so late in the day," said Daj as they stood outside the Founders Museum.

"That's okay, Daj," Lisa said with a smile.

He froze a minute, thinking how much she looked even more eerily like Nanci when she smiled.

She continued: "But this is certainly an unusual place to meet. I've been to the museum before. Wait a minute. The lights are off. Isn't it already closed?"

"That doesn't matter," he said, holding up a magnetic key card.

"Daj, how…?"

"I have my own key," he said. "I've done a lot of research here."

"Wow," said Lisa. "The administration must really trust you." Lisa, as a member of the administration, wondered why she didn't have her own card.

He slid the card into the slot, causing the door to swing open. The two of them walked through the door and Daj flipped the main light switch.

"Lisa, I appreciate you spending the last couple evenings with me. I've really enjoyed your company. But before we get to know one another better, there's something I think you should know."

He began to explain about his failed marriage to Nanci and showed Lisa the same 3-D records he'd shown his friends a couple weeks earlier. Afterwards, she didn't say anything for a while. She just sat and stared. He began to feel uncomfortable.

Finally, she said: "Daj, I've enjoyed spending time with you, too. I just hope you're going out with me for the right reasons. I'm glad you let me know about you and Nanci Batami. And I'm fascinated that you were married to her. She's not only my ancestor but she's always been a hero of mine. But you've got to realize...I'm not Nanci."

"I know. Your resemblance to her is what first caught my attention. But I've enjoyed starting to know you. Your hobbies, your mannerisms. Nanci lookalike or no, I've enjoyed spending time with you."

Her countenance brightened. "I'm glad to hear you say that!"

"But...regarding Nanci, there's something I've been wondering...."

"You can put your mind at ease," she said. "I am definitely *not* your descendant. I'm not descended from Ami, the daughter you conceived with Nanci. I'm descended from a later daughter, Evva, whom Nanci conceived through her second husband, Ron Batami."

He smiled. "So there's no reason at all why we shouldn't continue spending time together."

"I'm willing to keep going if you are," she said.

They left the museum and walked down the sidewalk. After they had gone a couple blocks, he suddenly stopped. Walking toward them was another woman who looked just like Lisa!

He shook his head. "There seem to be *so many* women in this city who look like you...or like Nanci or..."

She laughed. "Of course. I'm sorry. A little while ago you were very open with me about Nanci. Now, I need to tell you something about me...."

They kept walking until they found a park bench. They sat down. She turned to him, took a deep breath and said: "I told you before I'm Nanci's descendant, which is true, but you see...I'm also one of many clones of Nanci that have been made over the centuries."

"You're a clone...? Of Nanci?"

"It's true. I'll start at the beginning. When our colony almost died out three hundred years ago their biggest focus was survival. The colonists used several means to achieve that end...multiple spouses, large families, artificial insemination and…once they were able to build the appropriate medical facilities, cloning. Our ancestors lost many technologies in their struggle to survive. But our people became experts in the reproductive sciences. We had to. Today, you see the results all around you. We've grown into a large, thriving city. Quite a feat for what started out as a small band of people who almost died out! So, cloning was fairly common the first couple generations. Today, it's still done to some degree, even though it's no longer a necessity. And sometimes clones were made of great leaders to honor them. When Nanci Batami passed away, some of her tissue was preserved for cloning purposes. Many clones were made…and still are made…of her. The same thing with the other Founders."

Daj interrupted: "But…I thought you were Nanci's descendant. If you're actually her clone, with 100% of her genetic material, then you're more like her *twin*."

She smiled. "I know it's a little confusing. Actually, I'm *both*. Yes, I'm a clone of her. But the woman I call my mother is actually Nanci's descendant. A blood descendant, *not* a clone. I was always curious about that, so I checked the records. My mom, who *is* Nanci's descendant, provided the womb in which I grew. She wanted a little girl but she wanted one who looked like Nanci, as way of honoring her distant ancestor. So in that sense, I'm both her clone *and* her descendant."

Daj shook his head in wonder. "Nanci's clone! Yet you're so different than she was. Different in a *good* way."

Lisa shrugged. "Even identical twins can have totally different personalities."

Daj looked down and chuckled nervously.

Lisa looked concerned. "If this is a little difficult for you, I'll understand."

"No…it's okay. I'm glad you told me this. But it doesn't change the fact that we enjoy one another's company. If you can accept *my* ties to Nanci, then I can accept *yours*."

She sighed with relief.

It was then that he noticed a blue tattoo on her wrist. It contained characters consisting of Al'aaman letters and numbers: 12167NB. His eyes grew large. She had been marked with a number, almost as if she were some sort of mass-produced machine part. She became very self-conscious as he stared at the number in silence.

Later that day, Erik arrived back at the suite. Minj was staring at the wall. "Hey, buddy. What's wrong?" asked the captain.

The crew member continued facing the wall. "How long before our mission here is finished?"

The skipper was taken aback. "Finished?" he asked in shock. "It may take a while. Are you anxious to leave here?"

The crew member didn't respond.

"But you just started seeing that lady. I thought things were going okay."

Daj lowered his head. "It's nothing she did. I just...just can't deal with their society. She's a clone. A clone of Nanci Batami. I don't have a problem with that. In fact, it's kinda special." He began to tell Erik all he had learned about A'laaman clones. By law, all clones were required to be numbered. And it wasn't handled discretely, such as a tattoo that could only be read by infrared or ultraviolet light. Instead, the numbering was obvious. Daj compared it to the ancient practice of branding cattle. The 12167NB on Lisa's wrist meant she was the 12,167th clone ever made of Nanci Batami. Some brands were even more intrusive than Lisa's. Some numbers appeared on a clone's forehead. Or in the middle of the face. Daj and Erik each recalled seeing a few examples.

He also told Erik about the customs governing clones. Some, such as clones of historic figures, were accorded great honor. But the typical clone didn't fare so well. They frequently suffered discrimination. Even some of the Al'aaman's language taught prejudice against clones, as in: "I'm the original but you're only a copy." Clones weren't allowed into some of the better restaurants. They were barred from many of the better paying professions. In some cases, they were mass-produced and speed-grown in a matter of months just to fill a specific job niche. Sometimes clones were made of famous video stars to serve as stand-ins and stunt doubles. In other cases, a father or mother might clone themselves for vanity's sake. In some cases, the clone was treated better than the natural children. In other cases they were treated worse. Some people grew tired of their clones and outright abandoned them. And, although it was illegal for clones to be made as a source of spare body parts, there was a black market....

Erik put his arm around his friend's shoulder. Finally, Daj continued: "You know how I've made a record of our entire stay on this planet, often using hidden cameras...."

He pulled a tiny, handheld device from his pocket. He clicked a button and a large, 3-D image of their old prison cell appeared. Outside stood the three guards, Lila, Lola and Leela. "Now, look at this," he continued. He zoomed in. A closeup of Lila's wrist revealed a tattoo that said: 1 of 3. "Here's the sad part: I've found they'll never be able to get better jobs because of being clones. They'll never be any more than prison guards. See why I'm so disgusted?"

The captain shook his head. "Each planet has its moral blind spots. Some cultures over the millennia have condoned slavery. At least Al'aama's not involved in full-scale genetic engineering like some of the places we've visited. And the A'laamans treasure life."

Daj nodded. "On some planets, abortion is common. But it's rare here."

"Besides, all those cloning issues aren't your lady friend's fault."

"She's a nice person. But...I just can't get all this out of my mind."

Erik again placed a hand on his friend's shoulder. "Maybe at some point, you'll be able to give things another try," he said.

Minj nodded.

# 42.

Umni was pacing in the grass. Her boyfriend, Bobby, was watching her. He stood a few inches taller than she. He was powerfully built and had black hair that fell to his shoulders.

This giant village felt so strange. They were living in the shadow of an enormous building. Behind the structure was a vast field of unnaturally short grass. It was almost as large as the distant field where the battle had taken place a week and a half earlier. The lawn contained just a few stands of fern trees, and they seemed to exist merely for shade, as well as to break up the otherwise uniform landscape. Umni and Bobby each had a tent. There was no jungle. There was no hunting. And, worst of all, there were no other tribes people. That was the part Umni missed most.

Their needs were provided. The star man had brought them a portable toilet. Members of the chief's staff brought the couple meals three times a day and they were provided daily with a metal drum of water for bathing and drinking and a large, movable screen for privacy. Umni wasn't used to eating so much and thought she was getting fat. They had free run of a large section of the lawn. She had even marked it off as a circle that went about 100 paces in any direction. Then they ran into an invisible wall. The couple had requested some dried tree branches. They had stayed busy whittling new bows and arrow sets and spears. They also practiced with these weapons to keep up their skills. Bobby was a gifted woodcarver, and over their first several days in the city, he made walking sticks for the chief who lived in the giant house, the star man and several of his crew members. They kept hoping to meet with the tribal chief, but so far she had not come out to see them.

At least once a day, the star man visited them, talking with them in their native tongue. One day, Umni was sitting under a fern tree talking with her beau.

"Our tribe may have disowned us," she said, "but our families are in Batu country. And all our friends, too. This is a *terrible* way to live. I wish the star man had just left me in that trap."

"Don't say that! If he had left you alone, you might have been stung by an unfoonaba, just like the star man, except there might have been no one to rescue you."

She sighed. Trying to get her mind off her misery, she reached into her animal-skin bag and pulled out some parchment, a quill pen and some ink. She began jotting some thoughts on the paper.

Finally, the star man arrived at about the usual time. She looked up from her work. "What are you doing?" he inquired.

"Writing," she replied. "I write poetry."

"What do you write about?"

"Nature, the jungle, the stars."

Erik held out his hand. She gave him the parchment. He sat under the tree with the couple, got out his cosmic translator and read her poem. "This is good," he said. "Do you have any more?"

She reached into the bag and handed him several pieces of parchment. He took time to read each one. "You have talent," he said.

"Thank you."

A few days later, Erik had finally convinced Zama that she needed to meet with the two warriors. That day, when the couple would normally be expecting the star man to show up alone, a lady accompanied him. Umni immediately recognized her as the chief of the tribe that had been hosting them. Her stomach tightened like a fist as she recalled tangling with the duo in the jungle.

Erik beckoned the couple forward. The chief had her arms crossed and looked stern. The two warriors waited respectfully for her to speak. There was a long silence that was finally broken by Umni stepping forward. "Chief, my boyfriend, Bobby, and I would like to thank you for providing sanctuary for us and for giving us food and shelter." They both bowed.

Zama Elle continued to stand there with folded arms.

Bobby spoke up. "Chief, I've carved this walking stick and would like to give it to you." He held out the stick. The woman did not make a move to accept it.

Finally, the chief spoke, pointing a trembling finger at Umni. "You held a knife to my girl's throat and threatened to slay her like an animal!" she cried.

The warrior swallowed hard and looked at the ground. "Yes, I did, Ma'am. And I'm very sorry...."

"And I'm sure you remember me!" Zama continued. "When I was stuck in that outdoor meat locker, you kept trying to run me through with your spear. And now I'm supposed to give you food and shelter?" She turned away.

For a long moment, Umni was speechless. Then she blurted out: "But, Chief, the star man showed me kindness, and I was poisoned by the unfoonaba and almost died and all that made me re-think some things, and I don't feel like I used to toward your people, and I'm *sorry*, Chief." A tear rolled down the warrior's face. Bobby put his arm around her.

The local chief turned back toward them but her face was like stone. The warrior got down on one knee and began to weep.

"She's no longer your enemy. She wants to be friends," Bobby said in his deep voice.

The sobbing woman nodded.

Zama softened a little. She extended her hands and helped the woman to her feet. She said in a low voice: "I understand you also saved Captain Erik's life."

"Yes, Ma'am." She sniffed.

"The captain has been a valuable resource for us. I...uh, we could not bear to lose him. I understand you almost lost your life to save the captain's. That was very unselfish. I commend you, Miss Ott."

"Thank you."

"Tell me the truth. In the months leading up to the battle, your people raided our gannao ranches a number of times and killed several of our people. Yet, prior to that, *years at a time* would go by without much of that happening. We didn't have much more than occasional hint that your people even existed. How do you explain that?"

"For many years, our tribe lived far away from the nearest of your herds," Bobby explained. "We live off the jungle. Over the years, our take from the hunts had gotten smaller and we had to hunt over a larger area. Finally, several moons ago we were forced to move our settlement to a more plentiful hunting area. Our tribe now lives less than half its former distance from your gannao supply."

Zama nodded. "And…now that you're settled in your new location, how much of the land between your village and our herds do you consider your tribe's hunting ground?"

"A-*all* of it," Umni said sheephishly.

The chiefexec frowned. "What's that in your hand?"

Umni glanced down at a handmade item bound in animal skin. She held it out to the tribal boss. "A book of poems I made for you."

"A what?" The other woman accepted the book and began to leaf through it. It contained pages of a substance that felt stiff to the touch. "What's this stuff?"

"Paper," Erik said. "That's what people wrote on before there were systems.

"How quaint."

A shout in Erik's ear caused him to jump. "What is it, Irv?" he cried.

"Captain! We've tracked hundreds of Batu to a site in the jungle near the farm district. They're planning to launch a surprise attack tomorrow morning."

"What's wrong?" asked Zama, touching his arm.

He put the comm link on speaker mode. "We're back at war!" snapped Erik.

Once Zama knew the details, she glowered at Umni. "So! Your people are about to attack us!"

"B-but, Chief, I knew nothing of this! I've been here with you since the last battle."

The chiefexec turned back toward the captain and bit her lip. "I'll video my police chief and we'll re-assemble as much of our fighting force as we can on such short notice. Last time, we tried to avoid killing. But they want to massacre innocent people. There are new orders for this battle. It's now shoot to kill."

"No!" cried Umni.

"My orders stand!"

"Got that, Irv?" said Erik.

"Aye, sir. Shoot to kill per order of Chiefexec Elle."

# 43.

Hundreds of Batu streamed out of the jungle and toward the farm district, shouting as they went. Some of the warriors began setting fires in the wild, overgrown fields that occupied the area between the jungle and the farms. The fighters had gotten within a hundred yards of the cultivated fields ahead and only had to run that distance then go down a small hill to reach their destination. Many of the braves froze as they saw hundreds of defenders running up the hill toward them!

"Force fields!" Erik ordered to everyone through the comm link. "Drop as many braves as you can!"

Chief Laura cursed the star man. The two groups quickly closed the distance between one another and joined battle. The Batu, still unnerved by the unexpected resistance, began to fall in large numbers. But some of the flame bearers were successfully setting areas of crops on fire. As the battle progressed, Chief Laura shouted orders to her troops. The braves began to regain their confidence. The Batu were carrying small, polished metal shields that caused the Al'aaman light beam weapons to reflect back toward them.

Some of the Al'aamans were carrying a defensive weapon that had been developed after the first battle. It was a tube-like device that shot balloons filled with flat, black paint. As the paint bombs hit warriors' metal shields they were no longer effective against the Al'aaman lasers. The defenders had their weapons set on high power and the beams cut through the shields.

Many warriors in the front line dropped to the ground while Erik's group continued to fire. The advancing warriors slowed enough to step over or around their fallen comrades then continued forward. Some of the Batu broke past all the resistance and advanced onto another farm, continuing to set fires as they went. They also began to torch all the buildings in sight.

"Captain Houston," one of the field commanders called urgently, "we've just discovered a group of farmers who disobeyed the chiefexec's evacuation orders. They insisted on staying here to defend their properties and those of their neighbors."

"Where are they? We'll get them shields," he shouted.

Too late. A small knot of armed farmers ran into the field and began firing on the invaders. A few of the braves fell. But the farmers were quickly riddled with arrows and spears. From a distance, Erik saw the massacre. At his direction, the landing craft took to the skies and began firing blasts at the enemy. Erik assessed the situation. The number of braves who had been injured or killed appeared to number several dozen, but at this rate, it would take some time to win the battle. A strategic blast occurred in the middle of the warrior contingent, bowling over a number of their troops and causing the remainder to scatter in all directions.

"Thanks for evening out the odds, Irv," Erik called into the comm link.

"Aye, Captain."

On Erik's orders, the transports again took to the skies, this time spraying firefighting chemicals on the sections of blazing fields and buildings. His small army had been able to hold most of the attackers at the second tier of farms. He called the Al'aaman police chief and urged him to keep trying to round up any additional troops. Once a sufficient number was available, Erik would dispatch the landing craft to pick them up.

Erik had his battle tacticians on the lookout for the Batu chief. One of them spotted her in the distance. A handful of allies fought their way to her. They opened fire on the chief and the circle of defenders that surrounded her. The shots were all to no avail. Chief Laura, McTeague and the other tribal leaders stood there, arms folded and laughed at their attackers.

Captain Houston stepped forward.

"You don't frighten me, star man," she bellowed. "Not even you can overpower these magic shields."

"No, but I can stop them from working," he replied. He pulled a handheld device from his pocket and twisted a knob. Several blue sparks flew through the air. The iridescence surrounding the chief and her party dissipated.

"Do you really think I wouldn't notice these devices were missing?" Houston laughed. "You walked right into my trap!"

The Batu leaders tried to run but the allies gunned them down. Chief Laura collapsed to the ground and breathed her last. Several of her contingent also fell. McTeague turned to run but came face to face with the chiefexec's daughter.

"Hey! You threatened to kill me!" Omma cried, training her weapon on him.

"No one hurts my little sis," cried Andy, raising his gun as well.

The tribal leader hesitated. His eyes shifted between sister and brother. Andy fired. McTeague had already picked up a discarded shield from the ground. The polished metal deflected the shot. Omma shot McTeague from a different angle, searing his arm.

He shouted. Fell. Rolled some distance. His left arm and shoulder were red and swelling. He struggled back to his feet and ran off toward the jungle. "After him!" Erik cried.

A knot of fighters tore after the wounded leader. He burst through the foliage and began hobbling along a path that wound between trees. In his haste, he brushed against a vine that dangled from a tree branch. The vine shivered to the top, knocking half a dozen unfoonaba onto the hapless man. Erik and his crew hurried onto the scene. McTeague was writhing on the ground, his face and arms already turning purple from the deadly toxin.

Erik shuddered at the thought of so many of the painful bites. He drew his gun and was about to shoot McTeague as an act of mercy but the man quit struggling. His body went limp. Erik re-holstered the gun and shook his head. He scrambled back to the battlefield.

At the far end of the field, several landing craft touched down. Streaming out of them were a couple hundred fighters. The additional troops were firing relentlessly on the Batu. Erik directed the reinforcements and soon the braves were caught in a vice-like maneuver between the original defenders and the fresh troops. Additional warriors began to drop to the ground. The remaining ranks, now much thinner, began to break through the enemy lines and retreat. The defenders chased the enemy back to the jungle.

"We'll need to keep a number of troops in the field for now," Erik called to his squad leaders. "It's a long way back to their home and it would be easy for those who aren't wounded to regroup and attack again!"

A short while later, he noted that the battle was winding down around her while fires smoldered in the distance and dozens, perhaps hundreds, of people, mostly Batu, lay on the ground.

Omma was crying on her brother's shoulder as she sobbed: "I-I really didn't mean to *kill* anybody!"

"I know, sis, I know," he sighed.

# 44.

 

"Eleven farmers' lives lost, several more of our people killed, astronomical property damage!" exclaimed Lil Nemms. "How do you account for this loss, Chiefexec Elle?"

"I told you it couldn't be helped!" she replied. "In fact, we preempted a surprise attack *before it took place.* Otherwise, our losses would have been much greater. Our people and our allies did everything they possibly could…."

"But was all this violence necessary?" interrupted Harald Filb. "Wasn't there *some other way* to stop these scoundrels?"

"No, there wasn't!" Zama cried. "In fact, we were far too easy on the enemy in the last battle and I think that created the conditions for their counter-attack. They're a stubborn tribe."

"Well, I say we should just wipe out the whole lot of them out!" said Ana Fulton, the new science director. "It wouldn't take too much work to set up a solar energy collector near their village, turn it on them and get it to reflect heat that would burn them all up! Or, we could set up a giant mirror to focus the suns' rays on their village. Since they like fire so much...."

The chiefexec vigorously shook her head, unnerved by all the extreme viewpoints. "Look, there's already been too great a loss of life on both sides," she responded. "The last body count I heard from the field was over 100 for the Batu, and still climbing."

"All this has been so senseless!" cried Lill Nemms. "None of this would have happened if we hadn't attacked *them* in the first place!"

"We *had* to do something," the chiefexec insisted. "The Batu had killed several of our people. They'd brought A'laama's expansion to a stop... I've kept the best interests of our people in mind throughout this trying time. So, I'm going to the legislature to request funding for an ongoing security force for the foreseeable future, heavy electronic surveillance of the northern rim of the farm district, fortified watch towers...."

"We don't have that kind of money," said budget director Marla Stockholm. "Are you going to raise taxes?"

"And where do you plan the get the *people* for this security force?" asked the exec's new security chief. "We keep tying up hundreds of police officers."

Added Nemms: "And if you think *we're* being hard to deal with, wait until you meet with the legislature. They want a full-scale hearing!"

By the time she left the meeting, Zama's head felt like it was splitting. She strode back to her office to catch up on some online reports. Chief of Staff Alisa Conway was still at work. Her video screen was on, tuned in to a newscast showing live coverage of a protest going on in front of the exec mansion. Hundreds of people were marching, most with individualized holographic messages over their heads. Some signs called their leader a murderer. The broadcast switched stories and began discussing the day's battle in a negative light. The reporter also made innuendos about the star people and their involvement.

Alisa noted her boss standing nearby, arms folded as she glared at the screen. She shook her head and said: "Madame Exec, with all due respect, that star captain is in the thick of it again. Trouble seems to follow him."

The chiefexec bit her lip. She turned around and faced her chief of staff. "Yes, and I like that about him!" she responded emphatically. With a flip of her shoulder-length hair, she turned her back on her chief of staff, walked into her office and slammed the door.

# 45.

"Omma's missing!" the frantic chiefexec cried to her son.

"What?" shouted Andy.

"She told me she was going for a walk on the grounds. That was several *hours* ago. She seemed so upset. I've got my security detail scouring the city looking for her."

He slammed his fist into his hand. His mother jerked back. His eyes dropped to the floor. He was instantly ashamed at having startled her when she was upset. He walked over to his mother and put his arm around her shoulder. He looked into her eyes. "Don't worry, Mom," he promised. "I'll bring her home."

Andy went to his room and sat on the bed, running his hand through his bushy hair. He knew exactly where Omma would go when she was happy. But where would she go if she were deeply upset? He donned a pair of faded pants and a pullover shirt. Veins stood out on his prominent biceps. He grabbed the ener pistol he had recently used in battle, shoving it into his pocket. He hurried out his door, taking the shortest route out of the suite and out of the mansion. Practically running away from the grounds, he entered downtown. He blended into the rush of pedestrian traffic on the sidewalk. Andy dodged around slower-moving people and picked up speed. After a few blocks, the crowds began to thin. He started to run. His legs were pounding quickly and he began breathing rapidly. His lungs began to burn. He crossed the government district and entered the uptown area. The scenery changed to one of smaller buildings, many in various states of disrepair. He passed a vacant lot. A large mongrel walking down the street growled at him as he rushed by. Two seedy-looking men on a corner were engaging in a dubious business deal. Andy passed a cheap hotel. A woman in a tight outfit stood in the doorway, hand on hip. She called out to him. Darting past, he ignored her. Spying a small bar, he ducked inside. He quickly surveyed the darkened interior as his eyes adjusted to the dim light. He turned and headed back outside. He went to a second such club. Then a third.

Meanwhile, Omma sat on a stool in the dark pub, oblivious to her surroundings. She wasn't distracted by the noise of conversation or by the blaring video wall that had been running continual coverage of the battle that had taken place earlier that day. She was looking down at the floor. Her hair was falling into her face, which was smeared with tears. She felt as if she had been sitting there for days but felt no better than when she had come in. She had the bartender pour her another shot of gold-colored intoxicant and drained the glass in a single gulp. The liquid burned as it moved down her throat. She felt the warmth radiating out to her stomach then to her extremities, but the warmth didn't make her feel any better. Her senses dulled, she gradually realized a hand was on her shoulder.

"Hey, it's me!" She looked up and tried to focus on the blurred face in front of her.

"Hel-lo, brother!" she said, laughing giddily.

"Sis, we've been worried. I've been looking everywhere for you. Do you have any idea how late it is?"

"Shtop it. You shound like Mom," she moaned, slurring her speech.

"Well, this club doesn't look like the safest place and you're in a bad part of town."

"I-I can take care of myself. Maybe *too* well."

"I thought that if you wanted to cheer yourself up, you'd go jump dancing."

Omma continued to look at the floor. "Jumping is for people who are happy."

"Are you…all right?"

"No. No, I'm not all right. I *killed three people* today. Three people. I did it to defend our people, so more of them wouldn't have to die. But I didn't want to *kill* anyone…. One of them even looked younger than me. She couldn't have been more than sixteen. She had these big, innocent eyes. She kept trying to fire arrows at me. And it scared me so I…I…."

"Sis, listen to me. I killed that many people or more today. I'm not happy about it, either." He paused, swallowing hard before continuing. "Some people would consider you a hero."

"Don't feel like a hero."

"I'll stay here and have one drink with you. Just one. Then we have to leave, okay?"

"You're on, brother."

Andy bought a round. The two of them tossed back the intoxicant. He almost choked. He was normally the non-drinker in the family. The two of them sat there for several minutes without saying a word. Finally, he said: "Let's go, Om." He helped her to her feet and held onto her as she struggled to walk.

As they drew close to the door, two rough-looking men got up from bar stools and blocked their path. "You can leave, bud, but the little lady stays with us," the taller of the two snarled, flashing a grin that included a broken front tooth.

Andy felt fire in his stomach. Flexing his powerful arm muscles, he walked over to the speaker, almost standing on the other man's shoes. He pushed his face in close to the threatening man. He pulled out the weapon. "I've already killed several people today," he growled. "You don't want to make me mad."

The bartender, a man even larger than Andy, hurried over to the fracas. "I don't want any trouble," he said loudly.

"We were just leaving," Andy replied. "Make sure these two goons don't follow us."

The ruffians stepped away while he helped his sister out the door. The light of the two-sun night hurt their eyes. Fortunately, a train was due shortly and it would be just a two-minute ride back to the mansion.

# 46.

Minj was glad the battle had ended and that he was now back in the city. After freshening up, he took the maglev to the Ministry of Agriculture. He ran up the long, moving stairs that transported people from the sidewalk to the entrance of the stately building. He rushed inside and used an electronic directory to find a specific office. The vertilift took him to the proper floor. He sprinted down the hall and came to a large, glass-encased suite. A familiar name was painted in large, gold letters on the exterior wall. He tried to enter the door but there were no knobs. "Identification, please!" demanded the automated door.

"I need to see the undersecretary," he said.

"Identification, please," the door repeated, this time firmer.

The only Al'aaman ID Minj had was the government-issued card that had been given to all of Erik's senior crew members. He pulled it from his wallet and held it up toward the door.

"Mr. Dodge Minj, you are not authorized to enter this office. You will leave here at once," the door insisted.

"I need to see the undersecretary," he repeated.

A one-wheeled security bot zipped up the hallway, one of it hands grabbing Minj's arm. The hand felt soft and warm, like human flesh. But the voice was steely cold.

"Sir, you've been asked to leave the premises," the robot insisted. By now, a small crowd was gathering on the other side of the glass wall. A short, dark-haired woman came out of an inner office to find out what was happening. The woman waved her hand, causing a glass door to slide open. "Let him go," said the undersecretary of agriculture. "He means no harm."

"As you wish, Miss Undersecretary." The guard retreated.

The woman waved the gaggle of onlookers away. They reluctantly dispersed. Lisa looked Daj in the eye. "So…Mr. Minj. It's been a while."

"Yes, it has," said Daj, sheepishly.

"I'm…glad to see you're back from fighting the aborigines. You look well."

"Thank you. I'm…glad to have come back intact. A few of my friends were wounded."

She frowned.

"Lisa, you look good, too. I've…missed you."

"That took a long time."

"That's not true. I've missed you ever since…ever since that last time we saw one another. I haven't been able to stop thinking about you. That's why I rushed over here as soon as I got back from battle."

She stared straight ahead for a moment as she painfully recalled their last moments together. "So…*this* doesn't bother you now?" she asked, flashing the clone ID number on her wrist.

"Not anymore."

"Daj, it really hurt that you left me so suddenly that day. I never heard from you again. And …I can't change who I am.."

"I know. Lisa, I'm sorry to have hurt you. I haven't been the same since. Is there any chance we can…start over?"

"I don't know…."

He stared at the floor. He looked back up, his face brightening a little. "I noticed a café in the lobby…."

"I'm not hungry."

He turned to leave, stepped out the door and began to shuffle down the hall. "Hey!" she called after him. He turned around. "You still have my video code?"

Daj smiled. "I've got it memorized."

"My screen hasn't been working lately and I might need you to call me once or twice this evening to test it."

"What's a good time to call, Miss Undersecretary?"

"I should be done with all my meetings by seven."

"I believe I can fit in a quick call."

"Seven o'clock prompt, Mr. Minj. Don't keep me waiting."

Zama and Kelly had kept the secret of Minj's ancient history with Nanci Batami. They had managed to keep the media from learning of the romance between Daj and Lisa by having the couple meet in out of the way places, sometimes even wearing disguises. The top leader's official security force had been working plain clothes, handling the logistics.

But Zama kept feeling there was something in her own family background she needed to re-visit. Late one evening, during some private time in her sanctum, she pulled up her personal data file, something she hadn't viewed in years.

It began with the heading:

Elle, Zama Faye
CHIEFEXEC OF THE PLANET (Followed by the official seal of the chiefexec)
Born: 15/34/255
Age: 44
Primary Tribe: Paol

Her screen automatically took a quick med scan of her, projecting the results into mid-air as a six inch high, slowly rotating, 3-D schematic of her body. She always hated looking at the visual. No wonder she did this so infrequently. The figure dissolved into data about her height, weight and several vital signs. At least her blood pressure appeared under control.

She punched some tabs to get to Family History. The Summary Page listed extensive data that had somehow survived the crash of the starship *Endurance*, listing a dozen different star systems where various of her forebears had lived. She clicked on one of the names. A color, 3-D map filled in the air, highlighting A'laama, its two suns and a distant orb some sixteen light years away that was the home star to some of her ancestors. Most of the star names meant nothing to her, yet she felt blessed to have such an extensive pedigree. The large majority of A'laamans only had enough information to trace their ancestry back to the founding of the planet and perhaps a few generations further based on oral traditions.

Further down the page were names of several nation states on Ancient Earth where her ancestors had originated. She clicked on one of the country names. A 3-D of a blue and white planet, apparently Earth, appeared. How much it looked like A'laama. A certain portion of one of the land masses lit up. She touched one of the other nation names. The different piece of geography was highlighted. She touched other names, eventually learning her ancestors had come from a total of three different land masses on that fabled world. But otherwise, the text and even the visuals were meaningless to her. Perhaps some day she'd show that historian, Minj, and ask him to interpret the data.

Progressing past the summary, she pulled up the family tree. She accessed information on her parents then began tracing her father's line through time. She stopped four generations back.

Since the last battle with the Batu, the chiefexec had gradually been warming up to Umni. She had even hosted the warrior and her boyfriend for dinner in the mansion. Umni had told Zama why the two of them looked so much alike, a resemblance Zama had finally begun to notice. They'd had the same great-great grandmother. Umni's branch of the family had left A'laama sometime prior to the creation of the Forbidden Zone. They had migrated into the wilderness and eventually joined the Batu tribe.

Zama pressed a tab to access a 3-D photoid of their common ancestor. As the image of the woman rotated, Zama could, indeed, see the forbear carried some key physical features Zama had in common with her distant cousin.

Finally, she came to the part of her family tree she had dimly remembered. Yes, it was true! Zama almost fell out of her chair. This gave her a whole new perspective on things. Now she had one more secret to keep.

# 47.

"Chiefexec Elle is wrong! Dead wrong!" thundered Legislae Nathaniel Tuu. "She launched a premeditated attack on the Batu tribe, which resulted in them counterattacking less than two weeks later. More than twenty of our people died in the second attack. Dozens are wounded and we *still* may not have solved our problem. This is some of the worst mass violence we've seen. And it's all the chiefexec's fault. She's overstepped her authority. We should officially censure her!" Several legislaes murmured their approval.

"And not only that," Tuu shouted, "I'm calling for a no confidence vote to remove her from office!"

A number of legislaes noisily voiced their approval while others booed and attempted to shout down the dissidents

"I disagree!" cried a female voice. Legislae Monja Norris was on her feet.

"Order! Order!" shouted the female parliamentarian, striking an air gong to focus the group's attention. Once the notes stopped reverberating, the official continued: "If the esteemed legislae from Ferntreetown is finished, Legislae Norris can take the floor."

"I'm not yet ready to yield the floor and still want to call for a censure vote," Tuu continued.

"Why? What has Chiefexec Elle done except to defend our people?" cried Norris. "She's tried to ensure our safety and was even willing to send her own son and daughter into battle. That's more than any of us have done!"

"It figures you'd stick up for her, just like you always do!" Tuu shouted.

The parliamentarian rang the gong again, louder this time. "We will have order! One more outburst and I'll clear the floor and cite both of you with contempt." Silence again reigned in the chamber. "All right, Legislae Tuu, the floor is yours."

"I make a motion to censure the chiefexec."

"I second that motion!" called a female legislae from the back of the room.

The parliamentarian said: "Legislaes, each of you may vote electronically using your video screens." She waited a few minutes while the officials voted. "OK, here's tally. And…the motion is defeated 42-53 with two absent and three abstaining." Legislae Tuu, grimacing, left the floor to take his seat

Immediately after the official announced the results, the chiefexec strode into the chamber, just in time for a scheduled speech. Electricity was in the air as more than half of the legislaes stood up to show support. She gracefully, purposely descended the manual stairs that led to the podium. Her eyes met those of many of the legislators as she smiled at some, nodded at others, even some of those who had opposed her moments earlier. She smiled broadly at Legislae Norris then at Legislae Clayton. But her spine turned to ice as she locked eyes with Tuu. They'd had a long history, none of it pleasant. He was the one official she actually feared.

Despite her brief staring match, she strode confidently to the dais. Before starting to speak, she punched a button on her video screen that projected a giant, 3-D image of her head and shoulders into the air, better allowing the chamber to see and hear her.

"I object to the chiefexec enhancing her speech!" cried Tuu. Several legislaes shouted him down.

"Overruled!" snapped the parliamentarian. "It's common practice. You use it in your own speeches. Sit down, legislae."

Non-plussed, the chiefexec launched into her speech. She thanked the group for their support and passionately laid out her case for drastic measures to defend the northern rim. Tuu and a few of his colleagues hammered the her with questions and protests but they now seemed less persuasive in light of the failed censure vote.

By the time she left the legislature, Zama Elle was beaming. The legislaes had approved by a narrow margin an appropriation for the materials needed to build the watch towers and install the electronic surveillance equipment at a number of different locations. Within a few days, the funds had been transferred to an account earmarked for the project. The defense committee looked into the costs and found that the appropriation would, indeed, cover the cost of materials but not the labor. Dipping into her personal fortune as an industrial heiress, she hired a number of cybots to do the construction. Her action was perfectly legal according to Al'aaman law. The work began a few days later. At each of two dozen locations spaced a couple miles apart, a small crew of men and women housed in temporary, air conditioned sheds were lying down while technicians attached hundreds of sensors that would allow the crew members' brains, eyes, nerves and muscles to direct the construction equipment and robots that were outdoors. Finally, the equipment started into motion. Each tower was built on a wide metal base that rested on tall tractor treads. A motor in the base would allow each tower to be moved in its entirety as A'laama continued to gradually expand. The cybots worked efficiently, greatly multiplying the amount of work a human-only crew could accomplish with power tools. By late in the day, all the towers were completed. Technicians then installed and tested the surveillance equipment.

The next morning, the chiefexec was on hand to officially open Tower # 1, which directly overlooked the recent battlefield. Zama felt a sense of accomplishment as she rode to the vertilift up the tower, accompanied by several other officials and defense force leaders. At the top of the tower, several stories above the ground, she stepped into the sealed, air conditioned lookout area where volunteers stood at attention. While everyone waited, she threw the master switch activating the equipment. The officials and volunteers applauded while media people recorded the event. The chiefexec looked out the front plexiglass windows and saw the field below and jungle stretching miles into the distance. Technicians showed her how to use the power binocs, infrared, radar and other types of sensing devices. There were several gun ports from which sharpshooters could fire high-powered laser rifles. Technicians who were in video screen contact with groups at the other twenty-three towers told Zama they were all "a go" as well. The leader sighed happily, reveling in the feeling that Al'aama was now much safer. The media heavily publicized the opening of the watch towers, giving her a positive bounce politically.

—

# III: "Into Your Hands..."

# 48.

A'laama was in a dismal mood. The media continued to question the chiefexec's fitness to lead, as did some of the more outspoken administration members. Some called for her to resign. Several opinion polls gave her unfavorable ratings. The public was deeply divided on many issues: whether the city should have imprisoned the warriors who had raided gannao farms several months earlier, whether fighting the Batu had done more harm than good, whether everyone would have been better off without the arrival of the star people. There was a palpable feeling of anxiety and frustration over the citizens finding out that the Non-techs existed after all and that they represented a violent threat. Some vocal groups of citizens were interviewed by the media, calling for the "good old days" when the city *was* the whole world, no one had every heard of a gannao raid and everyone had felt secure. Every day there were protests in front of the fence that surrounded the mansion. Sometimes there were competing protest rallies at the same time. Some of the protests got ugly and a number of people were arrested. The chiefexec shook her head as the situation seemed to daily grow worse.

Finally, she decided what to do about all the unrest. She was going to speak with her people, heart to heart. This was going to be a bigger speech than what she used to call her annual State of the Planet address. This needed to be her most effective speech ever.

When she was in the middle of the second draft, a disembodied female voice announced: "Madame Exec, some important research only for you." Intrigued, she used her video screen to access the message. It was from one of her senior speech researchers. The message included an attachment purported to be centuries old. The chiefexec read the doc then re-read it. The researcher had included other docs to corroborate the first one. The information all agreed. Now the chiefexec knew more about early Al'aama as well as the *real* origin of the Batu.

Two days later, Zama and Erik were in the landing craft, flying over an area east of the farm district. She was holding a video screen several times the size of the one she normally used and was reading from the old-time doc. It included a map. "It should just be a couple more miles," she said. Erik slowed the craft a little. A few moments later, he cried: "Look. To the right!"

She gasped. Hundreds of feet below were several structures, buildings where there should have been none in a place assumed to be wilderness. He landed the craft in the overgrown brush a dozen yards from the nearest building. The structures were eight miles past the farm district, right where the doc had said they would be. He helped her out of the vehicle. The chiefexec and he strode over to one of the buildings. She stepped boldly into the large wood and stone edifice. Erik activated a pocket light globe that lit the building interior like a two sun day. Zama slipped her free hand into his and they wandered through the unfurnished structure. A thick layer of dust coated everything. She stopped occasionally and put the screen on Record mode so it would make a 3-D video of the site. They eventually came to a wall that was missing an uneven section of boards, letting in a flood of blinding sunlight. Perhaps someone over the years had hauled off some the boards for firewood.

The duo finally went back outside and headed for another building. The structures included what appeared to be a town hall, a public square with a gazebo, some booths that may have been intended as open air market kiosks and several single family homes. One building contained a metal box. Upon sensing the visitors' presence, it sprang to life, launching into a grade-school level lecture about A'laama's early history. Zama shook her head.

The chiefexec estimated it would have taken several decades before

Al'aama had expanded far enough to have found this ghost town by accident. She put the screen back on Record and panned the scene, zooming in on some of the individual buildings. She laughed as she realized that, in her upcoming speech, she was going to break an exclusive story that was unknown to any of the media. Again looking more serious, she glanced down at the screen, which still displayed the old doc and shook her head.

"This place is a long way from our flight path to the Batu settlement, so we've never before flown over this area," Erik said, interrupting her thoughts. "Did you know this was here?"

"No," she admitted. "And I can guarantee virtually no one else knows about it, either. Except for a few obscure historians who have speculated about it for years. They're the ones who confirmed the doc is legitimate."

"Did you notice anything unusual about some of the buildings?"

"Yes," Zama noted. "A few of them weren't quite finished, almost as if the builders ran out of materials or money."

Erik nodded. "Finding this town is certainly going to upset the status quo."

"That seems to be all I do these days," she sighed.

Over the next several days, the chiefexec worked exceptionally long hours. One evening, she was in her office past nine. Alisa had already gone home.

Zama's arm implant was connected electronically to her video screen and her eyes were closed. The machine was reading her thoughts, creating in mid-air a 3-D scene at her direction. It was a garden setting. Various plants and trees began to fill in with detail. Colors began to appear. The cries of birds sounded. The sweet perfumes of enormous wildflowers began to surround her. Her face muscles started to lose some of their tenseness. She smiled. Wait! Something was wrong!

Snapping back to reality, she jumped in her seat and gasped. Startled, she looked up. Erik was standing in front of her.

"Nice work," he commented, eyeing her creation.

"You scared me!" she cried.

"You all right?" he asked with concern.

"Yeah. Yeah…trying to relax. I'll just save this and finish it later." The 3-D artwork disappeared. She looked up at him, dark circles under her eyes.

She stood up but suddenly felt dizzy. She held her head and swayed, almost losing her balance. Erik grabbed her shoulders and steadied her. He eased her back into her seat.

"Go home and get some rest," he said.

She held her head again. She opened her eyes, which focused sharply on him. "Don't order me around."

He turned to leave.

"Will you join me for dinner?" she called after him.

He turned back toward her. "Where we going?"

"Nowhere. Come back in an hour."

He returned forty-five minutes later. She looked up from a budget spreadsheet that was in mid-air at her eye level. "Thought you'd never get here. I'm starved." She arose from her chair and stepped over to the far wall. She turned back, looking at him with mischievous eyes. She put her finger to her lips. She waved her hand and a section of wall slid up. She stepped through the doorway and beckoned him to enter.

He followed her, gazing around at the lair. She touched a wall panel, closing the doorway. "Welcome to my private world," she said.

"To what do I owe the honor?"

"I trust you."

They each took a seat at the small, round table. She waved her hand and a 3-D, visual menu appeared, complete with the aroma of each dish. She spotted a meal she liked and touched its hologram. Erik chose one as well. Within moments, the loaded plates and two beverages appeared from within the table. He laughed.

He pulled four small cylinders out of his pocket, handing two to her.

She wrinkled her face. "And these are...?"

"Energy utensils." He twisted one of the cylinders and a blue beam emerged. He grabbed the handle and used the blade to cut his entree into bite-sized pieces. He twisted the other cylinder and it produced a yellow beam. He directed the amber light to a morsel of food, which rose from the plate. Her jaw dropped and she knocked her utensils to the floor. He used the beam to direct the portion of food to his mouth.

She laughed. "You people are insane! You have ships that fly though space, landing craft that fly through the air, belts that let you fly like a bird and now you make your food fly?"

He chuckled. He ate a couple additional mouthfuls then encouraged her to try. She turned on the energy knife but it seemed to pull her along. She jammed it into the table, taking out a chunk of wood with a loud buzz. He put his hand over his face and shook his head. She tried using the levitation tool, raising a small piece of food a few inches then promptly dropped it onto her lap. Her face turning red, she grabbed a cloth napkin and began dabbing the stain. "Your technology's hard!" she said.

248

"Like learning to use a personal video screen?" He walked over and gently began guiding her in using the food tools. She started to do better and they began to converse.

She arose from her chair, took his hand and led him to the private chapel. "Will you pray with me?" she asked.

"I'd love to."

They crowded together on the kneeler built for one. He asked God to bless and protect Zama and her people from both known and unknown threats. He asked the Lord to give her a restful mind and the ability to again have some fun. She blushed as he thanked God for her dedication, good leadership and devotion to her kids.

She thanked the deity for sending Erik and for all the blessings that had come since his people's arrival. She confessed the bad attitude she'd had when the star people had first arrived. She asked God for forgiveness and squeezed Erik's hand. He gripped hers as well.

They concluded their prayers and he helped her to her feet. They lightly embraced. The one-time strangers with two different lives had never felt closer. He gave her a set of the power utensils to keep. They departed her secret refuge and he walked her back to her living quarters.

But in succeeding days, she became equally absorbed in work and could no longer be budged from her desk. One evening, Andy and Omma stormed into the office.

"Mom," Omma began.

"You're going out tonight," Andy said.

"I…what? No! I can't…."

Erik walked into the room. She eyed him suspiciously, asking: "Did you put them up to this?"

He raised his hands, palms up in denial. "Their idea," he insisted.

She sat back down at her desk. "I have work to do."

"You like to dance and you're good at it…" Erik said.

"I…uh…."

"C'mon. Let's walk, Mom," daughter urged.

Zama eased up from her chair. She set the electron lock on her office and the group hurried down a blur of hallways until they reached their private retreat. Erik passed a handheld device over the area to check for audio and video bugs.

"Here's the plan," Omma continued. "You know that new clone you use on occasion?"

"Yes," Zama replied.

"Well, she's shortly going to leave here with Andy and me to attend a play. Then we'll have dinner. The security people will think you're going out for a nice evening with your kids."

"The G men have been getting more sophisticated lately, so we've having to go to greater lengths to fool them," Andy laughed.

"While we're out, you'll be elsewhere with the captain," said Omma,.

"Here. Put this on your face," Erik said, holding a brown dot in his hand.

"What's that?" Zama asked.

"It's a fake mole."

"And I'm going to paint your face," said Omma.

"Just a touch of color is fine, honey."

"Mom, you don't get it. I'm going to paint your face." She picked up a makeup pencil and began drawing an outline.

"Guess I need to be in disguise if I'm traveling without security," she replied. She pulled a small case from her pocket, put a finger on a plastic lens and stuck the digit into her eye. She repeated the gesture with the other eye. "There. Now I've got different retinal patterns. So, who am I tonight?" she asked as her daughter brushed on makeup.

Erik held out a card and looked at it. "We've created new identities. You're Roxie and I'm Sean."

"This is outrageous!"

Omma ran a wand through her mother's hair, creating blonde streaks.

Zama pulled on transparent plastic gloves that immediately molded to her own skin. Gloves with a different set of fingerprints. She pulled a necklace from her bag and used a fingernail to adjust tiny controls. She fastened the jewelry around the base of her neck. "How do I sound?" she asked.

Erik wrinkled his brow. "That voice is too high for you," he replied.

She worked the mini-dials again. "How about now?" The sound was more sultry.

He laughed. "Are you flirting with me?"

She chuckled. "No, I'm not."

Omma blushed.

Zama left the vocal modulator on that setting.

Andy laid a bag at his mother's feet. "Here's your outfit."

Zama pulled a blouse out of the bag. It was a psychedelic print. Parts of the shirt were silver and had a mirror finish. The bag also contained some hip-hugging pants and a belt composed of hundreds of wooden beads. She shook her head in disgust.

"These clothes are trendy," said Omma. "All the old clubbers wear them."

"A metfab shirt? I'll sweat like a y'urranga."

Daughter clucked her tongue. "Mother! It's lined and has full AC."

Erik chuckled. Zama cast him a sidelong glance. "Don't you have something to do?"

Andy pointed him toward another room. He changed into his outfit for the evening: slacks, a snug-fitting shirt and a dark, boagoa skin jacket. The jacket also had built-in air. When he re-entered the room, Zama was now wearing her outfit, even the shiny blouse. She wore red lipstick. Omma had painted a blue, five-pointed star on the left side of her mother's face, with her eye at the center of the star. She had outlined the star in silver. Daughter proudly handed Mom a video screen, for once being used as a mirror.

"I look hideous!" she cried.

"You'll blend right in," Omma insisted.

"With who? The clowns?"

Erik eyed his date. "I actually like it," he said.

"Then, I guess I can live with it. And these pants make me look thin," she added, looking into a full-length mirror.

"Looking good, Roxie," Erik agreed.

"Sean, you do look good in that outfit," said Roxie.

"No star man clothes, Captain. You look like an Al'aaman," Omma agreed. "How about if I paint your face?"

"I'll pass."

Andy stood over Sean and glared at him. "Have her home by ten," he growled. He continued to glower for several seconds before breaking into a mischievous grin.

"Kids." Roxie signed with a wave of the hand.

"Let's get outta here," said Sean.

He had been given discrete directions to one of the mansion's several underground parking garages where a small vehicle was parked in a distant corner. Sean threw the electron pass to Roxie. "Here, you drive. My license is no good on this planet," he quipped. "Have you eaten yet?"

"No…Sean, I haven't."

"Then we're going to Binnja's place. They're supposed to have the best waa-anna sandwiches in the city."

"I've never eaten that kind of fish."

He shook his head. "And I thought you were trying to learn new things!"

She followed his directions to get off the mansion grounds and into the downtown area. They parked in front of a small establishment. "Now, you're going to meet some of your constituents, Madame Exec."

"Name's Roxie!"

They walked into the tiny restaurant, which was overflowing with a sea of people. Roxie felt some beads of perspiration at her temples. At least her torso felt cool. The polished metal on her shirt showed distorted reflections of her surroundings, like broken pieces of a fun house mirror.

A lady strolled up to her and complimented her on the blouse. Roxie smiled, using her hand to brush her hair from her eyes.

"Two waa-anna sandwiches and two chilled bottles of y'poni!" Erik yelled over the noise of the crowd. He produced an Al'aaman debit card, one containing Sean's name.

"Where'd you get that?" his date cried.

He laughed.

"Whatever you've done, I guess I can approve it," she said.

"Stay in character!"

"Anything you say, Sean!" She put her arm around him, turning his face red. "Hey, I'm playing a part, here!"

While they waited on their food, she glanced around the room. She spotted a man with red and yellow lightning bolts painted on his face. Nearby, a woman's face contained a large, green triangle. One lady had a drawing of the Ava sun on the left side of her face and the Zoe sun on the right. Sometimes both members of a couple sported painted faces. She also noted other metfab outfits, including one lady wearing a copper-colored print dress and another in a golden top. She sighed with relief.

The robot clerk brought out hot waa-anna sandwiches and the chilled, bottled intoxicant. Roxie wrinkled her nose at the thought of drinking y'poni from chilled bottles. She preferred other, more refined types of intoxicants in glasses.

"C'mon, you'll like it, " Sean insisted. She took a swig and found out that she did. He led her to an empty booth. "This hot sauce is supposed to be really good," he said, sprinkling some liberally on his.

"No food analysis machine, Mr. Picky Eater?"

"You knew about…."

"Nothing gets past me," she said with a smile.

Roxie poured the hot sauce on her sandwich. She took a bite and smiled. Sean was batting two for two.

Eyeing the couple from a distance was a man in a dark outfit. His face was mangy with three or four days of patchy beard stubble. He ducked into a more secluded alcove and punched a code into his video screen. "Boss?" he said. "Yeah, I am off tonight. But I'm at this hole in the wall downtown and I'm within fifty feet of Number One."

"We haven't been able to track the signal from her arm implant the past couple days," said the Boss. "She must be wearing a cloaking device."

"Or her security's on to us."

"Naw. Got that under control," the Boss insisted. "You say she's in some dive?"

"Yeah, of all places. Our in-tel said she'd be out with her kids, but I'm sure this is her. She's wearing an aging bar fly outfit and she's with that spaceman, Houston. I'd recognize him anywhere."

"Zip me a live shot," ordered the Boss.

The man ambled back to his previous location, pointing his video screen in the lady's direction. He zoomed in and transmitted. "That's not the exec," the Boss insisted. "Doesn't look like her or sound like her. The space jock's just trying to make out with some sleaze."

The informant turned his back to the couple. "I can't see him doin' that. Supposed to be a straight arrow."

"Get a scan on the babe. Use your de-scrambler to cut through any fake retinal patterns. If it is her, take her out. I'll get you some backup."

The Boss ended the call and the agent turned back toward his target. The couple's table was now empty. He hurriedly glanced around the room. They had vanished. The dark figure tore down the aisle and out the door, almost plowing into two people trying to enter. He ran until he was out of breath. He saw her about thirty feet ahead, walking beside that alien. He crept along behind the duo, like a carnivore stalking its prey. Moving quickly though the shadows, he was able to get ahead of the couple. He loitered nonchalantly on the street corner, pulling out a coin-sized device to telescopically take a retinal scan of the woman. Moments later, it came back positive.

Abruptly, Roxie stopped walking. She grabbed his arm. "An alarm's going off in my ear," she gasped. "My security's been compromised."

Sean turned on a pocket electronic device that pointed out the man who had taken the retinal scan. Sean grabbed Roxie's hand. They tore off, disappearing into the crowd. The dark figure hurried after them. He pulled out an ener pistol and shot, hitting Roxie in the back. But a shiny, metallic section of her blouse deflected the beam, sending it in another direction. The man aimed at her head and shot again. The shot was little off but singed a few ends of her hair, creating an acrid smell.

Sean ran and tackled the assailant. He hit the pavement with a thud. Sean pulled the man up by his collar, slamming a fist into his face.

Roxie's stomach turned to ice as he saw three other men running after them. "Let's get outta here!" she urged. They tore off.

"Car's over there!" she cried. A shot flashed by Sean, burning his left shoulder. He pivoted. Drew his stunner. Aimed. Fired. The attacker dropped to the ground. The duo reached the car, Omma's Red Streak. Roxie opened the electron lock. They crammed into the tiny car, as close as Siamese twins.

"Don't get fresh!" she cried.

"Do I have a choice?"

Roxie slammed the car into gear and squealed the wheels. The acceleration jammed them against the seat. Zama's adrenaline was pumping as the car flew down the road. She gasped as two dark-colored cars appeared in her mirror. She floored it. The little vehicle burst ahead. The pursuers faded into the distance. But within moments, they began to narrow the gap. Sean opened a window and fired at the other cars, missing. Arriving at an intersection, the car hit bottom with a thud. Roxie made a sharp right, almost hitting three pedestrians crossing the street. She made a quick left, then another. Her galloping heart seemed ready to jump out of her chest.

"Hang on!" she cried, wheeling the car into a one-eighty.

"Where'd you learn to drive like that?"

"Daughter gets it from somewhere!"

The two pursuers, trying the same maneuver, collided. Roxie made quick little clapping motions as she laughed giddily.

"Steer!" cried Sean, grabbing for the mechanism.

She returned her left hand to the steering and grabbed his arm with her right.

"Car's got hyper controls! You'd have rolled it and killed us," she snapped.

Another car whipped out of a side street, re-starting the chase. The red flash tore through an intersection as the light changed, hitting bottom again. The pursuer followed, narrowly missing some through traffic.

"All cars! Red Lady on the run! Red Lady on the run!" cried the other driver into his video screen. Two additional cars zoomed into the fray.

Roxie punched it, losing the larger, slower vehicles. She barreled onto a highway ramp. Within a few minutes, she cut onto an exit. She sighed as she pulled into a private, underground garage at the mansion. Sean hopped out of the car and helped Roxie out. She was panting rapidly. Perspiration beaded her forehead. Her underarms were damp.

"You okay?" he asked.

She nodded. She lowered her head a moment and caught her breath. She looked at him and pointed at the nearby vertilift. They raced over to it. Within moments, they were inside the exec suite.

"I want to stay here for now," he insisted

"I'd like that."

Erik, back in his normal persona, prowled around the suite, stunner in hand as he searched for any potential intruders. She disappeared into another room and had an automated table produce them each a cup of hot, herbal tea. She walked a steaming cup over to him. She finally noticed the large, oval hole burned through his jacket and shirt, revealing a patch of skin with all the hair singed off. The skin was red and blistered. She clenched her teeth in sympathy, put the cup down on a table and jogged away. She returned moments later with a tube of medicated salve and some bandaging. He took off the jacket and she gently treated the burn. He pointed out a small patch of singed hair on the back of her head. She rubbed the area and they laughed nervously.

Abruptly, she remembered her kids. She punched in each of their personal video codes. The numbers just rang and rang.

# 49.

The waitress was pleased her info had proven correct. Chiefexec Elle was in the restaurant with her kids. The waitress had cajoled a coworker into switching with her so she could wait on the leader. That had really taken a hard sell, especially coming from someone who had just joined the wait staff a week earlier. It took the payment of a hundred monetary units plus switching two work days for the coworker to agree to get to miss meeting the head of A'laama. The waitress had chosen this restaurant because it was rumored to be one of the chiefexec's favorite haunts. In reality, she alternated restaurants frequently for security purposes and more often than not ate at secluded clubs, arriving and leaving via private entrances. So, this was even more of a treat for the waitress tonight to be able to meet the chiefexec.

The server eyed her from a distance. Before approaching the VIP table, she quickly ducked into the restroom with her purse and headed for a stall. She removed the laser pistol from her purse and placed it in the holster on her leg garter. The waitress was already beginning to feel the adrenaline rush. Yes, she was going to meet the chiefexec. Her bosses would be pleased.

Sometime later, Omma and Andy were enjoying their dinner. They had a window view and Omma was gazing out at the lit skyline. The clone looked like Mom and sounded like her. In some uncanny manner she had already known her kids' favorite dishes and had ordered the food for them. She knew about the kids' hobbies and talked with them about them. This woman must have really studied hard to substitute for the chiefexec or, more likely, gotten a memory download. She an almost too-prefect replica. The woman even wrinkled her nose when asking a question, just like their mom.

Their waitress arrived at the table. "So, are you ready for dessert, Madame Exec?" she asked.

"Zama" was about to say something when the waitress pulled up her skirt, grabbed the laser pistol from her garter and pointed it at the "chiefexec." The waitress was about to pull the trigger. Andy picked up a lit candle that was burning in a glass jar. He threw the hot, liquid wax on the would-be assailant's arm. The woman shrieked. She fired. But the gun was now pointing into the air. A beam of light flashed. Hit a wall mirror. Reflected off it. Hit the floor, burning a small hole in it. Within seconds, several security people had the waitress surrounded. They ener cuffed her and hauled her away. The body double began hyperventilating. Omma screamed.

"You all right, Madame Exec? Mr. Elle? Miss Elle?" one of the remaining guards asked. Two others hovered over the double, trying to calm her.

"I...think so," Andy said, answering for them.

"Mr. Elle, you're a hero," the first guard continued. "That was some quick thinking, son. You *saved your mother's life!*"

Andy looked at the clone. He was glad his mom was safe in another part of town.

"I-I need to go to the restroom," Omma said nervously.

"Certainly, Miss Elle. Let me check it for you first to make certain it's safe," said a female agent. The guard hurried into the restroom then quickly came back out to tell Omma the room was unoccupied and she would stand guard until Omma left the room. The coed hurried inside.

She retrieved her video screen from her purse."Mom! Is that you?" she whispered frantically.

"Yes, baby! You all right?"

Back at the mansion, the chiefexec had turned pale."That was Omma. Someone's shot at my clone!"

Erik shook his head. "Do you feel you can trust your new security chief?"

"As far as I know."

"We'll work with him to get to the bottom of this." He reached into his pocket and handed her a coin-sized item."Keep this force field generator on at all times."

"Okay. But I need you to leave for now...."

"Just let me know when it's clear to come back. And I don't know about your making that speech in a couple days."

"Got to make the speech! Can't let people think I'm intimidated...."

"All right. We'll make sure you're covered. Get back to me soon as possible."

"I will."

He reluctantly walked out the door.

Zama walked to the spare bedroom at the farthest end of the suite and hid under the bed, Omma having told her that several guards would be accompanying the "chiefexec" and her kids back to their suite. If need be, she could always prove who she was via a retinal scan. But she was hoping she wouldn't be discovered so she could avoid the embarrassment of having to reveal her deception to the security agents. Her worst fears did not come to pass. About an hour later, Omma, Andy and Zama's double were all escorted back to the suite. The officers took some time looking over every part of the vast suite but never did look under the bed where Zama was hiding.

Finally, she heard a familiar voice. "Mom! Mom! C'mon out. The agents are gone!"

"I'm in here!" she called.

She carefully slid out from under the bed, eased to her feet and began brushing imaginary dirt off her clothing. "I think I swallowed a dust mite!" she spat.

"Mom, no dust mite could live in your germ-free environment," Omma scoffed.

Zama looked up. Her now-wrinkled shirt was coming out of her pants. Staring at her were both her kids, Erik, Kelly and a stranger who looked like she had walked out of a mirror. The double stepped forward.

"Madame Exec, I'm thrilled to meet you. My name is Annie Onalooka." She extended her hand.

"I—don't normally look like this," said the red-faced chiefexec, still in her colorful Roxie outfit and with her makeup smeared from having lain on the floor.

"No problem, Ma'am. How was your costume party?"

"Umm…it was fine. Thank you for, for…being there tonight. I'm glad you weren't hurt."

"I'm glad of that, too. It was scary."

"I-I'll make sure you get triple pay for this evening, Miss…"

"Call me Annie," the double said with a smile.

Erik kept looking back and forth between the two women. "Annie is one of two or three clones that I keep on retainer," the chiefexec explained. "She's the first of my clones I've actually *met* since I'm normally in a different place than any of them."

Annie nodded.

"Erik, if you'll excuse us, Annie and I need to change clothes. And Omma's going to put 'Roxie's' makeup on her. That way, if any security people see her leave they won't think the chiefexec's going somewhere."

"I'll wait in the next room," he said. "But once you're done, we need to speak with you about some safety precautions."

Kelly nodded.

A while later, Zama, Annie and Omma emerged from the room. Erik was still unable to tell original and copy apart. They looked at one another, laughing in spooky unison at his bewilderment.

"I'm glad I met you, Madame Exec," said "Roxie."

"Thanks again for helping keep me safe, Annie," said Zama, hugging her.

# 50.

Zama's adrenaline had been pumping for the past two days. She had the speech sounding the way she wanted. She was still worried about another assassination attempt, but she knew this was something she *had* to do. As she was preparing to leave for the legislature chambers where she'd be giving the speech, she glanced at her full-length mirror. She cocked her head and looked again. The woman in the mirror was different one than when the star people had first arrived. This new Zama looked slightly thinner, tanner and she stood up straighter. The chiefexec realized that perhaps all her adventures in recent months had had a more positive effect on her than she had realized. She knew her improved appearance and more confident manner could help her sway public opinion. Zama smiled a dazzling smile. She *knew* she was going to score big with this speech. Chiefexec Elle bounded out the door.

Meanwhile, as the assembled legislaes and other dignitaries awaited the arrival of the leader, dozens of plainclothes security agents were at their posts, alertly seeking to prevent any potential trouble. Several of them communicated back and forth with one another on private-band video screens. The officers and several robot counterparts had spot-searched a number of people prior to allowing them entry into the legislature chambers. The security people had electronically combed every square inch of the stage from which the chiefexec would be speaking. Behind and above the podium was an eighty by fifty foot screen that would carry the videocast live so that everyone in the vast hall could see the chief executive.

When she arrived at one wing of the stage, the entire legislature was gathered in the chambers. There was tension in their air. Zama had become a controversial figure. Everyone knew she would need to give an outstanding speech in order to preserve what remained of her power. But many residents of Al'aama were also sympathizing with her due to the assassination attempt. Some thought her courageous for even going forward with the speech. Several minutes before the appointed time, the video stations were already broadcasting. At the stroke of the hour, a high government official loudly announced her.

She strode onto the stage, accompanied by thunderous applause, more from respect for her office than for her as a leader. Many citizens had been anxious for their governor to address issues that had been brewing for months so the viewing audience was a large one. Many of the in-person audience and members of the viewing public observed the same changes in her that she had noted in her mirror. There was also a fire in her eyes the public hadn't seen for a while. She smiled a big smile. She was standing on her toes. Her countenance grew more serious and she took a deep breath and launched into the speech.

She spoke of the courage and vision of the original colonists, summarizing their travails in founding A'laama. She pointed out that as the modern-day descendants of those founders, her contemporaries had developed a safe, comfortable society, but had lost that pioneering spirit. They had shut themselves into a box. It was comfortable, it was beautiful, but it was still a box.

She described how she had broken out of that box and had gotten to see wonders beyond the farm district. She showed video of the beauty of the jungle, the Great Waterfall. She decried the loss of that pioneering spirit and spoke of the need to regain it. She described and showed online docs and video of the ghost town as proof the original settlers had longed for their descendants to grow, explore and spread out to other areas of the planet.

The chiefexec cited how the arrival of the star people had challenged the A'laamans' complacency and inspired them to expand their horizons. She spoke of the legitimate need for the fights A'laama had waged against the Batu. She called for legislation that would end the Forbidden Zone and encourage people to explore the outlying areas. She called upon her people not to be discouraged by the fierce demeanor of the Batu. There would always be risks and dangers but the rewards would be even greater.

She asked her citizens to not dwell on the past but to become worthy descendants of the pioneers.

"I can picture a day when our entire planet will be dotted with cities hundreds of miles apart linked by mag lev trains and air ships," she cried. "Some day we will explore our solar system and even go to the stars. My friends, in recent months, I've learned that there are no limits. Let's regain that pioneering spirit of our ancestors. Walk with me into this exciting new era. God bless our planet. All of it!"

Zama had been exhilarated while giving the speech. As she finished, there was dead silence for several long seconds. Then intense applause erupted. Several times louder than that which had greeted her upon her entrance. She was beaming as she waved to the gallery. The applause increased and was followed by a standing ovation and several more minutes of hearty clapping. Normally, at the end of the applause, the chiefexec would begin to move through the gallery, greeting the various officials. Following *this* speech, a number of them were anxious to congratulate her. But instead, once the appreciation died down, she merely waved to the audience one more time and walked off the stage. Uncertain what else to do, the audience applauded one more time. They waited for her to reappear and bask in her triumphant moment. She didn't do so. The attendees waited for several minutes then slowly began to disperse, some of them beginning to animatedly discuss the speech. The media had already started spinning their commentary.

Sometime later, back in her personal sanctuary, the chiefexec was sitting on a lounge chair. For security purposes, she hadn't given the speech in person after all. She had done a 3-D broadcast from a remote location using a set that was identical to the official podium and stage. The broadcast had been so realistic that even her live audience had assumed she'd been there in person. She was now sipping on a mixed drink.

Abruptly, a wall panel slid open. Three hooded men dressed in black burst into the room. Zama shrieked. Several security agents rushed out of hiding. A hail of weapons' fire erupted. One of the hooded invaders fired at her. A force field deflected the beam. One by one, the security people downed all three of the intruders. The protectors pulled off the masks off the wounded assailants.

262

They were all members of the mansion security force!

Erik and Montoya barged in, stunners drawn. Everyone's attention turned to the leader. She sighed with relief, turning off her force field. One of the wounded rogue agents lying on the floor lifted his hand. He aimed his laser pistol and fired. A beam of light hit the chiefexec. She slumped over. Two of the loyal security agents fired on the man, ending his life. Erik froze in his tracks and stared at the limp body. A deep burn hole smoldered in the upper part of her shirt.

Montoya retrieved a handheld diagnostic tool from his pocket. "She's dead," he said, looking at the ground.

Erik shook his head in disbelief. He walked over to the lady and rolled up her left sleeve. No pink, starburst birthmark. He shuddered as he looked down at the slain clone.

"We need to get to the real Zama before any more killers do," he declared. Monotya and he rushed out of the retreat. The two star men ran full speed along the quickest route to the mansion roof. Using their anti-grav belts, they launched into the sky.

Outside the penthouse at a plush, downtown hotel, a hooded figure dressed in black kicked open the door. Several people in similar dress scrambled into the room. Minj and Luci met them, weapons drawn. The intruders shot at the defenders. But the weapons were useless against the star people's force fields. The defenders quickly took out the people in black. But a number more arrived and a protracted gun fight ensued.

In the next room, the chiefexec had been watching a news video of her recently ended speech. In the oversized room was the mock stage and podium from which she had made the 3-D broadcast. She heard the commotion in the other room. She did as she had been instructed and hurried toward a closet. She reached into her pocket to turn on the force field generator. It wasn't there! Zama's stomach suddenly became queasy. An arm grabbed her around the waist. She gasped as she felt a cold, metal weapon barrel in her ribs. She jammed her elbow hard into her attacker. She broke free and turned to face…herself!

Zama shrieked. "Annie! I-I thought you were loyal!" Stone-faced, the clone aimed a pistol and pulled the trigger. A beam of light shot out. The chiefexec had already ducked. Still crouched low, she launched herself at her opponent's feet. The lookalikes fell to the floor with a thud.

Erik and Montoya ran into the room. The men saw two Zamas, one about to stab the other with a Star man laser knife. Erik fired his stunner at the would-be knife victim, who screamed in pain. Her assailant released her.

"What are you doing? That's the wrong Zama!" cried Montoya.

Erik rolled up the sleeve of the knife-wielder, who was trembling and breathing heavily. Adorning her shoulder was a pink, starburst birthmark.

Two hooded figures sneaked up behind each of the men and clubbed them in the head, knocking them out. The larger of the two figures eyed the shocked Zama, who was still holding the energy knife. The intruder pulled a weapon from a holster and fired. Zama's chest exploded. She collapsed to the floor, her upper body a smoldering wreckage of melted electronic circuits. "Stupid android!" spat the gunman, kicking it out of the way. He slipped the weapon back into the holster then pulled a different gun from his pocket. The black-clad duo prowled around the room like two cats. The leader crept up to a closet door on the far side of the room. He flung open the sliding door. Empty. The intruders continued to case the room. Nearby, a hiding woman strained to quiet her breathing and slow the pounding of her heart.

The two black-clad figures looked around the room. The larger figure had ocular implants. He tried the heat-seeking function. X-ray. Nothing. He scanned the area over his head. The larger person pointed to an over-sized ceiling vent. His companion boosted him up so he could reach it. He pulled off the metal cover and dropped it to the carpeted floor with a thud. He reached his arm into the vent and felt around. Just feet away, the hiding woman tried to still her breathing. A dust particle tickled her nose. She tried to stifle a sneeze but it came out, soft and high-pitched, like that of a pet. With another boost, the intruder's head and shoulders penetrated the cooling duct. He felt around and touched something warm and damp. He grabbed onto a wrist and felt hot, sweaty skin and a racing pulse. He clamped onto the person tightly and pulled downward with all his full weight. His companion yanked as well. The hooded figure and his prey fell through the vent. They crashed to the floor. A cloud of dust billowed out in all directions. Both hunter and hunted coughed violently.

The predator caught his breath. His prey rose to her hands and knees, trembling. "If this isn't a pitiful sight," a familiar voice sneered, sending chills up her spine. "The chiefexec of a planet, hiding like a rat. And knowing what a germophobe you are, I'm sure you're an emotional wreck. Don't worry. We have more treats in store for you."

His victim was still on all fours, coughing. The speaker kicked her in the seat, knocking her back to the floor as she cried out. His partner slapped the companion hard in the shoulder. The masked ones seemed to glare at one another for a moment.

Zama's antagonists jerked her back to her feet. Pain shot through her back. She gasped in disbelief as she spotted her fallen heroes from the stars. She tried to scream but no sound would come. The larger assailant got behind her. He grabbed her left arm and yanked it behind her back. Electricity shot up to her shoulder.

"Hello, Zama," snarled the voice. "That was a touching performance tonight. Your last performance."

She turned her head. Just inches away was the bitter, now uncovered face of her former security chief William Thal. She gasped a high-pitched note. A severe pain shot through her chest. She wondered what would kill her first: her heart or her assailants. But within moments, the meds were pumping through her bloodstream to give her relief. She took a deep breath. She chomped down on her lip. Cancel that thought. She wasn't going without a fight.

The second attacker put her in a headlock. William kept the gun in her ribs. Zama tensed her muscles from head to foot. She wrenched from side to side, trying to shake loose.

"You've been leading our people to ruin long enough!" William growled in her ear, offensive breath assaulting her nostrils. She kicked her heels into his shins. He hung on.

"Now it's all going to come to an end!" he cried. "By the way, since these will be the *last* seconds of your life, I want you to know that your *friend*, Tanna Bern, developed this new weapon."

"Tanna wouldn't do that!" she hissed through clenched teeth.

The other figure removed the hood. "Wrong you are, Madame Exec," Tanna said as she pulled a second gun from a holster. Zama felt her stomach drop. Her knees gave way. William held on to her, not letting her fall to the floor.

Tanna continued: "These weapons emit high energy pulses that will cook you from the inside out. You'll boil in your own juices. You'll have the honor of being the first human on which they'll be used. But don't worry, the weapon proved *quite effective* on lab animals."

"I have a better idea," William snarled. "If we really want to make her suffer, we can make her watch as we use the guns on these two worthless aliens. They've brought nothing but trouble."

"That's not true!" Zama cried. "I don't care what you do to me, but spare their lives!"

"That can be arranged," growled William. "With two of these pulse guns, we get to double your suffering."

"T-Tanna," shouted Zama, "we go back a long way. I-I cried my eyes out the night of the crash. The night I thought you might die!"

"She's lying!" cried William. "Pull the trigger!"

"Zama...I...."

"Fire the gun!"

"As you wish!"

William squeezed the trigger, making Zama howl in pain. Tanna let go of Zama, swivelled and fired at William. Both targets crashed to the floor and began writhing on the carpet. Tanna lowered her weapon. She collapsed to the floor and began to weep.

"Forgive me, Zama!" she sobbed.

The chiefexec moved her left hand an inch or two in Tanna's direction. Tanna grasped her former boss's hand. Zama squeezed it weakly then her hand went limp.

Several loyal guards ran into the room. They slapped ener cuffs on the female assailant and her pain-stricken companion, carrying them away. "I'm so sorry, Zama. So sorry," called the woman as they pulled her out the door.

Two guards jerked the wounded clone to her feet."Wait, you've got the wrong person. I'm the chiefexec! Arrest that other woman!" The guards began to pull the struggling female away.

The pain-stricken woman lay on the floor, holding her side. Her face was red and twisted in agony. Erik, having stirred back to consciousness, knelt down beside her. "Montoya!" he cried as the doctor rubbed the back of his head and slowly rose to his feet.

The lookalike continued to scuffle with her captors, who were each holding her under a shoulder. She partially jerked one shoulder free, ripping her shirt. As the guards forcibly hauled the woman out the doorway, the last thing Erik saw was an exposed shoulder that *also* had a pink, starburst birthmark. He looked back at the agonized woman on the floor then at the now-empty doorway.

# 51.

Pain shot through the woman's insides. The intensity was worse than childbirth. She heard excited shouts around her. Distant shouts.

In her agony, she remembered a familiar passage: *"My God, my God, why have you forsaken me? Why are you so far from helping me…?"*

"Look. She's moving her lips," said one of the distant voices.

"What's she saying?" asked another.

"Can't tell."

*"Our fathers trusted in you. They trusted in you and you delivered them…."*

She lost consciousness. What seemed like a long time later, she heard more voices. "Parts of several internal organs have…have *melted*. I've never seen…" said a male voice.

*"My heart is like wax. It is melted in the midst of my bowels…."*

A female voice said: "I don't care *who* she is, we've got to save her."

"We've checked her brain wave patterns. This is definitely the chiefexec."

The horrendous pain was still there. Eventually, it began to subside. At other times she was pain free and felt strangely at peace. Sometimes she sensed people around her. Perhaps even talking to her. She vaguely recognized some of the voices. There were also extended periods of silence. The one constant was some electronic humming and beeping that had become as familiar as the sound of her own heartbeat and breathing. She fantasized that she had somehow become part machine. Her arm implant kept cloning itself and had taken over her body.

One time, she had a sense of foreboding. It was totally dark. Darkness had never frightened her before. It did now. Her muscles knotted. She felt cold steel against her ribs. "You thought you could get away from me, " growled William Thal. "This time, I'll finish you off!"

She screamed. A nurse ran to help her. Zama gasped for breath. She was soaked with perspiration and breathing heavily. It had only been a dream! The room was totally dark and it was apparently late. She slept fitfully. Sometime later she awoke in a start, mumbling: "Why are you trying to kill me? I only want to help our people!" She pushed a button to summon the nurse, who gave her another sedative.

For a time, she had started to feel better, although she was still weak and groggy. She heard the voice of someone (Montoya?) talking with another doc about tiny bio-somethings working to rebuild her damaged organs.

Then the waves of pain washed over her again, worse than ever. She was vaguely aware that the docs had surrounded her again, talking worriedly about a relapse.

"Hope we can save her!" she hear a distant voice say.

"Would take a miracle…" said another.

."..shows she's brain dead…."

"Has someone contacted the nextexec?"

She felt cold hands on her head. The hands were soft and scented. She heard a voice that sounded like Kelly. Zama sensed time passing. People waiting. A young woman's voice started to sob. Other voices sounded like they were trying to comfort the young lady. Zama felt a sheet being pulled over her head. The young woman screamed.

"Tried our best…" said someone light years away.

Panic gripped her, overriding her pain. *Wait! Wait!* she thought. *I'm not ready.* Suddenly she was at peace.

*"Though I walk through the valley of the shadow of death, I will fear no evil. For you are with me. Your rod and staff comfort me…."*

She was a little girl picking flowers in a field. She looked up and smiled at the bright sunlight. She began to spin around until she became dizzy. She heard a choir singing. It was the most beautiful music she had ever heard.

*"Into your hands I commit my spirit."*

Everything went black.

# 52.

Her wrist and ankles bound in ener chains, Tanna was wearing a drab jail uniform. She sat in a beat-up wooden chair and was staring down at an equally worn table in an otherwise unfurnished room. It was hot and she hadn't had a drink in hours. A stocky detective with crew cut hair paced the floor.

"Mrs. Bern, so far you've been fairly cooperative," he said. "You've turned in the names of everyone involved in this conspiracy and you've led us to the specs of that hideous weapon you created. Yet you refuse to give us the most important name of all. The kingpin. You and William Thal were taking orders from someone."

The prisoner continued to look at the table. The interrogator glowered at her. "How long are you going to continue ignoring me?" he cried. "Tanna, you're in serious trouble. William may not survive so this will all fall on you."

She continued looking down.

"I need a name."

Tanna gritted her teeth. "I-I can't tell you. He's a powerful man. If I gave him up, he'd get to me. Even in prison.'"

"So you refuse?"

Silence.

"Very well. Here's a video I think you'll enjoy." He waved his hand. The wall facing Tanna filled with 3-D, infrared images of William, several agents and she firing weapons at the force field of one of the star man landing craft.

"Look familiar? I'll speed this up so we can get to the juicy part." Tanna continued to stare at the table. The officer slowed the video back down to normal speed. It showed the security personnel leaving while the two officials remained behind. The shot zoomed in on the images of William and Tanna. They stepped closer to one another. Their faces filled the screen as they indulged in a slow, passionate kiss.

She looked at the screen and felt her stomach drop. "And I thought I loved that pig! Why did I help him do that to Zama? Why?" She buried face in her hands and began to sob.

"William Thal may be past tense to you, but how will your family react when we show this to them? How will your kids feel seeing Mommy with another man?"

"All right!" she cried. "I'll tell you who put us up to it! He not only wanted to kill the chiefexec but also Dr. Farji, Legislae Norris, Legislae Clayton and others leaders of Zama's party. He was going to launch a coup to take over the government. He wanted to turn back the clock to the days before the Batu, the days before the star men...."

The detective clapped his hands together. "Now we're getting somewhere. Now talk into this screen...."

A short time later, at a private dock on the lake, a yacht was about to get underway. The smug owner was sipping on a cocktail, his hairy chest and stomach exposed to the suns. On either side of him sat a model in a bathing suit each also enjoying a drink. Two other women in bathing suits fanned the seated man. He flirted with the woman on his left, a brunette with thick hair flowing past her shoulders. Several bodyguards stood at alert. They heard a sharp sound from a dozen yards away. Pulling their weapons, they hustled over to investigate. Behind them, a dozen armed cops swarmed out of hiding, weapons drawn.

"Drop 'em!" the lead officer yelled at the guards. They tossed their weapons onto the deck and raised their hands while other police frisked them.

The watercraft owner jumped to his feet, his wild, greying hair making him look even more hysterical. "This is an outrage!" he spat. "Do you know who I am? I'll have your jobs!"

The commanding officer strode over to the man, pushing him back down onto his chair. "I know exactly who you are!" he shouted.

The brunette in the swimsuit stood up, flashed a badge and trained a weapon on her admirer. His jaw fell open.

"Sylvia! Even you?" the wiry-haired man cried.

"We've suspected you for a long time but now we've finally got the goods," she replied grimly, her gun still trained on him.

The lead officer pulled the chilled drink out of his hand and dumped it onto his lap. The man jumped in shock. Stepping onto the yacht was a somber-faced Chief Franklin. He had arrived just in time to hear the lead officer say: "Legislae Nathaniel Tuu, you're under arrest for conspiracy to assassinate the chiefexec!"

Prisoner Tuu had been in the Pit ever since his capture. It was max security solitary. Nothing was allowed in. Not even light. He had a bunk and a toilet. He received three meal trays a day. And worst of all there were no private stock intoxicants. Nothing with a bouquet.

He was trembling with rage as he lay on his rock-hard bunk. He had worn the same clothes the entire time. He had not been allowed to bathe. How uncivilized. But they couldn't keep him locked up forever. They'd let him out. His constituents would demand it. Or his network of underlings would break him out. Or he would buy the judge and jury. He was still the most powerful man on the planet….

He jumped. Someone…or something…was in the cell. His muscles tensed. He eased to his feet and balled his fists. Even his darkness-adjusted eyes couldn't spot anything. He heard a tiny noise from the corner of the cell. He lunged in that direction. He slammed into a wall and crumpled to the floor with a groan.

Laughter crackled through the air. It seemed to be coming from his right. He dove in that direction, sending him thudding to the floor. Now the laughter was coming from behind him. Now from overhead. From several places. No, everywhere. The volume soared until he held his hands over his ears.

Silence.

A foot jolted his stomach, doubling him up in pain. "Tuu!" a bass voice spat his name at two hundred decibels.

"Tuu," the voice repeated quietly, without amplification.

He recognized it. One of the assistant police chiefs. A weasel of a man.

"Answer me, you scum bag!"

A fist broke into his face. The prisoner tasted blood. He lay on the ground and whimpered. "Not so strong now, are you?" Pain exploded from a kick in the ribs.

"What a dignified career you've had," the cop went on. "Gang leader. One who beat up teenage girls. Con artist. Power broker. Murder conspirator. All the while looking respectable on the outside. What a fraud! You wanted to kill off some of the best leaders we've had in decades. That weapon your flunkies designed? You'll be its last victim."

"No!" he cried. His stomach spasmed in pain. Within seconds, it was over.

The official cause of death was a heart attack. That day, the last existing pulse gun was disassembled and its parts were melted down. The specs were permanently erased.

# 53.

Zama saw a white light up above her. Light so bright that she shielded her eyes. She was somehow drawn to the light and wanted to climb toward it. A silhouette appeared. There was someone up there! The light compelled her even more. Suddenly, she felt lighter than air. She began to float toward the light. The shadowy figure took on a form. It was a woman wearing a white robe. She looked at the women's face. It was her late mother! "That's it, darling," she said sweetly. "Time for you to come home."

The younger woman began to hesitate.

"It's okay," her mom said soothingly. "Let go of all your burdens. That's all in the past."

The daughter still held back.

Her mother reached toward her. "Everything will be all right. Just take my hand," she said.

Zama reached out her arm toward her mother's. Their hands were almost touching. Mom's hand grasped her daughter's. They held on to one another tightly. Zama saw her surroundings fall away. She was quickly rising through the air. She was high above the city, flying through the clouds. The light grew brighter. Mom's smiling face seemed only inches away.

"Wait!" Zama cried. "Our people need me!"

Mother looked startled as her daughter let go. Zama felt like she was falling a long distance. "I love you, Mom!" she cried. "I love you, Mom," she mouthed wordlessly.

Back in the emergency room, a small knot of people stood around the gurney holding the woman who was covered with a sheet. Some of the bystanders looked at the floor. Some had tears running down their faces. One person was on a video screen, about to break the news to the media.

"Look! I saw her move!" shouted a man.

"That's just the body's last motions," sighed one of the docs. "They're involuntary. She's already dead."

"No! She did move!" a woman insisted.

The doc pulled down the sheet down to the woman's waist. She was clad in a hospital gown. She did not appear to be breathing. Her face was ghostly pale but had the most serene look the physician had ever seen. "Madame Exec?" he gasped. "Madame Exec. If you can hear me, move your little finger."

By now, everyone was staring in silence. Eternal moments passed. Nothing happened. Then, the finger slowly moved. It was barely perceptible.

The doc swallowed hard. He pulled the sheet all the way down. "And now, Ma'am, can you wiggle your big toe?"

A pause for a moment. The big toe moved.

The room erupted into chaos. People were shouting. Hugging one another. The woman on the screen to the media began jumping up and down as she screamed the good news to the press. Zama, her eyes still closed, tried hard to smile before she slipped back into unconsciousness.

Sometime later, she noticed a scent. A sweet scent. No, *several* such smells. Where was she, in a field? She cracked open her eyelids and saw there were flowers. Many bouquets and arrangements. It looked like a florist shop. Next, she felt the several tubes that were attached to her, tubes leading to electronic equipment that was taking the place of her damaged organs. Someone was standing over her. She noted the concerned faces of Fred Montoya and three Al'aaman doctors. She opened her mouth.

"Don't say anything. Just rest," one of the docs cautioned. She closed her lips then closed her eyes.

What seemed like a long time later, she re-opened them. A figure sat nearby in a chair. She focused on the man as if she had never before seen him. He had dark circles under his eyes and a heavy, rough-looking beard stubble. It was Erik. She drifted off again. The next time she opened her eyes, she recognized Andy and Omma. Another time she thought she saw Kelly.

Hours later, she opened her eyes slightly. She sensed a figure to her right and opened her eyes a little wider.

Montoya stood nearby. "Still in pain?" he asked gently.

"A little," she said weakly. He looked at her sympathetically but said nothing further.

"H-*how am I?*" she asked.

"Greatly improved," he said, smiling. She smiled and went back to sleep.

The next time she awoke, she was much more coherent. Montoya was telling her: "You had us worried. I'm glad Tanna stopped that crazy man. A few more seconds and you'd have been dead!"

"I was dead," she mumbled, too low for the doc to hear.

Later that day, Erik visited again. He was clean-shaven and smelled of cologne. She asked him to pour her a glass of water. She drained the glass and said nothing further for a while. After Montoya left the room, she looked down again and said in a low voice: "We-we never fully appreciate how fragile life is...."

He nodded gravely. He looked into her eyes. She looked away.

"I brought you something," he said. He reached into a bag and pulled out a baseball cap that said: President. She smiled broadly, took the cap and placed it on her head. She hugged him.

"I lied to you," she said, still hanging on to him.

"What do you mean?"

They drew apart. "That day in the wilderness. The pink mark on my shoulder. I told you it was a birthmark. I-I lied. I was ashamed to tell you how I really got it."

His brow furrowed.

"It happened when I was a teenager. I had a fight with my parents and ran away. I got into a bad part of town. Stumbled onto this gang of boys. They tackled me. I landed on some pavement, which broke my arm and my nose. Scraped up my face. Knocked out two of my front teeth. My dentist helped me grow new ones. Anyhow, these gang members burned that mark on me with a laser. They were all going to carve their initials into me, too. But my dad was in his car, looking for me. He found me, pulled out his ener rifle and chased them away...."

276

He shook his head in sympathy.

"I could have had the mark removed. And I could have had my nose fixed. But I decided to leave these things alone. They remind me to always be strong. No matter what life throws me...."

He nodded.

She continued: "Those guys who started to attack me...the police found them and my dad filed charges. They went away to juvenile detention. Their leader, the one who burned me with the laser, later became 'respectable' and went into business. Then later into politics. Police Chief Franklin has also visited me here in the hospital. It turns out all these years later that former gang leader headed the conspiracy that was trying to kill me. Legislae Tuu."

Erik's jaw hung open.

Silence hung in the air. Then Erik changed the subject. "That clone who attacked you in the hotel had a pink marking on her shoulder. She must have had that done so she'd look even more like you."

"How did you know which one was really me?"

He shrugged. "Somehow, I knew."

"I know we were also using Annie as a decoy. Is she all right?"

Erik hung his head. "We tried to protect her."

Tears welled up in Zama's eyes. "Kelly once told me that although my clones are my bio twins, ethically they're my daughters. We'll give Annie a daughter's funeral. A hero's funeral."

A high-pitched beeping interrupted their discussion. The chiefexec retrieved her video screen from a nightstand. She spent some time answering and making various calls. Erik headed down the hall and returned a while later.

"When I gave my speech, I meant what I said about developing an Al'aaman space program."

He burst into laughter.

"What?" she said, missing the absurdity.

"You've never even developed airships. Now you want to go into space?"

Her eyes brightened. "Not just space. To the stars."

"You're crazy."

"Is this the same Erik Houston who said to expand my horizons?"

He balled his fists and said nothing.

"Well...are you going to help us?"

He rubbed his chin.

"Once again, you're Mr. Not Share My Tech. If you tell me this is another matter that's tied up in your interstellar politics, I'll scream."

"I told you there are limits." Burned into his mind was First Contact Protocol #14, which expressly forbid revealing near-light speed tech. "We'll be able to teach you more on successive visits."

"Successive visits? I'm not going to wait a century. We'll figure it out ourselves by then."

"Why don't you rest?"

He turned and left the room. By the time he returned, she was asleep. He sat by her side for a couple hours then left the hospital. When he returned the next day, she was sitting up in the bed and her color had almost returned to normal.

"Hi. You look a lot better," he said with a smile.

"You don't look so bad, either."

"How are you feeling?"

"A lot stronger. So…where are we on starships?"

"Realistically, we're starting from scratch. You don't even have so much as air travel. Not that you've *needed* it up to this point. It's amazing that you have a tech civilization but no air ships whatsoever."

"Well, no one's perfect," Zama replied, twisting her mouth into a half-smirk.

"We'll have to start with the basics. Teach your engineers some aerodynamic principles. We could start by doing things like building a one-person glider. Later, we can add an engine to it."

She frowned at him. "C'mon. That stuff sounds silly."

"I'm serious. You have to crawl before you can walk and you have to walk before you can run. Otherwise, you'll be crashing all your ships before they even get out of the atmosphere."

She thought back to that dreadful day in which Tanna and William had almost been killed in the crash of one of Erik's landing vehicles. She shuddered at the thought and knew she didn't want *that* to happen again.

He continued: "Once you've mastered the principles of flight, you could build a nuclear-powered ship that would allow you to explore your solar system and even farther. Or you could make a solar-powered ship using a giant solar sail. That big Ava sun gives off a lot of energy."

"But…from what you told me, those types of ships would be too slow…."

"Unless your people were willing to take a couple generations to make the trip. That's how it was with the earliest starships."

Zama bit her lip. "Okay, Star man. Let's get to work. And the next time your people visit, tell them to send one of their big honchos so we can do some real negotiating," she teased.

"You mean giveaways."

She rolled her eyes.

"We can't continue to stay indefinitely," he continued, "but we could take a couple months to teach your scientists, do experiments with them and help them develop a game plan."

"Okay. We have a deal. Besides, I wouldn't mind having you…uh, your people around a couple more months…."

"Good enough."

On the fifth day after the assassination attempt, the chiefexec left the hospital in an automated wheelchair. As she rolled out a back exit, a throng of thousands of people were waiting. Her security people tried to disperse them, but she insisted they stay. The crowd was cheering, chanting her first name. She stopped the wheelchair, gripped the armrests and struggled to her feet. The crowd roared. She held onto the chair with one hand while a security agent supported her. She waved vigorously with the other hand. She smiled and laughed until her face felt like it would split. "Thank you! Thank you all!" she cried. "I love you!" The throng erupted again.

She was wearing her cap that said: President. The reporters wanted to know what the word meant, but she was already being helped into the waiting limo. She eased into the car and an attendant closed the door, cutting off the sound of the throng. The window glass was a smoky hue. Zama could see the mass of people outside but no one could see in.

Sitting next to her at her request was Erik. "Glad to see you well enough to come home," he said.

She smiled again. As they leaned back on the plush seat, she turned toward him, closed her eyes and said softly: "I'm going to sleep a lot the next couple days. But once I'm feeling a little stronger, I need to get away from here."

He wrinkled his brow. "Where do you want to go?"

"Someplace far away. Take me to that beach you showed me months ago."

The last several days' opinion polls showed Zama's popularity had risen dramatically. Her speech a few days earlier had been a hit plus the public gave her high marks for pressing on despite the assassination threat. She also picked up several percentage points as a sympathy vote from people who were concerned that they had almost *lost* their chiefexec. After several days, her favorable rating dropped a few percent but then stabilized at a high, favorable number. It seemed she had done exactly what she intended to do—inspire the public and get them behind her. It wasn't only her words that impressed people, it was how she said them and her new, more dynamic appearance. The improved energy and confidence of the new Zama were playing well. She seemed to embody what she had said in speech. Her critics now had nothing effective for a comeback.

# 54.

Erik and Zama walked along the beach, their toes covered with powdery, white sand. The temperature in this area was much cooler than in A'laama. It actually felt good to be outside, warmed by Ava and Zoe suns that for once seemed benign. Occasionally, the tide would lap at their feet, the chilled water sending shivers up their spines. A lone sea bird flew overhead, its cry interrupting the rolling sound of small waves hitting the shore.

He looked over at her. She was smiling and seemed carefree for the first time in months. Her hair was frizzed out. He had never before seen it like this. He wondered whether it was due to the humidity of the ocean air or whether she hadn't used the ever-necessary conditioner. She looked good. Long and lean in her bathing suit, the bottom piece resembling a short skirt. The color of the suit complemented her skin tone. The suit had a white racing stripe down the right side running from the top of her ribs and following the curve of her hip. The edges of the top piece were trimmed in a different color.

She stopped walking and shielded her eyes with one hand as she once again gazed into the distance. Nothing but water all the way to the horizon.

She shook her head. "I've never seen anything so vast!"

He chuckled.

They sat down and fashioned little sand buildings with their hands until the tide came in and collapsed them. They got back up and started walking again.

"You sure some wild woman isn't going to pop up and attack us?" she laughed.

He shook his head. "I've checked. There are no people within hundreds of miles. We could be the first humans this place has ever seen."

"You've been wrong before," she chuckled, kicking sand at him. Abruptly, she broke into a run, her long legs pumping as she began to shrink into the distance.

He tore off after her, struggling to reach her speed. She maintained the lead. He re-doubled his effort and began to close the gap. He was almost up to her. His lungs burned. His feet pummeled the sand. He started to pass her. She tagged his shoulder as he flew past her.

"Hey, you can't show me up!" she laughed.

They abruptly stopped, almost losing their footing as the soft sand sprayed out in all directions.

"Not bad...for a four-hundred-year-old man," she laughed between breaths.

She trotted back to their blanket and picnic basket and sat down. She licked her lips. "This salty air is making me thirsty," she said.

He opened a bottle of self-chilled, sparkling beverage and filled two glasses. She took a sip, tilted her head back and looked at him. "We never did tell you the entirety of the Angel's Prophecy," she said.

He looked bewildered.

She quoted: "'And just as three women came here from the stars, before three hundred years have passed three men shall come from the stars and call fire down from heaven.' Now here's the part we didn't tell you: 'After they arrive, your people will never again be the same.' The angel said your visit here would totally transform our society. That's the reason I resisted your arrival so strongly. I was comfortable with the status quo and knew it was about to be swept away. You've changed us. You've changed me. I-I want to thank you."

He smiled broadly and spent a moment soaking in the implications of her comments. "What else did your angel say?"

Her brown eyes flashed with a mischievous look before she lowered them. "Now, Captain, we can't tell you all our secrets."

"So the angel did say something more about us. What is it?"

She remained silent.

"Tell me," he insisted.

She looked away and began to blush.

He finally gave up and changed the subject.

After they finished their drinks, she watched him as he walked away and built a fire using driftwood. He used the fire to cook some fish they had caught and he had filleted with a laser knife.

She drew close, watching him. A cool wind stirred, causing the fire to flicker. Zama's hair blew in all directions. She jogged back to their blanket, opened her beach bag, pulled out a warm cloak and threw it on over her swimsuit. She placed the hood on her head. "I know why no one lives here," she called, shivering. "Too freakin' cold!"

He shook his head and chuckled. "Some cultures would consider this mild weather."

Sometime later, when their stomachs were full, she was sipping another glass of effervescent beverage. "You're always talking about time and how quickly it passes," she said. "I wish this moment could last for eternity."

# 55.

Erik was alone in the suite, his stomach knotted inside. In his mind, he was mournfully singing a song he called "The Last Day on the Planet Blues." He had spent the day checking in with every member of the crew, making sure all was in order for their departure. There had also been a round of goodbyes to various planetary officials and speeches at three or four different functions. Kelly had thanked him profusely for all he had done for her people and asked a blessing on him. Umni and Bobby had dropped by and given him a stuffed unfoonaba and a carved wooden walking stick depicting the two suns, the moon, the Great Waterfall and the jungle, including several animals.

Finally able to relax a little, he eyed his five o'clock shadow in a mirror when a knock on the door startled him. He strode over to the door wearing pants and a sleeveless undershirt, his bulging arm and shoulder muscles in evidence. He opened the door. There stood a short-haired, red-headed woman barely his height. An explosion of freckles covered her face. She looked about twenty years old. The insignia on the left shoulder of her wrap outfit revealed she was junior member of the mansion staff. She looked at Erik and he smiled broadly.

The young woman smiled back. She bowed and he returned the gesture.

Without a word, she handed him a scroll of parchment and continued to stand in the doorway, waiting.

He slipped the ribbon off the small scroll, puzzled that one of Umni's poems had apparently gotten into the staffer's hands. Instead, as he unrolled the crude paper he found a message scrawled in ink in a shaky script as if the writer were used to making online signatures but inexperienced at printing entire letters by hand. The message read:

> To Starship Captain Erik Houston:
>     The honor of your presence is requested at eight o'clock this evening for dinner at Chiefexec Residential Suite 4B. (See map that follows.) Formal dress required. RSVP in kind immediately.
>                     (Signed)
>                     The President

He laughed aloud as he re-read the note. The messenger, sensing something special, chuckled too. Without a word, she handed him a quill pen and a small bottle of ink. He shook his head, took the proffered items and moved to a nearby counter to painstakingly scribble his response. He rolled the parchment back up, retied the ribbon, and handed it to the admin.

He was ready to conclude she was a mute when she said, quietly: "Honored to meet you, Captain."

"Likewise," he said.

She accepted the paper scroll, turned on her heel and headed down the hall. After a few seconds, she giggled.

Erik was still laughing as he returned to the bathroom mirror.

Five minutes before the appointed time, he showed up at the entrance to the suite. The automated door announced him. The door opened to reveal an enchanting lady, her hair fixed in an elegant style. Several thin, gold necklaces adorned her neck. A floral aroma surrounded her. He swallowed hard, feeling he was having an audience with royalty.

"Good evening, Madame President," he said with a smile.

"Good evening, Captain. I see you accepted my invitation."

"How could I refuse such a unique presentation?"

Her gown was sleeveless, boldly displaying her pink shoulder scar, which was encircled with rhinestones. She caught him staring at the mark. "It reminds me to…"

"...always be strong," he completed with her. Her arms encircled him for a few seconds.

He walked through the door and handed her a bottle of chilled, sparkling beverage. He noted the plush carpet, the stuffed living room furniture, the expensive-looking artwork on the walls. He hadn't previously seen this part of her vast living quarters.

"This is for you," he said, removing a metal object from his suit coat pocket.

She held out her hand. He placed into her palm a weighty gold sculpture of some sort of flying creature. Her brow furrowed.

"It's an eagle, like the ones on my dress uniform," he explained.

"What's an iggle?"

"A mythological creature. It symbolized strength and freedom. Minj tells me the first spaceship that ever landed on a planet's moon was called the Eagle."

She nodded thoughtfully. "You've taught me a lot about freedom," she said quietly.

"I also have a gift for you." She handed him a wrapped package a little smaller than a shoe box. He tore off the wrapping paper and pulled off the lid. He lifted out a white plush animal about the size of his hand. The stuffed toy was feathery soft. He stared at the present.

She laughed. "You don't know what it is. Erik! A well-traveled man like you. It's a mythological creature, too. It's a dove. A symbol of peace. I'd like there to always be peace and friendship between our peoples."

He nodded, thinking he had vaguely heard of a duv. "Here's to peace and friendship between Al'aama and the Association. Thanks. I'll cherish it."

She walked him over to a to a round table, one that looked much too small for a chiefexec. It was a table where she typically ate dinner. Alone. Alone except for those rare occasions when her kids didn't have plans. Or the infrequent times she invited Kelly and Legislae Norris over for a girls' night. In the old, pre-William days, Tanna had been there, too.

Zama ordered two dinners on the automated table. Erik opened the bottle of chilled intoxicant and filled two glasses. His hand trembled slightly as he handed a glass to her. She looked at him a little shyly.

"I'd like to make a toast," he said, raising his glass.

"What should we toast?" she asked, raising hers.

"To the continued progress and prosperity of your planet!"

"To the planet Al'aama!" They clinked their glasses.

"I have a toast of my own," she said. "To the health and safety of the starship *Initiative* and her crew, the best friends a leader could ever have!"

They clinked glasses again and each took a sip. They uncovered their dinners and began to eat. "You realize these are some of my favorite Al'aaman dishes," he said.

She nodded and smiled.

As he looked at the meal, a bolt shot through his stomach. He just sat there and pushed around his food with his utensils. She put her hand on his arm. "C'mon. Don't be sad. Let's *enjoy* the evening."

She walked over to a cabinet, opened a drawer and retrieved the energy utensils he had given her. She demonstrated her proficiency, having gotten quite good at using the power tools. She offered to feed him and playfully almost dropped some morsels of food on him. He laughed. They spent some time recounting the highlights of their experiences working together, even chuckling over incidents that had made them angry at the time. After they had talked for at least an hour, their conversation lapsed.

Finally, she asked: "Still have feelings for Kelly?"

Silence.

"She still drools over you."

He lowered his head and shook it. "Kelly has some good qualities. But she's not you."

She met his gaze then looked down, smiling. A few moments later, her face developed an impish expression. She snapped her fingers. Some slow dance music wafted through the air. She began to tap her foot in time to the music. "You know, Captain," she said, "we never did get to go dancing." He stood up and offered his hand. She accepted it and led him to another room, one with a hardwood floor. The furniture had all been moved to the edges of the room. She slipped off her shoes like she had the night of the banquet. He placed his arms around her and they began to glide across the makeshift dance floor. He was still maintaining that respectful distance. She gently pulled him closer. "Don't be so formal, Captain. We know one another too well." Several numbers later, she suggested: "Let's go out onto the balcony."

She strode over to the French doors and pushed them open. It was cool outside. She donned a lacy shawl. He shook his head and wrapped his suit coat around her. It was nighttime and the lights of the city obscured all but the brightest stars. They spent several quiet minutes gazing into the sky. The wind ruffled their hair.

Finally, she spoke. "When you…leave here tomorrow, *where* will *you go?*"

"See that bright star?"

"*That* one?" she said, pointing.

"Yes. Right there. It's about five light years from here."

She shook her head. "Five years...By then, I'll have finished my second term in office and will be doing something else for a living. It's a horrible thing."

"What is?"

"That Einstein's Law. You'll leave here tomorrow and I'll never see you again. And if you ever do make it back to this planet, my great-great granddaughter will probably be running the place and I'll have been many years in the grave." He swallowed hard and gripped the balcony's railing with both hands.

"Erik, look at me." The pale moon provided enough light for them to see into one another's eyes. "You and I have worked well together. We could be a *team* to develop this planet. I could make you my director of planetary development, complete with a salary. You could even help us finalize plans for our tricentennial in a couple months. Of course, this is...strictly a *business* proposition."

"Of course," he repeated. It was some time before he answered. "Zama, I'm flattered. But...I've been wandering the stars half my life...."

"I understand. It's just that...."

"Have you ever thought about going into space *with us?*"

She turned away and didn't say anything for some time. Finally, she continued: "It's too bad some cosmic hiccup couldn't have brought you here a few years later...I...I can't.... We've got to explore the planet. Omma's still working through her depression...."

"D-do you really think it could *work?*" he said. "Spending months at a time aboard a starship might seem like a prison to you. And I'm used to going to a different planet every several months. I *don't know* if I could stay on one place indefinitely...."

"Hold me," she whispered.

He did for a moment, feeling warm all over. His thoughts were getting away from him. He was tempted to....

"Be strong," said a voice in his mind. He took a breath.

He gave her a final, tender embrace. They kissed passionately, melting into one another. They parted and gazed into one another's eyes, only inches apart. He peered deep into those brown orbs and saw her soul. She was a beauty queen. An angel. "Goodbye, Zama," he said, his warm breath on her ear. "You're special to me. You always will be."

"I'll never forget you."

After his reluctant departure, she wandered around the suite, finally winding up on the balcony again. She went back to looking at the stars but was able to see little. There was something in her eye. Her left hand held something damp. She looked down and spied his handkerchief, moist from her earlier tears. She touched the gold necklace she always wore. The one she toyed with when in deep thought or upset. The one with a tiny gold cross on the end. "Lord, help me!" she prayed. She lowered her head, which began to bob up and down, her fountain of tears totally letting loose.

Sometime later, still on the balcony, she thought of the script for tomorrow. She'd planned a simple ceremony to thank him and his crew for all they'd done for her people. She would give him a gentle hug, but not too long. Few people other than Kelly knew of her feelings for the captain. The firstadvisor had remained supportive despite struggling with her own feelings.

Zama finally went inside, slipped out of her gown, brushed out her hair. Still wearing her slip, she dragged over to one of her dozen bedrooms and lay down. Her stomach knotted. Up toward the ceiling some lighted, digital numbers slowly moved in a large circle, displaying the date and time. Three fifty-six AM. Time to get up in an hour. She wouldn't have slept anyway.

# 56.

Zama, Umni and Bobby were relaxing under the shade of a fern tree on the back mansion lawn. Zama had set a cool zone around the area. Each of them was sipping on a bottle of self-cooling beverage.

Umni sighed. "I miss the star man."

Zama looked down.

"That day he rescued me changed my life," Umni continued. "I was his enemy. He could have left me stuck in the trap. He could have killed me."

"He's a good man," said Bobby.

"Zama, do you worship the same God as Erik?" asked Umni.

She looked up and smiled. Her hair fell into eyes that had a faraway look. "Yes, yes, I do."

"Sometimes he would talk with us about this God. I'd like to learn more about him."

"He's the Creator of our planet, the stars, everything that is. In fact, he Is. One of his names is I Am. He's always existed. He is, always was and always will be."

Umni pursed her lips. Zama told Bobby and her about Jesus and salvation through him. The two warriors said nothing, eyes full of wonder as Zama spoke. They had a number of questions. Finally, Zama had to leave.

Several days later, the chiefexec was again speaking with the duo. "The time has come for us to go," Umni said somberly.

Zama sighed. "I'd be glad to give you some land of your own...."

"No. We need to go back," Bobby insisted. "Back to our own country."

"But I thought your people hated you," said Zama.

"Not all of them," Umni replied. "It would really depend upon the new chief. Before the star man left, he found out it's Sam O'Toole. He's more reasonable than Chief Laura or Shane McTeague."

"We need to be with our people," said Bobby. "All we can do is try to go back. If we live, we live. If we die, we die."

"And it would give us a chance to tell our people about the Lord," said Umni. "They need to be saved."

The next day, the couple packed up their belongings. Silence cloaked them as they rode with Zama in her limo to the edge of the farm district. The three of them got out of the car. The chiefexec had offered to send an armed posse to ensure their protection but Bobby had insisted they needed to do this on our own. She had offered to give them riding beasts to carry on them on their long journey, a thirty-plus mile trip. But Umni insisted they had traveled the route several times before and it wasn't that bad.

Umni and Bobby shouldered their over-sized packs. Each one had a newly-carved walking stick in hand. Zama hugged each of them.

"Thank you," Umni whispered. "Thank you for teaching us about God."

"Thank you for your hospitality," said Bobby. The two of them tramped off into an overgrown field.

"When will I see you again?" Zama called.

"If our chief is agreeable to peace with your people, maybe soon," Umni called back. "Someday, we'd like to help you explore more of the outlying areas. There's a lot we can show you."

Umni waved and turned back around, trotting to catch up with Bobby, who was already trudging ahead. They tramped through the brush then vanished into the tall, golden prairie grass. As they plodded forward and got into the jungle proper, Umni noted the various types of vegetation and animals. As she hiked alongside her beau, she would occasionally stop a moment to look, smell, touch. It felt good to be back in the wilderness. Bobby looked at her and smiled.

She noted tiny lizard-like creatures scurrying around on the jungle floor, colorful birds and small leaping creatures moving from tree to tree. She enjoyed sniffing the scents of wildflowers, some of them as large as her head. Some plants had huge, floppy leaves. Others had tiny ones. She liked touching the different types of vegetation. Fern trees had smooth, slick trunks. One type of bush looked like a large, standing brush with thousands of bristles. They were soft to the touch but contained a sticky substance that held insects and small animals in place. The plant would grow a pod around the meal, eventually dissolving it. One tall plant, called a Whistling Rangus, was punctuated with numerous holes, causing it to emit high-pitched, musical notes when the wind was blowing. Another plant was armed with poisonous thorns, each several inches long.

As the day wore on, the two began to perspire heavier. Their canteen breaks and rest stops became more frequent. Umni's shoulders, arms and legs began to hurt. Her stomach knotted as she wondered what fate would befall them back home.

"Jesus will help us," Bobby said.

She smiled and nodded.

Seventeen and a half miles out, the jungle ended and the couple was back out in the open, the suns mercilessly beating down on them. The two figures staggered across the barren landscape. As far as the eye could see, there was nothing except hardened, red-brown earth splintered by countless inch-wide cracks that ran a foot or more deep. It was the dry bed of a seasonal lake. Every year, during the rainy season, the shallow area would fill with water only to turn back into a dust bowl during the torrid summer.

Umni was soaked. Her shirt, waistband and hat band were all caked with white from salt that had distilled from her perspiration. Bobby's face, arms and clothes were white. The ground burned under their feet. They were panting as they walked. They passed within ten yards of a canoe that had run aground when the water had become too shallow to navigate. Later, Umni almost stepped on an animal skull, realizing that, perhaps only a few months earlier, a living creature had stood there.

They each had less than half a canteen of water. Halfway across the dried up lake, Ava had arisen further into the sky. The heat was intensifying. Umni tried not to think of her thirst. As she walked, she looked down and started counting cracks in the earth. She lost count a little past a hundred. Her mouth was dry as cotton. Her throat burned. Her head throbbed. Her lips began to feel as hard and parched as the ground. Her pack was becoming too heavy to bear.

"We've gotten soft," she mumbled through cracked lips.

"Yeah," said Bobby.

Finally, up ahead—what was that? Something shimmering in the distance. Could it be? Summoning all her energy, she broke into a trot then a run.

"Where you going?" Bobby called.

She ran for two minutes solid. No water. More running. Still nothing. "No! A mirage!" she cried.

He caught up with her, shaking his head. "Hang on," he said. "A couple more hours and we'll be home."

Fifteen minutes later, Umni noticed a shimmering again. Newly cynical, she refused to believe her eyes. After several minutes of walking, she almost stumbled past it. There, about twenty yards to her left, was a small puddle, too shallow to be of much use.

Her stomach hurt. She eased to the ground and retrieved some bread from her pack. She tore into it, washing it down with a mouthful of water while her man stood guard.

Deep in a crack in the ground, some tiny creatures had detected Umni's presence. Hundreds of red insects each the size and shape of a thumb tip wound through a labyrinth of tiny, underground tunnels and up the to the surface. They swarmed onto the young woman's clothing. Bobby vigorously brushed a number of them off Umni, but their numbers were overwhelming. He pulled a metal whistle from his pocket and blew a note too high for human hearing. The countless red insects covering the woman quickly retreated back into the deep cracks that fractured the parched earth. Some of the white stains on her clothing and skin were now gone. "Stupid salt leeches," he spat

He offered a hand to help his lady back to her feet. She ended her break and they continued trudging across the barren land. After they had walked another forty minutes, they reached the edge of the dusty lake and brush began to appear. About fifty paces farther and they were back in the jungle, the canopy providing shade.

Eight and five-sixths more miles of jungle followed, as the couple remained on constant alert for unfoonaba. And giant spiders. And especially Batu. They broke into a clearing. Umni's throat tightened as they spotted the stream that became the river that fed the Great Waterfall a few miles away. The couple stumbled to the brook. They fell on their knees and scooped up water with their hands, slurping down the treasure. They splashed it on their faces. Splashed one another, laughing.

They continued on. Less than four miles later, they crossed the bridge that spanned the river. The waterfall roared, its spray dotting both their faces.

They each licked at the moisture. They spied a shadow in the distance. Ah, the Batu's wooden stockade. Gradually, the settlement grew closer. As they drew near the fence, the two warriors were exhausted, their faces streaked with dirt. Their backs were sore. Umni's heart pounded like rapid hammer blows. She prayed.

"Who goes there?"

She jumped at the burst of sound. It was a sentry from a walkway inside the top of the wall. He pointed his spear at them.

"Bobby Anderson and Umni Ott," Bobby called.

"Thought you were dead," yelled the sentry. "Dead or gone to the enemy." He spat, barely missing them.

"Neither," said Bobby.

The guard disappeared. Several voices cursed loudly from behind the wall. Fist-sized rocks flew over the wall followed by a hail of spears and arrows. The couple ducked. Dodged. A rock hit Umni in the arm, enraging Bobby, who picked up a spear. Missiles rained all around them. In anguish, Umni remembered how she had treated Zama months ago at the cave. Was she being punished? The attack halted. Bobby was poised to hurl the weapon but finally let it drop. Silence ensued.

What seemed like an eternity later, the massive gates swung open. The couple walked forward. Just inside, several armed braves were waiting. A tall man with long, blond hair pointed his spear at the duo. "You will meet with the chief," he said in a deep voice. The posse surrounded them and escorted them to the chief's tent. Curious passersby, many recognizing them, joined the group.

Chief Sam O'Toole stepped out of his dwelling and rose to his full height. He said nothing while he eyed the visitors. "You two have been accused of treason," he said.

"It's true!" cried a lady from the back of the crowd.

Umni's heart sank as she turned her head and saw the woman who had tried to spear her months ago in the jungle.

"I saw her consorting with that star man when she was injured."

"So did I," yelled a man from elsewhere in the crowd. It was the other warrior who had been on the scene. "Under Chief Laura, that would have meant death."

Chief Sam bristled. "I'm chief now and we go by my rules," he bellowed. "Miss Ott, give an account."

"A few months ago during our first battle with the giant village to the south, I caught my ankle in an animal trap. The star man freed me and treated my wound. At first, I fought his efforts because he was the enemy. But he insisted, and in my weakened condition, there was only so much I could do to resist him. He actually fought off these two," said Umni, pointing at her accusers, "when they tried to run me through with their spears. He knew I would be in danger as long as Chief Laura was in charge so he arranged for Bobby and me to have sanctuary with the southern tribes.

"We were grateful for a safe place to stay, but my heart is with our tribe. I missed everyone and thought of them daily. That's why we came back. We respectfully ask that you allow us to return."

The chief frowned. "Is all of this true, Mr. Anderson?"

"She spent a lot of time pining away, wishing to be back here," he replied. "I've missed everyone, too."

The chief stood there for long moments while he continued to eye the couple and the crowd, which had continued to grow larger. It looked like about half the tribe was now on hand. He turned his gaze back to the duo. "Miss Ott, you were a member of the Circle of Honor. Mr. Anderson, you led several hunts and are a skilled warrior. Neither of you had previously been in trouble with the tribe.

"Umni Ott and Bobby Anderson, do you each solemnly swear that you will defend, protect and, if necessary, give your life for the Batu tribe and that you will place it above your friendships with any other tribe?"

"I do," said Umni.

"I do," Bobby added.

The tribal leader squared his shoulders and raised his voice. "Hear my words, oh, Tribe of Batu. From this day forward, I declare the charge of treason against Umni Ott and Bobby Anderson be dismissed. These two braves will be re-instated into the tribe at their former positions and accepted as our brother and sister. Old grievances against them must be dropped. Anyone seeking to harm them must answer to me! The chief has spoken!" He jammed his spear into the ground for emphasis.

Umni jumped up and down with glee. Bobby hugged her. A number of friends and relatives surged forward to hug them as well.

The next day, the chief declared a hunt. The braves hauled their game back to the village. A savory flavor filled the air as dozens of animal carcasses turned on spits. The chief addressed the tribe, stating that the feast was in honor of Umni and Bobby. The eating, music, dancing and reverie lasted late into the night.

# 57.

Over a year had passed since the *Initiative* had departed Al'aama. Second term Chiefexec Zama Elle was remarkably leaner, having lost the remainder of her paunch and her double chin. She had been frequenting her private gym daily over the past several months and had been watching her diet. She had also gone back to running, an area where she had excelled in her youth. She had let her hair grow several inches and it was now halfway down her back. These days, the chiefexec was front cover material on the largest online news and business magazines. She even starred on the fitness and fashion ones as well. *Executive Week* was crowing about "Our New, Youthful Chiefexec." The cover featured a svelte Zama Elle clad in a skirt suit several sizes smaller than she had formerly worn. *Glamourous People* showed a closeup of the boss and Omma. The First Daughter's eyes looked somber but her lips were curled up in at least a hint of her former smile. The headline read: "Mom and Om, or Are They Really Sisters?" For some time, the media had been trumpeting her youth and vigor. That and her new development and exploration programs had impressed the public, strengthening her politically. She had bounced back from all her trials and had been re-elected in a landslide.

The chiefexec sat at the far end of the long table as various cabinet members arose from their chairs. After spending a few minutes deep in thought, she realized someone else had remained. It was Daj Minj. He sat to the immediate right of the chiefexec, a position of honor as the last remaining visitor from the stars. She had hired him as an advisor and made him an honorary cabinet member.

"Mr. Minj. Good to see you."

"Thanks, Madame Exec. Lisa and I want to thank you for your bridal shower gift."

"You're welcome. I can tell you two are very happy."

He was beaming. "I mean, we really…want to thank you. You were very generous. I don't know what we've done to deserve this."

Zama's face was reddening. Her secret was burning within her. She changed the subject. "I don't mean to be critical," she continued, "but progress on developing a space craft has seemed so slow. It could take us generations before we're ready to go to the stars."

He nodded. "It's a huge project," he agreed. "But your scientists have learned a lot about aerodynamic principles and before long you may be able to build a vehicle powerful enough to launch a small payload into space."

She sighed and looked away.

"Madame Exec, I want to show you something." He pulled out of his pocket what appeared to be a small coin inside a clear, plastic case. He placed the object on the table.

"What's that, space money?" she laughed.

"Not quite. Prior the *Initiative* leaving Al'aama, I talked Erik into copying of a massive file and formatting it for A'laama's system. It contains the entire known history of L ships."

"What kind of ships?"

"L ships. L stands for light and an L ship is one that travels at close to the speed of light, thus making it suitable for star travel. This file is comprehensive." He waved his hand. The air in front of them began flashing through pages of schematics and mathematical symbols. The pace picked up until data and pictures were flying by at a blinding speed. He waved his hand again and the info disappeared. He continued: "The file contains all the specs on propulsion systems, ship designs, construction materials, the works. Thousands of years of technology," he concluded, his eyes beaming. "Erik was forbidden from making this information available to you because he was part of the First Contact group. But you see, since I no longer work for the Association, I'm no longer bound by their rules."

Her eyes widened. "All that is on this little coin?"

"Yes. I made several copies and have formatted them for A'laaman systems. And in a sense, you're right. This really is space money because it's your passport to the interstellar community and all the commerce and culture that goes with it."

She looked puzzled. "I don't get it. What good will all this information do if no one on our planet understands it, not even you? You're not a tech guy; you're an historian."

He was grinning. "If all I did were historical research, I'd have never been sent on all these missions to the stars. There's only so much room on a starship so all adults aboard ship do some job that's vital to the mission. Plus, we all wear more than one hat. Don't forget, Montoya was our physician but he was also our chief science officer. Luci was our communications expert but she would occasionally double as a medical technician and a naturalist. She even helped with battlefield logistics. True, I was the ship historian and history is my hobby. But my main job was as the ship's chief engineer."

Zama gasped. "But...how could Erik afford to leave you here?"

"Another aspect of space travel is...always have a backup plan. There were two other people on the ship perfectly capable of stepping in if I were gone. Traveling the stars is not an easy life. Occasionally, someone will be killed on a mission or succumb to a native illness or, like me, decide to stay behind on a planet."

"So...you actually understand all this stuff. Well, why don't we start building our ship right now?"

"Because having the knowledge is one thing but implementing it is not so easy. Constructing a ship that actually works would take technologies you don't even have yet. I'm letting your scientists learn a few things then I'll take a more active role in helping you achieve your dream. It will take time. It may take a long time. But one way or another, we're going back to the stars!"

The chiefexec hugged the startled Minj and kissed his face. Her eye caught the data file, which was still sitting on the table. That dear man had just given her and her people something of immeasurable value. She swallowed hard. "Sit down, please, M-mr. Minj. There's...something I need to tell you...."

Daj, looking puzzled, eased into his seat.

She sat as well. She turned toward him and looked into his eyes then looked down. "There's something I never told you," she said. "I'm mainly from the Paol tribe, but one branch of my family is Batami. In fact, I come from Ami Batami, your daughter."

His jaw dropped. Finally, he wheezed: "Madame Exec...."

She laid her hand on his arm. "Please. We're family. Call me Zama."

"I-I'm honored that you're my great-great grandaughter."

"And I'm proud that you're my ancestor," she said, beaming. Her expression changed and she looked down again. "I-I haven't been fair to you," she confessed. "Your involvement with Nanci Batami makes you a key figure in our history yet I've kept that a secret. You deserve a place of great honor. With your permission, I'd like to make an announcement."

"Zama, I...."

She bit her lip, sensing the publicity would make him uncomfortable. "There's still a segment of my people who weren't happy about your crew's visit here but once they realize your tie-in with our history, I think they'd have a much more favorable impression of you and your Association."

He nodded. "Okay. But I need to talk with Lisa...."

"That's fine. And let me know if there's anything I can do for you. Anything at all."

He put his thumb and finger on his chin and thought a moment. "Yes. Your great-great grandad has a favor to ask. Remember when you had us in prison when we first arrived?"

The chiefexec looked down, ashamed of how she initially treated the star visitors. "Yes...."

"There were three female guards there. Triplets. Clones, actually. Their names are Lila, Leela, and Lola Leason. I want them to have an opportunity to advance their careers. To become anything they want to be."

Zama's face began to turn red. "Clones...given opportunity.... But that just isn't done."

"Not even if your beloved ancestor asks you?"

Her face began to soften. "All right. You win. After all, I wouldn't even be here without you. I'll have Kelly look into this."

"As you often say, we have a deal." He held out his hand for her to shake. They looked at one another and laughed then stood up and hugged again.

As she hurried out of the meeting hall, she stuck her hand in her pocket and felt the case that held the disk of starship data. She felt like the wealthiest lady on the planet. She already had a destination in mind for A'laama's first starship, that jewel of a planet two light years away that was supposed to have become her ancestors' home.

It was almost sunset. The once-in-three-weeks night was about to begin. After an inspiring temple service, she returned to the mansion. For a long time, she stood on the balcony. She focused on a special star five light years distant. As she often did when looking at the nighttime sky, she thought about the final part of the Prophecy, the part she had temporarily forgotten in the heat of the moment during Erik's last night on the planet: "*In that day, there shall be alliance between the leader of your seed and the leader from the stars. They shall be apart for a time, but they shall come back together in the end.*"

"We'll meet again, Erik Houston," she said., her face breaking into a smile. She continued to gaze into the heavens.

# Epilogue

It was quite late when the elderly star traveler finished his story. The bar would have normally closed hours ago. When the man finally finished speaking, he glanced up and jumped in his chair when he saw a crowd that was several people deep. Some folks in anti-grav chairs and lounges hovered at various heights in the cathedral-ceilinged bar. The floating eating booths were all filled as well. Halfway through the story, the proprietor had set up a sound amp. After the Story Teller finished speaking, the group remained spellbound for a long moment.

Finally, a dark-haired lady in a far corner of the room called out: "Do you think it was really an angel who appeared to the colonists?"

The bartender offered: "I've always heard that every inhabited planet has its own guardian."

The space wanderer smiled. "Actually, an entire legion," he said. "And every space station has a few. There could be some among us as we speak." Many mouths hung open. Other faces registered disbelief. A few were beaming. The sharp ticking of an ancient retro clock was all that broke the silence.

The elder began another tale, but a thin man in the back yelled: "What about the captain and the lady exec?"

"Did they ever see one another again?" echoed a woman from another part of the room. A few loud murmurs filled the air.

The story spinner froze in mid-syllable, his arm and hand stopped in a half-completed gesture. Silence cloaked the room. A hint of a smile creased his worn face. A twinkle lit his eyes but it was gone before most noticed. He took on the appearance of a master poker player. A full minute ticked by. Two.

"Tell us," insisted the man who had asked the question.

"Tell us," repeated the lady whose hand rested on the man's arm.

"Tell us. Tell us," the crowd began to chant.

The Story Teller shook his head. He eased to his feet and held his hands, palms up. "Thank you all for coming," he said. "I'm grateful for so large a crowd. And, bartender, you've been great. That's the reason I appreciate having a human bartender, not an android. They only pretend to listen. I'm glad you've all enjoyed these tales. But it's late and I'm an old man. I've got plenty of other stories, but they'll have to wait for another day." He flashed the debit chip to leave the bartender an extra-large tip. The crowd parted as he grabbed his ancient walking stick and headed out the door. The bartender and a number of patrons stood and watched the old man as he hobbled away.

Once he got a short distance from the pub, they saw him reach into his pocket and walk into the night. Alone and beyond their gaze, he pulled an object from his pocket and held it in his palm. A dainty, gold necklace adorned with a cross.

# Appendix:
# The Entirety of the Angel's Prophecy

You had planned to go to a world fresh and green and instead have come to this torrid place. You have traveled from afar to come to this world and at times your efforts have seemed for nought. Fear not, for you shall not perish. Rejoice, for you and your seed shall live. Within ten days the rains shall come and the drought shall end. Your land shall be green again. Your little group shall not perish but will take root and grow and bear fruit in abundance. You who started so small and weak shall become a great and mighty people.

And this is the sign that these things shall all come to pass: three women shall arise from your midst to become great leaders. And just as three women came from the stars, before three hundred years pass three men shall come from the stars and call fire down from heaven. And after they arrive, your people will never again be the same.

In that day, there shall be alliance between the leader of your seed and the leader from the stars. They shall be apart for a time, but they shall come back together in the end.

MAY 2 3 2008

DATE DUE

Printed in the United States
72864LV00005B/205-228

000245615M

9 781424 154036